DYLAN LOOKED AT STUDENTS AND KNEW THAT HE HAD NO CHANCE OF GETTING INTO YALE.

These other students were obviously better than he was: smarter, richer, braver. Yale was for people like this Polo here, someone who wanted to study semiotics and linguistics, whatever they were. Or for Allison, who wrote her songs. Dylan getting admitted to Yale was about as likely as getting Allison to take a second look at him. If you thought about it, girls and college were a lot alike: there was Early Decision, Regular Admission, and Wait List. The only difference was that with college you took SATs whereas with girls there were all these other secret examinations you took and failed without even knowing it. It would be nice, actually, knowing what your scores were in life. That way you wouldn't keep trying to ask out Stanford when in all probability you'd wind up married to somebody like the University of Las Vegas.

Also by James Finney Boylan

getting in

A NOVEL

james finney boylan

WARNER BOOKS

A Time Warner Company

AUTHOR'S NOTE:

This book is a work of fiction. Real colleges and universities are mentioned, but all of the characters, events, and dialogue described in the book are imaginary. Any resemblance to actual persons, living or dead, events, or locales is entirely coincidental.

Grateful acknowledgment is given for permission to reprint the following:

Material from *The Insider's Guide to the Colleges* copyright © 1996 by the Yale Daily News Publishing Company, Inc. From *The Insider's Guide to the Colleges*. Compiled and edited by the staff of the *Yale Daily News*. Reprinted by permission of St. Martin's Press, Incorporated. Copyright © 1998 by the Yale Daily News Publishing Company, Inc. From *The Insider's Guide to the Colleges*. Compiled and edited by the staff of the *Yale Daily News*. Reprinted by permission of St. Martin's Press, Incorporated.

The "Theme from *Gunfight at the O.K. Corral*" by Ned Washington and Dimitri Tiomkin is used by permission. Gunfight at the O.K. Corral copyright © 1956 by Paramount Music Corporation.

Material from "Bottle of Wine" by Tom Paxton © 1963, 1968 (copyright renewed) EMI U Catalog Inc. All rights reserved. Used by permission. Warner Bros. Publications U.S. Inc., Miami, FL 33014

Warner Books, Inc., 1271 Avenue of the Americas, New York, NY 10020
Visit our Web site at http://warnerbooks.com

W A Time Warner Company

Printed in the United States of America
First Printing: September 1998

Library of Congress Cataloging-in-Publication Data

Boylan, James
    Getting in : a novel / James Finney Boylan.
      p. cm.
    ISBN 0-446-67417-6 ISBN-13: 978-0-446-67417-1
    I. Title.
    PS3552.0914G48 1998
    813'.54—dc21   97-51216
                          CIP

Text design by Stanley S. Drate/Folio Graphics Co. Inc.
Cover design by Mary Ann Smith
Photo of top building by Arne Hodalic/Corbis
Photo of bottom building by Lee Snider/Corbis
Top vignette photo by Alexandra Bennett/Nonstock
Bottom vignette photo by Stefan May/Tony Stone Images

For my father,
who finally found his orchestra

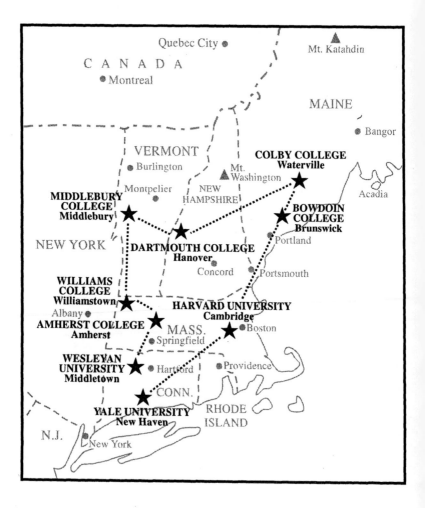

Yale University:	New Haven, Connecticut
Harvard University:	Cambridge, Massachusetts
Bowdoin College:	Brunswick, Maine
Colby College:	Waterville, Maine
Dartmouth College:	Hanover, New Hampshire
Middlebury College:	Middlebury, Vermont
Williams College:	Williamstown, Massachusetts
Amherst College:	Amherst, Massachusetts
Wesleyan University:	Middletown, Connecticut

Wyatt's lady fair
He left her crying there
He broke his vow and rode away to
Tombstone.

—''Theme from *Gunfight at the O.K. Corral*''

they were asleep, father and son, when the train pulled into New Haven and all the lights went out. Dylan opened his eyes, surprised by the sudden darkness.

"Where are we?" he cried. "Dad, we're lost!"

"I'm awake," said Ben. "We're not lost."

"You're asleep," Dylan said, accusingly. "Asleep!"

In Ben's lap were the catalogs of all the colleges they were going to visit: Yale, Harvard, Bowdoin, Colby, Dartmouth, Middlebury, Williams, Amherst, Wesleyan. These catalogs were slick, their pages full of kids in sweaters.

Ben Floyd was embarrassed by his son's anguish. "It's okay," he said. "I'm not asleep anymore."

They collected their bags and walked through the coach. "This stop is New Haven," said the conductor. "Next stop, Providence."

They stepped off the train and onto the platform. The air was rich with the smell of creosote and brake shoes. "You smell that, son," Ben said. "That's what it smells like."

"What what smells like?" Dylan said.

"College!" Ben said.

Ben looked through the crowd of people, most of whom were now moving toward large escalators. "We need to go up a flight," he said. "Down here is only where the trains are."

Dylan shook his head and walked toward the escalator. Some pretty girls were walking in front of them. One of them wore a sweatshirt that read YALE. Another was carrying a paperback book by Immanuel Kant titled *The*

Prolegomena to Any Further Metaphysics. They looked at Dylan, then at his father, then looked away.

"We're coming into the main station now," Ben announced, as they ascended into the waiting room. He jerked his head gently, which was one of Ben's annoying tics. To Dylan, it often looked as if his father were trying to shake some water out of his eardrums.

"Thanks, Dad," Dylan said. He was hoping the girls would look in his direction again, but they did not.

They entered the main waiting room. The place looked like a Greek temple, fallen on hard times. Marble columns stretched toward the distant ceiling. Long wooden benches stood in echelons beside the stairs that led below. There were billboards for the army. Sound echoed in the great space.

"I don't see Uncle Lefty," Dylan said.

"Would you recognize him?" Ben said. "It's been almost seven years."

"I don't know," Dylan said.

They stared into the moving crowd. Dylan tried rearranging the features of oncoming strangers so that they might, for an instant, resemble his uncle. It was possible, Dylan thought, that Lefty could have somehow changed over the years. It was something to hope for, anyway.

"Maybe they're outside," Ben said, looking toward the exits.

"Well, they're not here," Dylan said. "We're lost again."

"We're not lost," Ben said.

They walked out into the October sunshine. Cars were pulled up around the curb. A man with a white glove and a whistle was flagging down taxis.

An astonishingly loud horn blasted, causing father and son to jump suddenly. Dylan covered his eyes for a moment as if to wield off a crushing blow. Ben looked at his son, felt pity for him.

A voice cried out. "Hey!" it said. "Dickweed!"

Coming toward them was Cousin Juddy. He was wearing a baseball cap that bore the legend VILLANOVA WILD-CATS. He smiled broadly. A set of plastic rings bearing five cans of Budweiser dangled from one hand. The other hand held an open can.

The horn blasted again. Parked on the curb behind the impending Juddy was a Winnebago the size of a Burger King. At the wheel was Uncle Lefty. "C'man, c'man," he called. "I'm double-parked!"

"You're wrong, Dad," Dylan said. "We *are* lost."

"Dickweed," Juddy said again, fondly. He held up his thumb, which had a small scar on it, traversing the thumbprint.

Dylan held up his thumb, which had a matching scar.

"Hi, Juddy," said Dylan.

Juddy made a sudden, sweeping gesture with one hand, as if he were slashing the air with an invisible sword. "*Whsshst-whssht,*" he said.

"Hello, Judson," Ben said. "You're looking well."

"Whatever," Juddy said. He peeled a Bud off of the six-pack ring and handed it to Dylan. "Brewdog?"

"No thanks," Dylan said. It was strange to see his cousin after all this time. He had changed since they were kids. He had grown into a different person, somehow. He reminded Dylan of some sort of bug now, maybe the kind that makes potatoes rot.

From the curb, Uncle Lefty honked the horn of the Winnebago again.

Juddy pressed a beer into his cousin's hand. "Tell you what," he said. "You save this for later."

"Okay," Dylan said, taking the beer. The girls from Yale were stepping into a nearby cab. A woman with a kind face, one of their mothers, was getting into the front seat. She looked at Dylan for a moment as if she had forgotten his name. Somebody's mom, Dylan thought. It must be nice, to have one.

They turned to look at the Winnebago. "Is that your car?" Dylan said.

Juddy shook his head. "It's not a car, man," Juddy said. They walked toward it. "It's a great big thing. Burns gas like a airplane!"

Uncle Lefty blasted the horn again, even though they were standing right there. "Hey, we don't got all day," he shouted through the window.

"Well," Dylan said. "I guess we just climb aboard."

"Well, dude," Juddy said. "I guess you just."

They walked to the far side of the Winnebago and climbed up the stairs. Uncle Lefty turned from his position behind the wheel to shake their hands, although at first Dylan thought he was going to ask them for their tickets or something. He was a large man with thick stubble. In one hand he held a submarine sandwich.

"Lefty," Ben said, and reached forward to shake his brother's hand. Lefty had to move the sandwich from his right hand to his left before he could shake. As the men clasped hands, Lefty's lower lip began to move in a delicate vibration of sorrow.

He stood suddenly and hugged Ben, his arms wrapping around his brother. Oil from the submarine began to drip onto the back of Ben's shirt.

"I love this guy," Lefty said. "I love him." He broke the embrace to look his brother in the face. "Let's never fight again, okay? Okay?"

Ben nodded grimly. "It wasn't my idea, fighting." He looked into the guts of the Winnebago. A beautiful woman in her late forties sat at a table next to a picture window. She was wearing a leotard top and a pair of black jeans. Her blonde hair fell nearly to her waist.

"Hey," Lefty said, escorting the men into the camper. "Meet Chloë. The new Mrs. Floyd! You know what I thought when I first saw Chloë? I thought, *Hot diggity dog!*"

Chloë glanced at her husband as if he were a kind of toad, then looked back at Ben. "I wonder if you can guess what I thought when I first saw Lefty."

"Her friends thought she married me for my money," said Lefty, shaking his head. "Boy!"

Chloë shrugged. "Boy," she said.

"I'm Ben," Ben said, "and this is my son, Dylan."

"Hello, Mrs. Floyd," Dylan said, and stuck his hand out to shake.

"Baxter," said Chloë. "I kept my name."

"I'm pleased to meet you, ma'am."

"Oh, don't you ma'am me," she said, getting to her feet. "You make me feel like I'm fifty years old."

"Hey, Chlo," Uncle Lefty said. "You *are* fifty years old."

She shook her head. "I am *now*," she said, annoyed.

Ben's face twitched again. Dylan looked away from his father, embarrassed.

A door opened at the far end of the camper and a girl Dylan's age walked out. She looked like a less fermented version of her mother, with blonde hair and glasses. She wore a peasant skirt and a yellow sleeveless top.

"This is my daughter, Allison," Chloë announced. "Allison, say hello to everyone."

Allison glowered at the men and muttered, "Hello to everyone." She sat down in a chair next to the window and hid behind the curtain of her long hair.

"She wants to go to Middlebury," Chloë announced. "But I'm telling her to keep her options open."

"Good school, Middlebury," Ben said.

"What are you interested in, Allison?" Dylan said.

She turned and regarded Dylan. It was as if she were looking at him through a telescope.

"I write songs," she said, and looked out the window again.

Dylan felt the blood rushing to his face. He glanced around for something to look at other than Allison, and found nothing.

"Where'd you go to school, Chloë?" Ben asked, hoping that she had gone somewhere.

"Jarlsberg?" she said.

"Jarlsberg," Ben said, trying to think of where this was. He wasn't sure there was a Jarlsberg College.

"It's in Oregon," she explained.

"You guys want to go to Jarlsberg, Chloë here can tell you all about it," Lefty said. "Some wild times."

"Well, good," said Ben. He studied the interior of the Winnebago with some desperation. "Boy, Lefty, this is quite a rig you've got here."

"She's a beaut, isn't she," Lefty said proudly. "Fifty thousand dollars, used. This is her maiden voyage!"

"Me, I'm a go to that Harvard," Juddy said.

"I thought we were going to rent a minivan," Ben said softly. "That was the plan."

"This is better," Lefty said. "Now we don't have to rent motel rooms! We can just stay on the 'Bago!"

At this moment a young man wearing a black turtle-neck and a blue blazer stepped into the camper.

"Everyone," Allison said, standing up. "This is Polo."

"Polo MacNeil," the young man said, surveying his fellow travelers.

"Polo met Allison here at Flathead Art Work Camp,

last summer,'' said Lefty. ''Polo, this is my brother Ben and his kid Dylan.''

''Flinthead,'' Allison said.

''Polo here comes from New York City.''

''Upper West Side,'' Polo explained. ''Central Park West and Seventy-second. The Majestic.''

Dylan wasn't sure what he meant by ''the majestic,'' but he nodded anyway. Polo, a good-looking young man with curly blonde hair, walked over to Allison and put his arms around her. He kissed the girl. The others watched, then didn't.

Dylan glowered at Polo. ''You're an artist, too, I guess,'' he said. ''A musician?''

''Myself?'' Polo said. ''Not quite. My area of enthusiasm might more readily be described as *poetics*. Linguistics. Semiotics. Narratology. You understand.''

Dylan nodded. He pretty much got the picture.

''Well, I guess we're all here then,'' Lefty said.

''You want a brewdog, Polo?'' Juddy said. He swung the ring of beers toward him.

Polo looked surprised. ''A—'' he said, then smiled painfully. ''I think not.''

''Well, here's one,'' Juddy said, unpeeling a Bud. ''You can save it for later, like the little peckerwood here.'' He looked at Dylan with regret. ''Buncha goddamn squirrels,'' he muttered.

''Well, let's throw this thing in gear,'' Lefty said. ''You guys find some bunks. Those first three are already claimed. The rest you can grab. Whatever. Hey, this thing sleeps ten! We make some friends along the way we can just throw 'em on the pile!''

Ben and Dylan put their bags on a pair of bunk beds toward the back of the camper. A moment later the engine roared to life.

Ben lay down on his bunk and looked up at the ceiling.

Dylan sat in a chair and looked out the window at New Haven.

"Next stop, Yale University," Lefty called. He blasted his horn and pulled out into the oncoming traffic.

"Yale's a good school," Ben informed his son.

"Me," Juddy said. "I'm a go to that Harvard."

yale university

There is no dating at Yale. Either you're "married," or you just hook up, unless you count . . . coffee . . .
—*Insider's Guide to the Colleges, 1998*

New Haven, Connecticut
Number of applications: 12,620
Percent accepted: 20%
Mean SAT (1996): 657V, 703M
Most popular majors: history, economics, biology
Mascot: the Bulldogs

dylan was impressed—and would continue to be impressed over the course of the next week and a half—by the ability of college tour guides to walk backward and talk to a large group of people at the same time. The Yale guide was a healthy-looking backward-walking young woman named Lindsay. When they reached the curb at the corner of Cross and Temple, she stepped gently backward into the intersection and proceeded gracefully on her way in reverse.

"On your right is Saybrook, one of Yale's twelve residential colleges. All Yale undergraduates live in the colleges, which are like small schools within the university. Each has its own courtyard, cafeteria, and library, and there is a dean for each college who lives with the students."

"What do you mean, lives with the students?" said a man with a Southern accent. "Like he's their roommate or something?"

Lindsay smiled politely. "The dean has his own apartment within the entryway of the college."

They walked down Temple toward the Yale Center for British Art.

"He lives in the entryway?" the man said. "Like some homeless guy? That doesn't sound right."

"The door is off the entryway," Lindsay said. "I'm not saying he lives in the hall."

"Sounded that way," said the Southern gentleman. He shook his head. Dylan looked at the man with curiosity. It was the first time he'd ever seen a man wearing a string tie who was not on the front of a bucket of chicken.

11

"Captain, please," said the man's daughter, mortified.

"That's all yuh need, some dean runnin' 'round with his pants down," the Captain said.

"There is a great diversity within each of the colleges," Lindsay continued. "In each college you'll find students from all over the world, scholars of every stripe. There are no fraternities at Yale. Each college provides a wide range of inclusiveness and integration."

"What's this dean do when he's hanging around with students?" the Captain said. "He buys 'em beer, that sort of thing? Tells 'em about his war wound?"

"Dad," said the daughter.

"She said we could ask questions!"

"Of course you should ask questions," Lindsay continued, walking in reverse. "There's no question too stupid."

Allison looked like she was going to ask a question, but wasn't sure she believed Lindsay about the impossibility of stupidness. She put her hands in the pockets of her bomber jacket.

"What's New Haven like?" Dylan said.

"Well, you're looking at it," Lindsay said. "While it's technically a city, we like to think of it really as a large town. The Yale area is full of resources for students, including the Chapel Square Mall, the New Haven Green, and, of course, Toad's Place."

"Toad's Place?" the Captain asked sarcastically. "Who's this Toad? One of them deans?"

"No, sir," Lindsay said. "Toad's Place is a small concert hall for jazz, blues, and rock-and-roll artists. It's very popular."

"I bet," muttered the Captain.

"There's a lot of theater in New Haven, isn't there," Chloë said enthusiastically. "You always hear about shows closing here!"

"Yes," Lindsay said. "*Streetcar Named Desire* opened here, as did *Oklahoma!* and *My Fair Lady*. They all premiered at the Schubert Performing Arts Center down on College Street. And then there's Long Wharf. Anybody who's interested in the theater will find a lot going on. Each of the colleges, for instance, has its own dramatic troupe. It's quite impressive."

They walked back toward the admissions office.

"You still didn't say anything about this Toad guy," Lefty said.

"Well, that brings us full circle," Lindsay said. "I hope you all enjoy your stay at Yale, and good luck!" She disappeared into the door quickly, perhaps to avoid giving them the chance to prove that some questions, indeed, were stupid.

"This Yale sure isn't anything like what you hear," Juddy said.

"Lefty, darling," Chloë said. "Why don't we walk around the campus a little more. Dylan and Polo and Allison have their interviews."

"Some campus," Lefty said. "Lotsa cars and buses from what I see."

"You're not interviewing at Yale, Juddy?" said Polo. "I'm shocked."

"Yale?" Juddy said. "Yeah, right. Place is a dump."

"A dump?" Polo said. "Yale University?"

"What'd they ever do here besides invent that padlock. I'd like to know. Enlighten me."

There was a pause while some of them tried to figure this out.

"Come on, boys," Chloë said, pulling Juddy and Lefty by the elbows.

"I guess this is it," Ben said to Dylan. "Good luck, son." He patted Dylan on the back.

"Dad," Dylan said, embarrassed. "It's not a big deal."

"Oh, I should say it is a big deal," said Polo. "The interview is the most important part of the application. A mistake at this juncture puts the kibosh on the whole enterprise, don't you know."

"Let's just get it over with," Allison said, pulling open the door. "I can't feel any dumber than I already do, anyhow."

"Exactly," said Polo.

"We'll meet you back at the, uh, the van," Ben said.

"It's a Winnebago, Dad," Dylan said, dejected. "A Winnebago."

"We'll meet you there."

"Fine."

The teenagers walked into the admissions office and sat down in the waiting room. It was strangely quiet. Nine or ten other high school students sat in chairs around a table full of Yale bulletins.

Dylan looked at the other students and knew that he had no chance of getting into Yale. These other students were obviously better than he was: smarter, richer, braver. Yale was for people like this Polo here, someone who wanted to study semiotics and linguistics, whatever they were. Or for Allison, who wrote her songs. Dylan getting admitted to Yale was about as likely as getting Allison to take a second look at him. If you thought about it, girls and college were a lot alike: there was Early Decision, Regular Admission, and Wait List. The only difference was that with college you took SATs whereas with girls there were all these other secret examinations you took and failed without even knowing it. It would be nice, actually, knowing what your scores were in life. That way you wouldn't keep trying to ask out Stanford when in all probability you'd wind up married to somebody like the University of Las Vegas.

"Floyd, Dylan?" said a secretary, standing in a doorway.

"Here," he said, without thinking. All of the other kids in the room looked at him with irritation. He realized too late he wasn't supposed to say "Here," he was supposed to stand up and meet his interviewer. It was people like himself, obviously, that made it necessary to wait around all day to get interviewed, students who clearly had no chance but insisted on taking up Yale University's time anyway.

Dylan walked down a long, brightly lit hallway. There was an oriental rug on the floor. The secretary ushered him into an office and handed a man behind a desk a large folder.

"This is Dr. Kugelmaus," the secretary said.

"Floyd," Kugelmaus said. "Good to meet you."

"Good to meet you too, sir," Dylan said, realizing at this moment that Dr. Kugelmaus had his name backward. He thought his name was Floyd Dylan, not Dylan Floyd. He should have caught this when the secretary announced him in the waiting room, but Dylan thought that they were just being official about things, last name first, first name last. Now it was too late to correct the man. He'd have to endure the entire interview being called the wrong name.

"So, Floyd, have you had a good trip up here so far?"

Dylan felt his face growing hot. His palms began to sweat. He thought about explaining about the train ride from New Jersey with his father, about the Winnebago and Uncle Lefty and Allison and Polo, but didn't know how this could possibly make a good impression. He thought about Allison, wondered how her interview was going.

"It's been, I don't know, good," Dylan said. "You'd call it good."

"Well, fine, Floyd. You know, this is really just a chance for the two of us to talk informally, get to know each other. I hope you'll be able to relax and feel at home. That's what Yale is, really, if you come here. A place you might feel at home."

Dylan had a sudden insight. It was possible that there really was someone named Floyd Dylan out in the waiting room, and Dylan had jumped up so quickly that the real Floyd Dylan hadn't gotten a chance. He was in this office as an impostor, a fraud. Dylan wasn't sure, but there was a possibility this could even work out to his advantage, especially if this Floyd had done well on his SATs, which Dylan most assuredly had not.

"Well, I'd like that," Dylan said.

"You'd like what?" the interviewer said, his face clouding over.

Dylan couldn't really remember where they were. "What you just said."

"Ah," said Kugelmaus. "Fine." He flipped open the folder in front of him. "Now it says here you like English, is that right?"

"Yes, sir," Dylan said. Had he written this? He couldn't remember what he'd written on the card he'd had to fill out in order to schedule the interview. Whatever he'd said was surely the typical blur of half-truths, fudges, and just plain lies.

"What books are you reading this fall?" the interviewer said.

"Well, actually, I just finished *Blood Meridian* by Cormac McCarthy."

Kugelmaus did not respond.

"You know, the one with all the dead horses and everything."

"I read that," Kugelmaus said. "It failed to cheer me."

"Well," Dylan said. "It's not cheerful, that's for sure."

"Do you ever read books out loud?" Kugelmaus asked.

"Out loud?" Dylan echoed. He was trying to figure out where Kugelmaus was going with this.

"Yes," said Kugelmaus. "I'm just rediscovering the joys of reading out loud myself. I'm reading *House at Pooh Corner* to my daughter. She's six." Kugelmaus pointed to a picture on his desk of a very cute little girl. Little Kugelmaus had a balloon.

"My mother used to read to me," Dylan said. "I loved that when I was little."

"I know," said Kugelmaus. "It's such a joy, one of the best things a parent can do with a child. It's a shame we lose that."

"She used to read me *Tom Sawyer*," Dylan said.

"Isn't that wonderful . . ." Kugelmaus said, his voice trailing off. A strange look came over the man's face. "Isn't that—"

Kugelmaus froze for a moment. Then he stood and walked halfway across the room. He paused by the door and put out one hand, as if to steady himself, clutching the doorknob. He stood there swaying for a moment, then raised one hand to his face.

Dylan realized that he was now in a very unusual, possibly unfortunate situation. Kugelmaus was crying.

"Dr. Kugelmaus?" Dylan said, unsure. He wondered what the right thing to do was. Should he try to comfort Dr. Kugelmaus? Was the man crying because of Dylan's loss, or because of some tragedy of his own? And most importantly, how might the proper expression of human sympathy even now help to make the right impression?

He looked at the man's shaking shoulders. Dylan wanted to stand and rush over to him. Look, he could say. I don't care if I get into Yale. It doesn't matter anymore. All that matters is that we share some basic sympathy, that you feel some sort of solace for your pain, whatever it is. And perhaps, if Dylan proceeded in this manner, it would get him into Yale anyway. Kugelmaus would write on his folder, *Very Kind Young Man*. It was a possibility, the kind of thing that would make up for his SATs, perhaps. Something Dylan had not discovered yet was going to have to make up for them.

But now Kugelmaus was coming back to the desk. He was wiping his face with a hanky. "I'm sorry," he said. "My mother died last week. I was just thinking about her. I had this enormous wave of grief, just hit me unawares."

"That's okay, Dr. Kugelmaus," Dylan said. "We've all been sad."

"This is embarrassing," Kugelmaus said. "I don't know what to say."

"My mother died when I was eleven," Dylan said. "I know what it's like to miss her."

"When you were eleven?" Kugelmaus said.

Dylan nodded.

"That's rough," he said. "I'm glad my mother lived as long as she did. She was in her eighties. Passed away in her sleep." He looked at Dylan over the tops of his glasses. "What did your mother die of, so young?"

Dylan licked his lips. "Suicide," he said. Then, as if this did not fully explain the situation, he added, "She took her life."

Kugelmaus looked very sad, ashamed, perhaps, that he had asked. "I'm sorry," he said.

Inexplicably, Dylan felt tears burning in his eyes. He tried to suck them back in. Clearly, although it was all right for Kugelmaus to start weeping, it was less acceptable for Dylan to do so. He took a deep breath but the oxygen appeared to loosen several more gasping sobs from the place where they had lain waiting. In a moment's time he found himself shaking, feeling the sobs dissolve him into his separate pieces.

"It's all right," Kugelmaus said, handing him a tissue. "Don't worry."

"Damn!" Dylan said out loud, then realized that he had now not only begun weeping in his first interview for college, but he had sworn as well.

But even as he watched Dylan, Kugelmaus's face became pink again. His lower lip began to twitch. Kugelmaus blinked some more tears from his eyelashes. "Damn it all," Kugelmaus said. "Dammit to hell!"

So now Kugelmaus and Dylan were both sitting in their chairs, thinking about their mothers, sobbing and swearing. Dylan closed his eyes and tried to steady his head with his hand.

Kugelmaus swiveled around in his chair and looked out the window across the quad. There were students in sweaters playing Frisbee. The October leaves were just beginning to turn shades of yellow and red. A couple of students walked by the window, speaking animatedly to a professor.

"Well," Kugelmaus said at last, blowing his nose. He swiveled back toward Dylan. "That felt good, I guess."

Dylan, too, was coming to his senses. He wiped his face with the tissue. "I didn't mean to—" he said, apologizing for something. "It wasn't my intention—"

"Well, that's all right," Kugelmaus said. "You're a good boy. I can see that. You've made something of yourself, haven't you. I know your mother would be proud of me."

Dylan was about to point out the man's mistake, then decided against this. Maybe it wasn't a mistake.

"You know, in an odd sort of way, I guess this has given me a chance to get to know you," Kugelmaus said. "You're a kind young man. Sympathetic to others. Caring. I appreciate your graciousness. It's rare."

"Thank you," Dylan said.

Kugelmaus stood up. "Are you all right, then? You can take a few minutes to compose yourself before heading back out to meet your father, if you want."

"No," Dylan said, "I'm all right. It's like you said. It kind of felt good."

"It does," Kugelmaus said, smiling.

"Well," Dylan said. "Thank you."

"No, thank you," said Kugelmaus. "I think we've shared something important today."

"I do, too."

"I can't make any promises," Kugelmaus said, holding open the door. "But I hope to see you next fall." He clapped Dylan on the back. "As a member of Yale's class of 2003!"

"Thank you, sir," Dylan said, and thought to himself, *Yeah, right.*

"Good luck, Floyd," Kugelmaus said, and went back into his office.

The Anchor Bar, over on College Avenue, was a dimly lit dive. Ben and Lefty were drinking beers.

"Cheers, brother," Lefty said, clinking his pint glass against Ben's. "Doesn't get much better than this."

"Yeah," Ben said, miserably. "You're probably right."

"Aw, come on," Lefty said. "Buck up. This is one special time we all are having. Don't be a grumpy gus."

"I'm not grumpy," Ben said.

Lefty drank. "Still bad, is it?"

Ben nodded. "Yep."

"Well, damn. What can I tell ya. Maybe something good'll happen."

Ben shook his head. "Not likely."

Lefty looked across the bar. The place was almost deserted, except for themselves and two old men playing gin.

"Is there anything I can do, brother?" Lefty said. "You know I'd do anything if I could help."

"There's nothing," Ben said. "I'll be all right."

"Well, maybe you need a place to go for a while. Until you get on your feet."

"It's not that bad."

"I know. Still you know you got family. There's no reason you have to sit out in the cold."

"I'm not sitting in the cold."

"Next year all the kids'll be off at college. It'll just be me and Chloë. No reason you couldn't park yourself at our house at least until you get on your feet."

"I said I'd be all right," Ben said, annoyed.

"Hey, don't bite my head off, brother. I'm just offering a helping hand. That's what families are for."

"Yeah, well, your hands have offered enough already."

Lefty put his pint down and looked at Ben. "Man, you are an ugly drunk, aren't you."

"I'm not drunk."

"You should be."

"Give me some time, it's early."

"I hate to see you like this."

"Like what?"

"Like this. Hating yourself."

"I don't hate myself," Ben said. "I'm one of the few people I like, actually."

Lefty thought this over. "Well, good. You should. You got a lot going for you."

"I know," said Ben. "You don't have to tell me."

Lefty took a good swig. "So," he said. "You think these kids're getting into Yale?"

Ben shook his head. "I don't know. Dylan's kind of quiet about his plans."

"Yeah, I noticed. You think he's all right?"

"Of course he's all right. Why wouldn't he be all right?"

"I don't know," Lefty said. "It'll be good for him to get out, though. Get a fresh start."

"Yes," Ben said. "It will."

Lefty thought things over. "Allison wants out, too. She's not too crazy about me, in case you couldn't tell."

"She's not?"

Lefty smiled. "Come on, brother. You know. I'm not exactly Albert Fuckin' Einstein."

"No," Ben said. "You're not."

"She doesn't see much to admire, selling Pontiacs."

"You mean you don't exactly measure up to her expectations?"

"Yeah, well, her ol' man—Chloë's ex—was a rocket scientist. I mean, like, an actual rocket scientist. Worked for NASA and all."

Ben shook his head. "Imagine her, disappointed by you then."

Lefty put his drink down. "Well, say what you want. It's put a roof over our heads. It's sending ol' Juddy to Harvard, or whatever. Maybe it's not brain surgery, fine, but it's not nothing."

"I didn't say it was nothing."

"I know what you think. And I don't care, brother. If selling Pontiacs is what it takes, I give no shit. They're good cars."

Ben finished his beer. "Maybe I should have sold Pontiacs."

"Well, hell," Lefty said. "The ol' man wanted you to have the fuckin' lot. You had to practically spit in his eye to get your independence."

"I did," Ben said. "For all the good it did me."

"You did what you had to do," said Lefty. "You wouldn't a been happy."

"I know," said Ben. "I'm just being maudlin. Once I get myself clear it'll be all right."

"That high-tech bullshit is impossible to figure anyway. How are you supposed to know the difference between a gold mine and a swindle?"

"Well, I guess I didn't," Ben said. "Okay? I guess I didn't." Ben stared at his beer.

"What happened again?" Lefty said. "You want to give me the blow-by-blow?"

"What's the difference, I'm a goner, that's all you need to know."

"I'm just giving you the opportunity to take a load off. If that's what you want."

"They cut my legs off, okay? Goddamn Ventura Monmouth. Bunch of goddamn vultures is what they are."

"What did they do that for? You weren't doing so hot?"

"We were almost exactly on schedule. The deal was, they loaned us two million to do this expansion deal. We were supposed to increase our earnings by eighty percent, then they were supposed to give us the other three."

"And they got what, equity in the company in exchange?"

"That's the thing, they got a chunk of the business. It's insane for them to play hardball. Nobody profits out of this. Nobody."

"But if they had a contract—"

"We didn't make the eighty percent, okay? We spent the two million, ran into a hitch. Still, we were up seventy-five percent. We were very close. It makes no sense for them to shut us down, except for them to show what a bunch of assholes they are. We were up seventy-five percent!"

Lefty shook his head. "I'm sorry, brother," he said.

"Me too," Ben said. "I'm a fuckin' goner."

"Well listen," Lefty said. "It's not the end of the world. You want to work on the lot for a while I'd be happy for you. Give us a chance to get to know each other again."

Ben choked for a moment. "Me?" he said. "On the lot? You mean working for you?"

"If that's what you want. Until you get on your feet."

"I'm not working on the lot, okay?" Ben said. "I haven't sunk to that."

Lefty shook his head. "You can call it sinking," he said. "I don't mind."

"Yeah, well, I'm not working on the lot, okay? I'd rather mow lawns for heaven's fucking sake."

"Okay," Lefty said. "Mow lawns." He caught the eye of the man behind the bar. "Bartender? Two more." Lefty looked back at his brother. " 'Course it'll take a lot a lawns to pay for Yale. Let me think, twenty-five thousand dollars a year, divided by—how much do you get for mowin' somebody's lawn, like maybe ten bucks? I guess that comes out to about two an' a half thousand lawns. Say you mow each customer ten times a summer, that's two hundred an' fifty customers, takes about two hours to mow a lawn, so that's five hundred hours a week you got behind the mower. Sure, I guess you could do it that way. Why not?"

"Don't get snippy," Ben said.

"Hey, I'm not the guy mowing two hundred lawns a week. You know what else you could do, maybe open a lemonade stand."

"Fuck you," Ben said. "Just fuck you."

The bartender brought over two more beers. Ben dug around in his pocket for change.

"Hey," Lefty said. "It's on me." He handed the bartender a fifty.

"You like this," Ben said. "You think it's funny, me being broke, you rolling in the dough."

"I don't like it," said Lefty. "How could I like it?"

"You love it," said Ben. He ran his open palm down the length of his face. "Jesus, how did it come to this?"

"One step at a time," Lefty said. " 'We wear the chains we forge in life.' "

Ben looked at him. "What the hell was that?"

"Mr. Charles Dickens," Lefty said. "*A Christmas Carol.*"

"How do you know anything about Dickens?" Ben said.

Lefty smiled. "I seen movies," he said.

"Right," Ben said. "For a minute there I thought you'd actually read a book. Whoo—what was I thinking?"

Lefty looked at him for a second, then laughed. "I don't care," he said. "Laugh it up. I swear I don't mind. I never said I was smart."

"I never said you did."

"I don't blame you for being pissed. You can be as pissed as you want. I'm just saying I'm here to help if you want. If you don't, like I said, I give no shit. As long as you know I'm here."

Ben sighed. "I know. I hear you. I appreciate it. You just have to let me work all this out on my own. I'll let you know if I need your help. I'm not ungrateful, all right?"

"All right then," Lefty said. "Well all right."

The men stared at their pints of beer, nearly full. It was awkward to have reached the end of their conversation and still have this much beer to drink. They sat in silence for a while, drinking and not drinking.

"How's your health?" Ben asked. "Docs give you the green light?"

"I'm as healthy as I'm gonna be," Lefty said with a smile. "No use worrying about it."

"They have you on a special diet or anything?"

Lefty waved his hand. "They tried that, but you know what I say, the hell with it. I'd rather have another heart attack than give up French fries, you know what I mean?"

"Yeah, well, you gave us all a turn," Ben said.

"I'm all right, I told you," Lefty said. "I take a pill every morning, that's it. I don't think about it. You can't spend your whole life worrying about dying. It's better living when you're dying than being dead the whole time you're alive."

Ben nodded, trying to work this out.

"So," Lefty said, changing the subject. "How about that Chloë?"

"How about her," Ben said.

"I mean, what do you think? Is she hot, or what?"

Ben smiled. "She's very nice."

Lefty's face fell. "You don't like her?"

"She's great," Ben said. "Much more your type."

"Oh," Lefty said. "Now I get you. Boy oh boy, an elephant never forgets."

"You think I'm going to forget?"

"I guess I don't."

They each drank a large swig of beer.

"Maybe I'm stupid, but I kind of figured that was water under the bridge."

"You're right. Maybe you are stupid."

The men looked at each other angrily.

"I'm not having this conversation," Ben said.

"What conversation? We aren't even talking."

"You're talking," Ben said. "I don't want to hear about it."

Lefty shook his head. "You know what pisses you off

about me?'' he said. ''You hate the fact that I'm at peace with the world. The way you figure, the world won't work right until you're happy and I'm miserable. Well sorry, brother, life goes on. I'm not spending the rest of my life crying into my Rice Krispies.''

''I don't want you to be miserable, Lefty,'' Ben said. ''Maybe a little guilt would be all right, though. Some sort of regret, even.''

''I told you it's water under the goddamned bridge. What's done is done.''

''It's not that simple,'' Ben said. ''Just because something's over doesn't mean you don't think about it every day.''

''Well, fine,'' Lefty said. ''You live that way. I'm not talking you out of it, doesn't look like.''

Ben stared out the plate glass window into the brightly lit scene of College Street. It looked like a different world.

''Such a beautiful woman,'' Ben said at last, softly.

''Yeah,'' Lefty said. ''You got that right. Ol' Chloë knows how to beat the band!''

Ben looked at his brother sadly.

''I didn't mean her,'' he said.

Polo and Allison were walking through the Old Temple Street Cemetery. Allison looked at a campus map.

''This doesn't look like the Center for British Art,'' she said, worried.

''It's a short cut, my dear,'' said Polo. ''The fastest way. All the Bulldogs cut through the graveyard on their way to wherever they're going.''

''Bulldogs?'' Allison said. ''Is that what they call themselves?''

''Well, it's the vernacular.''

"Gives me the creeps," said Allison, shivering. "Look at these stones. They're old."

They paused before a row of long, brown headstones. The tops of the stones were carved in the shapes of angels with sad, open mouths. The names on the markers had worn away.

"I've always found cemeteries restful," Polo said. "Haven't you?"

"I guess," Allison said.

"Why don't we pause here? Take a moment to collect our thoughts."

Allison looked around nervously. "Okay. If you want."

Polo sat down on a marble slab buried lengthwise in the grass. THE REVEREND URIAH COFFINS, it read. 1742–1791. ONE WITH HIS MAYKER.

Allison sat next to Polo on the stone. He put his arm around her. Allison looked at her watch.

"They say there are monks in Ireland who sleep in coffins every night," Polo said. "To remind themselves of their last end." He cleared his throat. "Joyce writes about it in 'The Dead.'"

"Jeez, Polo," Allison said. "What's with you? You're creeping me out."

He squeezed her. "Allison. That is hardly my intention. It's a place of peace, though. A place of perfect solitude."

"I guess," Allison said. She looked at her map. "Is that the Center for British Art over there?" She twisted the map around, trying to get oriented.

Polo put his hand on the map, slowly eased it away from her. "A place of solitude," he said. "A place where we can be alone." He moved his lips close to hers. Allison looked at his handsome face, drawing nearer. She closed her eyes.

"Polo," she whispered.

"My love," he said, and kissed her.

The teenagers lay there in an embrace for a while. The young man's fingers rose to trace the length of Allison's hair.

"Polo," she said again, as his lips drew away from her.

"My love," he said. "My own."

Polo moved his hands down the front of Allison's shirt and paused on her breast. His thumb stroked back and forth over her nipple.

"Polo," she said quietly. "Quit it." Her eyes closed and her head fell back. "Quit it," she said again, more softly.

Polo unbuttoned the front of her yellow top and unhooked her front-clasp bra. He gathered her breasts into his face. Allison could feel the stubble on his cheeks.

"Oh," she said.

"Allison," Polo said.

He moved his hands up and down her rib cage, then swept beneath her peasant skirt. Slowly his fingers moved up her legs. Allison had goosebumps. His hand slipped under her panties.

"Oh," she said.

"Allison," Polo said.

For a few moments longer his fingers trembled upon her, as if he were playing the cello. Then he grabbed the waistband of her underpants and tried to yank them downward.

"Allison," Polo said. "Come to me."

Allison opened her eyes. "I'm not ready," she said. "Please, Polo."

"Of course you are," he said. "You're wonderful."

"No," Allison said. "Please. I want to wait."

"I know you do," Polo said. "You've wanted to wait for now. Here. In this place. The two of us together."

"No," Allison said, annoyed. She pulled up her underpants and smoothed down her skirt. "I said I don't *want* to."

Polo sat up. "There's nothing to be afraid of," he said.

"I'm not afraid," she said. "I just want to wait. Is that so hard to understand?"

"Allison," Polo said, taking her hand. "Of course I understand. I would never want you to do anything you're not ready for. You want to wait, of course we'll wait. That's all you have to say."

"Well, good," Allison said. "You're making me feel like some sort of, I don't know. Stupid."

"Of course you're not stupid," Polo said. "What a thing to say. You're the most intelligent woman I've ever known. You know I don't sleep with lots of different girls. You're practically the first girl I've ever loved, practically. I've never known anyone like you."

"You're not serious," Allison said.

"Of course I'm serious," Polo said. "I want us to be together for always. I want to remember every moment we've spent together as something magical and intense. I don't know, seeing you here in this beautiful place, it seemed like the time was ripe at last. For the two of us, together, to become one."

"Well, I don't know," Allison said. "I mean, anyone could just come along here."

"Have you seen anyone while we've been in here?" Polo asked. "Have you noticed another human being?"

"I thought you said these Bulldogs walked right through."

"Well, perhaps," said Polo. "But I believe they're all in class now. We're quite alone."

Allison looked around the old graveyard. The maples above an obelisk were turning red.

"It's so quiet," she said.

"It is," said Polo. "Except for the pounding of my heart."

Allison looked over at him. He looked so earnest in his black turtleneck.

"Don't you want to feel it?" he said, taking her hand and placing it on his chest. "Don't you want to feel my beating heart?"

As a matter of fact she really *didn't* want to feel his beating heart, but there she was, her fingertips being pressed into the warm black cotton of his turtleneck. His heart was pounding away beneath her fingertips. She could feel it.

"Now let me feel yours," Polo said, and placed his hands on her breasts. "Yes," he said. "I can feel it pounding. Pounding with the life force."

"Come on," Allison said. "Quit it."

"Ssshh," Polo said. "I want to listen to your heart."

Allison said nothing and sat there with his hands on her breasts. He closed his eyes. "Buh-bump, buh-bump, buh-bump," he said.

"How did your interview go?" she said. "Okay?"

"I'm sorry, my love," Polo said. He was still holding her breasts. "I can't hear a thing with your heart pounding. He lowered his head onto her chest, put his ear right up against her heart. "I want to be filled with the sound of your beating heart!" he whispered. "I want to be consumed with the percussion of your animation."

"Okay, fine," said Allison. "Whatever."

He raised his lips to her breast and began to kiss her nipples again. Allison looked around to see if there was anyone coming along the path. Why did boys insist on this? Was it so wrong just to sit there and talk about their interviews, watch the leaves change colors? Why did everything have to be breasts and underpants all the time?

And yet, at the same time, it was not unpleasant to

have her breasts kissed. The more she wanted to object to his view of the world, the more reasonable it became. She wished that there was some way of slowing everything down.

Her nipples puckered. "Yes," Polo said, "that's right," as if she had some sort of control over this event. "Now you are my girl. My only."

"Polo," she said, trying to sit up again. She pushed him back.

"Allison," he said.

For a moment they wrestled like that, Polo pressing down, Allison pushing back. Then Polo relented. Allison sat up.

"Do you know how hard you make me?" Polo said. "Do you know?"

Allison didn't want to know how hard she made him, didn't have any interest in finding out. But Polo grabbed her hand and placed it on the fly of his pants. His wiener was giant in there, like some burrowing gopher trying to dig its way out of his underwear. "Yes," Polo said, as if she'd asked him a question. "Yes, yes, yes."

"Darn you," Allison said, grabbing her hand back and standing up. "I wish you'd just quit it. Why can't you quit it when I say so?"

"Darling," Polo said. "I thought you loved me."

"I do love you," Allison said. "Don't you believe that?"

"I thought I did," Polo said, looking dejectedly down at the grave of Uriah Coffins.

She kneeled down next to him and took his hand. "I don't want to have sex," Allison said. "I'm waiting until I'm married. Is that so wrong?"

"It's not wrong," he said. "It's just that I'm worried for you."

Allison looked nervous. "Worried? About me?"

"Yes, you're so tense. I'm afraid it's destroying you."

Allison thought about this. "I don't feel tense," she said.

"Of course you don't," Polo said. "That's why I'm so worried. It's not good for you to be this tense and not be aware of it."

"What do you mean, destroying me?" Allison said.

"I mean you've become so nervous and unhappy that people can tell. It's as if people can see the invisible burden that you bear. It's hurting you."

"It's invisible, this burden I have?"

"It is," Polo said. "And I'm just—well, forgive me for saying this, my love, but I'm afraid you're not going to get into college like this. I'm afraid all the interviewers can see what I see."

"Which is what?"

"A girl with a private sorrow."

"You can see that?" Allison said. "My private sorrow?"

"Yes," Polo said. "And it makes my heart break for you."

"You're lying," Allison said. "You just want to have sex with me. You're just trying to screw up my mind."

Polo opened his mouth, then shut it. He looked astonished. Tears seemed to gather in the corners of his eyes. He got up and walked several feet away, then paused.

"Polo?" Allison said. She got up and went over to him. "Polo?"

"I can't believe you said that," he said, his voice breaking. "I don't know what to say to you."

"I'm sorry," Allison said. "But you really bug me sometimes. I'm totally confused."

"That's what I've been trying to tell you," Polo said. "And here I am trying to help you, and what do you do but say something like that." He shook his head. "Sometimes I feel like I don't know you."

Allison looked at him. Maybe he was right. Maybe he didn't know her.

Polo took her hand and the two of them walked across the cemetery toward the Center for British Art.

As they came to the iron gates they saw Juddy, peeing on a grave.

"Yo," he said, turning and zipping. "Do it up!"

"What?" Polo said, astonished. "What?"

"What's going on?" Juddy said. "You do your interviews and shit?"

"We did," Allison said. "We're all done."

The stream of Juddy's urine trickled down an old stone. AMOS HUDSON, the stone read. MAYFLOWER PASSENGER.

"Boy," Juddy said, looking around at the cemetery. "This Yale is nothing like you hear."

Chloë sat in a chair in the empty Winnebago, holding a pair of needle-nose pliers. It would be simple enough, she thought, to cut the brake cables. Then if she could make up some sort of explanation for getting herself and Allison off the camper, that would be that. The whole busload of Floyds—and Polo—would go careening off of a large suspension bridge and plummet into the waters of the Connecticut River. It was a soothing image to think about, everybody screaming.

People often did such things on television, Chloë thought. The moment they were alone they slid under buses on dollies and pinched a wire here, unscrewed a bolt there. For a moment she imagined her face, illuminated by the light of a blow torch. Hot solder dripping onto the pavement.

She put the pliers back in her husband's tool kit. With

some regret, Chloë realized she wouldn't even know what a brake cable looked like. She'd probably cut the one wire that wouldn't do anything. The wire she cut would probably improve the gas mileage, for all she knew. It was impossible in this world to do anything as succinctly as they did on TV.

Well, Christ. I'm not the only woman who's ever thought about murdering her husband, Chloë thought. It's the most normal thing in the world, as long as you don't do anything about it. There isn't a married woman in the universe who hasn't contemplated, some rainy afternoon, what life would be like if a piano suddenly fell on her husband's head. That doesn't mean you want it to happen, or that you're a bad person. It's a natural part of marriage, to imagine the other person assassinated. The great circle of life.

A mother with a newborn baby in a Snugli walked down Temple Street. Jeez, Chloë thought. The devices they have for parents these days. If they'd had half this stuff when Allison was young things would have been so different. Even now the memory of how terrible it had been was enough to take her breath away, make her clap one hand to her forehead and shudder.

Allison had developed a heart arrhythmia several hours after she was born. This was seventeen years ago, in 1981. They'd had to take the baby, by ambulance, to the big hospital up in Baltimore. For a day or so they didn't know whether the child would live or die. Chloë, meanwhile, wasn't allowed to leave the hospital, since she was still healing from the cesarean. She had to lie there in her room, wondering what was happening to her baby, fifty miles away.

That was the thing she'd never recovered from, she thought. Her newborn baby being taken away from her, wearing a tiny oxygen mask, IV tubes running into her navel and foot. Gary followed the ambulance all the way to Baltimore and paced up and down the corridor of the IICU, waiting for word. He had to come back that night to Chloë's bedside, ashen-faced, and say they still don't know what's wrong with her. They can't get her heartbeat down. A normal newborn's heartbeat is about 150 beats per minute. Little Allison's heart ran at over 240. If they couldn't get it down, the child might suffer heart failure, enlargement of the heart.

In the end they figured it out, of course; the child had been born with a secondary bypass tract, which caused the tachycardiac nerve to short-circuit. They gave Allison two syringes full of Digoxin each day for the first year of her life, and then that was it. They got into a routine of preparing a syringe for their baby, at eight in the morning, at eight at night. Eventually she outgrew the condition. One day Allison found the old syringes piled up in a medicine cabinet and threw them all away. Allison didn't even remember anything about it.

Hell if I'll ever forget it though, Chloë thought. That's the terrible thing about parenthood. You endure these crises, weird medical situations, your child wracked with fever in the middle of the night, and eventually the crisis passes and your child has no idea that each of these events is a spear in your heart that you carry with you the rest of your days. Then they wonder why you worry, why you're afraid of eventualities that couldn't possibly transpire, and all you want to say is, I've seen it happen. You think this is bad? I've seen this and worse.

Chloë went into the galley of the Winnebago and made herself a cup of coffee. The air was rich with the smell of hazelnut. It was amazing, the changes in the world in the last eighteen years, since the time of Allison's birth. In 1981 coffee was just coffee; it wasn't an entire field of study. Same with a lot of things that once had been simple. Where once there had been Budweiser and Miller, now there were raspberry wheat porters and honey lagers. Where once there had been just three networks and UHF, now there were satellite dishes and home shopping channels. Where there had once been a little girl playing with Barbies and a Big Wheel, now there was a young woman with three earrings in one ear and a boyfriend who studied narratology.

Before he'd died, Gary was working on a NASA project called Copernicus II, which was a probe designed to take pictures of a something called Planet X, the tenth planet in the solar system, out beyond Pluto. Although the planet had never been seen on any telescope, the irregularities in the orbits of Pluto and Neptune made its existence highly likely. *Copernicus II*, scheduled for launch in fall 1998, was supposed to actually take pictures of Planet X for the first time.

Gary used to come home seething with excitement over the project. It was infectious. He'd barrel through the door at the end of the day, unable to contain himself. *You won't believe this, Chloë. We've solved the problem of the trajectory vectors.* They'd sit there in the living room, looking out through the bay windows at the Chesapeake, drinking wine and talking about Planet X, while their daughter played with a Play-Doh Fun Factory on the floor, making purple hot dogs and spaghetti.

It was strange how she'd come to believe in Planet X. It was Gary's enthusiasm for this theoretical place that made it real for her. It was Planet X that had built their house, that paid for the Play-Doh, that kept Allison and her mother rolling in juice boxes and merlot, Big Wheels and Volvos.

She found out just how theoretical Planet X was a few years later when Gary dropped dead of a heart attack. A week after the funeral she discovered how much he'd been hiding from her. Loans he'd taken out. A second mortgage. Wild speculations on real estate in places she'd never heard of. Three months after his death she had to sell the house. By the fall she had to pack up her daughter and move back into her mother's house in Bridgeport, Connecticut. She and Allison slept in bunk beds in the room Chloë had occupied as a child.

She'd spent the fall looking for work, but no one wanted a woman in her forties with no experience doing anything besides making macaroni and cheese. They lived off of her mother's pension, and Chloë collected AFDC. By the spring she learned to type, got menial jobs temping at offices in Bridgeport. On the one-year anniversary of Gary's death she was working part-time in the office of the cafeteria of a veterans' hospital. Even then she was aware that college was less than five years away for her daughter. She thought about the thirty thousand dollars in tuition money she'd need every year for four years, and felt sick. Planet X was a long way off.

She'd gone down to Lefty's lot pretty much at random, to sell the Volvo and try to get something used. He was kind, helpful, excruciatingly jolly. He wound up selling her a Firebird. When she went for the test drive, he sat in the back and told her about his empire. They drove south along the river, through the beautiful hills. It was depressing, all those wealthy people living in all their huge houses with all their green lawns. "I tell you something, Mrs. Baxter," he'd said. "You know what they say about Pontiacs? We Build Excitement."

Six months later she was walking down the aisle at the Deep River Lutheran Church to the sound of her daughter playing "Moonshadow" on guitar.

So: at the age of forty-eight she'd become Mrs. Lefty "Flat Foot" Floyd Pontiac Oldsmobile Mitsubishi. *Have we got a deal for you.*

It didn't take very long for Chloë to realize what kind of deal he had for her.

Chloë sat down in the driver's seat of the Winnebago. She looked out at New Haven. Yale students were walking down the street wearing day packs. A boy with a goatee sat on a fire hydrant tapping on a PowerBook. From a tower came Westminster chimes. Go on, Allison, Chloë thought. Disappear into this world.

The question, of course, was what world Chloë would inhabit once Allison went off to college. Would it be necessary to stay with Lefty for four more years, to make sure the tuition got paid? Or could she gradually assume her own life, move her things into the spare bedroom, for instance. Lefty wouldn't take his disappointment out on his stepdaughter, would he? She knew he had this streak. It was the same streak that had led to the trouble seven years ago—the trouble that even now hung above the brothers like a satellite.

What if she just started feeding him high-fat dinners and waited for him to have another heart attack? Lefty was fifty pounds overweight anyway, made no effort to watch his cholesterol. The man had never seen a hot dog that didn't have his name on it, written out in relish. She could just give up on vegetables, start feeding him these he-man dinners, and who knows, maybe in a week or two he'd turn purple and keel over.

Or she could poison him. Surely there was something in the medicine cabinet already that, if taken in the proper dosage, would make his brain explode. You could grind it up with a mortar and pestle and stick it in his coffee and the next thing you know you've got a little peace and quiet.

Then there were all sorts of less subtle approaches—stabbing, shooting, blowing him up with nitroglycerin. Maybe it was better just to get it all over with, sink a knife into his liver or tie him up and slip a stick of dynamite in his mouth. The good thing about blowing him up would be that you'd get the drama of the detonator.

But then there'd be the inevitable aftermath. Cleaning up the mess. Disposing of the body. Being questioned by police. Sitting by, pretending to be innocent while guys went through all her stuff, reporters camped out on the front yard. And in the end, she knew she'd be caught. It's impossible to do anything in the world that leaves no trace, especially murdering people.

She remembered leaving the hospital with Allison, five days old by the time they finally let her go. It was like getting sprung out of prison. And yet she also felt guilty leaving with her newborn baby, as all the other infants had to remain behind. The kid who'd swallowed Drano, Duncan, who could not speak because his esophagus was burned out. They were building him a new esophagus out of a piece of his small intestine. The tiny pale baby, Gina, with the tiny pale mother. Another baby, a week old perhaps, with both its legs in traction. All the other parents congratulated Gary and Chloë on Allison's discharge, but there was no joy in their wishes. Gary helped them to the elevator, and the doors opened and a person with deformed features walked out of the elevator onto the children's ward. She had huge purple lips and deathly pale white skin. Her bald head was ringed by fringes of singed orange hair. Her nose bulbous, bloody red. For perhaps three seconds Chloë looked at the woman with unflinching sympathy, thinking, Women like this have become my sisters. And then, a moment later, realizing the obvious truth: it was a normal woman, dressed as a clown.

Chloë watched the members of her family approach from down the street. Her brother-in-law, Ben, and his son, Dylan. Allison and her boyfriend, Polo. Her husband,

Lefty, and her stepson, Juddy. They walked toward her like members of some lost and ragged army.

They climbed up the stairs that led into the Winnebago. Ben and Dylan lay down on their bunks. Polo sat in one of the bucket seats next to the picture window. Allison came in, sat down in the galley, and picked her guitar up out of its case. A moment later she was softly singing. *Oh, Shenandoah, I love your daughter. Away, you rolling river.*

Lefty came in last and looked proudly upon his people. He hugged his wife and smiled. Chloë smelled beer. "How'd it go?" she said.

"Good," he said. He looked around. "What do you say, gang? Good?"

Polo nodded resentfully. Ben stared at the ceiling. Allison played guitar. Juddy opened a beer. Dylan said, "Good, Uncle Lefty."

Allison was still singing. *I'm bound away, across the wide Missouri.*

"You see?" Lefty said to Chloë, as if he'd just proved something. "We're good."

He smiled so proudly that Chloë's heart had to go out to the poor man. She reached forward and kissed her husband, squeezed him around the waist. Maybe this was it, then. She thought of his face, squinched up and purple, consumed with his own passion. People died like that all the time. Nelson Rockefeller, for instance. A massive coronary in a rented hotel room with a woman not his wife. What were the last words Nelson Rockefeller heard? *No, Nelson. You're going.*

That was the answer, Chloë thought. A Christian kind of assassination. She would murder him with love.

harvard university

"I took a literature and arts course on symphony and music, and I am now a pretentious classical music snob with an ever-growing library of make-out music," reported one (student).

—*Insider's Guide to the Colleges*, 1998

Cambridge, Massachusetts
Number of applications: 17,852
Percent accepted: 12%
Middle 50% SAT range, 1996: 630–730V, 660–770M
Most popular majors: government, economics, biology
Mascot: the Crimson

d ylan woke up unsure of the time. The Winnebago was moving. From somewhere nearby came the sounds of his father clacking at the keys of his laptop computer. Juddy was singing softly to himself in the bunk over Dylan's head. *We're poor little lambs who've lost our way. Baah, baah, baah. We're little black sheep who've gone astray. Baah, baah, baah.* This much was clear: Dylan's cousin was no Whiffenpoof.

Dylan saw himself, ten years old, running down a dirt road near a farm. Juddy was running just ahead of him. They ran until they collapsed on the banks of a small stream. A covered bridge crossed the stream a few hundred feet from where they sat. Juddy looked back in the direction from which they had come. Dylan started to cry.

"You stop crying, Dickweed," said Juddy. He grabbed his cousin by the collar of his shirt. "You hear me? Shut up."

Dylan tried to stop crying but couldn't. Juddy shoved him. Dylan shoved him back. A few moments later they were wrestling, rolling down the bank. Dylan felt the water of the stream soaking into the back of his shirt. "Okay?" Juddy said, pinning him down. "You ready to stop crying now?"

Dylan nodded, and Juddy let him go. They crawled back up on the bank.

"You listen to me," Juddy said. "We never tell anybody about this, ever, you understand?"

"What was that?" Dylan asked. It still wasn't clear. "Who were those people?" He knew who they were.

"I said shut up, okay? We never talk about this again, to anybody, as long as we live. Got it?"

Dylan wasn't convinced. Juddy grabbed him by the collar again. "Okay," Dylan said.

Juddy reached into his pocket and got out a penknife. He clicked open the long blade and ran it over his thumb. "Okay, Dickweed, now you do just what I did." Dylan looked at his cousin, unconvinced. "I said, do it."

Dylan took the penknife and cut his thumb with it. A small red line appeared.

"Okay," Juddy said, pressing his thumb against Dylan's. "Now you repeat after me. I promise . . ."

"I promise."

"Never to say a word about this to anyone in my life."

"Never to say a word about this to anyone in my life."

"For as long as I live."

"For as long as I live."

"On threat of death."

"On threat of—*death*?"

"Forever."

"Forever."

Juddy pushed his thumb into his cousin's, hard, then let go. "All right then," he said. "We're blood brothers now."

Dylan nodded. Juddy looked at him, and for the first time, it looked as if there was pity in his eyes.

"It's okay, Dickweed," he said. "We just gotta keep our mouths shut. That's all. If we want to help them."

"I don't like having secrets," Dylan said, wiping the tears away from his cheek with the bottom of his shirt.

"Yeah, well," Juddy said. "You got one now."

In the Winnebago he heard the sound of Ben's fingers, clacking against the keys of his laptop computer.

Dylan thought of his father, whom even now he protected with his silence, and hated his guts.

*   *   *

By the time they were bearing down on Boston it was nearly noon. The others woke up, drank coffee. Dylan's father used the Winnebago shower. Just before noon traffic on the Mass Pike became heavy, then slow, then slower. Red taillights of crawling cars shone for miles ahead of them. Juddy checked his watch. His interview at Harvard was at two. The Winnebago came to a halt now. A light rain began to fall.

"Little traffic tie-up," Lefty said, shaking his head.

"Man, lookit all these cars," said Juddy. "There's nobody moving for miles."

Polo rubbed his chin. "This is unfortunate, to be sure."

"We'll get there," Lefty said. "Don't worry."

Juddy cracked his knuckles. "I'm not worried," he said.

"Well, you don't want to be late for your interview," said Polo, whose interview was not until 4:30. "Talk about making a bad impression. It would be hard to imagine a worse thing than being late for your own interview."

"Hey," Juddy said. "If we're late, we're late. We can't fly there."

"Atta boy," Lefty said.

"Anyway, they're the ones who want me. I could care less. It's either this or working on the lot with Pop. Hell, Pop's half hoping they won't take me."

"Did I say anything?" Lefty called, smiling. "I didn't say anything!"

Ben Floyd, sitting at the table in the midst of the Winnebago, looked up from his computer. He thought about the Pontiac dealership their father had founded nearly fifty years ago, how he had spent his whole life trying to get away from it. Now, in his middle age, he felt his father reaching out from beyond the grave, to drag him back. Unless he found some unlooked-for godsend, he would have to work for his brother. His mouth filled with acid.

Then, he thought about Juddy, going to Harvard. An unpleasant realization was forming. In the bar yesterday, Lefty had offered Ben the job under the assumption that Juddy was heading off to college. Ben knew enough about the finances of the dealership to be dead certain of one thing: if Juddy stayed on the lot, there would be no room for Ben. With a sudden horror, Ben now understood: it was Juddy's job Lefty was going to give him.

Everything, therefore, now hinged on Juddy going to Harvard.

If Juddy didn't go away to school, there'd be no job for Ben, no tuition money for Dylan. Ben looked at Juddy. He was wearing the same stained shirt as yesterday, the same backward-facing cap that read VILLANOVA WILDCATS.

"You're going to change before your interview, Judson?" Ben said. "Now'd be a good time, while we're all stuck here."

"Change?" Juddy said. "I don't think so. Come on, Uncle Benny, they're the ones who are courtin' me, not the other way around."

"Still," Ben said. "You ought to make a good impression."

"Forgive my asking," Polo said. "But what is it you're being courted for exactly?"

Juddy looked at Polo with pity. "Harvard, man," he said. "They're courtin' me for Harvard."

Polo's ears turned red. "I understand that, my good man. But what exactly among your many strengths is it that has captured the attention of the university?"

Juddy shrugged, as if the answer were already known. "Fencin'," he said.

"I'm not applying to Harvard," Allison said, holding her guitar in her hand. "I figure, why bother."

"Exactly," said Chloë. "Who needs them?"

"Excuse me," said Polo. "Did you say fencing?"

"Yeah," Juddy said. He was looking into his navel, as if something might have fallen into it. "That's what I said all right."

"I still wish you'd look at Jarlsberg, honey," Chloë said to her daughter. "There's a lot to be said for a women's junior college."

"Mom," Allison said, rolling her eyes. "I mean really. *Jarlsberg?* I mean, who wants to go to a college named after a kind of *cheese?*"

There was silence for a moment. "Colby's a kind of cheese," Dylan said.

There was some nodding at this. Allison, though, wasn't convinced. "Colby's a better kind of cheese than Jarlsberg," she said.

Uncle Lefty leaned on his horn. "C'man, c'man, c'man." He slapped himself in the forehead with the meat of his palm. "I'm not sittin' here all day!"

"Fencing?" Polo said, still trying to understand this new aspect of Juddy's personality.

"Yup," Juddy said. "The ol' épée and saber deal."

Polo looked like he had swallowed a nail. "What?" he said. "What deal?"

Juddy glanced up from his navel. "I said saber," he said. "That's not why they're recruitin' me, though. They want me for the épée. That's Fenelon's specialty."

"Who?" said Polo. His face seemed contorted with pain.

"Fenelon. François de Salignac de la Mothe Fenelon." He belched. "Winner of the gold medal, individual men's fencing, Munich 1972. Harvard's fencing coach. He's one big froggy honcho. That's why they want me to do épée, man. Them Frogs don't like the saber so much. Ya wanna do saber, ya gotta go to Stanford, work with what's his name, the little Hungarian dude. Ruki, his name is.'' Juddy shook his head. ''Like I'm gonna go all the hell out to California to fence with a saber! Get real!''

The color had drained out of Polo's face. ''So you fence,'' he said.

''Yeah,'' said Juddy. ''Some guy at school got me into it. I liked it 'cause it reminded me of *Star Wars* and all.''

''*Star Wars*,'' Polo whispered softly.

''Hey Polo, man,'' Juddy said. ''Like, don't go over to the Dark Side!'' He laughed.

Dylan looked over at his cousin, remembering that even when they were children, Juddy had been obsessed with swordplay. They used to play superheroes together: Juddy was the Secret Swordsman. Dylan was his loyal sidekick, Dickweed. Now, years later, Juddy had become, in reality, the person he'd pretended to be as a child. As a result, the only one of them with any chance to get in anywhere was turning out to be Juddy. Somehow, it figured.

Uncle Lefty honked his horn. ''C'man, c'man, c'man!'' he shouted. ''Jesus, we might as well put out a mailbox!''

''What's eppy? That thing you said?'' Dylan asked. Once you got over how unfair it was, it was kind of interesting, Juddy having a talent.

There was the crisp sound of a beer can opening. ''Épée, dude,'' said Juddy. ''It's a weapon. Like a rapier, only straighter and narrower. Got no cutting edges, is what I mean. A button tip. Ya can get points from touches using the whole body, unlike foil, where you only get to whack 'em in the torso.''

''You're good at this?'' Polo said. ''Swordplay?''

''It's cool, Polo. You'd like it. You want me to show you the routine, I'd be glad!''

Polo's face darkened still further. Dylan watched him, half hoping that Polo would agree, and then the two of them—Polo and Juddy—would stand there in the middle of the stalled-out Winnebago stuck on the Mass Pike, wearing facemasks and padded jackets and gloves and trying to murder each other with swords. It almost looked as if Polo thought it was a good idea, too; Dylan could see him imagining Cousin Juddy falling backward, a sword sticking out of his guts.

But then something stiffened in Polo; Dylan thought it was the begrudging realization that Juddy was probably pretty good with a sword. He had to be good enough, anyway, to get this François de Salignac de la Mothe Fenelon to consider enrolling Juddy Floyd at Harvard University. If there was anything more humiliating than his current situation, Polo probably figured, it was being in this situation a half an hour from now after Juddy had practically slain him through his turtleneck.

"No thank you, Juddy," Polo said. "Maybe some other time."

"I'm telling you, you'd like fencin'," Juddy said. "It's like a whole sport, where you pretend you're murderin' somebody."

Chloë looked at him suddenly. "You know, I've never seen you play," she said. "I'd love to watch some time."

"Well, next time I get out the swords I'll let you in on it, Chlo!" He sucked on his beer. "'Course, women are only supposed to use the foil. That's the rules, anyway. Go figure."

"I think it's interesting," Chloë said.

Allison rolled her eyes and strummed her guitar. *Oh, Shenandoah, I love your daughter. I'm bound away across the wide Missouri.*

Dylan was impressed by how well Allison played. He wished he were musical. About the only thing he had ever played was the autoharp. He'd gotten pretty good on it, but no one cared. It wasn't the kind of instrument that would get you anywhere.

"This is throwing off the whole schedule," Lefty cried. "We miss Harvard today, we'll have to cancel out on Colby and Bowdoin. We cancel out on them, we'll have to use Sunday to make 'em up!"

"So we use Sunday," said Chloë.

"But Sunday's the day I was going to climb the mountain with Ben!" He looked in the rearview mirror. "Remember we talked about that, Ben? Climbing Mount Katahdin?"

"Yeah," Ben said, uncommitted.

"Well, Sunday's the day, unless we want to throw off Dartmouth on Monday. Or Middlebury on Tuesday!"

"We'll be okay," Chloë said. "This can't go on forever. I mean, how bad could traffic in Boston be?"

Uncle Lefty jammed his thumb down on the horn of the Winnebago. "I can't believe this," he yelled, as the horn blew like a factory whistle. "I can't believe we're just *sitting here*!"

Chloë got up and stood behind her husband. "Come on now, Lefty," she said, rubbing his neck with her hands. "Your heart. Your blood pressure. You've got to learn to relax."

"Relax. I'll relax when we get to this fuckin' Harvard!"

Ben sat in the rear of the Winnebago, watching the cars stranded and unmoving for miles ahead, and in an instant saw, stretching before him, his entire miserable future.

An hour later, the Winnebago was moving again. The rain that had begun as drizzle was now a raging downpour. The massive wipers of the Winnebago were slapping back and forth. Lefty peered into the storm, trying to maintain his course. Drivers from the state of Massachusetts swerved around him at ninety miles an hour, flashing their lights, honking their horns, and giving him the finger.

"They sure drive like maniacs up here," Lefty said. "Jesus!"

A man in a black BMW moved up behind the Winnebago and started flashing his lights on and off at Lefty. "Jeez, what the hell do you think he wants?"

"He wants you to pull over, Dad," Juddy said.

"Pull over? Why? He should just pass me. I'm sitting in the middle lane."

"He doesn't want you in this lane, I guess," Juddy said.

The guy in the BMW swerved around the Winnebago, passing them on the right. The window rolled down and the driver yelled something at Lefty, his face contorted in unforgiving vitriol.

"Boy," Lefty said. "They sure take driving seriously."

"How fast are we going, honey?" Chloë said, trying not to sound nervous.

"Seventy-eight, seventy-nine."

"Why's everybody passing us?" Chloë said. "It's like we're the slowest people on the road."

A Mercedes flashed its lights at Lefty and screeched around him on the right. Another car, an Audi, passed them on the left, and for a moment it looked as if the Mercedes and the Audi were going to collide directly in front of them as the two cars merged into the same space. The driver of the Mercedes gave the finger to the driver of the Audi, who flashed his lights back at the other car and swerved at ninety miles an hour into the breakdown lane.

"Dylan," Ben said, coming over to his son. Ben's face

seemed ashen and pale. "My I speak with you for a moment?"

"Sure, Dad," Dylan said.

Allison and Chloë looked over at them.

"In private," Ben said.

Dylan looked around the Winnebago. He wondered where exactly his father had in mind. Ben turned and walked toward one of the captain's chairs that faced the rear window. Dylan followed and sat down in a chair adjacent to the first.

"What's up, Dad?" Dylan said.

"I've been meaning to speak with you," Ben said, and he could tell even before he'd come to the crisis that his son was already battening down the hatches. How had it come to this, he wondered. How was it that his own son only expected the worst from him?

"What?" Dylan said, now clearly worried. "What is it?"

"I wasn't certain until recently," he said. "But now it looks final."

"What?" Dylan said. "What's final?"

Ben glanced toward the front of the Winnebago. The attention of the others seemed glued on the road in front of them.

"Our situation," Ben said.

"What about our situation?" Dylan said. "What?"

"Well," Ben said, "it's like this. Floyd CyberTech isn't doing so well. You know this. We've discussed it."

"You said things were slow," Dylan said.

"Things are more than slow," Ben said. "I know this now."

"You know what now?" Dylan said. "What are you saying?"

Ben took a deep breath. "I'm selling the company," he said. "I have to give it up."

Dylan's eyes were huge. "You're selling it? Like, to investors you mean?"

"No," Ben said. "Not to investors. It's bankrupt. The state's approving my filing for bankruptcy. It's all gone."

"Gone?" Dylan said. He couldn't imagine his father's business being gone. "But can't you get, like, a loan or something?"

"I got a loan. Nine months ago. Remember when I was telling you about those guys from Ventura Monmouth? They put up the money for the expansion."

"So what happened?" Dylan said. He still didn't understand.

"They cut me off," Ben said. "Sons of bitches decided to play hardball."

"But why?" Dylan said. "Why would they do this to you?"

"Because they can," Ben said. He looked at his son, defeated. "I'm sorry. I've been holding off telling you 'til now because—" He looked out the rear window, awash with rain. Furious people were passing them on the left and right. "Because I don't know why. Because I've been afraid to tell you."

"Afraid to tell me?" Dylan said. "Afraid?"

"I'm sorry, son," Ben said.

"What's going to happen?" Dylan said. "What are we going to do?"

"Well, you," Ben said, clearing his throat. He put one hand on Dylan's shoulder. "You are going off to college, young man. You're going to get yourself a future. Me, I'm not sure yet. I'll land on my feet, though. Don't worry about that."

Dylan looked at his father's face. He had never seen his father look so sad, so used up, at least not since his mother had died. Still, he didn't know what to say. He couldn't believe that his father had lost his business. It seemed reckless and irresponsible. Maybe it wasn't that much of a surprise, if you thought about it.

"Anyway, I know this is a setback, but I want you to know I'm still proud of you, Dylan. More proud of you than I am of myself."

Dylan wasn't sure what to do. His father was trying to be soft and vulnerable, and it was kind of creepy. Dylan wasn't all that sure he wanted his father to be in touch with his feelings.

"It's a good thing you aced those SATs," Ben said softly. "At least now you'll be able to take your pick of schools. What with your grades and those scores, you can pretty much sit back and see which school offers you the most aid."

Dylan felt a sudden tightening in his throat. He hadn't thought about this aspect of things. He figured he'd break the news about his SATs to his father a month or two from now, after things had calmed down. Now didn't seem like a good time for the truth.

The truth was that something terrible had happened during Dylan's SATs. He had accidentally skipped one of the first few lines on the answer sheet, and thus had filled in the answer for question five in the space left for question six, and so on. He had discovered his error only moments before the end of the test. He had begun hopelessly trying to erase his answers, to move them all up a row, but his eraser had been corroded and had smeared the graphite across his test. In panic Dylan had started filling in spaces at random. The last thing he knew, a stern-faced proctor was forcibly taking his test away from him. Other test-taking students had looked at him with pity and horror. It was as if they were all in Vietnam together and the others were gathered around his body after a mine had exploded. Shame about Private Floyd, the lieutenant said. He didn't make it.

The section of the test he had botched was the verbal section, the only section he had ever had any chance of doing well on. The math section he'd already written off as a loss. The verbal, though, was his last chance. When the scores came in, he took the unopened envelope up to his room. He said a prayer before opening it. The results: math, 350; verbal, 277.

Two hundred and seventy-seven. Out of a possible eight hundred. If he had filled in blanks at random without even reading the questions, he would have done better. Now he was going around to the small colleges of New England telling people he wanted to be an English major. With a verbal score lower than that of most orangutans and rhesus monkeys.

And now, if he understood his father correctly, he was being told that the only way he was going to get into college was on a scholarship. He'd somehow have to convince them that there was some other reason they ought to take him. Dylan looked out at the rain and tried to think of a reason why he was unique, a person worthy of special consideration. Nothing came to mind.

He glanced toward the front of the Winnebago. There was Allison, the musician. Polo, the scholar of narratology. Juddy, a fencing champion.

The rain sloshed against the window. "It's okay, Dad," he said. "We'll be all right." He put his hand on his father's shoulder, and hated his guts, hated him forever.

"I love you, Dad," he said.

What Dylan was thinking was that he could work on Uncle Lefty's Pontiac lot next fall. After Juddy got into Harvard, he'd be needing somebody.

Lefty Floyd stared hopelessly through his oscillating wipers at the line of crawling cars. They were stuck on some sort of giant bridge on 93 south, hanging above the city of Boston. Lefty had never been on such a highway in his life. Exit ramps led out into space and simply stopped there, a few concrete blocks standing in between the highway and a desperate plunge into thin air. Apparently they'd run out of money while building this thing, Lefty figured. Boston drivers surrounded him, scowling and muttering.

The lane Lefty had been in merged into the one adjacent to it with no warning or sign. As Lefty attempted to merge the giant Winnebago to the left, other drivers swerved around him, gesturing at him with their loathing and derision, giving in to their hate. Jeez, Lefty thought, you'd think I was trying to murder somebody.

"Hey, Chloë," Lefty said. "You seen my heart medication?"

There was a pause. "I know where it is," Chloë said, in a distant voice. "Would you like some?"

"Yeah," Lefty said. "I'm getting palpitations."

A few minutes after he finally merged, this lane was joined on the left by another line of cars driven by furious people, flashing the lights of their BMWs as they barreled toward the stalled traffic at ninety miles per hour. The air filled with the sounds of blasting horns.

"Boy oh boy," Lefty said. He felt a little guilty for their current situation. He'd made a mistake, turned north on 95 from the Mass Pike, wound up circling the city a quarter of the way around to the north, before realizing his error. Now he was coming into the city on the north-south freeway, 93, this hideous central artery. Lefty checked his watch. It was quarter after two. Unless a miracle occurred, his son was going to be late for his interview.

Juddy looked out the window and hummed softly to himself. *Baah, baah, baah.*

*   *   *

Polo was surprised by Boston. It didn't look anything like it was supposed to. There wasn't a single church spire visible from the turnpike, no girls in sweaters, no fields of blowing tweed. Instead, people in expensive cars were merging in and out of lanes of traffic that mysteriously veered off into emptiness, or, worse, were suddenly closed down by traffic cones and blocks of concrete. A half a mile ahead something appeared to be on fire, a Volkswagen bus, maybe. The Winnebago was trapped in endless traffic, suspended on a two-tiered bridge. Over their heads was another highway, supported by rotting, rusted girders. On this highway were even more cars, jammed up and stalled, facing the opposite direction. Gushing water poured through holes in the roadway above and fell in furious columns onto the road before them.

Allison lay to his left, her eyes closed. Polo could see her eyeballs moving around behind translucent eyelids. Her soft lips were slightly open. The girl's blonde hair fell over one shoulder.

He wondered what she was dreaming about, hoping it was himself. Sure, she was saying to him in her dream world, I would love to fuck you. I have been waiting for my entire life for you, Polo MacNeil—you and your special brand of magic. They were walking through a field of flowers, their clothes tearing off in the wind. He saw Allison's head, resting on the daisies and the Queen Anne's lace. Yes, she was whispering, as Polo pulled off his silk boxers. Yes, Polo, you are the perfect being, she said. At last all my dreams are true.

Something along these lines, Polo thought. He stared at the side of her face. The earrings he had given her were looped into her earlobes. Emeralds. Oh, Polo, she'd said. No one ever gave me emeralds before.

The night after he gave her the emeralds he was all but certain her resolve would finally crumble. And yet here, too, he had been wrong. He managed to get her shirt and bra off, but when he started feeling her crotch through its panty hose, she got all sore at him. Please, Polo, she said. You know how I feel.

Well of course I know how you feel, Polo thought. What do you think I gave you the earrings for?

He'd never encountered such resistance before. Lisa O'Brien, Allison's best friend, had been so agreeable. It was funny how quickly he got to be close with the girls at Allison's school, considering that the only time he saw them was when he drove up from Manhattan for the weekend. Still, there was something about him that women found educational. The two of them had been up in Lefty and Chloë's bedroom, that weekend that the parents went away and he'd talked Allison into having the big party. Eleventh graders from as far away as Waterbury had invaded the place, and by midnight kids were having sex in nearly every upstairs room. He remembered lying there with Lisa afterward, Lisa who turned out to have a giant birthmark on one breast. This is a secret that the two of us will keep forever. If either of us ever tells, it will destroy Allison, bring her pain. And we cannot hurt our friend. Out of love for her we will never mention this. Our silence will be a testament to our respect.

He'd kept his end of the bargain but then Lisa's friend Rose McQuillan came up to him at a party over at Carabasi's a month later and said, So, heard you did it with Lisa. He was shocked. It was a secret, he said. Something sacred. Rose said it was a secret all right, a secret from Allison. Still, said Rose, it made her sad. She looked at Polo. I don't have any secrets like that.

Would you like your life better, Polo said. If you had secrets?

Rose shook her head. It would be a terrible burden.

Polo explained about secrets and how sometimes a burden gives complexity to your soul. It's a measure of how deeply we experience our lives, how well we carry the things in our own hearts. It's the kind of thing that can really help you feel grown up at last, increase your sense of independence. If you want to live that kind of life, Rose, I can help you, said Polo. But you have to be willing to say farewell to the life of innocence that you have known. I don't know, Rose McQuillan had said. I don't know if I'm strong enough.

Sex with Rose had been better than sex with Lisa. It was the first time he'd told the woman to sit on top of him. It was better, Polo figured, when you got to see the woman. When you were on top of them it was hard to see sometimes because your own body was in the way.

When he slept with Mrs. Dilworth, he'd done it exactly this way again, although the experience was really different. She had this black bra and panty set that surprised him. Mrs. Dilworth taught social studies and was always trying to get her students to feel bad about the Indians. Polo figured anybody who wanted you to feel bad about the Indians probably had pretty plain underwear, but this turned out not to be the case. It was interesting, learning about people.

Then there was that time with his college counselor, Miss Amran. She was Middle Eastern, or something. She owned this little dog, too, named Bakarusso, that kept yipping the whole time. You'd have thought that this was distracting, but in fact it just made the experience more colorful. He wondered if Miss Amran had heard Bakarusso barking, or if she was used to it by now. She made a lot of noise, Miss Amran did, and Polo wondered if that's what got the dog upset. It figured he was hurting her.

Polo looked at his Portable Nietzsche on his lap. It certainly was wonderful being an intellectual, he thought.

Polo glanced at his watch. If the traffic didn't start moving soon, he was going to miss his interview. He couldn't bear the idea of having to go to school somewhere other than Harvard. What if he wound up going to a safety school, like Bates or Denison, or something? That kind of mishap could affect your whole life. You met a Harvard man, you shook his hand, you told him you'd gone to Denison, you knew what he was thinking. And he'd be right, too. There was no excuse for people who did not go to Harvard. Only pity.

Allison, still asleep, turned in her chair, her head rolling toward him. One of the buttons of her shirt had come undone.

He opened the book he was reading, Nietzsche's *Man and Superman*. "We do not want what we desire," he read. "We only aspire to the state of desiring."

Boy oh boy, he thought. Isn't that the truth.

It was nearly seven o'clock now, and the rain was still coming down. Uncle Lefty was still driving around Boston, attempting to find Harvard. Chloë sat behind him with the map in one hand. Now and again she offered her husband counsel, but he would not listen. Finding his way by any means other than intuition was not in Lefty's nature.

They'd been stuck on the Mass Pike, going east, for maybe an hour. Then, when things got going again, he'd gotten confused, took the I-95/128 beltway to the north. Instead of correcting his mistake, he followed the beltway until they were well above the city, then headed south on 93. Ninety-three, of course, got all jammed up on the central artery, and they sat in that nightmarish double-decker bridge with the off ramps leading into space for another hour. Finally Lefty turned off of the central artery, figuring he'd worm his way through the back streets toward Cambridge, but somehow he'd wound up in the Callaghan tunnel, and the next thing they knew they were underneath Boston Harbor and they didn't emerge from the darkness until they were at Logan Airport. Lefty had to follow the airport road all the way to the United terminal, where he finally turned around, headed south on Route 1A, trying to avoid the tunnel this time, when he wound up on some causeway that took him toward Lynn and a series of traffic circles that spun them around and around until, finally, Lefty's spirit broke. They wound up trapped in a tunnel beneath the harbor again, and came back to the hopelessly clogged central artery about an hour and a half from the time they'd first gotten off of it. Traffic, if anything, was worse now. They sat at the end of an on ramp for fifteen minutes as they waited for an opportunity to merge into traffic. But no one wanted to make room for their horrible Winnebago. What they would have preferred, actually, was for everyone on board to slay themselves samurai-style.

At last they'd gotten back on 93, went down into a tunnel and missed the entrance to the Mass Pike again, which was not marked. They'd gone south toward Cape Cod for a few exits until finally Lefty got the Winnebago off the highway in Quincy and turned around and headed north again. This time he made the exit for the Mass Pike, but traffic here, too, was jammed, and they sat on the highway for another hour, with the rain coming down and everyone in the Winnebago silent and angry. Now they were headed north again. Lefty squinted through the rain, hoping for a sign that read, HARVARD UNIVERSITY: TURN RIGHT HERE, YOU GUYS.

"You know, I don't think they figure we're showing up today," said Juddy, drinking a beer.

"They don't think *you're* showing up," Polo said, anxiously. "I'm only two hours late."

"Two and a half," Juddy said.

"They probably aren't even there anymore," Allison said. "Seven o'clock on a Friday night? Probably went home."

"Home?" Polo said. "Home? But we had an appointment!"

"You didn't show up, dude," Juddy said.

"But we are still en route!" Polo said. "They can't imagine I would simply not show up! That's inconceivable!"

"It's what happened, man," Juddy said. "You stood 'em up."

"We'll call them, dear," Chloë said. "We'll explain what happened."

"Oh, yes, I'm sure that will make it all very clear. We'll say we spent six hours lost like *morons* in the city."

"It's my fault, okay?" Lefty said from behind the wheel. "If there's a problem, I'll just explain. I'm the one who's to blame here."

"Oh, Lefty, it's not all your fault," Chloë said. "These highways aren't very well marked."

"It's still my fault," Lefty said. "I'm admitting this."

"What's the diff," Juddy said. "If they want you so bad, they'll call you back."

"If they want me—" Polo said.

"Don't worry, Polo," Allison said. "There are other schools."

"Other—"

Dylan spoke up. "I don't see what the big deal is about Harvard, anyway."

"The big deal," Polo said. "I think I can explain about

the big deal. There's Harvard, okay, and there's everywhere else."

"So go somewhere else," Juddy said. "What do you care?"

"I'm not having this conversation!" Polo said, getting up and storming toward the back of the Winnebago. "I can't believe this!"

They all watched him stomp toward the back of the vehicle. Dylan's father, Ben, was sitting, slumped, in one of the two captain's chairs at the back, his eyes closed.

"He's upset," Allison said. "I should talk to him." She got up.

"I don't know," Dylan said. "Maybe he wants to be alone right now."

"You think you know him pretty well?" Allison said. "You got a deep understanding of what makes him tick, I guess. You've read a lot of philosophy and psychology, just like Polo."

"No," Dylan said. "I didn't say that."

"Maybe you should mind your own business, then," Allison said.

Allison brushed past him and walked toward the back of the van.

Dylan opened his mouth, then shut it. He looked sad.

"It's all right, honey," Chloë said to Dylan. "She didn't mean anything by it."

Dylan looked at Chloë. He didn't know how to feel about her.

"She hates me," Dylan said. "I didn't even say anything."

"She's upset for Polo, dear," Chloë said. "It's hard. Imagine if you wanted something very much, more than anything in the world, and you thought you'd lost it forever. Can you think what that's like?"

"I know exactly what that's like," Dylan said, hotly. "I don't need it explained."

Dylan looked out the window at the darkness. He remembered running away from the farmhouse with Juddy, his heart beating in his throat. He saw the line of red as Juddy cut into his thumb with a penknife. Dylan looked at his thumb, examining the scar. The Winnebago lurched suddenly in a pothole and he looked up. There was Juddy, sitting across from him. He was looking at his thumb, too.

In the back of the Winnebago, silhouetted by the headlights of the cars behind them, Chloë could see her daughter and Polo, holding hands. Polo looked upset, like someone had stolen his underpants. Allison was trying to soothe him. She was experiencing Polo's loss as if it were her own.

There are some things you don't want to witness, Chloë thought. This would be one of them. Having children, she concluded, is nothing but heartbreak. She wished she'd had more of them.

Juddy looked out the window at the darkness, singing. *We're poor little lambs who've lost our way. Baah, baah, baah.*

"You know, I think we should treat ourselves to a motel tonight," Lefty said from the driver's seat. "Get ourselves a hot meal, shake off this day, you know what I mean?"

"That's a good idea, Lefty," Chloë said. "The next Howard Johnson's or something you see, why don't we pull in? It will be nice to sleep in a real bed."

Already she saw it—the motel room with its pleasing and maddening blandness, the coverlet thrown upon the floor. She would have to begin her plan tonight. They'd order onion rings and cheeseburgers from room service, make sure that Lefty finished them all. Then she'd take off her shirt, walk around in her bra.

Lefty honked the horn.

"Hey, honey," she said, turning to her husband. "How are your palpitations? You feel anything more like yourself?"

"I'm all right, I guess," Lefty said. He sounded shaken. "Kind of strange."

A sign on the highway ahead of them rose out of the rain and fog. NOW LEAVING THE COMMONWEALTH OF MASSACHUSETTS. GODSPEED.

"I know I feel like somebody," Lefty said. "I'm just not sure who."

bowdoin college

Brunswick, Maine
Number of applications: 4,435
Percent accepted: 29%
Mean SAT: 670V, 670M
Most popular majors: government
biology, English
Mascot: the Polar Bears

"There is a dinner hotline which you can call to find out what each dining hall is serving. Then you just pick the one you like best," one student said.

—*Insider's Guide to the Colleges*, 1998

the admissions building at Bowdoin College was very old, nearly as old as the man who was interviewing Dylan. They'd been sitting in this lavish and antique room for some time now, an oriental rug on the floor, a portrait of General Joshua Lawrence Chamberlain, the Civil War hero, on the wall. This old guy, whose name was Gladstone, might have served with Chamberlain in the Twentieth Maine during the fight for Little Round Top. Actually, Dylan thought, if it was up to Gladstone, the Twentieth Maine might have looked the oncoming Rebels in the eyes and thought, *Aw, the hell with it. We didn't know you guys wanted slavery* this *bad.*

Gladstone peered down at Dylan's file through tiny, Benjamin Franklin–style glasses. Dylan could hear him breathing. Down the hallway a clock chimed. It seemed very silent there in Gladstone's office.

"Dylan Floyd," Gladstone said, after some time. He seemed very far away.

"Yes, sir," said Dylan, trying to be both natural and casual. It was hard to be either while wearing a tie.

He waited, expecting this Gladstone to ask him a question, to give him a chance to start selling himself to Bowdoin College. But Gladstone just kept staring down at Dylan's file, squinting. The man's breathing seemed slow and deep. Dylan hoped Gladstone wasn't falling asleep.

They had had a long night. Uncle Lefty decided to find a motel after the debacle in Boston, but they didn't find one that met Uncle Lefty's specifications until they were already in Maine. Dylan had to share a room with Polo and Juddy, both of whom snored. It was sort of like sharing a room with a couple of shop vacuums.

Dylan's interview was early, just after 9:00 A.M., so he'd gotten up alone, put his tie and jacket on, and had breakfast in the Brunswick 24-Hour Truck Stop across the street from the Maine Idyll Motel. After that he'd walked across the campus, largely deserted at that hour, and was struck by Bowdoin's beauty. The autumn colors were at their peak, and the leaves falling from the blue sky among the centuries-old buildings gave him a feeling of warmth and hope. He saw professors and students walking toward academic buildings. One girl was gesturing with her hands as she tried to describe something complex to her teacher. The professor smiled as they all walked into an old granite building. Yes, the man seemed to be saying. Your thesis is compelling.

"Dylan Floyd," the interviewer said again. He cleared his throat. "Unusual name, Floyd."

"Yes, sir," Dylan said. "I suppose so."

"Dylan," Gladstone said, looking up at the ceiling, stroking his chin. "I wonder if you'd indulge me for a moment."

"Indulge you," Dylan said. "I could do that, certainly."

"Well then," said Gladstone. "Imagine you had, say, three wishes. From a genie, for instance. What would you wish for? Eh?"

Gladstone put Dylan's folder down with what seemed like relief. He whisked his glasses off his face.

"Wishes?" Dylan said. His college counselor, Mrs. Midgely, hadn't told him anything about wishes. Just be yourself, she'd said. Try to relax. It was maddening, the way adults advised you to be yourself. As if you had any idea who that was.

"Yes, from, as I said, a genie, for instance."

"Oh, well," Dylan said, his mind racing. How could he move from this trick question back to the business at hand? "Let me think."

"Ah," said Gladstone. The man rubbed his hands together. "You're thinking it over. Good! Good!"

Dylan was glad he appeared to have won some points for thinking. He decided to stay with the thinking for a few minutes. Dylan rubbed his chin. "Three wishes," Dylan said. "Let me see."

"Lots of things to wish for, aren't there," Gladstone said. "Not an easy question, is it? Not by any means!"

"Well," Dylan said. "I suppose the first thing I would wish for would be, you know, world peace and all."

"World peace," Gladstone said. "A good choice! Brotherhood among nations! An end to internecine strife! Excellent, excellent!" Gladstone picked up a large clipboard with a yellow legal pad attached to it and began to scribble some notes in pencil.

After a few moments, Gladstone put the clipboard down. "It is as you wish, Mr. Floyd. The world is at peace. Your second wish, then, is what? Still many things to wish for, aren't there. Which do you choose? Eh?"

"Well," Dylan continued. "On a personal level, I suppose I might wish for the ability to get the most from my college education."

"Your education, you say?" Gladstone said. "Tell me more about this wish. I am not at all sure your desires here are clearly stated."

"I want to get the most from it," Dylan said. "I want the next four years to be fulfilling. To study things that are, you know, important, and for me to be able to take part in those things in a way that is good."

Gladstone looked at Dylan, unsure. He was waiting to see if Dylan was done. Then, since no more words came forth, Gladstone picked up his legal pad again and began to scribble. Dylan could hear the graphite scratching against paper. Gladstone seemed to be writing an awful lot, considering how little Dylan had said.

"Dylan," Gladstone said, after a while. "What is it exactly that makes you different from everyone else?"

"Different?" Dylan said. He felt his head spinning. It sounded as if Gladstone was giving up on the third wish. He'd heard enough.

"Yes, each of us is unique, don't you know. So when I meet a potential freshman I wonder, what is it about this person that makes him an individual? How might you answer that question, if it were asked of you?"

"If it were asked?" Dylan said. "I don't know. I mean, I'm curious, I guess. About things. And I try to, I don't know." Dylan had to pause for a moment to swallow a large glob of spit that seemed to have gathered at the back of his throat.

"You're curious, then," Gladstone said. "Curious about what sorts of things, what sorts of things, you say you're curious about, but what exactly?"

Gladstone seemed to be getting very excited.

Dylan thought and thought but he wasn't sure he could narrow this down. He heard the ticking of the clock down the hallway. He remembered the professor he had seen, walking with his students in the morning at Bowdoin, and began to realize he would never receive this kind of attention from anyone. There was nothing about him that made him special.

"I don't know," Dylan said, trying not to sound anguished. Gladstone looked surprised. "There's so much stuff in the world. I don't know how any of it is connected. I mean, I want to make things better for people, but I don't know how. There's so much I don't know. Things are so weird, if you think about it, how can you know where to begin, if you don't even know what you don't know. I mean, that's why you don't know it." He rubbed his hands together. They were moist with sweat. "So I guess that's what I'm curious about."

"Ah," Gladstone said. "So you're curious about the world, then."

"Exactly," said Dylan.

"What did you call it, 'weird,' you said, you said things are weird."

"Yeah," said Dylan.

"Perhaps you could give me an example, of something being weird."

Dylan thought about Polo and Allison kissing in the back of the Winnebago last night, as the RV sailed on, lost on the Boston highway system.

"People," Dylan said quietly. It was over now, he knew. He would not be going to Bowdoin.

"What about people," Gladstone continued, relentlessly. "What about people is weird?"

Oh, leave me alone, Dylan thought. We both know I'm not going here. You can see it as clearly as I can, I don't know how to talk, at least not about myself. I don't know how to sell myself to you, like I'm a car or a television. Why does it all have to hinge upon this, the ability to successfully pretend you're on a talk show?

Gladstone was still waiting. He tugged on his little bow tie. Dylan blew some air through his cheeks.

"They don't know what they want," Dylan said.

"People," Gladstone said. "You're saying people don't know what they want."

"No," Dylan said. "Or the things they do want don't make any sense."

"What about the things people want doesn't make any sense?" Gladstone said.

Dylan thought he was going to pass out. "I don't

know," he said. "They want things they can't have.
Things that are impossible."

"Like world peace?" Gladstone said. "Like an education?"

"Those things aren't impossible," Dylan said. "I don't
think they're impossible, anyway."

"Still, they seem unlikely to you? They seem like
things that one might need a genie's aid to achieve?" Gladstone smiled the smile of a hunter who knows his prey
has been snared.

At this moment, however, a miracle occurred. Something Dylan had learned in his eleventh-grade English
class materialized in his brain, at just the precise second at
which it might be useful. Dylan had no idea where this
thought came from. It simply arose before him, and he
reached out his hand and closed his fingers around it.

"Well," Dylan said, thoughtfully. "As Robert Browning said, 'A man's reach should exceed his grasp, or
what's a heaven for?' "

Gladstone's eyes grew suddenly wide. "Browning, yes.
Browning!" Gladstone grabbed his clipboard in excitement and began writing furiously.

Well well well, Dylan thought to himself. Bowdoin
was suddenly back on the map. It would be nice to go to
college in Maine. He saw himself wearing a yellow rain
slicker, eating lobsters.

"What about your third wish?" Gladstone said, finally. They were back to the wishes now. Gladstone was
still clutching the clipboard. "Before you only mentioned
two wishes. What would be your third wish, if you could
have one? Something impossible, perhaps? Something
you've lost and would like to regain? Eh?"

Dylan felt his heart beating quickly. He wasn't out of
the woods yet. He tried to think about some of the things
he'd had and lost. For some reason he thought about

going to Colonial Williamsburg with his parents when he was six or seven. He'd put his mother in the stocks and taken her picture. Later they all went out to dinner at some pancake house. They had a dozen different syrups, arranged on a lazy Susan. Maple, strawberry, blueberry, honey, boysenberry. So many different syrups for his pancakes.

"I don't know," Dylan said at last. "I don't know what I'd wish for. It doesn't make any sense."

"What doesn't make any sense? Wishing? Eh?"

"No, no, wishing is fine, it's just frustrating. That's not the way you get things."

"Ah. How do you get things then?"

Dylan shrugged. "You have to work. That doesn't mean you get what you want, exactly. But it makes more sense than wishing."

"I thought you said a man's reach should exceed his grasp," said Gladstone. The smile of the hunter returned, cautiously. "Robert Browning, you said."

"I said that," Dylan said. "But that's how you get things, you work for them, you work all the time. You don't get things by wishing."

"Very good," Gladstone said, writing on his clipboard. Their work seemed nearly concluded.

"If you had to describe yourself in one word," Gladstone said, with finality. "What word would that be, I wonder? Eh? What word?"

"One word," Dylan said slowly. "To describe myself." He thought. All sorts of bad choices came to mind, like *hopeless, hapless, stupid* . . .

"Nice," Dylan said at last. "I'd say nice."

"Nice you say?" said Gladstone. "Nice?"

"Yes, nice," Dylan said. "That's what makes me different, I guess. Remember before, you were asking me what makes me special. I'd say it's because I'm a nice person. I try to look out for people. Be nice to them."

Gladstone didn't know what to make out of this. He sat there with his head tilted to one side like the dog on the RCA Victor label.

"Nice," Gladstone said quietly. "I'm writing down nice."

There were a few moments while Dylan sat there and listened to Gladstone's pencil scrape against the paper. Then Gladstone stood up and extended his hand toward Dylan over his messy desk.

"I'm wishing you luck, young man. You are correct in your estimation of yourself. You are a nice young man indeed."

"Okay, thanks," Dylan said, feeling the man shake his hand. He turned when the shaking was done and walked out alone into the hallway.

Son of a bitch, Dylan thought to himself, as the front door of the admissions building swung open suddenly. He was out on the quad again, and now the place was full of students, walking around with L.L. Bean backpacks, Polartec vests, Frisbees.

He couldn't believe what he'd just been through. *Nice*, Dylan said to himself, hearing his own embarrassing words come back to him. Jesus God in heaven, I told him the one word in the universe to describe me is *nice*.

Dylan walked across the campus toward the student union, where a tour was beginning in an hour.

I'll tell you what my wish is, you goddamned fucking moron, Dylan thought to himself. I want my mother back.

Chloë Floyd sat in front of a mirror in a room in the Maine Idyll Motel, trying to find the holes in her ears. She wore a knit black dress with a scoop neck, a gold necklace, and as soon as she found her earholes, would be wearing gold seashell earrings. Chloë looked at herself in the mirror; even beneath her not-inconsiderable makeup, her expression was taut, strained.

Lefty, naked, lay in the double bed, covered by a tangled sheet, a wide smile on his face. A platter containing several empty plates lay next to him. Lefty looked tired, but happy.

"Man oh man, Chloë," Lefty said. "I musta died and gone to heaven."

"I'm glad you're happy, Lefty," Chloë said, curling her earrings into her ear.

"Happy, hell," he said. "Forget it. I'm stayin' in Maine. The Way Life Should Be! They're not kidding."

Chloë smiled a tight-lipped smile.

"I don't know what I like better," Lefty said. "French toast before sex or waffles right after!"

"Well, I'm pleased you got to have both."

"Exactly," Lefty said. "I got both!" He looked toward the ceiling and waggled his feet to the left and right. "Maybe some time I can have the waffles first, though. I think if you're going to have both it's good to have the waffles, then the French toast. That way you have a base."

"Well, whatever pleases you, honey."

"Man, Chloë," Lefty said. "Something's gotten into you!"

Chloë turned around to look at her husband. "What do you mean?"

"You know what I mean. You're out of control!"

Chloë imitated someone smiling. "There's some law I can't make love to my husband?"

"Yeah, but, you know," Lefty said. "There's makin' love, and then there's makin' love!"

"I just want you to be happy."

"Happy!" Lefty said. "I'm happy all right!"

Chloë patted her husband's large and hairy belly. "That's my boy!"

"I hope you're happy too, Chloë," Lefty said.

"Of course I am," Chloë said. "I'm married to you, aren't I, Lefty?"

"I know, I know," Lefty said. "But really. I want you to be happy."

"I am."

"Well," Lefty said, "good. I'm glad." He looked at the empty dishes. "I know I'm not— I don't know. I'm glad you're happy."

"What?" Chloë said. "What are you trying to say?"

"I don't know. It's just, well, you know. I'm probably not like Mr. Wonderful Husband of the Year every day."

"What are you talking about? Of course you are."

"Now, come on, Chloë, you don't have to give me all that goo. I'm—well, you know what I am. I do my best, you know?"

"Of course you do."

"It's not like—I mean, okay, there are probably better husbands in the world."

"I'm not married to those other husbands," she said. A muscle in her jaw seemed to be pulsing.

"Yeah, well, listen, even if you were they wouldn't love you like me, Chloë. I just want you to know. I love you like nobody does."

"I love you, too." Chloë stroked his giant belly.

"Listen, Chlo, did you, you know—did you get everything you—you know. When we were doin' it, were you all done and all?"

Chloë smiled. "Of course, Lefty. Can't you tell?"

Lefty shrugged. "Sure, Chlo," he said. "I can tell. I just

wanted to make sure. 'Cause if you wanted more I could, you know, help you finish up."

Chloë looked at him mischievously. "Lefty Floyd," she said, "you're not trying to seduce me again, are you?"

"Aw," Lefty said. He wiggled his toes and sat up. Lefty reached around his wife's back and pulled down the zipper of her dress.

"Oh, Lefty," Chloë said. "You're like, a magnet. A love magnet!"

Lefty grinned, then reached forward to embrace her. Chloë kissed him from his mouth to his ear. When she reached the ear, she paused. Lefty seemed to lose his bearings.

"Holy cow," he said. "Here we go again!"

Chloë unhooked her bra, stepped out of her panties. One hand rose to her hair. "You know what, Lefty, can I comb out this hair spray first? It's like straw."

"You want to comb your hair out, you go ahead," Lefty said.

"Tell you what, while I'm getting myself ready, why don't you get yourself a treat? Call up room service and have something?"

"You're serious? I already had two breakfasts."

"How about some eggs benedict, some bacon?"

"I don't know, I mean, I had the two breakfasts, like I said."

"Lefty," Chloë said. "Hollandaise!"

Lefty thought about it. "Where's the phone?"

A moment later, Lefty was dialing. Chloë reached for her hairbrush, began combing her hair down. She looked at herself in the mirror. So this is what you've become, she said to herself. Chloë shook her head.

Lefty hung up the phone. He was looking at his wife watching herself in the mirror. She was lovely.

"I love you, Chloë," he said.

"I love you, too, Lefty," she said. "I'll love you till the day you die."

The phone rang in Polo and Juddy's darkened motel room. Juddy's hand felt around for it.

"Hello?" he said. A moment later he sat up in his bed, ran his palm down over his face.

"*Bonjour, Monsieur,*" he said. "*Comment allez-vous?*"

Polo opened one eye, gazed over at Juddy with horror.

"*Pas mal,*" Juddy said. He cleared his throat. "*Bien.*" Juddy's hand was clapped to the side of his head, as if he was afraid his brains were going to start leaking out.

"*Parlons en Anglais, Monsieur Fenelon?*" Juddy said. For a moment it looked as if Juddy were going to be crushed beneath some giant weight. Then, suddenly, he smiled. He had escaped.

"Well good," Juddy said. "I know. I'm sorry." There was a long pause. "He did? Well I appreciate that. We got tied up, to tell you the truth. Turned all around."

M. Fenelon spoke rapidly into Juddy's ear. Polo could hear the nasal voice squawking through the receiver. He couldn't quite make out the words.

"Well I'm not sure," Juddy said. "We're up here in Maine, seeing some college." The voice on the other end started speaking rapidly. M. Fenelon was alarmed. "Naw, naw, I'm not interviewing. Honestly, I'm not. I'm just along for the ride. Seein' the sights and all."

Polo stood and opened the curtains. The room filled with light. Outside there were pine trees, blue sky.

"We might get back down there, I don't know." Juddy had to pause again. It looked like he was having a hard time getting a word in edgewise. "Okay," he said at last. "Okay. Sure. You can put me through. Yes. It's a pleasure talking with you too, Monsieur. *A bien tôt.* Okay. I'll hold."

Juddy put one hand over the mouthpiece. "He's puttin' me through to some guy named Barker."

"Hensleigh Barker," Polo said slowly, turning back toward Juddy. Light dawned. "Hensleigh Barker? That's Harvard's dean of admissions! You're talking to Dean Barker?"

"Yeah, hello," Juddy said. "This is Juddy Floyd. Monsieur Fenelon said I should talk to you."

There was the distant and miniaturized voice of a man of good breeding.

"Well that's awfully nice," Juddy said. "Henny."

"Let me speak to him when you're done," Polo said urgently. "Juddy?"

"Aw," Juddy said. It sounded like Dean Barker was ribbing him. "You guys are nuts!"

"Juddy!" Polo whispered.

"Get outta here, you crazy Dean Barker, now come on!" Juddy said, and laughed.

Polo sat on the floor next to Juddy. "Juddy! Let me talk to him when you're done."

"All right already," Juddy said, loudly. "Sorry, Henny, I got a pal up here wants to talk to ya."

"Don't tell him I'm here!"

"Now he says to tell you he's not here."

Polo buried his face in his hands.

"Anyway," Juddy continued. "I don't know if we're going to get a chance to get back down to Cambridge this trip. Yeah, we got all these other schools to look at."

The dean of admissions at Harvard University said something to Juddy Floyd.

"I know, well blame my pop. He got all turned around, next thing you know we missed the whole kit an' caboodle. Believe me, I'd rather have been walking around Cambridge than stuck on the Winnebago!''

There was a pause.

''Yeah, we're all riding around in a damn Winnebago!''

''Don't tell him about the Winnebago!'' Polo cried. ''In the name of God, Juddy!''

There was the sound of Hensleigh Barker laughing from his office at Harvard.

''Well listen, let me see if they'll let me off the bus here for a couple days, maybe I can come down there, meet with you all. Sounded like Monsieur Fenelon was gonna pee in his pants if I didn't come down.''

Polo moaned.

''Okay, I'll be in touch,'' Juddy said. ''Now, wait, hang on a second, Henny, I got a pal here wants to talk to ya. No, he doesn't fence. He's just—well, wait, here he is. I'll let him talk for himself.''

Juddy held out the phone toward Polo. ''Here ya go,'' he said. ''Dean of admissions, Harvard.''

Polo looked at the phone for a long moment. He swallowed, then gently reached for it.

''Hello,'' Polo said. He stood up. ''Dean Barker. Yes. This is Polo MacNeil.''

There was a pause.

''MacNeil,'' Polo said again. ''Yes. Yes, I'm traveling with Judson. Yes.'' There was a pause as Polo's features assumed a deathlike pallor. ''Yes, I'm on the Winnebago,'' he said in a very small voice.

The dean of admissions at Harvard laughed, briefly.

''Well, yes, I had an interview yesterday at four-thirty. No, four-thirty. Yes, and well, as Judson explained, we just got, ah, with one thing and another, yes. I'm aware of that. I'm very sorry.''

Polo's features assumed an even more horrific expression. The dean of admissions seemed to be taking a moment to explain something to Polo.

"No, it's not my intention to waste anyone's time, Dean Barker."

There was another moment as the dean spoke, and Polo listened.

"Yes, I'm aware of that. I'm very truly sorry. As Juddy explained, however—"

The dean explained some more things.

"I am sorry," Polo said in a small voice. "I really am extremely sorry."

Polo grew quiet for a moment as the dean spoke at some length.

"Well then," Polo said finally. "I understand. Yes, I'll be there. You can be certain of that. You won't regret this, Dean. Yes."

Polo listened for a few more moments then held the phone out toward Juddy.

"He says he wants to talk to you again," Polo said.

"Yo," Juddy said. In the meantime he had pulled on the same shirt as yesterday. "What's that, Hen?" he said. "Oh, don't mind him. He's just a little mental."

The dean of admissions said something else.

"Right. Yeah, well later!" Juddy hung up the phone.

"How about that guy!" he said.

Another backward-walking woman was speaking to the group. She had blonde hair, tied into a braid, and ruddy pink cheeks. "On your right is Hubbard Hall," she said. "The departments of history, economics, government and legal studies, and Arctic studies are located here. It's also the home of the Arctic Museum."

They walked past Hubbard Hall. Allison looked over at the old building with a troubled expression.

"What is that exactly?" said a man with a Southern accent. "An *Ahtic* museum?" He tried to withhold his derision, and failed.

Dylan scrutinized the man. He had seen him before. The Captain, from the tour group at Yale.

The tour guide was prepared for this. "The Arctic Museum is the gift of two Bowdoin alumni, Robert Peary and Donald MacMillian. The museum holds most of the equipment, records, and artifacts associated with their trips to the Pole."

"Which pole was this?" the Captain said.

The woman looked confused. "Which pole?" she said. "I don't know. North, I think."

"Well that's a surprise," the man said sarcastically. He turned to his daughter, who had short black hair. It needed washing. "You want to study the Nawth Pole, you can hang out here, I guess."

"On your right," the tour guide continued, "is the Hatch Science Library, built in 1991. It's also home to the environmental studies and neuroscience programs. The library contains study carrels, science books and periodicals, CD-ROM directories, meeting rooms, and Bowdoin's neurology and sleep labs."

They walked past the science library. "Sleep labs?" the man with the accent said. "You're sayin' sleep labs?"

"Yes," she said tersely. "The Bowdoin Sleep Laboratories. The College has contributed significantly to the study of sleep."

"I reckon so," said the man. He turned to his daughter. "This heyah's the place to go if you wan'em to *study* yuh when yuh *sleepin'*."

"It's actually important research," the guide said defensively. "You'd be surprised how many people have trouble sleeping. Our research labs have helped many people."

" 'Somniacs, that kinna thing?''

"Insomniacs," the guide said. "Somnambulists. Sufferers of night terrors. Persons with—snoring disabilities."

"Snorin' disabilities," said the father to his daughter. "You getting this all down, Welly?"

Welly looked at her father with humiliation and desperation. "Yeah," she said miserably.

"We're going to head over to Matilda White Riley House now," said the guide. "Home of the departments of sociology and anthropology."

As they walked toward Matilda White Riley House, Allison looked back at the Bowdoin Sleep Labs. She walked to the front of the group and asked the guide, "Aren't we going to see the music department?"

"Gibson Hall," the guide said. "We don't have time for Gibson on our tour, actually." She looked at Allison. "Are you a musician?"

"Yes," Allison said with a small voice. "I play guitar. Some piano."

"Well," said the guide. "Bowdoin's a good place for musicians. Lots of people play."

Allison thought this over. "What do you mean, lots?" she said.

"Oh, jeez," the guide said. "Practically everybody plays something. My roommate plays the bagpipes!"

"Wow," Allison said. "Bagpipes." She fell back into the tour, allowing the guide to walk on ahead.

"Boy," Dylan said. "Imagine having someone playing bagpipes as your roommate. All that noise."

"I like bagpipes," Allison said. "Actually, I like small pipes better. Northumbrian pipes. The sound's sweeter."

Dylan didn't know what to say. He wasn't aware there were different kinds of bagpipes.

Toward the front of the tour, Welly's father was ask-

ing the guide about Arctic studies again. "Lots a call for
Arctic studies majors, out in the world?" he said. "Most
of them have jobs just *waitin'* for 'em once they bust out
of here?"

Welly fell back in the tour, joining Allison and Dylan
at the rear of the pack. Westminster chimes pealed from
the chapel. A gust of wind blew through the campus,
sending a cascade of bright leaves toward the green grass
of the quad.

Dylan couldn't believe how beautiful the Bowdoin
campus was. It was like some movie set. It seemed surreal,
students and professors walking around, talking to each
other, everybody hanging out. He remembered his SAT
scores and felt a hot sensation of shame. Well this is as
close as I get to it, he thought. Next year, I'll be working
on Uncle Lefty's lot, giving people test drives of Firebirds.

He looked over at Welly, who had a run in her hose.
The girl seemed depressed. Dylan tried to think of something to say.

"Is that your dad?" Dylan said, nodding toward the
front of the group, where the man with the accent was
complaining about something else.

Welly nodded miserably. "That's him all right. Cap'n
Bedford."

"Captain?" Allison said, wrinkling her nose. "You call
him Captain?"

Welly shrugged. "That's what people call him."

"He's funny," Dylan said.

Welly looked like she'd been stabbed. "Funny," Welly
said. "I guess."

Allison looked over at Welly. "Do you want to go to
Bowdoin?" she asked.

"I don't care where I go," Welly said. "As long as it's
far away."

The tour group passed a kiosk covered with posters.

There were announcements of concerts and lectures, requests for roommates, offers of instruction in guitar and shiatzu massage. Scores of fliers were stapled on top of each other, covering every square inch of the kiosk. Allison stopped to look at it, and Dylan stopped, too. Somehow college seemed very real, standing here reading all this junk. Visiting Scientists Lecture Series: Dr. Vikram Singh, Hydrogeologist. Open Mike Night, Coffeehouse. Rape Counseling. Baby-Sitter Needed. Sensual Massage Therapy, Call Bruce.

Dylan looked up suddenly to realize that they'd lost their tour. Wherever the tour had vanished off to, Welly had vanished with it. "Where'd they go?" he said. "Allison?"

Allison didn't seem concerned. "I don't know. I want to find Gibson Hall. There's probably a reason why they aren't showing it to us." She consulted a campus map on the kiosk, then started walking off in another direction. Dylan ran after her.

"You want me to come with you," he said, a little out of breath.

"Whatever," Allison said. His presence didn't seem that important to her.

They passed a set of buildings that looked like dormitories. From an open window came the sound of the Grateful Dead. This particular recording didn't seem high-fidelity.

Dylan looked at his watch. They were supposed to be back at the motel in forty-five minutes.

Allison took a deep breath. "Man," she said. "Smell that air."

Dylan sniffed loudly. "Yeah," he said. "Smell it."

"You can smell the ocean," Allison said. "We're near the coast."

"I've never seen the ocean," Dylan said.

Allison stopped and looked at him. "You're kidding," she said.

"Well, I don't know," he said. "We went once when I was little, before my mom died. We have all these pictures of us at some beach, Barnegat Light, I think. But I don't remember anything about it."

Allison thought this over, then started walking again. She didn't say anything for a while.

They approached the college chapel. The cornerstone was inscribed 1845.

"Cool," Allison said, and walked up a couple of steps to the chapel door. They walked inside.

The chapel was dark and deserted. Some light filtered through long stained-glass windows. Over their heads were giant paintings of scenes from the Bible. Adam and Eve were ashamed of themselves. David held Goliath's head aloft. Above these were the flags of the original thirteen colonies.

The pews in the Bowdoin College Chapel faced each other. There were two round windows, one above the front door, the other above the sanctuary. A concert grand piano stood near the altar. Allison walked up to it and sat down on the bench.

Her fingers fell upon the keyboard. A moment later she played a loud and dramatic minor chord. The sound of it scared Dylan.

"Boy, you're jumpy," she said.

"Sorry," he said. "You go ahead."

"You like Beethoven?" she asked.

Dylan nodded. Sure, he liked Beethoven.

Allison played the same melodramatic chord again, followed by some others. A moment later she was playing some sort of sonata. It sounded difficult.

Dylan sat down on one of the pews and listened to Allison play. It was annoying, in a way, that she had this talent. Her eyes were closed, her face contorted in an expression both ecstatic and pained. He made a face like this himself sometimes, when he played the autoharp. Sometimes the people that were listening to him play made faces too.

Dust moved through the shafts of sunlight slanting from the stained glass. There was a book on the pew next to him. Dylan reached for it and read the cover. *A Bowdoin College Hymnal.*

Another bunch of songs I'll never get to sing, Dylan thought mournfully. He closed his eyes.

For a while he sat there listening to Allison play Beethoven, feeling sorry for himself. When she stopped playing, he kept his eyes closed.

Her footsteps echoed in the quiet church. He heard her come over and sit down on the pew next to him.

Dylan wanted to ask her the name of the piece she had been playing, but he knew that to do so would be to confess his ignorance. Instead he sat there with his eyes closed, as if to duplicate the kind of meditative trance he presumed was common to college students.

She didn't say anything, though, and Dylan began to feel a little self-conscious just sitting there with her next to him. He wondered what she was thinking about.

After a long while he opened his eyes, expecting her to be staring at him. Instead he found her with her head pressed down into her hands. She was weeping.

"Hey," Dylan said. He stretched his hand out and felt her back. Her hair was soft. "Hey, Allison."

She lifted her head and looked over at him. "Hey," she said, and wiped her eyes with one hand. She smiled, self-conscious and embarrassed. "Sorry."

"Don't be sorry," he said.

"I don't know what's wrong with me," she said.

"It's okay," Dylan said. "You don't have to explain."

She puffed some air through her cheeks. "I guess I'm kind of tense."

"Me too," said Dylan. "You don't know the half of it."

She looked over at him, embarrassed. "Well, I'll get the hang of this sooner or later. I guess you could tell me a thing or two about how to do it."

"What?" Dylan said. He had no idea what she was talking about.

She seemed to withdraw into herself. After a moment she said, "When did your mother die?"

Dylan thought about it.

"Five years ago," he said. "No, six. Six years ago."

"My father died four years ago," said Allison. "He used to love the *Pathetique.* Made me play it all the time."

"I'm sorry," Dylan said. He wondered what the *Pathetique* was. Something in him wished that she would continue crying so he'd have an excuse to keep rubbing her back.

"Do you talk to your mom much?" Dylan said. "About your dad? She must miss him too."

"Yeah, well, we don't talk much since she married your Uncle Lefty. The human potato." She looked at him apologetically. "Sorry. I know he's your uncle and everything."

"That's okay," Dylan said. "He is kind of like a potato." He took his hand off her back. "What did your dad die of?"

"Heart attack," Allison said. "Just like that." She snapped her fingers. "What happened to your mom?"

Dylan licked his lips. "You really don't know the story?" he said. "Your mom or Uncle Lefty haven't told you?"

"Are you kidding?" Allison said. "They don't even know I'm alive. The only person who cares about me is Polo."

Dylan took her hand. "I care about you, Allison," he said. "I mean, I don't know you very well, but I care about you. I wish I knew you better, is what I'm saying."

Allison squeezed his hand. "You're nice," she said, then stood up. "Come on. We better get back to the motel. We're supposed to be at Colby by three o'clock."

"Colby," Dylan said, standing up to join her. "Where is Colby?"

"I don't know," Allison said. "Bangor, or something. Polo doesn't think much of it, you know."

"Why not?" Dylan said. "They have a good Italian department, I heard."

"Whatever," Allison said. "I hope Polo gets into Harvard. It'll kill him if he doesn't get in."

"Are you going to Harvard, too?" Dylan said.

"I don't know," Allison said. "Polo doesn't think we should go to the same school. He says we'll love each other more if we're free." They opened the door and walked into the sunshine.

"Do you think that's true?" Dylan asked. He felt his heart beating in his shirt. "You think you'll love him more if you're free?"

"Free," Allison said, as if she didn't believe in the word. For a moment they stood on the threshold, letting their eyes adjust. "I don't know," Allison said. "I guess I don't really understand boys sometimes."

"I know what you mean," Dylan said. "Sometimes I think I don't understand anybody."

Allison smiled and gave him a sisterly pat on the back. "Let's go," she said, and began to walk rapidly across the campus back toward the motel. Dylan struggled to keep up with her. All around them were more ruddy-looking youths and their encouraging teachers. A clock tolled. Allison's hair blew off her shoulders in the autumn wind.

Nice, Dylan thought, bitterly. *I'm nice.*

colby college ★

Waterville, Maine
Number of applications: 4,601
Percent accepted: 31%
Mean SAT: 640V, 640M
Most popular majors: biology,
    English, economics
Mascot: White Mules

One of the older athletic traditions
at Colby, throwing fruit and other
objects (including, on one notable
occasion, a cow's head) onto the ice
at the annual Bowdoin hockey
game after an opposition goal, was
recently abolished by the
administration.
—*Insider's Guide to the Colleges*, 1998

they stood in a grove of trees near Lunder House, Colby's admissions office. There before them was a large piece of granite with a plaque attached. The plaque read, THE BABSON ANTI-GRAVITY STONE. Beneath this was a rendering of a set of scales in balance.

THIS MONUMENT HAS BEEN
ERECTED BY THE
GRAVITY RESEARCH FOUNDATION
ROGER W. BABSON, FOUNDER
IT IS TO REMIND STUDENTS OF
THE BLESSINGS FORTHCOMING
WHEN A SEMI–INSULATOR IS
DISCOVERED IN ORDER TO HARNESS
GRAVITY AS A FREE POWER
AND REDUCE AIRPLANE ACCIDENTS
1960.

"What do you say, kids?" Ben said. "You ready?"

Allison and Dylan looked at the incomprehensible inscription. Dylan nodded miserably. "I guess," he said.

"Don't worry," Chloë said. "You'll do fine."

"Yeah," Lefty said. "Just be natural!"

Allison and Dylan walked toward Lunder House in their interview clothes. Dylan's neck itched where it made contact with the tight collar. Polo and Juddy were already miles away, driving in a rented car back to Cambridge.

The adults stayed behind, watching their remaining children walk toward the office of admission.

"That's your philosophy," Ben said, in an irritated voice. "Be natural?"

"It's good advice!" said Lefty. "Works for me!"

"Maybe that's why you work on a car lot," Ben snapped.

Lefty shot Ben an angry look. "Maybe that's why you're bankrupt," he suggested.

"Boys," Chloë said. "Come on. Don't do this."

"Hey," said Lefty, slapping his brother on the back. "We're just mixing it up! Me and Benny, we love to mix it up."

Ben nodded. He and Lefty sure loved to mix it up.

Polo looked out the window of the rental car. They were heading south, down I-95, back toward Cambridge. A sign by the side of the highway read, NOW LEAVING MAINE. THE WAY LIFE SHOULD BE.

"We should stop at the liquor store in New Hampshire," Juddy said. "They got the cheapest booze in the country, right on the friggin' highway."

"I don't feel like drinking," Polo said. "I want to be fresh for tomorrow."

Juddy smiled. "Your idea is, they'll like you better fresh?"

Polo felt the collar of his black turtleneck with one finger. "I don't know," he said. He looked out the window abstractedly.

"Hey, man!" Juddy said. "Polo dude! You gotta focus. You got the wrong attitude about this Harvard, the wrong attitude entirely."

Polo rolled his eyes. "Yes, I suppose I should be like you, a drunken Visigoth."

Juddy shook his head. "Sticks and stones, dude," he said. He thought about something.

"Exactly," Polo said.

"Anyway, listen," Juddy said. "You gotta get real. Face it: Harvard hates ya. You dissed 'em."

"I did not *dis* them. We were stuck in traffic, through no fault of my own. Once this is explained, they'll understand."

"Like they give a shit," Juddy said. "All they know is, you had an appointment and you didn't show up. Now you got another one, barely, on account of your girlfriend's stepbrother is being recruited by the fencing team. It's not like they're looking forward to seeing you. Henny already thinks you're a flake."

"I am not a flake," Polo said. He was having trouble breathing.

"They don't know that," Juddy said. "Listen, I'm trying to tell you something. The only way you're going to get into this Harvard is to act like you don't give a shit."

Polo shook his head. "You don't understand. I do give a shit. I most certainly do."

"Duh," said Juddy. "But that's not how to play 'em. You can't get anything if you act like you want it too much."

Polo smirked. "That's your philosophy, Juddy?" he said. "That's the secret of your existence?"

Juddy smiled. "One of 'em," he said.

"I should be writing this down," Polo said.

"You should," said Juddy. "It's true for everything, not just college." He honked his horn at a car in front of them. "You think you'd be havin' such a hard time gettin' Ally's panties off if you stopped beggin' her for it all the time?"

"What are you talking about?" Polo said. He knew what he was talking about.

"Little Ally," Juddy said. "It's so obvious, dude! The only reason she won't let you do the nasty is 'cause you keep buggin' her about it. You pretend like you don't give a shit, two seconds later, she's throwin' her panties on your head. I swear to God, man, that's how it works!''

''I don't want to talk about this,'' Polo said. ''Jesus, Juddy, she's your sister!''

''Stepsister,'' Juddy said.

''Regardless. It's none of your business. You don't know our private life.''

Juddy laughed. ''Yeah, man! It's like some big top secret! I better whisper, okay? I don't wanna give anything away! Hey! Maybe I should call up that *X-Files* dude!''

''Shut up,'' Polo said. ''Just shut up.''

''You want me to shut up, I can shut up. I'm just figurin' we're in the car together. We got this long drive down to Cambridge, tomorrow we got a long drive back up, all the way to Dartmouth. I was hoping we might be pals by the time we link back up with everybody.''

''Pals,'' Polo said, with loathing. ''You and me. Pals.''

''You'd be surprised the kind of people you got in common with,'' Juddy said. ''You're more like me than you think.''

''Well, yes, maybe you're correct,'' Polo said. ''I mean, we're all descended from monkeys, aren't we. Chimpanzees.''

''Ow,'' said Juddy, laughing again. He honked his horn. ''That was another zinger, wasn't it? Polo, man, you slay me!''

''I'd like to,'' Polo said.

''Go on,'' Juddy said. ''I don't care, man. But I bet you a case of Bud you wind up liking me before we get back to the 'Bago. We'll be like the best friends in the fuckin' world. What do you think, Polo man? A bet?''

Polo thought about it. ''What do I get if I still loathe you?'' he said. ''When we get back to the others? What do I get then?''

Juddy smiled. ''*Two* cases a Bud,'' he said.

* * *

Dylan was shown into a room in Lunder House, the admissions office at Colby College. Lunder House felt sort of like somebody's grandpappy's cabin, with secretaries.

A woman about thirty was sitting behind a desk. She stood up to shake Dylan's hand.

Some words came out of the woman's mouth that were not immediately decipherable by Dylan. It sounded like *Hooshey Cootin.* He wondered if that were the woman's name.

She looked at him as if she were expecting a response.

"Excuse me?" he said lamely.

The woman said it again. This time it sounded like "How's she cuttin'?"

A nameplate on the woman's desk read, *Fiona Mahoney.*

His heart began to pound. He could not make out a word she was saying.

"Wellbee sated, with ye." Dylan sat down in a soft chair.

" 'Tis fierce outside, isn't it," she said, amiably. Dylan felt sweat trickling down his temples. He wasn't going to be able to last the full twenty minutes like this.

"Fierce?" Dylan said. "It's fierce all right."

" 'Tis a soft day," Fiona said, nodding. "Well then. Are ye set? D'ya need to go to the bog?"

"The bog," Dylan said. He felt very pale. "No, I don't want to go to any bog." He figured they had some famous bog here.

"Well you're high and dry now, like," said Fiona Mahoney. "What d'you think of the place anyway?"

"Colby?" Dylan said. He hoped they were still talking about Colby. "It's pretty. I'd love to go to school here, if we can afford it."

"Well it's dear enough all right," she said. Fiona Mahoney cocked her head to one side. "Do'ja mix well at all?" she said.

"Mix?" Dylan said. "I don't know."

"Go on away out of that!" Fiona Mahoney said, smiling.

Dylan smiled. He appeared to have made a point.

"I'll be askin' ye a few things now but perhaps ye'd like ta be askin' a few things a yer own, like." She looked at him.

"Ask a few things?" Dylan said.

"Yeh-yeh-yeh."

If he understood her correctly, this Fiona Mahoney was trying something wickedly crafty on him, getting him to ask the questions. This Fiona Mahoney was crazy like a fox.

"Yes, well," Dylan said. The questions he had were ones he couldn't actually ask, like, *Is there any way in hell I can get in here, or should I just jump off a bridge?*

"I suppose I'm interested in your English department," Dylan said. He was totally improvising now. "I was wondering about the kinds of courses they offer."

"Oh, havoo no notion ah the curses," Fiona Mahoney said, surprised. "Well, you could study writin' with Professors Phinneas or Russeaux. They're ahead o' the game, that crowd."

"Oh, sure," said Dylan. "I'm a big fan of theirs."

"Well Professor Russeaux is all the rage, since his book was made into a movie. Did'ya see the movie of *Feckless Codger*? With Clint Eastwood and Mary Tyler Moore? Ye see it on cable once in a while."

Dylan had missed *Feckless Codger*, figured it was one of those movies that went straight to video. "Yes, I saw that," he said. "But I liked the book better."

"Did you now," said Fiona Mahoney. She looked out

the window. "Well, they're dear enough all right, the pictures."

"Yup," said Dylan.

There was a moment's pause. Fiona Mahoney looked at his folder, then up at him. Then she said something completely incomprehensible, and smiled.

Dylan smiled back.

Fiona Mahoney waited for a response. Getting none, she began to write on the paper before her.

"Hold it," she said. "The Biro's after runnin' out."

Dylan swallowed. He wondered if he was going to make it through the interview without screaming.

She looked, annoyed, at the nib of her pen. "Stupid little fecker," she said. "Now then, supposin' we could see you in some other way, like. The bollocks with the interview. If we could see ya when you're yourself, what would we see then?"

"Some other way?"

Fiona Mahoney nodded. "When you're yourself, like."

He thought. If she wanted to know, he would tell her. He wasn't getting in here anyway. "I don't know if there's a place where I'm most like myself. I mean, I'm not sure who I am yet, in a way. That's sort of why I want to go to college."

Fiona Mahoney was listening. "But maybe, I don't know, there's these woods near my grandparents' house where I walk sometimes with their dog. I go there and walk along these trails, and look at things."

"What sarts of tings d'you see?"

Dylan decided the hell with it. "It's hard to say. Trees, streams. Deer sometimes."

"That's brilliant, when ye see deer. If you come to Colby, you'll see moose, like."

Dylan wasn't sure if she meant this as a positive or a negative.

"I have this thing," Dylan went on, "where I don't tell anybody if I see a deer while I'm out walking. I keep it secret, so it's just this private thing, between me and the deer."

He figured this Fiona Mahoney had concluded he was nuts now.

"Good man," she said.

"It's like you're more alive in the woods. It probably sounds weird, but I feel more alive there than anywhere else. If I ever die it'll be like the one thing I can look back on and say, I was alive then."

Fiona Mahoney smiled slowly. "Dylan Floyd," she said. "Yer quotin' Thoreau."

He was just about to tell her, of course he was quoting Thoreau, but then he thought better of it. "Oh, I don't know who I'm quoting," he said. "I wasn't trying to quote anybody to tell you the truth."

"*I came to the woods because I wanted to live deliberately, like,*" Fiona Mahoney said. "*So that, when it comes time to die, I will not discover that I have not lived.*" She smiled. "See? Yer a philosopher and you don't even know it." She paused for a moment, to hack deeply into her fist. As he looked at her, Dylan realized he liked this Fiona Mahoney. She wasn't so hard to understand.

"Sorry," she said. "I've an awful chesty cough."

Dylan nodded. "I like Thoreau," he said.

"He's the bee's knees, now. Anyhow, the land around here is brilliant, to be sure. Mountains. Deer. Moose. If you're wantin' to be livin' deliberately, you can do it here."

Dylan looked her in the eyes. "I wouldn't mind living deliberately," he said, and it was true. It would be a change, anyway.

*   *   *

Lefty, Ben, and Chloë were standing on something called the Two-Cent Bridge, which was a suspension footbridge across the Kennebec River. On one side of the river was Waterville and Colby. On the other side of the river was a massive Kimberly-Clark pulp mill. It looked closed.

"Say, this is some town," Lefty said. "I could see going to school here."

"It's something," said Ben.

"So what's the decision?" Lefty said. "We're still doing Katahdin like we said?"

Ben exhaled. "I don't know. Remind me what's involved again."

"Katahdin. Highest mountain in Maine," Lefty said. "End of the Appalachian Trail. Five thousand two hundred and sixty-seven feet. It's supposed to be awesome."

"How far is this from here?" Ben said. He looked tired.

"A couple hours north," said Lefty. "Baxter State Park."

"Well, Allison and I are going to L.L. Bean," Chloë said. "That was the plan, anyway."

"If we want to do it, we should get an early start tomorrow," Lefty said. "Way I figure we want to be on the road by four A.M."

"You're kidding," said Ben.

"Yeah, we get in the 'Bago, drive three hours north to Baxter. Then it's a five-hour hike up the mountain, we spend an hour at the top, then four hours down. We start climbing around seven, say, we're up top by noon, on our way down by one, we're on the ground by five, we have dinner in Millinocket, then drive back here and meet up with everybody by ten. Next day, it's on to Dartmouth!"

Ben looked tired just hearing about this.

"I don't know, Lefty," he said. "I didn't know it was such a long haul."

"Ah, Ben," Lefty said. "We gotta do it!" He looked sad

for a moment. "It's supposed to be somethin' else. The mountain's this long ridge that connects two peaks. There's a trail between the two peaks called the Knife Edge Trail. It's only like a foot wide in parts. On either side of you there's a huge drop down thousands and thousands of feet."

"It sounds dangerous," Ben said.

"It is dangerous," Lefty said. "People die up there all the time!"

Chloë looked up suddenly.

"Well, I don't want to die," Ben said.

"We won't die," Lefty said. "It's totally safe if you stay on the trail."

"What kind of hike is this?" Chloë asked. "Do you need ropes and all that stuff?"

"No no," Lefty said. "It's just like a long walk. It's hard, though. Whizzer said it was the most physically challenging thing he'd ever done in his life. Said it was incredible. You remember Whizzer, don't you, Ben?"

Ben tried to think. He wasn't sure he remembered Whizzer.

"Whizzer's the one, whenever it snows," Chloë said, "writes his name with pee."

"Yeah!" Lefty said happily. "Ol' Whizzer!"

"I don't know," Ben said. "I don't want to rain on anybody's parade. But it sounds like an awful lot of work, all that driving, then ten hours of hiking. I wouldn't mind just staying here in Waterville for a while, maybe walking around Colby some more. They sure have a pretty campus here."

Lefty squeezed his hands into fists, then released them. He looked at his short stubby fingers.

"Listen, Ben. It's important to me, that we do this together."

"But, Lefty—"

"No, listen. As your brother, I'm asking you to climb this mountain with me. It would mean a lot."

Ben knew only one thing for certain in this life: he did not want to climb this Mount Katahdin with Lefty any more than he wanted to take out his own appendix with a pair of pinking shears.

"Okay," Ben said. "Fine."

"Boys," Chloë said softly. "Do you think I could come too?"

"What, up Mount Katahdin and all?" said Lefty. "You're kidding."

"I want to go," Chloë said.

"Aw, I don't know, honey, I was thinking this was just going to be me an' my brother," said Lefty.

"I know," Chloë said. "But I think it would be good for us, too. I think it would be good for our marriage."

"Our marriage?" Lefty said. "Our marriage is fine!" He looked worried. "Isn't our marriage fine?"

"Oh, it's fabulous, honey. Fabulous," said Chloë. It looked like she'd just bitten down on some small rolled-up balls of aluminum foil. "I just wanted to share this thing with you. It sounds breathtaking."

They stood there on the suspension bridge several hundred feet above the Kennebec. A large chunk of mysterious and possibly toxic foam floated on the river beneath them and disappeared over a waterfall.

"It's breathtaking all right," said Lefty. "The great outdoors."

Juddy and Polo were driving at eighty-five miles an hour down some street in Boston whose name they did not know. On all sides of them were red-faced people behind the wheels of expensive cars. Someone behind them was flashing his lights. A man in a Volvo passed them on the right, swung violently in front of them, then swerved into the left-hand lane. A moment later the Volvo disappeared down a left-lane exit ramp.

"Juddy, look out!" Polo shouted. The lane they were in ended, without warning, fifty feet in front of them. All other cars in this middle lane effortlessly glided to the left and right. These two lanes rose up small inclines and merged into other lines of traffic going in opposite directions. Neither exit was marked in any way.

"What do we do, what do we do?" Polo yelled.

"I don't know," Juddy said, unconcerned. "Hell, I'm going left. Why not?"

"Because maybe it's the wrong way," Polo said. "That's why not!"

"Well, hell, if you know the right way to go, you tell me."

Polo squirmed around in this seat, trying to see what the name of the highway was they had just merged onto.

"Son of a bitch," Juddy said softly. A moment later Polo felt himself being thrown against the dashboard. They had come to a sudden stop. Something was on fire in the middle of the road. There weren't any fire trucks or ambulances. Whatever it was was just sitting there burning.

Juddy attempted to get around the burning thing by moving into another lane. Immediately cars on his left seemed to speed up. Someone gave him the finger.

"Okay, okay, I think I know where we are," Polo said, looking at a road sign. "This is Memorial Drive. Let me check the map and I'll find out where that is."

"Better hurry, man," Juddy said, looking at the burning wreckage in front of them. "Looks like this thing is going to blow up. Whatever it is."

Juddy pulled into the left lane. A car behind them flashed its lights, then sped up so that it was less than a foot behind the rental car's bumper. "Okay," said Polo. "There's the river. On the map here's this Storrow Memorial Drive. So we must be on Memorial Drive, going south."

"Okay, excellent," said Juddy. "Now just find Harvard, and we'll be all set."

"I got it," said Polo. "We should be able to see it coming right up. We can't miss it."

The lane they were in suddenly ended, disappearing into an exit that was itself blocked off with orange barrels. Juddy merged right, speeding up to about ninety miles per hour. Cars behind him honked angrily.

"Sure is some town for driving around in," Juddy said, smiling.

"It's nuts," said Polo. "These people are nuts!"

"Aw, I don't know," Juddy said. "It's kind of fun, once you get the hang of it."

"You've got the hang of it, have you?"

"Well, sort of," said Juddy. "One thing I figure is, you should never look in your side mirrors in this town. You have to just figure that everybody else will make room for you. If you slow down and wait for them to let you in, it's like they can smell the fear. You just have to barrel ahead."

"We should be seeing Harvard any second now."

A sign ahead of them read, THIS ROAD IS LEGALLY CLOSED.

"You'd think there'd be signs or something," Polo said.

"I'm not worried," said Juddy. He looked at his watch. "We should stop somewhere, get ourselves a beer. It's getting late. Hey, you ever heard a this place Cowboy Bob's? I heard it's awesome."

"I don't want to go to Cowboy Bob's!" Polo said. "I want to go to Harvard!"

"Hey man, relax," said Juddy. "You're forgetting everything I told you! Just sit back and start *floatin'*, Polo. You think you can do that?"

"Floating?" said Polo. "You're talking about floating?"

"Yep," said Juddy. "Sting like a butterfly, float like a bee."

"I don't understand why we don't see Harvard," said Polo. "We should be right in the middle of it."

At that moment, the spires of Harvard University appeared, distantly, shining for a single moment, out of reach. Harvard was on the opposite side of the river from where they were, moving rapidly away from them.

"Hey," Juddy said. "What's it doing over there?"

"No, that's the wrong question," Polo said. "The question is, what are we doing over here?"

"We're not over here," said Juddy. "Look at the map again."

As Polo got out the map a sign zoomed past them. MEMORIAL DRIVE, it read, 1/2 MILE. "Hey wait," said Polo, as the exit flew by. "That's what we want. We want to be on Memorial Drive."

"We're on Memorial Drive," said Juddy. "Where did the map say we were?"

"Right here. We're on Storrow Memorial Drive."

"Well then we're where we're supposed to be. Except that they must have moved Harvard to the other side of the river."

Polo shook his head. "They wouldn't do that."

"Well there's no explanation," Juddy said. "Unless there's two Memorial Drives, one on one side of the river, one on the other."

"Or two Harvards."

Polo tried to think. "You don't think Storrow Memorial Drive and Memorial Drive are two different roads, do you?"

"They wouldn't do that," said Juddy. "Everybody would get confused."

"Yeah," Polo said bitterly. "And it's really important around here that nobody feel confused."

A man going ninety-five miles an hour in the break-down lane pulled in front of them suddenly. He honked his horn, then rolled back his sunroof and stuck his middle finger out the window at them.

Polo and Juddy looked at each other for a moment, thought about it, then started laughing. Juddy honked back and sped up.

"You know, I could get to like this town," he said.

A moment later they saw a large sign in front of them. COWBOY BOB'S NEXT LEFT.

Juddy veered, without signaling, into the left-hand lane, at eighty-four miles an hour. They pulled in front of someone with out-of-town plates driving a Camry. Juddy flashed his lights and honked at the Camry, then rolled down his window and gave the driver the finger.

"Yee-hah!" Juddy said.

"Where are we going?" asked Polo. He knew where they were going.

Allison and Dylan followed their student guide, Shawna, into a large lecture hall.

"What class is this again?" Allison said.

"Introduction to Literature and the Imagination," Shawna said. "Professor Phinneas." She nodded to Allison. "You'll love Professor Phinneas. He's awesome."

"What's awesome about him?" Dylan said.

"He just knows so much—about life!"

"Great," said Dylan.

They sat down in chairs in the middle of the room. The lecture hall had a gentle rise in the floor. The students in the back row looked down on the room like emperors watching the gladiators.

About seventy-five students filtered in and took their seats. They threw their coats on the floor. I always wondered about that, Dylan thought. Where do you put your coat in college? If you don't have lockers and everything.

A man about thirty-five swung into the room. He had a mop of dirty-blonde hair, little John Lennon glasses, and the pointiest nose Dylan had ever seen on something that was not a woodpecker. This Professor Phinneas looked like he would stick straight in a dartboard, if you ever threw him nose-first toward one. Looking at the man, Dylan had a sudden desire to do exactly this.

"Greetings, boys and girls," the man said, dropping his briefcase with a sudden flump onto a small desk at the front of the room.

"Hello, Professor," a good many of them said. Everyone in this lecture certainly seemed chummy.

"Well—whoa, where am I?" He blinked and stumbled for a minute. Out of one pocket he pulled a can of Fruitopia. Reading the side of the can, he said, "Shake gently."

Professor Phinneas put the can down on the desk, then began to gently shake. "Whoo boy," he said. "I'm feelin' *wiggily*!"

Shawna turned to Allison and said, "Did I tell you? He's awesome!"

"Now then, baboons," Professor Phinneas said. "For today I asked you to read T. S. Eliot's poem 'Burnt Norton,' the first of the *Four Quartets*." He took off his tweed jacket and threw it in the corner. He cracked his knuckles and rolled up the sleeves of his pressed starched shirt. Professor Phinneas had arms that were both tiny and strong, sort of like the arms on a tyrannosaurus rex. He had somewhat revolting transparent skin, so that without much effort, a student could trace the path of the veins and arteries in his arm, if she wanted.

"Now we all know what 'Burnt Norton' is, and it's not a horrible accident that happened to Ralph Cramden's pal." His voice shifted suddenly. *"Help me, Ralphy boy, I'm on fire! Help me, Ralphy boy!"* No one laughed. Professor Phinneas paced around the room. "Ah, you kids are too young to know about *The Honeymooners*, aren't ya. Man, I used to love that show. When I was living in New York with this girl—*whoa! The wrong woman! Somebody help me!*—I used to stay up, watch channel eleven. Eleven o'clock, *The Three Stooges*, eleven-thirty, *The Honeymooners*, twelve midnight, *The Twilight Zone*. Boy oh boy, now that was living. This woman I lived with didn't like the Stooges, though. Maybe that's not a surprise. Women hate the Three Stooges, did you ever notice that? Well, why shouldn't they hate them, these three guys beating each other over the head. Nyuk nyuk nyuk. You know, when I used to watch the Stooges you never knew which one you were going to get, like whether it was going to be a Curly, a Shemp, or, God forbid, a Curly Joe. When the credits came up and it turned out it was a Shemp, I used to get sad sometimes that it wasn't a Curly. But you know what? The older I get, the more I realize this one essential truth: *When you get a Shemp, don't be sad it's not a Curly! Just be glad it's not a Curly Joe!* Are you guys getting all this down?"

Professor Phinneas cracked his knuckles, took a sip of his Fruitopia. Allison looked at Shawna in shock. "What did I tell you?" Shawna whispered.

The professor opened his book and began to read. "Burnt Norton." He cleared his throat. *"Time present and time past are both perhaps present in time future."* He paused for a moment and looked up at the class with a lost, discouraged expression. "I know what you're thinking.

You're going: *Haaaah?* Like, *Haaaah?* Like, *What's he talking about?* Well, baboons, let's answer that question. Anybody?''

He looked around. Nobody moved. He started walking
down the center aisle, ascending the slow rise in the classroom until he reached the gladiator-watching level in the
back row. He sat down in the back row next to a guy who
was wearing a baseball cap backward on his head.

''All right, Weezums, you read this, right? What's it
all mean, all this stuff about time past and time future?''

Weezums blushed and shrugged. ''I don't know. It's
kind of a mystery.''

''Yes yes,'' Professor Phinneas said, excited. ''That's exactly right! It's a mystery!''

Weezums looked suspicious. Had he hit on something,
or was the professor making fun of him?

''Now what exactly is mysterious about this passage,
Mr. Weezums, do you suppose you could articulate
that?''

''Well, I don't know,'' Weezums said.

''That's right!'' Phinneas said again, still excited. ''You
don't! None of us do!''

Some of the students were attempting to take notes.

''Now what is it we don't know anything about? Mr.
Weezums, could you try to explain this once more?''

Weezums shook his head. ''This poem,'' he said.

''Exactly!'' Phinneas shouted again. ''The poem is
about something we do not understand. You're doing
very well, Weezums. So what is it that we don't understand?''

''Time,'' said a woman in the front row. She had apple-
red cheeks and long, blonde hair.

''What, what, what was that?'' said the professor. He
flew down the aisle toward the front row. ''I could have

sworn I heard someone say something intelligent. Was that you, Annie, I do believe it was."

"It was me," said Annie.

"So this poem is saying something about time."

"It's saying that time is all interconnected."

"Exactly," said Professor Phinneas. "The poem is asking whether time can be redeemed. It suggests several different ways of looking at time, in an attempt to make sense of things, in an attempt to make sense of the insensible. Is that the right word, *insensible?* Man, I'm just not sure."

Phinneas seemed to have worked himself up into a sweat. "I don't know," he said, sitting down on a desk at the front of the room. "Maybe this poem is too hard. Maybe we're going about this the wrong way. When you think about time, what do you think about? Your earliest memory? A moment of illumination? A moment when your life made sense? Are there such moments?"

He got up and looked out the window. For a moment he stood there, as if deep in thought.

"Hey, I know that girl," he said, pointing to someone outside.

He seemed to think some more.

"She was in this class, last year. I just saw her walk by. For that moment I was thinking about last year. For a moment I was transported to the past. It was like I was living there, and while I was there, this moment, here, now, with all of you, this was the future."

There was the sound of a few more people taking notes.

Professor Phinneas smiled. "Ha, ha," he said, laughing at apparently nothing. "When I was living in New York with that woman—*the wrong woman!*—there was one night when I was walking up out of the subway, arm in arm with you know who, when this other woman came walking down the subway stairs and our eyes met, and then we passed each other and just as I got to the top of the stairs I looked back down at her, and there she was, standing at the bottom of the stairs, looking up at me. Our eyes froze, then we walked on. We never saw each other again.''

He looked into the class. The place was silent.

''We do this, travel in time, every day. We are living our lives, the moments we are living at this moment, as well as living the whole rest of our lives, in memory, in reverse. Then there's the future, which exists only in the imagination, at least for now. In our hearts all of these moments exist simultaneously, don't they? The imagined future? The remembered past? But can you imagine the past? Can you remember the future? Hm, I don't know, let's just think about this. Well dee well dee well! It's a mystery, just as Mr. Weezums articulated!''

He pointed, suddenly, without warning, at Dylan.

''Now you, young man. Pick a moment from your life.''

Dylan looked around, stricken with horror.

''Yes, you. I know you're not in the class. It's all right. We're all friends here.''

Allison looked over at him reassuringly. It's all right, she seemed to be saying. We're all friends.

''A moment from my life,'' he said.

''Yes, a moment. Close your eyes and think of something at random.''

Dylan felt like he was going to pass out. All these college students were staring at him. There was nothing from his life that seemed to fit.

Everyone was waiting.

''I don't know,'' Dylan said.

''Don't think about it,'' the professor said. ''Just tell us the first thing that comes to your mind.''

Dylan tried to think of the first thing that came to his mind, but the only thing coming to his mind was terror and embarrassment.

"It's okay, Dylan," Allison said, rubbing his shoulder. "There's no wrong thing to say."

"Exactly," said Professor Phinneas excitedly. "Relax. Close your eyes. Let your mind wander, free as a little skunky-wunky."

Dylan's mind wandered, free as a little skunky-wunky.

Dylan and his father were driving toward Uncle Lefty's house. It was nine years earlier. "It's just for the day, son," Ben said. "While I go into the office and work." They drove through a covered bridge, and Dylan thought about the Headless Horseman. Ichabod Crane slain by a pumpkinhead.

"Well well well," said Juddy, sitting on the front porch of the house. He was holding a catcher's mitt. "If it isn't my trusty sidekick."

"Is it okay if Dylan stays over here today?" said Ben, not getting out of the car. Dylan walked over toward his cousin. "I have to go into the office and my wife's in Ohio this week."

"Ohio, huh," said Juddy.

"Yes, Ohio," said Ben, looking at his watch. "So Dylan's going to stay with you and Lefty today. I'll be back tonight to pick him up. Okay?"

Juddy didn't say anything. Ben drove off quickly, everything settled.

"Hey, Dickweed," said Juddy.

A moment later another car came by, an Impala station wagon.

"Come on, Juddy," shouted some kids from inside. "Let's go."

"Can't go," Juddy said. "Gotta stay here with my cousin." He nodded toward Dylan. "Peckerwood."

"You have to come!" the other kids shouted. "We need you!"

Juddy shrugged. "Can't," he said. "Not now."

The man behind the wheel, also wearing a Little League uniform, said, "Are you sure you can't come, Juddy?" he said. "You want me to speak with your father?"

"He ain't here," said Juddy. "He's at the lot."

A few moments later, the Impala was vanishing down the road, carrying off Juddy's disappointed teammates.

"You can play," Dylan said. "Don't stay here on my account."

"Yeah?" said Juddy. "An' what would you do if you stayed here by yourself? Rummage round my stuff? I don't think so!"

"I'm not going to touch your stuff," Dylan said, annoyed.

"Come on, Dickweed," said Juddy. "Let's play our game."

"You're sure?" Dylan said. It didn't sound like he wanted to play.

"I'm sure," said Juddy. He picked up a stick and held it out like a sword. "En garde!"

"Can I have a sword this time?" said Dylan.

"No, man," said Juddy. "*I'm* the Secret Swordsman. You're my sidekick!"

"If I'm your sidekick, I want to have a sword."

"Hey," said Juddy. "Knock it off. You don't want to have to spend the whole afternoon invisible again?"

Dylan shrugged. When they pretended Dylan was invisible, he wasn't allowed to talk.

"C'mon," said Juddy. "Let me show you this place I heard about."

Dylan followed Judson through a sea of wildflowers. His uncle and Juddy lived in a country house near the river, where they'd moved after the divorce. Nobody talked much about Judson's mother, Elio, anymore. She lived in Williamstown, Massachusetts.

"What's this place we're going to?" Dylan said.

Judson shrugged. "I don't know, Dickweed. It's a big mystery, isn't it?"

They walked through the field into deep woods. They followed a trail through pine and maple and beech.

Ahead of them was a rusted-out car, its doors torn off, beer cans strewn in the backseat. It was a 1956 Rambler. "You see this," Judson said. "The people that drove it here died."

"They did?" said Dylan.

"Yeah, there was this couple necking and shit and this guy who escaped from prison came and found them and blew them away with a shotgun."

Dylan stood there, believing his cousin.

They looked at the burned-out car. There were more beer cans inside. The shattered window, its shards hanging together in a spiderweb pattern, lay on the ground nearby. The Rambler appeared to have been here for a long time.

"What's necking?" Dylan said.

Judson looked at Dylan with pity. "Man," he said. "You're pathetic."

A raccoon walked out of the woods and paused in the path, looking at them.

"Look," said Judson. "An Iranian spy!" He charged the raccoon, brandishing his sword. The Iranian vanished into the woods.

Judson walked down the path, away from the car.

Dylan lingered next to the wreck for a moment, then ran after Judson, afraid of being left behind.

They walked through the woods until they came to an overgrown field. In the distance was a farmer's windmill, the sails motionless in the heavy summer air. A ruined house stood near the windmill, its broken windows peering out at the long grass.

"Who lives there?" Dylan said.

"The Hitches. Used to, anyway," Judson said. He began to walk through the long grass toward the house.

"What happened to them?"

"Guy blew his wife away with a shotgun," Judson said. "Then he poisoned himself."

Dylan looked at the house. Curtains blew through the open windows.

"You wanna go in?" Judson said.

Dylan looked at the house. He didn't.

"I don't know."

"The basement is totally weird. The whole house is built on lodestone. You know what lodestone is, don't you, Dickweed?"

Dylan nodded. He remembered something about this from school. Lodestone was magnetized rock.

"You drop something in the basement, it falls up," Judson said.

"Bullshit," said Dylan.

"This kid at school saw it," said Judson. "It's awesome."

"Things don't fall up," Dylan said, frightened, hoping that he was stating a fact.

"C'man, Dickweed," Judson said. "Let's check it out."

They walked up the stairs. There was no wind.

The front door creaked upon its hinges.

The house, while ruined, did not appear to have been abandoned long, and fragments of its owners' possessions still littered the place. There was a chandelier, all of its lightbulbs broken, hanging in the front hallway. A long staircase directly in front of them rose to the second floor. To the left was an archway that led into a parlor. A piano, covered with dust, stood in a bay window. There were a few books upon a bookshelf, a torn portrait of a man in pince-nez hanging above a fireplace.

The floors were strewn with empty cans of beer, broken glass. There were some rusted farm tools leaning against the wall. Spiderwebs hung thickly from the ceilings. The floor was made of warped, dried boards. Some of them were missing altogether.

To the right was a dining room with a long table. There was a fireplace behind the table, filled with garbage and broken glass. Vines from outside grew through an open window.

"C'man," Judson said.

They walked into the parlor, past the broken baby grand. Dylan imagined it suddenly beginning to play, by itself. He felt his heart pounding in his chest. Crickets chirped from somewhere in the house, the only sound in the intense summer heat.

A small door at the end of the parlor opened into what at one time might have been the gentlemen's smoking room. There was another fireplace, a small table, a couch with the springs broken through. On the table was a pile of magazines.

"Here's something to check out," Judson said. From the way he said it, Dylan had the distinct impression that his cousin had been here before.

The magazines were not recent. Some of the covers were ripped off; others were discolored with mildew and sunlight. The pages stuck together. One of them looked as if it had been partially burned.

The magazines contained almost no print. The pages

were covered with pictures of naked women. Judson and Dylan did not speak. They sat down on the couch and looked at the magazines. Judson looked at one, then handed it to Dylan. Dylan looked at the magazine that Judson had just seen. Now and again Judson would say something like "Whoa" or "Oh man!" and then Dylan knew that an especially disgusting picture would be coming his way in about five minutes. Dylan had never seen anything like this. It was like falling through a trapdoor into another universe. He did not want to look at these magazines, but it was impossible to look away. He felt the oppressive, heavy air weighing on him, with its faint smell of decay. This is a terrible world, he felt, looking at these naked people. A terrible, wondrous world.

After Dylan had looked at the last discolored, burned magazine, he looked up.

"C'man," said Juddy, and opened a door on the far wall. It exposed a long hallway. Judson and Dylan walked down the hallway, past disheveled bedrooms. At the end of the hallway was a crooked staircase, leading downward.

Dylan felt an agonizing terror. He did not want to walk down these stairs.

"What's the matter, Dickweed?" Judson said. "Scared?"

"I'm not," Dylan said. He stepped forward.

The stairs were very steep. He had to hold on to the stone walls in order to keep from falling. At the bottom of the stairs was a faint glow of light cast from small windows near the cellar ceiling.

"Where's this antigravity place?" Dylan said. "It's in the basement?"

"Yeah," Judson said. "That's what Whizzer said."

There was a small room off to one side of the cellar

that contained a coal chute. The wall behind the chute was sheer rock.

"That's it," Judson said. "That's the lodestone."

Dylan looked around. "I don't feel any different," he said.

Judson shook his head. "You got anything metal on you?" he said.

"Metal?"

"Yeah, it's gotta be metal."

Dylan wasn't wearing any metal, except for his belt buckle. "All I got is my belt," he whispered.

"That'll do," Judson said. "Take your belt off."

"My belt?"

"Go on, take it off. Throw it at the wall."

Dylan felt stupid, but he did as his cousin told him. He took off his belt. Immediately his shorts began to fall down.

"Throw it," Judson said.

Dylan threw his belt against the wall.

It clattered against the rock, then fell onto the floor.

The boys stood there, crestfallen.

"It's probably not real metal," Judson said.

"What do you mean, not real metal?"

"We have to find something that's all metal, like those paint cans."

Dylan picked his belt back up and started looping it through his pants. Judson went over and picked up an empty can of paint.

"Let's try this," he said. "Ready?"

"No," Dylan said. "Don't."

Judson threw the can at the wall.

It hit the rock with a hollow clunk, then rolled onto the floor.

And at that moment, they heard a human voice coming from upstairs, a low moan. It started off quietly, then grew louder. It sounded like a woman. For a moment her voice rose in pitch, almost screamed, then stopped altogether. The house echoed in silence.

"**U**m," Dylan said. He was sitting in a classroom at Colby College. Everyone was looking at him. He'd been silent for a long time.

"It's really okay, Dylan," Professor Phinneas whispered. "It's all right."

Dylan shrugged. "I can't think of anything," he said.

The professor sighed and went over to the window again. He stood there for a moment. "That girl wasn't in this class," he said. "I'm thinking of someone else. I don't even know that girl." He played with some coins in his pocket. He was silent for a long while.

"When the space shuttle blew up, my father was having brain surgery. I used to love the space program, boy, I used to. I remember this guy came up to me, the night the shuttle exploded, he said, 'The Shuttle blowing up just about serves you right.' Can you believe that? Boy."

Professor Phinneas checked his watch. "Hokey smokey, I'm running out of time. I got a lot of material to cover. Are we just about done with 'Burnt Norton' now? *Hiya, Ralphy boy.* Better move on to 'The Wasteland.' *Address the ball! Hello, ball!*" He looked up at the class, which was both enraptured and frightened.

He pointed at Dylan.

"*Ridiculous the waste sad time stretching before and after.*"

Dylan felt his heart pounding in his throat.

There was a long silence. Finally Weezums raised his hand.

"Yes, Weezums," Phinneas said, mopping his forehead with a bandanna.

"Professor Phinneas, is this going to be on the test?"

"Oh yes, Weezums," Phinneas said, bitterly. "This is on the test all right. Not the test you *take*, the test you *live*!"

Weezums nodded, unsure. "Okay," he said. "Good."

"Remember—don't be sad it's not a Curly! Just be glad it's not a Curly Joe! Whoo! Whoo!" He looked worried. "Jeez, I *knew* today was gonna be wiggily!" He looked confused. "You're all getting this?" Phinneas asked his class.

The class nodded fearfully. They were getting it all right.

A little after midnight, Juddy and Polo were sitting in a booth at Cowboy Bob's. A woman in white vinyl cowboy boots, leather hot pants, a white cowboy hat, and a halter top decorated with fringe came over to them bearing a platter.

"Here you go," she said. "Two more margaritas."

"Thanks," said Polo. He smiled handsomely.

The waitress put the drinks down, disregarding Polo's suaveness. She gave them more salsa and chips, then walked away. Polo watched the woman's remarkable buttocks as they moved away from him.

"She likes me," Polo said.

"Polo, dude," Juddy said. "You still don't get it."

"What don't I get?" Polo said. "What?" He took a sip of his margarita and closed his eyes. Things seemed kind of odd to him, like he was sitting on the deck of an ocean liner moving up and down in a rolling sea.

"You want that girl, man, you have to let her know you don't care!" Juddy said. "Jesus, it's like you think women are going to have sex with you because they like you!"

"Sure they like me," Polo said. "What's wrong with me?"

"You?" Juddy said. "The only reason a woman is going to sleep with you, Polo, is to get even with you."

"Even with me? For what?"

"For not liking her."

"Oh, you're fulla hooey," Polo said. "I've been with lots of women." He started counting on his fingers. His tongue ticked out of the corner of his mouth as he concentrated.

In the corner of Cowboy Bob's, a young man was climbing onto a mechanical bull. A moment later he started whooping.

"Fifteen," Polo said. "Sixteen if you count Mrs. Dilworth."

"I don't wanna know your tally, dude," Juddy said. "Spare me."

"No, wait," said Polo. "I forgot Tippy."

"I told you I don't wanna know."

"Well I'm just saying I know a thing or two about women."

"Yeah, you know maybe two things."

"Shut up, Juddy," said Polo. "I can't believe I'm even talking to you."

"Well, it's me or nobody, dude," said Juddy. "Anyway, it's like I told ya. You and me got lots in common."

"Oh, yes, I'm quite pleased with all our common ground so far," said Polo. "Pleased as punch."

"Why do you think women sleep with us, Polo? Tell me that."

"I don't know about you," said Polo. "As for myself, perhaps they find me interesting, someone different than the usual person they're familiar with. They like my knowledge of things. That's what attracts them, I mean, and then after that one thing leads to another. I think that's pretty much the process, yes." Polo finished his margarita and put it on the table.

"You're livin' in a dream world, man," Juddy said, smiling. "The magic kingdom!"

"Thank you," said Polo, rubbing his large chin.

"I didn't mean it as a compliment, dude," Juddy said.

"I know how you meant it," said Polo. He thought. "How did you mean it?"

"Why would women sleep with us?" said Juddy. He shook his head. "No reason!"

"Speak for yourself," said Polo. He was now seeing two Juddys in front of him. They were both laughing.

The waitress came over again. Looking at their empty glasses, she said, "One more round, boys? My shift is ending. I gotta settle up your bill."

"I don't know," said Polo. "I want to be fresh tomorrow."

"Tomorrow?" said the waitress. "You got a big day?"

"He's gettin' married," said Juddy suddenly. "We're both gettin' married, in fact. To sisters."

Polo opened his mouth, and shut it. The walls were breathing.

"Sisters?" said the waitress.

"Twin sisters," said Juddy. "Angelique and Dominique. They're Danish."

"Whoa," said the waitress, smiling. "Well then you'll definitely want another round."

"You got it," said Juddy. "This here is our last night as single men."

"Poor things," said the waitress.

"Aw, we're not poor things," said Juddy. "We're the two luckiest men in the world. Marrying the girls of our dreams, tomorrow at sunset!" Juddy winked.

"Tell you what, I'm bringing you one more round, on

the house." The waitress put down the tab. "You settle this up, I'll get you two more margaritas. I'll be back."

She walked away. Polo was amazed again by the movement of her four buttocks.

"What the heck was that?" he said. "We aren't getting married."

"Exactly, man, now you're catching on."

"You're a menace," Polo said, standing up.

"Come on back, dude," Juddy said. "The night is young."

Polo walked toward the men's room. Cowboy Bob's was full of young men, some women, many of them college students from the looks of them. Polo was surprised that they didn't have their books with them. When I go to Harvard, he thought, I'll sit in cafés, reading, eating biscotti, drinking cappuccino. I'll discuss great works with great women. With any luck, Juddy would be many miles hence at this time next year, giving people test drives of Trans Ams, while I sit in the tower of Lampoon Castle, reading the comic works of Swinburne and Burke.

For a moment Polo felt a strange kind of nausea creeping up on him. He reached the men's room and moved toward a sink. Polo splashed cold water on his face, then looked around for a towel. Unfortunately, there weren't any towels, only a hot-air blower. Polo turned on the blower and stuck his face in the stream of blasting air.

A moment later he backed away from the blast, looked in the mirror. His face was still somewhat wet. Is this me? he thought, looking in the mirror. Is this the face of a Harvard man? For a moment he remembered the sneer in the voice of Hensleigh Barker. What happens if they don't let me in? Who am I then? He felt the creeping nausea in his guts again. I disappear, he thought. I vanish from the face of the earth and turn into somebody else. Who do I become if I don't become the person I imagine?

Polo left the men's room. His cheeks were the color of spoiled milk.

It took a while for him to get across the room and find their booth. When he got there, the waitress was sitting on the bench next to Juddy. Another woman with long brown hair sat across from them. They were both wearing cowgirl costumes.

"Howdy, Polo," she said, and smiled.

"This here is Sandra," Juddy said. "And her friend Dawn."

"We just got off," said Dawn.

"Quite a place you got here," Polo said, sitting down. "Man!"

"It's some joint all right," said Sandra, shaking her head.

"So you boys are getting married tomorrow!" said Dawn.

"Yep," said Juddy. "Right at sunset!"

"God, your last night as bachelors!" said Dawn.

"I don't suppose I'll be back here," said Polo. "I don't suppose so."

"Yeah, me and you got bold new horizons!" said Juddy.

"Yes, I'll be going to other places from now on," said Polo. "Places where you can read. Places where you can discuss ideas."

Dawn smiled, pulled on an earring. "That's what I used to think," she said. "Back when I went to Harvard."

At 3:30 in the morning, the clock radio went off in the motel room of Chloë and Lefty. Chloë opened her eyes. Lefty was asleep on her shoulder. He snored softly.

She stared at the ceiling, thinking about Planet X. Right around now was when they were supposed to launch

Copernicus II. There hadn't been anything in the news about it, though. She wondered if they'd had to cancel it. It wouldn't be a surprise. On her shoulder she felt something wet. Lefty was sleeping with his mouth open. *Come on down to Flat Foot Floyds. Have we got a deal for you.*

She got her arm out from underneath Lefty. It was asleep. With her other hand she lifted the receiver of the phone next to the bed and ordered room service. "Yes," she said. "Three eggs over easy, three pieces of bacon, three pieces of sausage, a plate of waffles, and coffee. And one low-fat yogurt. Thank you." She hung up.

I must be insane, Chloë thought, getting out of bed to comb her hair. It's impossible. What I ought to do is be honest, sit down with him and tell him my feelings. It's not like I'm the only woman in the world who ever fell out of love with her husband. Would it be so wrong if she asked him for a divorce? But even as she asked herself this she knew the answer. He'd never pay Allison's college tuition if she left him. Allison would be left high and dry. She'd spend the rest of her life blaming Chloë for the opportunities she'd lost.

A little while later, there was a knock on the door. Chloë got up and opened it. A bellhop walked in and put a large platter on the bed, and Chloë signed her husband's name.

The smell of eggs and bacon filled the room.

Chloë sighed, pulled her nightie over her head, let it fall to the floor. She went to the mirror and looked herself in the eyes. Look at you, she thought. Pathetic. There must be a better way of killing him than this. "Lefty," she said, getting out the K-Y jelly. "Wake up, love. It's time for waffles."

*   *   *

At 7:30 in the morning, Dylan opened his eyes. His father was not in the room with him. During the night, Ben had put on his clothes and departed for the mountain. Dylan opened the curtains and let the room fill with light. He looked over at his father's unmade bed, thought for a moment about crying, then decided against.

At 8:15, fifteen minutes before Polo's interview with the dean of admissions at Harvard, Dawn opened her eyes and looked around the chaos of the room Polo had rented late the previous evening at the Cambridge Guest Quarters Hotel. Her bra was hanging from a ceiling fixture. A smiley face had been drawn with shaving cream on the screen of the television. A bottle of Jagermeister, nearly empty, stood next to the table, along with an open carton of orange juice.

Dawn gently put her feet on the floor, reached up, and got her bra off the chandelier. The rest of her clothes were scattered around the room, although it took a while to find them. When she was dressed, she sat down on the side of the bed, looked again at Polo's sweet face. He looked like a little boy dreaming there. It had been nice to sleep with him. She remembered guys like this from her hall when she was a freshman—so full of their own belief in themselves, so convinced that the world was about to open before them like a flower. It was a wonderfully romantic quality you found in boys just before they became men, this belief that their own invention of themselves might be true.

She thought about asking him about his fiancée, but decided not to embarrass him. Dawn felt the side of his face with her cupped fingers. His stubble tickled against her palm.

"Good morning, honey," she said, and leaned forward

and kissed his cheek. "I have to go, darling. Wake up. To-day's the day you get married!"

But Polo just kept sleeping. He breathed heavily in dream.

Dawn wasn't sure what to do. She looked at his wallet, which was lying next to the bottle of Jagermeister. There was a lot of money in it. Dawn smiled, remembering Polo and Juddy singing last night as they did the shots. *We're little black sheep who have lost our way*, they sang. *Baah, baah, baah.*

Dawn looked at the sleeping boy, trying to decide whether or not to wake him. She envied his innocence, his youth. And his friendship with Juddy was sweet as well. It would be nice, Dawn thought, as she took all the money from Polo's wallet, to live your life guided by that kind of love.

Ben, Chloë, and Lefty signed the register in the ranger's cabin. *Time in, 8:30.* A dozen hikers had already signed the book before them. "Here's our route up," Lefty said, pointing at a map on the wall. "Helon Taylor Trail, a slow rise, up to the top of Mount Pamola. That's the lower peak. Then we climb down the notch here, then back up Chimney Peak, following the Knife Edge to South Peak, then Baxter Peak. From Baxter, it's down the Saddle Trail, down to Chimney Pond, then the Chimney Pond Trail back to Roaring Brook Campground and the parking lot."

Ben nodded. "You think there's somewhere we can get a cup of coffee?"

The ranger, sitting at his desk nearby, smiled. He was a brisk young man with a handlebar mustache and a Smokey-the-Bear hat. "Sorry," he said. "No coffee here unless you packed it in."

"I'm excited!" said Chloë.

"You all be careful up there today," said the ranger. "We got twenty-mile-an-hour gusts on the Knife Edge. If it looks too dicey, you stop at Pamola, come down the Dudley Trail. Use your heads, okay? I don't wanna have to pick you off the peak with a chopper." He smiled good-naturedly.

"Does that happen often?" Chloë said. She looked at Lefty.

The ranger blinked, as if to say, *Of course it happens.* "Just last week some old guy had a heart attack. A group of through-hikers had to carry him down on their shoulders." He shook his head. "The mountain doesn't kid around. You stay on the trails, be careful, you'll be all right."

"Come on," said Lefty. "Let's move out!"

They turned and left the ranger's cabin. For a moment the ranger stared after them, thinking. Then he returned to the task at hand.

Dylan and Allison were driving south on I-95 in a loaner car from Callahan Waterville Pontiac Audi Maserati. The sun was shining brightly. Red and yellow leaves fell through the morning air.

"I can't believe they actually did it," Allison said. "Four o'clock in the morning, and they all piled into the Winnebago."

"Yeah," Dylan said. "It was weird waking up this morning, finding them gone. I didn't even hear my dad get up."

"I heard them," Allison said softly. "Mom and Lefty were up for a while." Her nose wrinkled in disgust.

"What?" Dylan said. "What's that face?"

"Nothing," she said. They drove on in silence for a while.

"You're nice to come with me," Allison said.

"Well, you didn't want to go alone."

"My mom was supposed to take me, before she decided to climb mount whatchamacallit. They have a lot of outlets here. You like shopping, Dylan?"

Dylan thought about the words he'd told his interviewer, about wanting to live deliberately.

"Sure," he said. "Sure I like shopping."

Allison shook her head. "My mom is so messed up," she said.

"Messed up how?"

"She's lost," said Allison.

"Do you guys get along okay?"

"Pretty much. As long as I don't have to hear about your uncle. That's not a happy topic."

Dylan nodded. "You can say that again," he said.

"So does your dad ever date?" she asked.

"Dad?" Dylan blinked, as if the question had never occurred to him. "No. Of course not."

"Don't say of course not," Allison said. "He could date."

"He could," Dylan said. "But he doesn't."

They drove on for a while. On either side of them were thick pine forests, punctuated now and again with maples, beech trees.

"That class we were in yesterday sure was weird," Dylan said.

"Yeah, it was weird," said Allison. "But I liked it. That teacher was pretty funny."

"You thought he was funny?" Dylan said. He shook his head.

"Oh, but you could like, see the way his mind was working. It wasn't like any class I'd ever been in."

Dylan was silent for a while, then said, "I didn't like

the way he called on me. In front of everybody. That wasn't fair. I felt stupid."

"You shouldn't," Allison said. She sighed. "When's your birthday, Dylan?"

"June."

"June what?"

"Twenty-second."

"Ah," she said. "You're on the cusp."

Dylan looked at her blankly. "I guess. When's yours?"

"February thirteenth." She flicked some hair out of her eyes. "Aquarius."

"What's Aquarius? The bull?"

"Water carrier."

"And Cancer is a crab."

"Exactly."

He didn't know what to say. Being the crab pretty much fit.

"They're probably having their interviews by now," Dylan said. "Juddy and Polo."

"Was Juddy interviewing too? I thought it was just Polo."

"Polo's interviewing, but I think Juddy is supposed to meet the fencing coach. That French guy." He smiled. "They sure take him seriously, don't they?"

Allison said, "Yeah. Well, that's only because they don't know him. They're under the false impression that, you know, he's like—a human being."

She looked at Dylan, then started laughing. Dylan laughed too.

"I'm sorry," she said. "I don't know what to say. Your family is just too weird."

"I know," Dylan said. "Sometimes I don't feel like I'm related to them."

"I can't wait to go to college," Allison said. "Get away,

on my own, where I can finally be myself instead of somebody's little . . ."

She did not finish.

"Me too," Dylan said. He thought about his father's
unmade bed. The laptop computer was sitting in the middle of his sheets.

"I just want to get away," he said, and knew it was
impossible.

Juddy walked back to his room just before ten. It had
been fun, meeting with M. Fenelon. It was one of the few
times in his life he had been with anyone who did not
find fencing ridiculous. M. Fenelon, who turned out to be
younger than Juddy had thought, understood everything
Juddy said about épée. The irony was that Harvard was
just about to hire a new assistant coach, a specialist in
saber work. Ruki, the guy from Stanford. M. Fenelon
shared Juddy's contempt for saber play, and Juddy understood that getting him to join the team would somehow bolster M. Fenelon's position against this Ruki. It
was odd for him, as he sat there in the man's office at the
athletic complex, to realize that M. Fenelon, the Olympic
champion, was worried about his position, and that
Juddy somehow was part of the man's great plan for
smothering Ruki. He'd left without committing himself.
Well, Monsieur, he'd said. We'll just have to see how it
goes.

The cab ride back to the hotel took fifteen minutes.
Now, as he walked back up to his room, he felt a sudden
optimism about the future. For the first time, it occurred
to Juddy, maybe he could go to this Harvard. In spite of
everything, maybe it would be fun to go someplace where
people didn't think he was a fool. He smiled as he thought

about the fencing coach. First thing I do once I get here, Juddy thought, is switch over to sabers.

He paused in the hallway before opening his room. He looked at Polo's door, thought about things. So far everything was going according to plan.

Juddy swung open the door to his room. Sandra was sitting in bed, wearing one of Juddy's T-shirts, watching television. A large platter full of empty plates lay by her side, and she smiled at him.

They were above the treeline by midmorning. Shortly after 10:30, Chloë and Lefty and Ben sat on large rocks on the shoulders of Mount Pamola. In every direction stretched the green horizons of Maine. There were lakes and forests, light shining through clouds. Ahead of them the trail ran straight up the pink granite of Katahdin.

"How are you feeling, Lefty?" Chloë said.

"Better," he said. "I think I found my rhythm."

Chloë looked disappointed. "Good," she said.

"Me too," Ben said. "I don't feel so winded. It's as if my body is used to what I'm asking of it now."

"Well, my body thinks my brain is nuts," Lefty said, tearing the wrapper off a Snickers. "But my body has thought that for years."

"How are you doing, Chloë?" Ben said. He looked over at her as if seeing her for the first time. She was a beautiful woman, Chloë.

"I'm all right," she said sadly, looking up toward the peak.

"I'm glad we're doing this," said Lefty, finishing his Snickers. "I'm glad we're all together."

*   *   *

At 10:30 Allison and Dylan were walking through L.L. Bean. The place was huge. There were stuffed bears, stuffed moose, stuffed deer. Largemouth bass swam in a pool that curled around the base of a large staircase. Hundreds of people were scurrying around, carrying down jackets, gumshoes, the paddles of canoes.

Dylan remembered a time when he was six or seven that he and his father had gone bass fishing. They hadn't caught anything.

"Do you like this shirt?" Allison said, holding up a plaid flannel.

"Yeah, it's okay," Dylan said. He hated shopping, and thought about his father and the others, probably on top of the mountain by now, looking down on creation.

"You don't sound convinced," Allison said.

"I don't know, I don't usually wear shirts like that," Dylan said. He was wearing a shirt nearly identical to it even at this moment.

"I didn't mean you, I meant me. Do you think I'd look good in this?"

She held it in front of her. Dylan looked at the shirt, draped over Allison's body.

"You'd look good in it," he said.

"What about this one?" She held up another shirt with a slightly different pattern.

"You'd look good in that too," Dylan said.

Allison looked at him with annoyance. "You're no help," she said.

A couple passed by, with a child in a stroller. The child held a balloon in one hand. Dylan thought about little Kugelmaus.

They walked into a large room full of camping equipment. Dylan was amazed to find an entire wall full of compasses.

"You like those?" Allison said.

"Yeah," Dylan said, looking at one. It had a rotating dial mounted on a clear plastic base, so you could orient yourself in the wilderness using a USGS map.

"I think I'm going to get this one," Dylan said.

"You need a compass?" she asked.

"It's good to have a compass," Dylan said. "This way I won't get lost."

Allison smiled. "You think having a compass will keep you from getting lost?"

Dylan did not reply. His tongue ticked out of the corner of his mouth.

Allison looked at Dylan and wondered what world he was lost in. Dylan stared at the compass, moving its dial around.

At noon Ben and Chloë and Lefty stood on the pinnacle of Mount Pamola, looking across the spine of Mount Katahdin and the Knife Edge Trail. The surface of the earth was unspeakably distant. Chloë thought about the fact that she had flown in planes at heights much lower than this. For miles and miles the horizon stretched before them. The world was silent up here, gorgeous, breathtaking, pristine. It was a lovely spot, Chloë thought, for somebody to turn purple, fall over.

"So that's the Knife Edge Trail," Lefty said, looking nervously at the thin ridge of the mountain before them. It disappeared down a notch a few feet away, and fell nearly a hundred feet before rising again up the next peak, the Chimney. From the Chimney onward, they saw the thin spine, only a foot wide in parts, bending upward toward the distant peak of Baxter, the top of Katahdin.

"How long will it take us to get up there?" Chloë said.

"About an hour I think," Lefty said, not moving. "We should get going."

A gust of wind blew suddenly against them. Chloë's hair blew out over her shoulder.

"Boy, you feel that," Ben said. "You think it's safe?"

Lefty looked at the Knife Edge Trail. Several distant figures, specks really, were visible ascending the summit.

Chloë could see her husband thinking it over. Sweat shone on his cheeks. "Sure it's safe," he said at last. "Let's do it! The Three Floyds, onward to the Knife Edge!" He looked at Chloë and Ben. "Ben, Lefty, and Chloë!"

"Moe, Larry, and Curly," Ben said.

Polo opened his eyes. He looked around the room. The digital clock next to the bed read 11:30. He was alone.

He sat up. Eleven-thirty? It wasn't possible. *Eleven-thirty?*

His heart began to beat wildly in his chest.

"Oh no," he said. "No, no, no."

He picked his wristwatch up off of the nightstand. Eleven-thirty.

Polo felt something escaping from him. All around him were the souvenirs of the previous evening. The long night at Cowboy Bob's. Singing those idiot songs with Juddy, getting louder and louder until they'd been asked to leave. Coming back here with the girls, Juddy and Sandra disappearing into Juddy's room, Dawn coming here into his. The Jagermeister. Dawn slowly peeling off his clothes. Kissing and tickling her, chasing each other around the room. Her insistence on wearing the cowboy hat. Sex on the hotel bed, his wild series of inventions.

Polo looked at the telephone, imagined himself picking it up, imagined himself trying to explain things to Dean Barker. I'm sorry I missed my interview a second time, but I was way hungover from this orgy I got myself into.

You wouldn't have believed this girl, she's a waitress at Cowboy Bob's.

He thought about Allison, sitting on the gravestone at Yale, telling him she wanted to wait. He thought about the love he had for her, about the future life he had imagined for them together, he a professor of linguistics, she a musician, an artist, his love.

Yee-ha, Dawn had said, sitting atop of him, crushing his ribs with her knees. She'd torn the cowboy hat off her head and raised it with one hand high into the air. He could still see her waving it around. *Weee*, she said. *You're a little bronco!*

Polo sat on the side of the bed, holding his head with his hands, feeling his future rushing rapidly away. Oh my god, he thought, miserably. I'm a little bronco.

Allison and Dylan sat on a wall eating Ben and Jerry's ice cream cones. Allison's cone was Wavy Gravy. Dylan's was vanilla.

"So are you and Polo going to get married, do you think?" Dylan said.

Allison licked her cone. "I hope so," she said. "He's got a good future."

Dylan looked at his cone, a little ashamed it was vanilla. "What about your future?" he said.

"What about it?"

"You think it's good?"

"Oh, it's going to be great," Allison said. "Once I'm free, finally. I can't wait. Don't you think it's going to be great?"

"I don't know," Dylan said. "I can't imagine the future. The way people talk about it."

"But you have to believe good things are going to happen," Allison said. "Eventually, I mean."

"I believe there's a future," Dylan said. "I just don't know if I believe there's going to be a good one."

Allison considered this.

"That's kind of depressing," she said.

"Yeah, well," Dylan said.

Allison looked at him. "Hey, are you okay, Dylan?" she said. "You seem a little out of it or something."

"I don't know," Dylan said. "Maybe I'm just tired."

Allison looked down. "It's not me, is it?"

"What's not you?"

"You're not mad at me?" she said. "I mean, I'm sorry if I was rude to you when I first met you. I'm kind of distracted myself right now, actually."

"You weren't rude," Dylan said. "You're great. I'm just homesick, or something."

"Homesick?" Allison said. "But your whole family is right here."

"Yeah," Dylan said. For a moment it looked as if he was going to say something else.

Allison licked her cone. Then she said, "You miss her, don't you?"

Dylan looked up. "Who?"

"You know what I mean."

For a moment Dylan looked as if he had been slain with a bow and arrow. Then he shrugged. "Yeah," he said. "I still think about it, like all the time. You must think that's nuts."

"I don't think that's nuts," Allison said. "I think about my dad the same way."

"I'm so mad at him," Dylan said suddenly.

For a moment they sat there licking, as Dylan's words hung in the air.

Then, "Who?" Allison said. "Who are you talking about? Your father? Why are you mad at him?"

Dylan stood up and threw his vanilla cone in a trash

can. "I don't know," he said, angrily. "Come on, let's get out of here. Isn't there more shopping you want to do?" He looked at her with desperation.

Allison ate the point of her cone and stood up. They walked away from L.L. Bean, toward a corner where people were waiting to cross over toward the Dansk outlet.

As they waited for the light, Allison said, "I didn't mean to piss you off."

"What?" said Dylan. "I'm not pissed off."

"Okay, well good," Allison said. The light changed and they walked across the street. They passed the Dansk outlet and turned left, walked past the Ralph Lauren and the Timberland stores.

Allison paused in front of the Maidenform outlet. "Listen," she said. "I need to buy some underwear. Can you stand it if we go in here?"

In the window mannequins were wearing brassieres. They didn't have any hair.

Chloë, Ben, and Lefty were climbing along the Knife Edge now. It was harder than they'd expected. Ben was in front, ascending the narrow granite ridge. Chloë was ten feet behind him, negotiating the boulders, trying not to look down. Lefty was fifty feet behind her. Even at this distance, Chloë could hear his labored breath.

If they'd known the climb was this difficult, Chloë thought, they probably wouldn't have undertaken it. Now they were pretty much stuck. It was six hours down the mountain no matter which direction they went.

For a moment she paused, looking all around. It was strange how oblivious, in some ways, she was to the incredible view. In every direction was heart-stoppingly beautiful scenery. And yet you couldn't look at the scenery. You had to keep watching where you were stepping, and holding on to the side of the peak with one hand, lest you make one misstep and fall six thousand feet. The wind gusted hard again, and Chloë felt a wave of exhilaration and fear.

She reached into her pocket and pulled out a red bandanna and mopped her brow. Lefty's heavy breathing drew near. A moment later he overtook her. ''Hey,'' he said, and trudged past. Ben was far away now. He was climbing up the ridge, growing small.

Chloë watched her husband, trying to catch up with Ben. It clearly irked Lefty that Ben was so far ahead. As he labored toward his brother, Lefty's pants were riding lower and lower, exposing the man's exceedingly unpleasant lower cleavage. Just a little bit farther and his pants were going to fall off altogether. There he goes, Chloë thought. The man of my dreams.

Chloë had a sudden memory of Gary, climbing the Appalachian Trail in the Smokies with her, years and years ago, before they were even married. The Appalachian Trail begins at the top of this mountain, she thought, and travels all those hundreds of miles down to that same ridge where Gary and I once were. She had a strange image of herself beginning to climb a long trail in her twenties, and now, nearly twenty-five years later, she was at the end, all the way up here in Maine, crow's feet around her eyes, Gary dead of a heart attack. If I had known that this was the person I would become, that this version of myself was waiting for me at the end of the journey, maybe I wouldn't have started it. Or maybe I wouldn't have become this person if I'd done some things differently. She remembered using her bandanna as a headband on that trip, tying back her hair. Was this the same bandanna, even? She held the red paisley material in her hand, played with it loosely in her fingers. It was possible.

A gust of wind blew it suddenly out of her hand. The

bandanna drifted ten, fifteen feet below her onto some rocks. It lay there, some distance from the trail, fluttering in the wind. One more gust and it would disappear down the side of the mountain.

Chloë thought about calling Lefty, but something in her did not want his help for this. She lowered herself off the Knife Edge Trail and crawled, spiderlike, down the side of the mountain. A few loose rocks skittered away from her.

Chloë felt her heart beating in her throat. It didn't seem that dangerous, and yet she knew it was wrong to leave the trail. She edged closer to the bandanna, slithering toward the precipice.

There was another good gust of wind, and the bandanna moved again. It fluttered ten, fifteen feet farther down the side of the mountain. Chloë was already most of the way there. She looked back up at the trail, and was surprised to see how far she had come.

She moved down the side of the mountain again. The bandanna was only five feet away now. It was fluttering in the wind against a large pink rock. Before her was a sudden sharp drop, which opened onto a bowl-shaped canyon several thousand feet below. She rested her foot against the rock the bandanna was on, and slowly bent her knee to get closer.

The rock suddenly gave way and disappeared off the edge of the precipice. An avalanche of stones rolled loose, and Chloë found herself sliding down the side of the mountain. There was the sound of a woman screaming. Her hand scrabbled madly at the loose rock as she went over the edge, trying to find purchase.

Chloë Baxter was disappointed to find that there was nothing solid to hold on to.

*   *   *

Dylan and Allison were having lunch at a picnic table by the ocean. They were eating lobster rolls and drinking iced tea. Several large bags from L.L. Bean and Maidenform and Timberland and Bass were gathered around their legs.

"This is fun," Allison said, looking toward the marina. There weren't a lot of boats docked here now; most of them had been hauled out of the water for the oncoming winter. A boat pulled into the wharf and some men began unloading large wooden crates black with wriggling lobsters.

"It's like some dream," Dylan said.

"You know what Polo says, a dream is the fulfillment of a wish. Do you think that's true?"

Dylan shrugged. "How'd you meet him again?"

"We were both in the same summer camp. Flinthead?"

"Oh yeah." The way she said it, it sounded as if Dylan was supposed to be familiar with it. "Flinthead."

"I was doing music. He was directing."

"Sounds like fun."

"It's hard for me to remember what I was like before I met him," Allison said. "It's like he helped me discover a part of myself that I didn't know existed." She took a bite of her lobster roll. "Do you think that's weird?"

"What's weird?"

"That you could love someone not so much for themselves but for the person you are when you're with them?"

"I don't know," Dylan said. "It would be nice if you could feel that way and also love the person."

"I do love him," Allison said. "I mean, I love him for himself, too. It's just that I—" She faltered. "I don't know," she said. "I can't explain it."

The lobstermen were still flinging boxes of lobsters onto the dock. A man from the restaurant came out and spoke to them. The lobstermen laughed.

"Can I ask you something?" Allison said. "Do you think guys think about sex more than girls do?"

Dylan swallowed. He looked at the bag full of bras and panties, then looked toward the dock. The lobsters were wriggling in their cages. He looked at the bag of bras and panties.

"I don't know," he said.

"Sometimes," Allison said. "I feel like there's nobody who understands what it's like. Then, when I'm with Polo, it's like I'm not alone anymore, it's like I'm part of something finally. I love that feeling, just sitting around, not even talking. We've had so many cool hours where we just, you know, sit." She paused. "Then he starts getting all weird about everything."

"What do you mean weird?"

"I mean he starts, well, you know, it's like he just wants to have sex all the time. Like that's all there is to the relationship."

"You have sex a lot?" Dylan said, hating Polo more than ever.

Allison didn't answer. "I don't know. Probably the normal amount. What about you? How often do you sleep with your girlfriend?"

Dylan wasn't sure what girlfriend she was talking about. She just assumed he had one.

"Same here," he said. "Normal amount, I guess."

Allison pushed the ice in her drink around with her straw. "What's her name?"

"Whose name?"

"Your girlfriend."

Several thoughts went through Dylan's mind at once. "Brenda," he said, finally.

"What's she like?"

"Oh, you know," Dylan said. His heart was beating quickly. "She's tall, you know. Long hair."

"How tall?"

"I don't know," Dylan said, and it was true. "Six feet at least."

"What else does she do?"

Dylan tried to think what else this Brenda might do.

"Plays the harp."

"Jeez," Allison said. She sounded depressed.

"What's wrong?"

"Nothing," said Allison, miserably. "And she likes sex and everything. The two of you, doing it pretty regularly I guess."

Dylan nodded. He hadn't meant to depress her. "Yep," he said. "Pretty regular."

Allison shook her head, as if this were about the worst news she'd ever heard.

"What's wrong?" Dylan said.

"Listen," she said quietly. "What would you think if you found out I was, like, a virgin?"

Dylan felt his heart beating in his throat.

"What would I think?" he said.

"Yeah—would you think I'm incredibly stupid?" she said.

"No," Dylan said.

"It's just like, I want to save that until I'm sure."

"Sure of what?"

"Sure of, I don't know, sure he won't disappear."

"You think he's going to disappear?"

"No, but that's what people do."

Dylan thought for a moment. She was right.

Allison looked at her watch.

"We should get in the car soon," she said.

They crumpled their paper plates into a ball, but they didn't stand up. Allison was still thinking.

"Dylan," Allison said. "Do you think Polo will break up with me if I don't sleep with him?"

"I don't know," Dylan said. "I don't know him like you do."

"Sometimes I think I should sleep with him just to get it over with. Just so I won't have to keep thinking about it all the time."

"That sounds romantic."

"He says I have an inner sorrow. Like, being a virgin is this thing I carry around with me, that people can see. He says it's going to keep me from getting into college even, because people can see how sad I am."

"He said that?" Dylan said.

"What, you don't believe me?"

"I'm sorry," Dylan said. "I just think he's full of shit."

Allison opened her mouth, then shut it.

"You don't know him," she said.

"I'm not trying to hurt your feelings," Dylan said. "I just think he'd say anything."

"Sometimes I think he's right," Allison said. "I do have an inner sorrow."

Dylan looked at her. She had a strange face, if you saw her the right way. She had beautiful features, like something poured from a glass.

"There is something sad about you, Allison," he said.

"Oh no," she said. "Don't say that."

"It's nothing to be ashamed of. It's nice, it makes you very real."

"Real? Oh my god."

"No, listen. What I mean is, maybe you have something sad about you. But it's not because you're not doing it with Polo, I mean come on."

"It's not?"

"No, it's because—" The captain of the lobster boat started up his engine. Other men untied the boat from the dock. "Oh, don't listen to me. What do I know about why you're sad?"

"But you think I'm sad?"

"Maybe. There's an air of being sad maybe."

"Oh my god, really?"

"It's not a big deal."

"I can't believe it. He's right! People do think I'm sad. They can look at me and tell."

"That's not what I'm saying."

Allison shook her head. She looked angry. "Maybe I *should* sleep with him then."

"No," Dylan said. "Don't."

"When are we going to Middlebury, day after tomorrow?"

"Tuesday."

She sighed. "That's my first-choice school," she said. Allison looked out at the sea.

"I'm not following you."

"I have two days," she said.

"Two days for what?" Dylan had no idea how they had reached this point.

"You know, two days to do it." She sucked on her iced tea. "Man, I hope Polo is in the mood."

"Allison," Dylan said. "You're talking like a crazy person."

"I know," she said. "That's because I'm sad. Once I get this over with, I won't sound so crazy. That's my theory, anyway."

"Allison, please don't sleep with him," Dylan said. "Please."

Allison looked at him. "Why? What's the difference?"

"There is a difference," Dylan said. "The first time you do it, it ought to be with somebody who loves you."

"He loves me. You don't think he loves me?"

Dylan shook his head. "Not enough."

Allison shrugged. "Yeah, well, if I meet somebody single, who's better than Polo, in the next two days, I'll sleep with them instead, okay? Otherwise, it's Polo."

Dylan's heart was beating so quickly it made his shirt vibrate. "You're serious about all this? You'd sleep with somebody other than Polo if you met him?"

Allison looked at him sarcastically. "Like where am I going to find somebody better than Polo in the next couple of days? That doesn't already have a girlfriend, I mean?"

Dylan shook his head miserably. "I don't know."

Allison reached out and squeezed his hand. "You know, Dylan, you're a good friend. That Brenda of yours is a lucky woman."

"Thanks," he said, squeezing back, hating Brenda, wishing it were possible to break up with her.

"I haven't been able to talk like this with a guy before. It's nice, having you as a friend."

Dylan thought about the Babson Anti-Gravity Stone. It would have come in handy right about now. "Yeah," he said. "It's nice all right."

Ben neared the top of South Peak, the last peak before the summit. From behind him, growing nearer, came the heaving breath of his brother. Ben paused for a moment, and in this second Lefty climbed past. "Hey," Ben said. "You want to take a break?"

"No time to stop now," Lefty said, stopping. He got out his water bottle and drained it. "Almost there."

Ben looked down the Knife Edge Trail back toward the Chimney. The trail was empty. "Hey," he said. "Where's Chloë?"

"Chloë," Lefty said, turning around. "She's—"

Chloë was not visible.

"Chlooo-eeee," Lefty shouted. The wind blew his voice away.

"You think she's resting?" Ben said.

"Resting, maybe," Lefty said. "That's weird though, she was right behind me."

Ben looked back at the trail with a worried face. There weren't a lot of places to hide. "How long ago was she right behind you?"

"I don't know. I passed her like ten, fifteen minutes ago."

Ben stared at the Knife Edge. "You think we should go back, look for her?"

Lefty looked, annoyed, at Baxter Peak, the summit of Katahdin, very near now. He glanced at his watch. "How far back do you suppose she is?"

"Well, you passed her fifteen minutes ago? So she was on that ridge there, right?" Ben pointed.

"Yeah," Lefty said. "I guess."

"Come on," Ben said.

Lefty looked worried. "You don't think anything happened to her, do you?"

"I don't know," said Ben.

They began to climb back down the Knife Edge. On either side of them small pebbles rolled off into oblivion. Lefty was red in the face, breathing hard.

"You want to wait here?" Ben said, "I'll find her and we'll meet you?"

"No," Lefty said. It sounded as if he was finally convinced that something might be wrong. "We gotta find Chloë." His voice cracked. "If anything happened to her I'll—"

"Let's just find her," Ben said. "You take it easy."

"Don't worry about me."

They climbed down the ridge for five, ten minutes. There was no sign of Chloë. The brothers moved quickly, Ben in front, jumping from rock to rock in the midst of the sky. Lefty lumbered on behind him.

After fifteen minutes, Ben paused. It took Lefty a while to catch up with him. "Is this about where you passed her?" Ben said.

Lefty looked around. "I don't know. It all looks the same."

On a rock a hundred feet below them was a red bandanna.

"Look," Ben said, pointing. "That's Chloë's, isn't it?"

"Jesus," Lefty said. "Where is she? Chloë!" He shouted her name into the wind. "Chloë!"

"Should we go down there and look?" Ben said. He looked at the side of the mountain. Some loose rock appeared to have been dislodged.

"We have to," said Lefty. "If she fell—"

"Yeah, but look at it," Ben said. "All those marbles. It's dangerous."

"We have to find her," Lefty said, starting to climb down. Stones began to roll down the incline toward a sudden drop-off.

"Be careful," Ben said.

His brother scrambled down the side of the mountain. Ben stayed on the trail for the moment, watching.

Lefty edged closer to the bandanna. As he reached it, he suddenly heard the voice. It sounded as if she was weeping. He grabbed on to a large boulder and peeked over the edge of the drop-off.

There, twenty feet below him, was Chloë, holding on to a rock. She wasn't moving. Tears were running down her face.

"Chlo," Lefty called. Chloë looked up.

"Lefty," she said. "It's Lefty."

"Are you all right?" Lefty said. "Are you okay?"

"I'm peachy," Chloë said. She didn't sound peachy.

"It's okay. Benny and I are here to get you. You're going to be okay."

"You see her?" Ben called from the trail.

"Yeah," said Lefty. "She's hanging on to a rock."

Ben opened up his pack and threw a coil of rope to his brother. "Here," he called. The rope landed at Lefty's feet.

Lefty picked up the rope and uncoiled it. "I'm going to lower this to you," said Lefty. "You just grab on, okay?"

"I'm scared," Chloë said.

"Just sit tight."

Lefty played out the rope. Chloë wasn't very far away. "Tie it around your waist, okay?"

Ben started edging down the trail toward his brother. Small stones began to roll toward the precipice.

"Be careful, man," Lefty said. "Jesus, Benny, all you want to do now is start an avalanche!"

"I've tied the rope," Chloë said.

"Okay," Lefty said. "Now I'm tying the other end around me. You're going to be all right."

Lefty tied the rope around his waist. Ben watched as Lefty grabbed the rope that led off the precipice toward his wife.

"Okay, now when I count three," Lefty said, "you start to pull on the rope. You pull yourself up while I stand here."

"Lefty—" Ben said. He was close now.

"One—two—three!"

As Lefty said the word *three*, something strange happened. There was the sudden tightening of the rope around Lefty's waist. For a moment it looked as if Lefty was trying to resist some powerful force. Seconds later, Lefty toppled over, and he slid down the side of the mountain, rolled off the precipice, and disappeared.

Ben stood there, looking at the place where a moment ago his brother had stood. "Lefty?" he said softly. "Chloë?"

Oh my god, Ben thought. I've lost both of them.

The red bandanna fluttered softly in the wind.

Ben began to move down the mountain toward the edge. This is insane, he thought. This is how I kill all three of us.

Holding on to a large rock, he peeked over the edge. It was not immediately clear what he was looking at.

There was a large boulder about fifteen feet down the drop-off. On either side of this boulder ran a length of rope. At the two ends of the rope, respectively, were Chloë and Lefty, hanging like spiders. Their hands and legs wriggled in mid-air.

"Chloë?" Ben shouted. "Lefty?"

"I'm here," Chloë said, softly. She was trying to clutch on to some small stones.

"I'm here," Lefty said. He was swinging freely in space, looking thousands of feet down toward Chimney Pond.

Jesus, Ben thought. What am I supposed to do now? Should I run and get help? Leave them dangling here until I get back?

A sudden hard gust of wind came up. Lefty and Chloë, suspended at opposite ends of the same rope, swayed back and forth like the scales of justice.

It was late in the afternoon. Juddy and Polo were driving north through New Hampshire, toward Hanover. They hadn't said much since they'd left Cambridge.

Polo watched the pine trees sailing past. He sighed.

"You okay, man?" Juddy said.

"No. I am not okay."

"Sorry, Polo, dude," said Juddy. "What can I tell ya? Ya fucked up."

"Just don't talk to me," said Polo. "I don't even want to hear your voice."

"You don't want to talk to me, fine. All I'm saying is that it's not as bad as you think."

"It's not. You're saying it's not as bad as I think. Well I don't see how it could be worse."

"Polo, dude. You aren't thinking straight. Listen. Why'd those girls fuck us last night? You figure that out?"

"I don't want to talk about them."

"Why not, man? They were awesome!"

"They were scum," said Polo. "Bottom feeders."

"What are you putting 'em down for?" said Juddy. "Just 'cause they slept with you is no reason to hate 'em! They were a couple a nice girls; we all had a good time!"

"Listen, you may not have realized this yet, Juddy, but I no longer have a future. None. And this is a direct result of the events of last night, okay?"

"Exactly, man! Things are finally starting to head your way!"

Polo looked out the window at New Hampshire. "I'm sitting here with an insane person."

"Answer the question, dude. Why did those girls sleep with us last night? Was it because they liked us?"

"I don't know about you. But sure. That Dawn liked me, I suppose. I'm not the kind of person she encounters."

"Polo, man, wake up. They slept with us because they thought we were getting married today. They knew we didn't want them!"

Polo looked over at Juddy. He was wearing a Villanova Wildcats hat backward on his head.

"We didn't?"

"No, man. We were unavailable! Women love that!"

Polo shook his head. "You really do live in your own little universe, don't you?"

"Don't you see, Polo?" said Juddy. "Same thing is going to happen with Harvard!"

Polo looked out the window again. "Now I know you're insane."

"Think, man, think! First time you missed your interview, you told 'em you got lost in traffic. What do they conclude? You're an idiot. Second time you miss your interview, you didn't call 'em at all! You didn't even explain the situation, did you?"

"Because they'd have hung up on me."

"No, man, it's 'cause you're finally making the right decisions. You don't call 'em, they gotta start wondering, how come this Polo MacNeil won't interview with us. We're a good school, what's so wrong with us this kid keeps blowin' us off?"

Polo looked over at him.

"I don't think Dean Barker is going to lose any sleep over my whereabouts," said Polo. "Harvard isn't going to exactly miss me."

"Of course he's going to lose sleep," said Polo. "You got it all wrong. How come you think Harvard's Harvard? Because they worry more than anybody. They're constantly looking over their shoulders, wondering if the best students are going somewhere else."

Polo closed his eyes. "So your theory," he said, "is that the more interviews I don't show up for, the better my chances are of getting in?"

"You just watch," Juddy said. "Next couple of days, Barker's going to call. He's finally started worrying about you. Yes sir, things are just about to start going your way, man."

Juddy looked pleased with himself.

"Did your mother take lots of drugs when she was pregnant with you?" Polo said. "Or do you think you wound up like this all on your own?"

"Hard to say," said Juddy. "I'm like, a work in progress!"

Polo looked out the window. "Poor Allison," he said.

"Hey, you don't have to worry about her," Juddy said. "Once she gets a whiff of the new you, she'll be throwin' her panties at ya."

"You know I think I'm going to swear off sex for a while," Polo said.

"Huh huh huh," said Juddy. "Funny."

"I'm serious," said Polo. "I think I've made some mistakes. I haven't been paying attention to what's right in front of my nose. Poor Allison, she deserves better." He sat up in his seat, as if gathering resolve. "She's going to get better. From now on, I don't sleep with anyone until the night I'm married. Until Allison is Mrs. Polo Mac-Neil!"

Juddy thought for a moment.

"Interesting," he said. "Interesting. That could work. That could be very effective!"

"What are you talking about?" Polo said.

"You're smarter than you think!" said Juddy. "It's just like I been saying. You tell Allison you don't want to have sex with her until you're married, next thing you know, she's gonna be beggin' for it."

"You don't understand. I'm serious about this."

"Yeah, well, whatever. It's a great strategy. I bet you, two days after you tell Allison you're going celibate on her, she's going to be down on her hands and knees."

"It's not a strategy," said Polo. "It's a resolution. I'm turning over a new leaf. I might not be going to Harvard, but I'm definitely going to have a future. I'm going to be a good boyfriend to the woman I love. I'm going to treat her with respect. I'm going to be the man she's always dreamed of, finally!"

"You know what I was saying yesterday? It's totally true, man. You and me are like peas in a pod."

"What are you talking about? What do you and I possibly have in common?"

Juddy smiled. "It's obvious, man." He shrugged. "We're both assholes."

They slowed as they approached the New Hampshire tollbooth. It was a dollar.

"Speak for yourself," Polo said. He got out his wallet to hand Juddy a buck.

"I got it," Juddy said.

"No, come on," said Polo. "This one's on me." It was important for him to show Juddy that he was wrong.

"Okay, fine, have it your way, brother," Juddy said.

With his last ounce of pride, Polo pulled out his wallet and opened the billfold. He had great hopes of handing Juddy a fifty, making him get change. But this plan, Polo soon saw, would not come to fruition.

"My money's gone," Polo said. "It's gone!"

Juddy reached into his pocket, pulled out a crinkled and soiled bill.

"Hey, man," he said to the toll collector. "Sorry about this. A hundred's the smallest I got!"

"That girl," Polo said. "She stole my money!"

"Of course she did," said Juddy, as the toll collector counted out his change. "Why wouldn't she?" He shook his head. "No reason."

Chloë gritted her teeth, pulled herself up the rope another foot, and wondered what it would be like to be someone else. Above her was Ben, standing on the Knife Edge, holding the end of the rope that she was now using to steady her ascent. Below her was Lefty, sitting on the same rock that she had cowered on earlier. It had taken nearly an hour to get the two of them disengaged from their scales-of-justice configuration and move them each, rock by rock, to a position of less immediate peril. Chloë had thrown the rope that had previously joined her to her husband up to Ben, who was now reeling her in, foot by foot. Please, God, Chloë thought, if you just get me out of this, I'll change. You won't even recognize me.

She paused for a moment to catch her breath. Ben shouted down to her. "You're doing fine. Just another twenty feet or so."

Chloë nodded. As she hung there, exhausted, the events of the last several days recurred to her in sudden and heart-stopping clarity. The idiocy of her fantasy of doing away with Lefty. I didn't mean it, she thought. I mean, I considered what the world would be like without him, but I didn't really do anything to hurt him, besides order him fried eggs and make him have sex three times a day. That's not the same as stabbing someone with a knife, not by a long shot.

Given her current situation, though, perhaps the difference was less theoretical than she thought. Maybe giving someone a plate of eggs and bacon and then giving them a blow job was *exactly* the same as stabbing them with a knife, on some level. Wasn't that the difference between venial sin and mortal sin—the issue of intent? She tried to remember the seven deadly sins; lust and gluttony came immediately to mind. Pride was another. That left four others—rudeness, maybe? Irritability? Scorn and contempt? What would you call giving eggs and bacon to a man with a heart condition? Whichever sin this was, it didn't seem venial.

"Come on, Chloë," Ben shouted. "You can do it."

"Yeah," said Lefty, from below. "You're doin' fine." He didn't sound convinced.

Dear God, she thought, taking another step up. If you just get me out of this, I promise I'll change. I won't try to kill him anymore. I'll be a good wife, maybe even try to get him on a diet. I'll cook vegetables in a steamer. Switch over to margarine. What was the name of that stuff? *I Can't Believe It's Not Butter!*

Ben began to pull her toward him. All at once her ascent seemed easy, like pulling on the drawstrings of a curtain. Look at that, she thought, feeling for a moment like she was floating somewhere above her own body. The trail was inches away. My prayers are answered. Now I have to hold up my end of the bargain and become someone else. She wondered who she was going to be from this moment forward.

"Chloë," said Ben, suddenly in front of her. "You're okay." He put his arms around her. He had a great smell, her brother-in-law, like cherries and wood smoke. It was funny how she hadn't noticed before.

She looked up at him and wondered what he'd look like with his shirt off. She thought about his boxers, folded neatly in a drawer. He was looking at her with a strange expression.

"Yes, Ben," Chloë said. "You're right. I'm going to be fine."

"Hey!" said a voice below them. "What about me?"

Chloë and Ben looked down the side of the mountain at Lefty. There he was, stranded and hopeful. Then she looked at Ben.

Chloë stood there, thinking about the words her husband had spoken. What *about* Lefty, anyway? It was a good question.

Dylan and Allison were driving north. The setting sun cast long shadows across I-95. Dylan was sitting in the front seat. From the back came the sounds of the Maidenform bag rustling on the floor.

"Okay, don't look, all right?" Allison said.

"I can't look. If I look I'll drive off the road," Dylan said.

There was a minute or so of silence.

"Okay, tell me what you think of this," Allison said. Dylan looked in the rearview mirror. There was Allison, wearing a pink bra she'd bought at the outlet. Dylan swallowed.

"It's all right," he said.

"Just all right? Tell me honestly. Do you think this'll do the trick?"

Dylan took another look. Yeah, it would do the trick all right.

"It's good," he said.

"Okay, listen, pretend I'm Brenda, okay? If Brenda were wearing this, would you want to sleep with her?"

Dylan thought about Brenda again, even now trying to think up a good way of doing away with his girlfriend. He'd thought about a sudden car crash, a slowly wasting disease. Maybe a terrible harp accident. One of the strings on her harp snapped without warning and sliced her head off at the neck. Everyone else in the orchestra was surprised about her head suddenly rolling around the pit. It was a shame about Brenda, if you thought about her. It seemed sad that he'd gone to all this trouble to invent an imaginary girlfriend, only to have her die so suddenly, so soon. If you were going to be in love with someone who didn't exist, it seemed unfair that they'd wind up decapitated only a few hours after you'd invented them.

"Yes, I think so," said Dylan. "I probably would. Sleep with her, I mean."

"Good," Allison said. "Okay now, wait a second. Let me try this other one. Don't look."

Dylan didn't look. Behind him he heard rustling.

"All right," Allison said. "You can look now."

This one was black. It seemed to cover less surface area

than the first. Dylan looked her up and down. "Uh-huh," he said. "That's good, too."

"Oh, I'm so glad," Allison said. She threw a leg over the seat and crawled back to the front. She picked her white T-shirt up off the floor and pulled it on. Dylan glanced over at her.

"I hope Polo goes for this stuff," Allison said.

"Yeah, well, I don't think you have to worry about Polo."

"Yeah," Allison said. "You're probably right. Like he cares what I wear, as long as he can get it off of me."

They drove on in silence for a while. "Hey, can I ask you something?" Allison said, after a few minutes. "How come guys are so weird about sex?"

"Weird?"

"I mean, you know, like with Polo it seems sometimes like that's all he thinks about. It's like an obsession." She itched herself. "Man, the cups on this thing are really scratchy."

"Well not all guys are like that," Dylan said.

Allison itched herself some more. "Well the guys I know are all the same. You wouldn't believe the things Polo says to me. The way his mind works. Sometimes I think it's all he thinks about."

At this moment, Allison performed a strange and sudden miracle of engineering. One arm withdrew into the armhole of her T-shirt. There was movement below her shirt. A second later, like a magician suddenly producing a rabbit, she pulled the bra out of her other sleeve. Dylan had never seen this done before, and for a moment his mouth hung open in stupefaction.

Allison reached into the backseat and stuffed the bra back into the bag with the others.

"Well, guys aren't the only ones obsessed with it," Dylan said. "Sex, I mean."

Allison looked over at him. "Brenda's like that, huh?"

Dylan shrugged, wondering where Brenda stood on this subject. After a few moments of consideration, he said, "She's kind of mature for her age, I guess."

"How do you mean, mature?"

Dylan thought about Brenda with loathing now, furious that she had intruded herself yet again into the conversation. "Well, she's Scandinavian and all," he said, hoping this explained things.

Allison muttered to herself. "Maybe Polo's part Scandinavian."

Dylan tried again, this time in a voice tinged with regret. "You know, if it was up to me, we would have waited. Waited until we were ready. But I don't know. She was kind of insistent."

Allison looked at him with sympathy, touched his arm with her fingers. "Do you really wish you'd waited?"

Dylan shrugged. "Too late now," he said.

"Do you miss it?" said Allison. "Being a virgin and all?"

Dylan's head was swimming. He was being asked if he missed something that in reality he hadn't surrendered. But let's just give her the benefit of the doubt, Dylan thought. If I were going out with this Brenda, would I ever regret it, not being the person who I am right now? Was it possible to imagine, in some other world of invention, a certain nostalgia for reality?

"Yeah," he said. "I miss it sometimes. The old me."

Allison shook her head. "Boy," she said. "You're a pretty honest person, you know that, Dylan? Polo would never admit something like that to me."

"Well, he probably doesn't miss it, either," Dylan said.

"That's not what I mean. You're just a really interesting guy, Dylan, is all. I admire that, your honesty."

"No, you don't," Dylan said.

She smiled. "Sure I do."

"Yeah, well," Dylan said. "Sometimes I wish Brenda were more like you."

Chloë and Ben stood on the top of the Knife Edge, reeling in Lefty. It was a much harder job than reeling in Chloë had been. Ben and Chloë stood there, sweat pouring off of them, as Lefty slowly ascended.

He was about twenty feet below them now. Suddenly a pile of loose rocks gave way beneath Lefty's foot, and he fell, face forward, against the sheer wall of the mountain.

"Oof," Lefty said.

"Are you okay?" Ben called. Lefty was just hanging there, like a dead orangutan on a vine.

"I'm alive," he said.

"Come on, brother," Ben said. "Give it one last try. You're almost here."

He turned to Chloë. "I'm going to see if I can't get down to him. Can you hold him steady for a second?"

"I think so," Chloë said. As Ben crawled down the other side of the Knife Edge, Lefty began to move again. He clutched the rope and started to climb toward his wife. Chloë looked at her husband, slowly rising before her like the sun. He was only fifteen feet away now, and for a moment he paused to catch his breath, and to look up at his wife.

Chloë was looking at her husband with a strange expression. She was looking at the rope in her hands, her husband at its nether end.

"Chloë?"

Chloë was thinking.

Lefty looked at his wife, still contemplating her own hands. He could almost imagine her thoughts. It wouldn't be that hard, opening her fingers. There'd be the long, drawn-out wail as he disappeared down the mountain. Everyone would say it had been a terrible accident. A shame, really.

"Chloë?" he said, almost in a whisper. "Please."

Chloë looked at him the way you'd look at a photograph of someone you'd known a long time ago. She seemed sad.

"Honey," Lefty said. "Please. I can change," he said.

One corner of her mouth rose, as if Lefty had said something vaguely funny.

Lefty stared at her, and in that single instant felt a tremendous ache in his heart. Oh my god, he thought, stunned. It wasn't the fact that his wife was about to murder him that amazed him, turned his heart to vinegar. It was a different realization. Jesus Christ in heaven. She'd be happier if I fell.

J uddy looked over at the sleeping form of Polo, the boy's cheek resting against the window of the car. He thought back for a moment to a night earlier, recalling Polo's joyful expression as he rode the mechanical bull in Cowboy Bob's. Sandra and Dawn looked over at him, admiring his joy. Juddy hadn't seen Polo with this look on his face before. For the first time since Juddy had met him, Polo had looked surprised by his own happiness.

"*Whssssht-whssht,*" Juddy said to himself.

This sound effect was a variation on the old Zorro signature, a sword whipping elegantly through the air. It was a sound that belonged to Juddy's mysterious and lonely alter ego, *the Secret Swordsman*. He smiled for a moment, remembering the summers he had played superheroes with his cousin. Dylan had been the Secret Swordsman's faithful sidekick, *Dickweed*. Looking back on it now, Juddy felt a little guilty that, as the Secret Swordsman (a catalyst for universal goodness), he had done so poorly by his own sidekick. Dickweed didn't even have a weapon, didn't have any superpowers whatsoever, with the small exception of the ability to make himself invisible when necessary. When Dickweed became invisible, though, he wasn't allowed to talk, couldn't even make a sound. And reappearance wasn't as easy as you'd think, either. Poor Dickweed couldn't even rematerialize unless he caught the sun's rays with a magnifying glass and set his own hair on fire. Sometimes when they were playing, Dickweed spent the whole afternoon silent, simply to avoid the humiliation and pain of reappearance.

He remembered the last time he and Dylan had been superheroes, the day they went down to the old Hitch farmhouse and looked for the antigravity chamber in the basement. As usual, he'd invented some wild hooey and his innocent and gullible cousin had believed him. They were down there in the basement and that's when they heard the scream from upstairs. The next thing you knew, their days as a duo had come to an end.

As he drove north, in the dark, Juddy wondered to what extent he and his cousin had become the people that they currently were as a direct result of that day. You could see it easily enough in Dylan: he still had that wounded look, the look of a boy who expects the world to disappoint him. But Dylan wasn't the only one who had been transformed. In his own way, Juddy thought, he had actually become the Secret Swordsman that day, had crossed over at that hour from the land of childish invention and into reality. Very well then, he remembered saying to himself. I'll become the Secret Swordsman.

And so, by doing good works in private, gently working, unnoticed, to destroy evil, Juddy exacted his revenge upon the world. In his slovenly, beer-swilling sloth, he had found the perfect disguise. No one suspected Juddy of being a force for good because they believed him incapable of a moral act. Juddy reached down and opened another beer. The character of "Juddy" was the perfect disguise to protect his secret identity.

He looked over at Polo again. It wouldn't take much longer for Polo to destroy himself. Just a few more gentle encouragements in the wrong direction, a little whispered flattery. It was a good thing he was doing, Juddy thought, taking out this asshole.

Juddy took another swig of beer, swallowed, and made his sword-slashing sound again. *Whsssht-whssht*, a giant *J* in the air. The Secret Swordsman expected no thanks, was untroubled by the contempt that society held for him. The life of an outlaw was what a man of justice expected.

Driving north, he did have a moment's regret about the way he had treated his invisible sidekick. Poor Dickweed deserved better. He remembered walking across the long field with his cousin, the blades of the farmer's old windmill spinning around. Actually, if you thought about it, Dickweed had it better than he'd figured at the time. It wouldn't be so bad, now and again, to be able to disappear, to pass silently and unseen through this world of despond.

Before them was a sign. MT. KATAHDIN. 5267 FEET. NORTHERN TERMINUS, APPALACHIAN TRAIL.

Ben stared at the sign. It was weatherbeaten, cross-hatched with people's initials, carved with penknives. All around them were other hikers, their boots off, holding their aching feet. Some of them were eating bananas.

Chloë looked toward the south. Another sign read, SPRINGER MOUNTAIN, GEORGIA. 2160.4 MILES. Before them the

Appalachian Trail descended a softer slope of the mountain and disappeared over the horizon.

"Which way is Harvard?" Ben said.

"That way," Chloë said, pointing in the direction in which she was facing.

"And Dartmouth and Middlebury, they're to the west." Ben turned to the right. Chloë, standing next to Ben, turned with him. She lost her balance for a moment and reached out to steady herself against Ben's arm.

Lefty glanced over at his brother and his wife. He didn't look good.

Behind them was a sloping grassland, and a trail that led through it. This region was called the Saddle, and after a half a mile hike across it, Chloë and Lefty and Ben would begin descending rapidly. The Saddle Trail, as it vanished down the long drop-off from the grassland to the earth, looked like a waterfall in small stones.

"Well," Ben said. "Here we are. A little more exciting getting up here than we expected, eh?"

Chloë grimaced. "I'm so sorry," she said. "I can't believe I almost got us all killed."

"We're okay," Ben said. He looked at his brother. "Aren't we all okay, Lefty?"

Lefty swung his arms back and forth, nodded. "Sure," he said. "We're fine."

Chloë looked toward the Appalachian Trail again. "How long does it take to hike all the way to Georgia from Maine?" she said.

"Months, I'd guess," said Ben. "Most of a year."

"I'd love to do that some day," Chloë said. "You ever want to do that, Lefty?" said Chloë. "Take a summer hiking?"

"I don't know," said Lefty. "Maybe if I was younger."

"You were right," Ben said. "About doing this, together. This was a good idea."

"You think so?" Lefty said.

"Hey, let me take your picture?" Chloë said. "You guys stand there, next to the sign."

"Okay," said Ben. The brothers stood next to each other, awkwardly.

Chloë took a couple steps backward to frame the picture properly. There they were, the Floyd brothers.

"Smile!"

They didn't.

"Okay," Chloë said. "Say cheese."

"Cheese," Ben said.

"Cheese," Lefty said.

Chloë took the picture, walked back to her husband, hugged him. He knows, she thought to herself. Her heart started pounding. He knows.

She put her arms around him and squeezed again. "I love you, Lefty," she said. Lefty just looked at her with his disappointed face. For the first time, Chloë suspected, it was occurring to her husband that his wife was a woman he did not really know, that he had lived these last few years with a stranger.

But then, as she looked over at Ben, her nerves suddenly calmed. For heaven's sakes, what is all this ruckus about, all this heartache and commotion? There was nothing to know. She thought about Ben's boxers again. At least not yet.

dartmouth
college

Hanover, New Hampshire
Number of applications: 11,398
Percent accepted: 20%
Mean SAT: 711V, 704M
Most popular major, 1996: government
Mascot: the Big Green

Students have mixed opinions of the Greek system at Dartmouth. One student said that it "makes for strange gender relations" at the college.
—*Insider's Guide to the Colleges*, 1996

dylan's heart was beating quickly as he sat in the empty office. This will be the fourth one I screw up, he thought. Assuming I screw it up. He looked out the window, saw the beautiful Dartmouth campus. A brick clocktower stabbed into the blue sky. There were bells ringing from the carillon in Baker Library.

Well, this is when they do it, Dylan thought. Juddy was looking at the Berry Sports Center. Ben and Chloë were walking around the campus. Lefty was asleep in the Winnebago. That left Allison and Polo alone, having sex in the Hanover Inn, in the room Polo and Juddy had rented after they arrived here from Cambridge yesterday. He knew he had lost her now. By this time, Allison had irretrievably entered the lost world of grown-ups, a place that more or less resembled the last age of the dinosaurs, before all the chewing and devouring began. An Allosaurus looked over at his brother and shrugged. *Sorry about this, bud. Gotta eat ya.*

Dylan squirmed in his chair, waiting for his interviewer, who was named Specter. It seemed odd that they'd leave him stranded here, cooling his heels, alone in Mr. Specter's office. Was it possible they'd put him in the wrong room? Maybe Mr. Specter had gone to lunch, had no idea Dylan was even in here. He tugged on his tie.

Of course, the failure of Mr. Specter to show up might actually work in Dylan's favor, if you thought about it. It was already clear that the college interview was not Dylan's strong point. He'd gone to pieces in three of them so far. If Dartmouth made some kind of mistake and stood him up, then at least maybe the college would feel like they owed him something. And in the absence of an interview, maybe they'd give him the benefit of the doubt, assume he had some talents they hadn't heard about. Which talents might those be, anyway? Dylan wondered. What parts of him exactly were the strong points?

On the desk in front of him was a folder marked FLOYD, DYLAN. He saw some notes written on a pad of paper, and underneath that some typed pages on the letterhead of his high school. His recommendations! There they were, the mysterious, top-secret recommendations written by Mr. Peebles, his headmaster, his college counselor, Mrs. Midgely, and his English teacher, Mrs. Henson. Dylan looked toward the door. No one appeared to be coming. How hard would it be for him to just gently lift the pages and find out what people really thought about him?

Dylan felt his heart beating in his throat. No, it was impossible. He'd get caught for sure. Picking up his recommendations was as certain a way as any to get this Mr. Specter to come bounding in here. He could imagine the scene already: Specter standing in the doorway with a look of disappointment and accusation. Dylan, sitting there behind the desk, his pants down around his ankles.

He sat up higher in his chair, craning his neck to see some of the other papers on Mr. Specter's desk. Next to his folder was a green sheet marked FOR DARTMOUTH ADMISSIONS USE ONLY. There was a header that read NAME: Floyd, Dylan. Sex: M. Date of Birth: 6/22/81. Secondary education: Camden Hills HS, Camden Hills, NJ. Beneath this was a large, empty box. At the top of the box were the words *Interviewer's Impressions.* At the bottom of the form was a line: Interest in Dartmouth: (A) Extremely strong; (B) Strong; (C) Moderate; (D) Weak; (E) Not interested in applying. The last line of the page read: Interviewer's Recommendation: (A) ADMIT; (B) WAIT LIST; (C) REJECT.

Here it was, Dylan thought. My future. How immoral

would it be for me to lean over and make a few notes? *Applicant seems strongly motivated. Capable of independent thought. Potential for extraordinary scholarship.* He could just jot down a couple lines like this, then circle (A) ADMIT, then get the hell out of here. Whenever this Mr. Specter showed up, he'd assume Dylan was someone he'd just lost track of and put him on the pile.

But wait, he'd know something was wrong since Dylan's handwriting wouldn't match his own. No, if he really wanted to pull off the stunt, he'd have to roll the sheet into the typewriter.

An IBM Selectric stood at right angles to Mr. Specter's desk. Dylan imagined himself going over to it, rolling the paper into the carriage.

Damn it all to hell, Dylan thought, remaining in his chair. The imagination appeared to serve no useful purpose.

He thought about Allison, lying down next to Polo. Sweetheart, she'd say, please make love to me. I have to do this before my interview. I don't want them to think of me as a child.

You're not a child, Allison, Dylan thought to himself. You're a beautiful woman. With wonderful hair that smells like oranges and a gorgeous face with sad eyes and a mole just above your mouth.

Please, Allison. Let me help you get into college.

A clock ticked softly from a mantelpiece above a fireplace in Mr. Specter's office.

It suddenly occurred to Dylan that maybe he could do exactly this. He stood up and went over to the desk. No one was coming. There was a whole stack of those green sheets of paper next to the typewriter. Dylan rolled one into the carriage and began to type.

NAME: Baxter, Allison. Sex: F. Date of Birth: 2/13/82. Secondary Education: Bridgeport HS, Bridgeport, CT.

He looked up. The sound of his typing seemed impossibly loud, like gunfire. Dylan walked over to the door and peeked gently out into the corridors of McNutt Hall. The place was deserted.

He went back to the typewriter. It was making a soft electric humming sound. Dylan felt his heart beating. He looked at the box headed Interviewer's Impressions.

He began to type: **Allison Baxter is a wonderful girl.**

Having typed this much, he stopped. He felt as if he had said everything he had to say, and yet there was a lot of space left. It wouldn't look right if he didn't fill it all in.

He continued: **She is a very talented musician with beautiful**

Dylan stopped, looked up. This wasn't right. He hit the auto erase button and eliminated the word *beautiful*.

a real ear for music. She is an excellent performer both on the piano as well as on the guitar. She also has a very good singing voice. It seems likely that she would become a major contributor to the musical life of the college.

Dylan hit the return key.

More important than this though is the sense I get from her as a person. She is very sympathetic. Allison Baxter has experienced personal loss in the form of her father dying at an early age. This has made her sad and yet she seems to have learned from that sadness and grown from it which is hard to do. This sad thing she has experienced seems to be a source of strength which is very impressive seeing how most people who would experience such a loss would get sad and not be able to move on from it. But Allison has and that is one of the things about her that I think is so very amazing.

Dylan looked at what he had written. Not bad, he thought. Not bad at all.

At that moment, a man appeared in the doorway. He looked at Dylan. Dylan looked at him.

"Mr. Specter," Dylan said.

"Mr. Specter," said the man, who seemed pretty young, now that Dylan looked at him. "I'm a little early, I guess."

"Early?" Dylan said.

"I can wait outside if you want."

Dylan looked at the man, not sure what to do. He didn't quite understand why he wasn't yelling at him for being behind his desk.

"Do you want me to wait outside?"

"No," Dylan said.

The man came in and sat down in the chair Dylan had occupied earlier. He looked very nervous. Dylan looked at him in fear and confusion.

"Oh my god, I didn't even introduce myself," he said. "I'm Tobin Stroud."

"Tobin Stroud," Dylan said softly.

"Everybody calls me Toby."

"Toby," Dylan said.

"Anyway, you should finish what you're doing, Mr. Specter. Like I said, I'm early. I didn't mean to interrupt you."

"What I'm doing," Dylan said. He looked at the piece of green paper in the typewriter. At the bottom was the line *Interest in Dartmouth.*

"Actually, I'm just finishing up," Dylan said. He removed the paper from the carriage and circled (B) Strong. Beneath this were the words *Interviewer's Recommendation.*

Dylan circled (A) ADMIT, and placed the paper in the corner of the desk.

"This certainly is a beautiful campus," Tobin said.

"Yes," said Dylan. "It is."

"It's pretty different from my school."

"Which is what?" Dylan said.

"Episcopal Academy. In Philadelphia."

"Ah yes," Dylan said. "Episcopal."

Dylan shuffled through some papers on the desk. He was trying to figure out how to get out of here now. If he just got up and ran, this Tobin Stroud would smell a rat, report him. Then they'd find the sheet of Allison's he'd fudged, and that wouldn't be any good. He'd just have to proceed.

"So, Toby," Dylan said. "What would you wish for if you had three wishes?"

"Wishes?" Toby said. Dylan could hear the fear in the boy's voice.

"Yes, wishes," Dylan continued. He put his hands behind his head and looked out the window. It was bizarre, this Toby Stroud mistaking him for a person of authority. But who knew? Perhaps Dylan looked older than he felt.

"Three wishes," Toby said. Dylan knew that the boy's mind was working quickly, desperately trying to figure out a way of turning the question to his advantage. "Well, I suppose the first thing I'd wish for would be world peace."

Son of a bitch, Dylan thought.

"Ah yes," Dylan said. "World peace. Very good. The wish is granted. The world is at peace. What is your second wish, then?"

"Hm," said Toby. He had short blonde hair, a square jaw, and acne. "Well, I suppose I would wish for something personal. I guess I'd wish that I might get the most out of my college education."

Dylan opened his mouth, then closed it.

"What I mean," Toby said, "is that I wish that I have the patience, the strength, and the moxie to do the kind of scholarship that is necessary for me to achieve my goals. I know from personal experience, Mr. Specter, that that kind of gumption is hard to achieve. I learned this on the Episcopal *Scholium*, our high school newspaper, on which I have served as the editor in chief. I also learned it on the junior varsity lacrosse team, which I'm one of the co-captains of. I also learned it in our Drama Club, where I played the Stage Manager in Thornton Wilder's *Our Town.* All of these experiences have helped me to learn how hard it is to achieve one's goals unless one has the wherewithal to really do your best, all the time. It's that kind of spirit I wish for, and which I hope will carry me on through four years of college, here at Dartmouth.''

Dylan listened to his amazing barrage of hooey with amazement and shame. This is the thing I cannot do, he thought. I cannot explain to anyone why I deserve to be paid attention to. It's why Tobin Stroud here is going to Dartmouth next year while I work on my uncle's Pontiac lot. It's why Allison is making love to idiot Polo MacNeil right now, while I sit here imitating someone who, when I was the person being interviewed, didn't even show up.

''Well, fine,'' Dylan said, irritated. ''What's your third wish then? If you know so much.''

Toby looked a little surprised.

''Well, I don't know,'' he said. Perhaps it was occurring to Toby Stroud at this moment for the first time that Dylan Floyd was not a member of the Dartmouth College admissions staff. Again Dylan could almost hear the gears in the boy's mind spinning around. He knew that Toby wanted to ask whether or not Dylan wasn't a little young to be working here, wanted to ask whether or not he was even in the right room, but Dylan also knew that poor Toby Stroud could not ask these questions now because there was the minute possibility that Dylan indeed was this Mr. Specter, and his sudden rudeness in the middle of the interview would almost certainly be taken into consideration when it came time to make the final decisions.

"I guess what I want is to be able to know people," Toby said, still looking at Dylan with suspicion. "When I meet someone sometimes I'm too trusting. Too gullible. What I hope is that by meeting a large and diverse group of students I'll learn more how to deal with people. Be able to see into them and judge them with respect."

"Well," Dylan said. "That all sounds very good."

"Did you go to Dartmouth, Mr. Specter?" Toby said.

"No," Dylan said. "I went to Bowdoin, actually."

"Did you just graduate there? Recently, I mean?"

"Yes. Just this last spring."

Toby thought this over.

"I know somebody who went to Bowdoin. Mickey Zacks. He was the captain of the wrestling team at Episcopal. Editor of the yearbook. President of the Episcopal Volunteers."

Dylan got out another sheet of green paper. Stroud, Toby, he typed.

"I didn't know him," Dylan said. He cleared his throat. "Well, listen, it's been a pleasure talking with you, Tobin. I wish you all the best."

"Yes?" Toby said, getting to his feet. He shook Dylan's hand. "Yes. Well, thank you very much, Mr. Specter. Thank you very much."

"I hope we'll see you here next fall."

"Really? You do?"

Dylan patted Toby on the back, escorted him toward the hall. "Sure," Dylan said. "You're a nice young man."

Toby walked away, beaming. Dylan went back to the desk and picked up a pen.

This Tobin Stroud represented everything Dylan hated. The little Schweinhund.

Dylan's hand hovered over the line *Interviewer's Recommendation*.

God dammit to hell, Dylan thought, and circled (A) ADMIT. Son of a fucking bitch.

He left the office and walked down the hall. Well you got in, Tobin Stroud. I hope next year you and Allison are very happy together.

Ben and Chloë stood before the Hanover Inn. A plate in the sidewalk below them announced their intersection with the Appalachian Trail.

"Can you imagine going to college anyplace where the AT cut through?" Chloë said. "If it was me, I'd never finish."

Ben thought about this. "What do you mean?"

"I'd always be thinking about heading off, instead of doing homework." She looked across Wheelock Street at the campus. The white buildings of Dartmouth Row stood there, resplendent in the autumn sunshine. Chloë looked distantly toward Rollins Chapel. Her blonde hair was piled high on her head.

"Somehow I never pictured you as the outdoors type," Ben said.

"I know, I know," Chloë said. "I wasn't always like this."

"Yeah, well," Ben said. "I wasn't always like this either."

Chloë looked at him, embarrassed. "What should we do, Ben?"

Ben caught something strange in her voice. "About what?"

For a moment she didn't answer. "I don't know," she muttered. With one hand she reached out and clasped the edge of his jacket.

"I don't know either," said Ben.

"There are some murals, somewhere," she said, hoarse. She cleared her throat. "You want to see them?"

"What murals?"

"In Baker Library. The murals by Orozco. Supposed to be something worth seeing."

"Sure," Ben said, stepping across Wheelock. "Why not." They walked toward the green. "Orozco? Who is that?"

Chloë shrugged. "I don't know."

Bells pealed from a carillon.

They passed Reed and Thornton Halls and sat down on a bench in between Thornton and Dartmouth Hall. To their left were Webster and the Baker Library.

"You know Dr. Seuss went here."

"I believe it."

The carillonneur was playing "Shenandoah."

"Hey," Ben said. "That's the song Allison sings."

"Is it?" said Chloë. She stared off at the horizon again.

Ben looked at her. "You okay?" he said.

"Ah, what am I going to do?" Chloë said, vaguely.

"About what?"

"About everything." Chloë crossed her arms in front of her. "I'm cold. Are you cold?"

"No, I'm wearing a jacket," Ben said. "You should be wearing one too."

"Yeah, well," Chloë said.

"Do about what?" Ben said again.

"Lefty, Allison, my life."

"What's wrong with your life?"

Chloë looked at him. "I don't know, Ben. I don't know where to begin."

"Well it sucks, being our age," Ben said.

Chloë looked at him. "Do I look like fifty to you? Honestly?"

Ben looked at her. "I don't know what fifty is supposed to look like."

"Thanks," she said, irritated.

"What, you're fishing for compliments?"

"Forget it."

"You look great," Ben said. "Don't tell me you don't know that."

Chloë shook her head. "I don't know anything anymore."

"Me neither."

"Our kids, interviewing at college. Can you imagine that? Christ. I thought I'd be smarter than this by the time Allison went to college."

"Me too," said Ben. "I thought I'd be—" Chloë was shivering. He took off his jacket and draped it around her back.

"Thanks, Ben," said Chloë.

"You looked cold."

"Hey, it has your smell."

"I smell?" Ben said. "You're saying I smell?"

"It's a good smell," said Chloë. "I like it."

Ben shrugged. "I didn't think it would be like this," he said.

"You didn't think what would be like this?" said Chloë.

"Being fifty." He looked at her. "I guess Lefty told you my situation, huh?"

"A little. He said your business wasn't doing too well."

"It's bankrupt," Ben said. It sounded so final, saying it that way. "I had to sell the whole thing. I'll probably wind up working at the lot next year, unless something else comes up."

"You're kidding," Chloë said. "You'd work for Lefty?"

"I have to work somewhere. Even if Dylan gets a scholarship there'll be bills."

"You don't have any savings? A college fund?"

"No," said Ben. "I spent it all on the company, trying to keep afloat. Can you imagine that? I blew my kid's tuition money."

"I can imagine that," Chloë said.

The carillonneur finished "Shenandoah" and started playing something else.

"What's he playing now?"

"I don't know."

Chloë smiled balefully. "You talk to Lefty much this trip?"

"A little, mostly about my business going down the drain."

"He misses you," Chloë said. "I think in a way he's hoping you'll work on the lot again, so the two of you can be friends again. He doesn't have many friends."

"Well, he doesn't need friends," Ben said. "He has you."

Chloë looked at Ben. "That was a nice thing of you to say," she said. "I think."

"Well, you know what I mean. If you're married you have someone to talk to. I can't tell you how much I miss that."

They sat there, listening to the bells peal.

"When you were married," Chloë said, after a while. "You and Faith got along, until the end anyway?"

Ben thought about it. "Yeah," he said. "We did. You would have liked her, Faith. She was an amazing person."

Chloë felt Ben retreating into himself. "I'm sorry for your loss," she said. "You still think about her a lot, I guess."

"I'm thinking about her more on this trip, actually. Being with Lefty, back in New England. Brings back a lot of memories."

"That's what my marriage to Gary was like. My first

husband. I was so in love with him. Even now, when I'm with Lefty, I think about him all the time. Isn't that weird?''

''It's not weird at all. It's normal.''

Chloë shook her head. ''It sure is sick, is all I can say. Being normal.''

Ben stood up and took her by the hand. ''Come on, Chloë,'' he said. ''Let's get out of here.''

They walked down the hillside, from Dartmouth Row, down toward the quad. A flag snapped on a flagpole. Chloë pulled up the flaps of Ben's lapels, to protect her from the cold.

Ben looked at her. Chloë's hair was collapsing over her ears, where the wind had blown it loose. A couple walked by, arm in arm. Ben and Chloë watched the young lovers, stumbling across the campus, oblivious to the world.

''Sometimes I wish it was me, going to college,'' Ben said.

Lefty looked out the window of the Winnebago. There were his wife and his brother, walking together across the green quad. From here they looked like a couple. For a moment he thought of something, then he dismissed this.

Son of a bitch, Lefty thought. He went into the bathroom and looked at himself in the mirror. ''You're a bad man,'' he said. The man in the mirror didn't seem impressed, so he said it again. ''A *very* bad man.''

He remembered the expression he'd seen in Chloë's eyes as he'd hung, suspended, from the side of Mount Katahdin. For a single moment he'd been convinced she was going to let him fall. He understood it all then—the sudden escalation of cholesterol and sex in his life. Funny how easy it was to mistake the actions of someone who loved you with those of a person who was trying to make you die. Still, if you thought about it, maybe it wasn't a surprise that his wife thought the world would be a better place without him in it. No one knew him as well as Chloë, and by now the truth was obvious. He was a bad man.

It wasn't his intention to be a bad man. Even now if it were possible to undo some of the things he had done, he would try to make amends. Still, it was impossible to live your life backward. You had to take responsibility for your verminiverousness.

He'd first heard about Ventura Monmouth from one of his customers, Bob Cuttner, who bought a new Alfa Romeo every spring whether his old one was running or not, which it usually wasn't. Cuttner made his cash on the venture capital market; that was how he was able to spend his days playing golf and driving Italian sports cars that constantly broke down. He had millions in the VC market, *millions*. About eighty percent of his investments went belly-up, he said, laughing, taking the test drive. But the other twenty more than made up for it. Hoo-boy, he said, honking the horn. They swept around a curve. You don't know the half of it. You oughta get a piece of this, Lefty.

So Lefty got a piece of Ventura Monmouth, more than a piece in fact. The Pontiac lot, which had been such an albatross in the late seventies and early eighties, was now making money hand over fist. Minivans and sport utility vehicles. Convertibles. It was shocking, really, how much money he had. Since he never figured Juddy would be interested in college, there wasn't much to spend money on, besides getting jewelry for Chloë, taking her to Europe now and again. The Ventura people welcomed him with open arms. Put him on the board. A few months later he'd seen that they were going to finance his brother's business. Give him five million to expand. Two mill up front, the other three when his earnings increased by eighty percent, nine months later.

He kept expecting somebody to ask him about his brother, to vouch for his character. But no one said a thing. One day it hit him: they didn't know. As far as they were concerned, Ben Floyd was just a stranger who lived in New Jersey who had his hand out. Which—who knows?—maybe was what he was now. He and Ben hadn't talked in nearly six years.

So they bankrolled Ben's company. For a while things looked good. Then he hit a snag with the software for his new line. He had to hire on staff to debug the whole thing. He got behind. He spent all the dough.

For a while it seemed as if Ben would go belly-up right then and there. But leave it to his scrappy brother to scrape his way out of the jam. After seven months he was making money again. At the nine-month review point he was just five percent short of the target. Everyone figured the Ventura board would give him the slack.

But then some other major investment of theirs—an amusement park in upstate New York—went belly-up, and the next thing you knew the board was spooked. They weren't taking any chances. Half the board voted to hold Ben to the exact terms of his contract. He hadn't made the eighty percent, so they wanted to cut him off. The other half wanted to give him some room to wiggle. Lefty Floyd had the deciding vote.

Lefty had sat in the big room, no businessman, just a fathead with a lot of cash, really, who had bought his way into the company, holding his own brother's fate in his hand. He did not know what he was going to say when he opened his mouth. He thought about his youth, growing up with Ben, always being the older brother, teaching the boy to fly-cast, how to thread a worm onto a hook. He remembered being drafted, one of the last of his generation to get called up during the war, spending the two years sitting on a base in Germany. He recalled coming home, spending the summers with his brother, working on the old man's lot.

The other men looked at Lefty. "Well," he said slowly. "A deal's a deal."

The following Monday they told Ben they weren't going to provide the next round of funds. Two Fridays after that, Lefty had been standing on the lot at lunchtime, eating a sub, when he felt the sudden crushing in his heart and fell to his knees.

He spent a week and a half in the hospital, breathing through tubes, having the bypass. He couldn't talk for a long time. Chloë came in to see him every day, her eyes full of love. One day she said, "Don't be angry, Lefty. But I called Ben. I thought he should know." He nodded. "He says he wants to talk to you."

An hour later the phone rang. "Hello, brother," Ben said.

Lefty, lying there in the hospital, felt the tears coming to his eyes. He suddenly understood something of the motivation for his own actions, a rationale that had escaped him even while he had done these terrible things.

You want to know why I screwed you out of your company, Ben? he thought, lying there, unable to talk. You really want to know the reason? Okay, I'll tell you. I was figuring if you went belly-up, you'd come to me for help. Maybe you'd work on the lot for a while. The two of us in business together. Brothers, like we were when we were kids. That's why I did it. I fucked you out of your company because I miss you, because I was hoping we'd wind up together again, friends at last. Don't you get it, brother? I ruined your life because I love you.

*   *   *

Polo lay on his stomach in his room in the Hanover Inn. He and Juddy had stumbled in here yesterday while waiting for the others to drive up in the Winnebago. He was watching *Gunfight at the O.K. Corral* on the TV. There was a song that ran through the movie, sung by Frankie Lane. Every twenty minutes they sang a new chorus. *"O.K.—Corraaalllll—O.K.—Corraaaaallll. Here they lay side by side, the killers that died, at the Gunfight at O.K. Corraaaaal."*

"Polo," said Allison, rubbing his back. "Turn it off, will you?"

"Just a sec," Polo said. "I want to hear this song."

"Please," Allison said. "I want you to hold me."

Polo sat up, gave her a hug, then rolled back down on his stomach.

"Oh, my dearest one, Must I," Frankie Lane sang. *"Lay down my gun, or take the chance of losing you forever? Duty calls, my back's against the wall! Have you no kind words to say, before I ride away!"*

"Polo," Allison said. "I need more than that. I want you to really hold me."

"Ally," Polo said. "I told you. I don't want to tempt you."

"It's okay," Allison said. "You can tempt me."

"I'm serious," Polo said. "I had an insight. A moment of illumination."

"Yeah, well, I had one too," Allison said. "I'm ready now, seriously I am."

"Ready?" Polo said. "What are you talking about?" He looked up at her.

"I want you, sweetie," Allison said. "I want you to make love with me."

"You do?" Polo said.

"I can't explain it," Allison said. "But it's like you said. I had an insight."

Polo sat up in bed. "You did?" he said.

Allison put her arms around his waist and pulled him to her. "I did," she said, and kissed him. She felt a great gust of wind blowing through her, like a flue or an open window. "I did," she said again.

She got up on her knees and kissed the side of Polo's face. He had a wonderful smell, like mushrooms. Polo's stubble brushed against her cheek. It gave her goose bumps. On television guys were shooting at each other.

Allison reached down and unbuttoned her shirt. Polo's hands pulled it down. She felt her breasts against his chest, her cotton bra moving against his skin. Her hands fell to the clasp and undid it.

"Polo," she said. "My love."

Polo held her in his arms, pulled back a little bit to look at her. She was beautiful, her long blonde hair curling into her navel.

"Allison," he said.

"Please make love with me," she said. "I'm ready."

Polo looked at Allison, her eyelids heavy with love for him. Her body was a warm ocean, waiting.

"I can't," he said.

"Can't?" Allison said. "Can't?"

"Please," Polo said. "I want to wait."

"Wait?" Allison said, smiling. "Yeah, right."

"I'm serious," Polo said. "I'm not the man I was."

"It's all right," Allison said, "I liked the man you were."

"Oh, you didn't know the man I was," Polo said.

"Wait," Allison said. "You're serious? You really don't want to make love to me?"

"Of course I want to make love to you," Polo said. "Don't you see how I'm on fire for you?"

"You don't look like you're on fire," Allison said.

"But I want to wait until we're married," Polo said. "I want to be the man you deserve, not some scumbag."

"You're not a scumbag," Allison said. "Of course you're not a scumbag, sweetheart." She sat up.

"Oh, I am! I am! I'm disgusting!"

"What are you talking about?"

"The things I've done, you don't want to know about them!"

"I don't care about the things you've done," Allison said. "I just want you to love me." She thought for a second. "What sorts of things?"

"Oh, the drunken stupid orgies, the meaningless stupid trysts with strangers! But you deserve better, I know you do! From now on I am going to be the man we both want me to be."

Allison moved her finger up and down the hairs on his arm. "Strangers?" she said.

"I can't even believe the sex I've had sometimes," Polo said. "It was so disrespectful!"

"You mean like, people you didn't even love?" Allison said. "You had sex with people you didn't have any feelings for?"

"Feelings, ha!" Polo said. "Boy oh boy, the old me would just about do it with anybody."

Allison stopped caressing his arm.

"So you're saying that you'd do it with a total stranger but you won't do it with me? I thought you loved me!"

"I do love you," Polo said. "That's what this is about."

"That's what what is about? I swear to God I'm totally lost!"

"That's why I don't want to sleep with you! Because I love you!"

"So you sleep with people you don't love, but me, you won't. That's what this insight amounts to?"

"You deserve not to sleep with me, that's what I'm saying."

Allison looked at him, trying to understand the complexity of Polo's thoughts. She was used to not following him, since he was so advanced.

Then she thought about what he had said about the drunken orgies. The meaningless encounters with strangers. In an instant she saw her lover in a new way. For the creep he had always been. He had lied to her, all this time. It was like suddenly being with someone she did not know.

"Listen, you goddamned son of a bitch," she said, and unzipped his fly. "If I say we're going to have sex, we're going to have sex, okay?" She reached into his pants and found his penis.

"Please," Polo whispered. "Don't!"

"Shut up," Allison said, pulling his pants down. She looked at his disgusting thing, and kissed its purple tip. "You think I like this?"

"Please," Polo whispered. "This isn't who I want to be."

"I don't care who you are," Allison said. "I'm being interviewed tomorrow at noon by my first-choice school. You understand me? And if I'm still a virgin when they talk to me, they're going to know it. So if I want to lose my virginity, you're going to help me, okay? I don't want to hear another word out of you. I just want to get this over with."

Polo looked at her and felt his resolve crumbling. He heard a little smacking sound. God dammit, Allison, he thought. It didn't seem right to keep her from getting into college.

At that moment the telephone rang. Allison kept kissing him.

"Hey," Polo said. "I should answer that."

The phone rang again.

"Ally—" said Polo.

"Would you forget the phone already?" Allison said. "Don't you want to make love with me?"

"I do," Polo said. "Good God, I do!"

"So let's do it," Allison said. "Come on!"

Polo looked at her, his heart breaking, trying to figure out what course of action his new self would take. The important thing was to treat her with respect and honor. Proceed only with the sort of action that would do justice to their love.

Allison looked up at Polo, wondering what she had ever seen in him.

Polo reached over and picked up the phone.

"Hello?" he said. The color drained from his face. "Dean Barker," he said, "Yes, this is he."

Polo studied her boyfriend. There's only one thing about boys you can be sure of, she thought. They are revolting.

"Well, yes. I'm sorry we missed you again. We—"

Allison put her clothes back on. If she couldn't have sex with her boyfriend she would have to have sex with someone else. She quickly tied her shoes, put on her bomber jacket, and left the room.

Polo watched her go, feeling pity. "Yes, I suppose we could try to schedule one last interview," he said. Quickly he remembered his new philosophy. "Ah, but wait. I'm not sure we can get back down there." He cleared his throat. "In fact, I'm no longer certain that Harvard is on—" His throat closed up suddenly, and he swallowed. "Is on my list of first choices."

There was a furious, desperate voice on the other end of the phone. Dean Barker was down on his hands and knees, begging Polo to change his mind.

On the other bed in the room was Juddy's cap. VILLANOVA WILDCATS.

"Actually, I'm thinking of Villanova," Polo said.

There was an apoplectic squawk from the other end of the phone.

From the television came the soft sound of Frankie Lane singing. *Wyatt Earp, they say, saved Doc Holliday.*

Polo reached over and placed Juddy's cap backward upon his head. It was a perfect fit, as if it had been waiting, all these years, for the brains of Polo MacNeil.

middlebury college

Middlebury, Vermont
Number of applications: 4,599
Percent accepted: 27%
Middle 50% SAT range: 660–730V, 650–710M
Most popular major: history, English, international studies
Mascot: the Panthers

Though rare, "gut" courses such as
Earthquakes and Volcanoes
("Shake and Bake") are available.
—*Insider's Guide to the Colleges*, 1998

allison got up before the others and showered. The Winnebago was parked in front of Emma Willard House, Middlebury's office of admissions. She put on her good clothes, checked her watch, and stepped outside. It was eight o'clock. The interview was at nine-thirty.

I must be out of my mind, she thought, walking toward Procter Dining Hall. An hour and a half to go. Surely there must be someone on this campus who wants to have sex. It was a shame about Polo, about Dartmouth, where she'd walked around for two hours and found no one. It was a shame about everything.

She walked into the dining hall and was suddenly surrounded by students. They wore backpacks and Birkenstocks. Most of the men were experimenting with facial hair. The women had big boots.

Allison got a cup of coffee and sat down at a table by herself with a copy of a newspaper, *The Campus*. There was a story about a sophomore being arrested for driving his car into Lake Dunmore, which appeared to be a large body of water some miles from here. The sophomore wasn't drunk. He said he had driven his car into the lake in order to make a statement about water pollution.

"Hi," said a male voice. Allison looked up. There stood a fresh-faced young man holding a platter of eggs and bacon. "Can I sit here?"

Allison felt her heart pounding. "Sure," she said. "Sit." It was too good to be true.

"What's your name?" said the dude.

She thought for a moment. "Brenda," she said.

"Brenda." He smiled. "I'm Marco."

"Hi," she said.

"Where do you live?"

Allison sipped her coffee. "Off campus," she said.

"Yeah?" said Marco. "I'm in Painter."

"What's that like?"

He smiled. "You know. Sketch, I guess."

She nodded. "Sketch," she said.

"Last night there was a whole crew, pretty shit-housed."

"Shithoused, huh?" she said.

"Shit-*hammered.*"

A young man with large muscles and waist-length hair walked by.

"Dude," he said to Marco.

"Who's that?" said Allison.

"You're serious? You don't know Wailer? I thought everyone knew Wailer."

"Well," Allison said. "Like I said, I live off campus."

"Dude is totally jacked."

She smiled. "I guess."

"I don't mind guys being all buffed and shit, but Wailer, man, he's just like, a total steakhead!"

She shook her head sadly. "He sure is," she said.

"I mean all the dude thinks about is getting huge."

"I hate that."

"I don't know, he's not so bad, if you can stand a trustafarian."

Allison shrugged. "I can stand it."

"So what do you do here?" said Marco.

"I'm into music," she said. "I write songs."

"No shit," said Marco. "Me too. I'm doing modal."

"Uh-huh," Allison said. "That's a good thing to do."

"What else you up to?" said Marco.

"Well," Allison said. Her heart was pounding. "I'm

doing this project for psych. About, you know. Guys and girls. The way they, you know. Connect."

"Sounds outré."

"Oh it's outré all right," she said.

"What's involved."

"Well, I like, you know, have sex with people and everything. Then I have them fill out this form."

Marco looked like an asteroid had just hit him on the head. "No way!" he said.

Allison nodded, with the seriousness of a social scientist. "Way," she said.

"Whoa," he said. "I mean, that is just nutrageous."

"What do you think?" she said. "Are you interested?"

"In what?"

"In being part of my research."

"Whoa!" he said again. "Well. I'm telling you. I'd like to."

At that moment another young man came over, holding another platter of eggs and bacon. He put down the tray and said "Hi" to Allison. Then he leaned over and kissed Marco on the lips. It was a long kiss.

"Brenda, this is Jonah," said Marco. "We're married."

Allison nodded. "Well, what do you know about that," she said.

"Brenda here is doing a psych project on couples having sex," Marco said. "She had just asked me if I'd help her."

"That sounds so interesting!" said Jonah. He opened his napkin and placed it on his lap.

"She interviews people after they have sex," said Marco. "Says she has this whole form."

"Well, for heaven's sakes."

"You're including gay couples of course," said Jonah, momentarily concerned. Then the concern vanished from his face. "Of course you are! What am I thinking?"

"Of course I am," she heard herself say.

"Well, what are we waiting for!" said Jonah.

"What do you mean?" said Allison.

"Come on back to our dorm. Marco and I can make love, then you can have us fill out the forms. I mean, I'm in the mood. Aren't you?"

"Sure," said Marco. "Is this okay? Do you want to do the research right now?"

Allison finished her coffee. "Sure," she said. "Whatever."

"Come on, Marco," said Jonah, standing up and taking his lover's hand. "Time to make the donuts!"

Ben walked around the Middlebury campus, lost in time. He hadn't been here in nineteen years, but being back amid the familiar landscape of his youth transported him effortlessly to the late 1970s. The hostage crisis. Inflation, recession. Jimmy Carter and the swimming rabbit.

He walked over toward Painter and stood in front of the dorm. Grateful Dead played out of the windows. *Jack Straw.* Jeez, Ben thought. It's even the same music.

He remembered coming over here, a few weeks before graduation, to wake up Faith. Her door was open, and he went in to the nuclear devastation of her dorm room and woke her with a kiss. The sleepy-eyed, rosy-cheeked woman opened her eyes and smiled. "Hi, honey," she said, and it occurred to him at that moment he could ask her to marry him. He had never thought about marrying anybody before, but he thought about it then.

On a Tuesday in February, twelve years later, she left their house in Connecticut and drove up to Vermont, rented a cabin on the banks of Lake Dunmore. I need time to think, she'd told her husband. I can't even remember who I am anymore. Her crisis hadn't come at a very good time for him. He had to take a whole day off from work, just so they could fight. *How could you do this to me?* he'd yelled at her, long distance. *I don't know*, Faith said. *It wasn't something I did on purpose.*

God damn, Ben said, shaking his head. *You're really something.*

I screwed up, all right? Jeez, Ben. You know what drives me nuts? It's not that you ignore me. It's that you can't forgive me for my mistakes.

Some things you can't forgive, Ben said.

You can say that again, said Faith.

So she spent the week in a cabin on a lake not far from where they'd gone to college, trying to determine her next move.

They found the note on the cabin's kitchen table. She'd left it there just before she went out on the surface of the frozen lake to ski.

Dear Ben,

I know that this is going to hurt you, but I have given this a lot of thought. We have been together a long time. Sometimes it seems as if the time we've spent together is the only life I've known.

But you know I'm unhappy. I am not so good at hiding it as I used to be. I'm hoping you will understand that I have to do this, and that in time you will forgive me. You know that I will always love you. Don't forget those days we shared, at Middlebury. For a while you showed me what it can be like, being in love.

Your darling, Faith

When they found the body, nearly a week later, the hole in the ice had already frozen over again. She hadn't drifted far. Faith was suspended in the ice, just below the surface. You could see the pale frozen lips, the hair floating around her face, her eyes wide open. If she hadn't been wearing the long skis, perhaps, she might have been able to climb back out of Lake Dunmore, out of the hole that had suddenly opened around her.

Ben was left to ponder the note she'd left. When she talked about "doing this," did she mean suicide, or divorce? Was the thing she wanted to get away from their marriage, or life on planet Earth? It still wasn't clear to him if her disappearance was something she'd intended.

He'd had to come up to Vermont to identify the body. He didn't stop in at Middlebury. He just kept looking at the place where his wife had last been, at the tracks of her skis, still imprinted in the snow. They led away from him, across the dark ice, until they came to a jagged place and stopped.

"Ben," said a voice.

He looked up. It was Chloë, standing behind him. She was wearing a black sweater and gold earrings. "Are you all right? I was looking for you."

"I'm okay," Ben said. "I was just thinking back."

"You used to go here, huh?" said Chloë, sticking her hands in her pockets, squinting up at the dormitory.

"Yeah," said Ben. From inside Painter came the sound of young people laughing. "A long time ago, I guess."

Juddy and Dylan sat in the Winnebago, drinking coffee. Polo and Lefty were still asleep in their bunks. Ben and Chloë were gone, walking around the campus, looking for things.

Allison came stomping back up the steps.

"Hey, Allison," said Dylan. "How'd it go?"

"I don't want to talk about it!" she shouted. She stormed in. A rolled-up Middlebury catalog was in one hand.

"Jeez," said Juddy. "She doesn't want to talk about it."

"Polo, wake up," said Allison. She opened the folding door. Polo opened one eye.

"Huh?" he said.

"You stupid, stupid, stupid," she said, whacking him with the Middlebury catalog. "Stupid stupid stupid idiot!"

"Hey," Polo said. "Quit it!"

"Ally," Juddy said, going over to her. As she raised the catalog to whack Polo again, Juddy grabbed it away from her. Allison was left striking Polo with something that no longer existed.

"Give that back," she said. "You moron. You stupid fuckhead."

"Now, now," Juddy said. "Don't say things you don't mean."

"She means it," Polo said, sitting up, rubbing sleep from his eyes.

"You're all a bunch of stupid fuckheads," she said, looking each of the young men in the eyes. "Do I make myself absolutely clear?"

The guys looked at each other. It seemed pretty clear what she meant.

"Well, good," she said, and got her guitar. A moment later, she stormed down the steps and out again.

"Boy," said Juddy. "Looks like somebody isn't getting into Middlebury."

"Poor Allison," said Dylan. "I wonder what happened."

"She's disappointed," said Juddy. "If you ask me, she seems disappointed."

"Well," said Polo, getting out of bed. He was wearing paisley silk pajamas. "Disappointment is a part of life, isn't it."

"Come on, dude," Juddy said. "You oughta go to her. Help her out."

"She is beyond my help," said Polo, shaking his head.

"Polo, dude. Focus. She's your girlfriend. You gotta look out for her. If she's disappointed, it's your job to take care of her, man."

"My job?" said Polo. "My job is to prepare myself for Harvard. I'm supposed to phone them in a half hour, schedule one final interview!"

"Polo," said Juddy. "Come on, man. She's cryin'!"

"I know what she's doing," said Polo, and walked toward the shower. A moment later came the sound of running water, and a young man's voice raised in song. It sounded like Polo was singing something out of Gilbert and Sullivan.

Juddy looked at the space through which Polo had walked for a moment, then sighed. "How do you like that," he said.

Dylan didn't say anything.

"You think you know a guy," said Juddy.

"You mean Polo?" said Dylan. "You thought you knew him?"

"I don't know, Dickweed," Juddy said. "Him and me, we had some good times this last week, down in Boston. You should have been there doing shooters in Cowboy Bob's!" He laughed.

"Maybe I should have," Dylan said.

"Well, it would have been a lot more fun if it was you and me, Dickweed. At least you and me got something in common."

Dylan nodded.

At that moment, Allison came back to the Winnebago. She stood at the bottom of the steps. "Dylan," she said, still crying. "Can I talk to you for a second?"

Dylan looked over at Juddy. "Go on," said Juddy. "She needs you."

Dylan got up, walked down the steps. From the shower came the distant voice of Polo singing.

"Listen, I'm sorry, okay," she said. They were outside now. "You're not a shithead."

"Allison," Dylan said. "Are you okay?"

"You can't do anything without everything going haywire, did you ever notice that?"

"What happened?"

"I screwed up my interview," she said, miserably. "I sat there like a moron. I couldn't even remember half the things I wanted to tell them. I got into this stupid situation just before I went in there. I'm such a total loser!"

"You're not a loser, Allison," Dylan said.

"Oh, Dylan," Allison said. She reached forward and collapsed in his arms. She leaned her head on his shoulder. Dylan felt the hot moisture of the weeping woman on his neck.

She looked up suddenly and kissed him. It was a soft, lovely kiss.

"Yow," said Dylan.

"Listen," Allison said, breaking the embrace. "Your friend Brenda is a lucky women."

"My friend Brenda," Dylan said. He couldn't remember who this was.

"You're like the only straight guy I know who isn't a psycho or a liar."

"Really?" Dylan said. It was a nice thing to say.

"God, I hate how guys lie to you sometimes." She blinked. "You must think I'm nuts."

"No," said Dylan. "You're just sad. That doesn't make you nuts."

She nodded.

"Listen," Dylan said, "About Brenda."

"What?" Allison said. "What?"

He tried to think what it was he could tell her about Brenda.

"Nothing," he said.

"Listen, I'm going to go sit in front of the library and play my guitar for a while. If you want to come with me, I'd like that."

Dylan looked at the beautiful girl. Her eyes were all red from crying.

"I have to go to my interview," he said.

"Right," she said. "Well, you'll do fine. You won't have any trouble. You'll knock them dead."

"I'll knock them dead," Dylan said, unconvinced. Allison leaned forward and kissed him again. "Sorry," she said, and walked away.

Dylan stood there for a moment, watching her recede, then walked back into the Winnebago.

Juddy was watching him. He shook his head. "You're something, Dickweed," he said.

"Leave me alone," said Dylan. The sound of water in the shower ceased. Polo was drying himself off. He was still singing.

"There isn't any Brenda, is there, dude," said Juddy.

"Huh? What?"

"Brenda," said Juddy. "There's nobody named Brenda. Is there?"

Dylan thought about perpetuating his lie, but he was too tired. "No," he said. "There isn't."

Juddy rubbed his belly. "You're kinda old for an imaginary friend, aren't you?"

"Listen, just don't tell Allison, okay? She'd be hurt if she knew I'd been lying to her. I don't know how I got myself into this."

"Don't worry, Dickweed," said Juddy, coming over to his cousin. "I can keep a secret. Can you?"

The two boys looked at each other for a long time.

"Yeah," Dylan said. "I can keep a secret. You know I can."

Juddy nodded. "You never told anybody, huh. About that time."

Dylan thought about it. "Nope," he said. "You?"

Juddy shrugged. "Nah," he said. " 'Course it was easier for me. It wasn't my pop we were trying to protect."

"Yeah," said Dylan.

"It's a shame about what happened to your mom and all," Juddy said. "I guess I never said anything to you about it, dude. I should've. But I didn't."

"It's all right. Nobody knows what to say."

"Well, I'm still sorry, okay, Dickweed? I am." He looked thoughtful. "You're all right. There's a lot more to you than meets the eye."

"Thanks," Dylan said, trying to figure out if this was a compliment.

"You know what I'm going to do for you, Dickweed?" Juddy said. "I'm going to do you a favor." He raised one hand, as if holding an invisible sword. *"Whssht-whsst,"* he said, making the sign of the *J.*

"Please, Juddy," Dylan said. "Don't do anything." He thought about it for a moment. "What are you going to do?"

At that moment, Polo came out of the shower, a towel wrapped around him. He didn't look so impressive wet.

"Hey, Polo," Juddy said. "Guess what. Dylan's girlfriend died!"

"No," said Polo. He stood there, stunned. "No!"

"No," said Dylan.

"Yep," said Juddy.

"Juddy," said Dylan.

"What happened?" said Polo.

Dylan looked at Juddy. Juddy explained. "Got bitten

by this chimp," he said, sadly. "Some research experiment."

"No!" said Polo.

"No," said Dylan.

"Yep," said Juddy.

"My dear fellow," said Polo. He was still standing there in his towel. "I'm so sorry."

"Me too," said Dylan.

"I didn't even know you had a girlfriend, Dylan."

"Yeah, well," said Dylan. "We kept it quiet."

"Is there anything at all I can do for you?" Polo said. "You name it!"

"Oh, don't you worry," Juddy said, looking off toward the quad. Allison was still visible in the distance, walking along the green campus with her guitar. "He'll think of something."

Lefty opened his eyes and found his wife missing. He hadn't had his waffles today. He looked at the clock, tried to remember where they were. Middlebury, he reckoned. Middlebury was where Ben had gone, a long time ago. Middlebury was where his brother had met Faith. It was funny how he never thought about Faith anymore, her wild eyes, the jet-black hair. There was a time when he'd thought of nothing else.

On a Sunday morning nine years earlier, Ben had called him up and said, "Lefty, can you pick up Faith at the airport? She's coming in from Ohio and I can't get her. I have to work."

"Sure," he'd said. "I can drive up there."

"And I want to drop Dylan off, too. You think he could hang out with Juddy today while I'm at the office?"

"Juddy's got a Little League game. I guess Dylan could go watch him play. Tell you what, you drop the kid off here, I'll head up to Hartford. I have to stop by the lot today anyway."

"Thanks, brother. I owe you."

That phrase stayed with him as he drove up to Hartford/Springfield International. *I owe you.* He thought about his two years stuck in Frankfurt while his brother went to parties at girls' houses. The old man gave Ben a barely used Camaro off the lot, gave it to him, just as a gift. The whole time Lefty had worked on the old man's lot, never once was he allowed to keep a car overnight, not even a junker. By the time Lefty got back from Germany, Ben was off at Middlebury, majoring in economics. A college boy.

Yeah, if you thought about it, it was the absolute truth. Ben did owe him.

Faith was surprised to see him, standing there by the baggage return.

"What are you doing here, Lefty?" she said, hugging him.

"Gettin' you, darlin'."

"Where's Benny?"

"Working."

"Working?" She looked upset. "Well, jeez."

"What's the matter?"

The muscles in Faith's jaw clenched and unclenched.

"Nothing."

"Doesn't look like nothing."

"I said it's nothing, all right?"

Lefty shrugged and took her bag. The two of them walked out toward Lefty's car.

"Listen, I'm sorry, okay?" Faith said. "I just wasn't expecting you."

"Sorry if I disappointed you, Faith."

"It's not that. It's just that it's so typical. I was thinking the whole way back how I never just hang out with

Ben anymore, never stay up talking, listening to music like we used to."

"Well, you're not kids."

"I know, but—what can I tell you? I'm just pissed off at him. I really wanted to see him. Maybe take the day and do something for a change."

"Well hell, you got me," said Lefty, slowly. "If you want to do something, I'm free."

"Jesus Christ," Faith said, still pissed off. "I can't believe he's working. On a Sunday. It's so typical."

"Well, you know Benny. Always got his nose to the grindstone."

"Yeah," she said. "I know Benny."

They drove out of the airport, down the highway past Hartford. Faith looked out the window, lost in thought.

"So who were you visiting? Your college roommate?"

"Huh? Yeah. Her name's Thayer. She's out in Dayton."

"You keep in touch?"

"No. That's what was so weird. I hadn't heard from her in forever." Faith gathered her long hair behind her head and fastened it in place with a scrunchie. "You know it's funny, when you see people you know from adolescence, you really revert."

"Revert?" Lefty said. "To what?"

Faith shook her head. "She's not married. Got no kids." Faith smiled. "Spent this last week staying up, listening to music, drinking wine. I felt like I was twenty years old."

Lefty nodded.

"Don't you ever miss it," she said. "Being young, not having everybody depending on you?"

He shrugged. "I was never young," he said.

"Oh, Lefty, don't give me that shit."

"I wasn't. Second I got out of high school, I was in the

army. Got back from the army, I was working on the lot, married to Elio.''

''Well, all I can say is, I miss it.''

''Me too.''

Faith looked over at him. ''I thought you said you were never young.''

''I did,'' said Lefty. ''Hell, darlin', I can miss something I never had, can't I?''

''Sure,'' said Faith. ''I guess.''

''Tell you what,'' said Lefty. ''Let's blow off today. Let's go get a bottle of wine, go have us a picnic or something.''

''You're serious?'' said Faith. ''What about Benny?''

''Ah, screw him,'' Lefty said, good-naturedly. ''He owes us.''

''Yeah,'' said Faith. ''Screw him.''

They sat in the barn of the deserted farm, drinking Almaden from a cork-stoppered jug. They were surrounded by bales of old hay. Spiderwebs hung from the rafters.

Lefty was laughing.

''The Worm?'' he said, choking on his wine. ''That's what they called him?''

''Yeah,'' Faith said. ''Benny the Worm.''

''Boy oh boy,'' Lefty said. He dug into the blue box of stoned wheat thins, got out some crakers. Then he cut off a wedge of cheese and placed it atop his cracker. ''This is all new to me.''

''I don't think he ever left the library until his senior year.''

''Benny the Worm,'' Lefty said happily.

''If I hadn't perverted him, he'd probably still be in there.''

Lefty drank some wine from a Dixie cup. ''How'd you

pervert him, anyway? These are some details I'm interested in."

"Oh, Lefty, you wouldn't have believed me in college. I was totally out of control."

"You?" Lefty looked at his sister-in-law, her elegant features, her silk floral dress. "You're putting me on."

"Well, it was a bad time for me. I didn't know it at the time, but it was. I partied a lot." She shook her head and blushed.

"A lot, huh," said Lefty.

"I had three abortions by the time I was a junior. One time I broke into the zoology department and stole this stuffed kangaroo. Another time I stole this cane—Gamaliel Painter's cane—it was this sacred object at Middlebury. I used it to pound some veal. I don't know, I had some kind of attitude then. I used to wake up all the time and not have a clue who it was I was waking up next to."

Lefty's brow wrinkled. "What'd you do that for?"

She shrugged. "I don't know. My parents got divorced in my senior year of high school, maybe I was rebelling or something, I don't know. Who knows why people do the things they do?"

"Sounds like you were having fun, though," Lefty said, hopefully.

"I thought it was fun at the time," said Faith. "Now, I'm just embarrassed. I kind of wasted my time in college, to tell you the truth. I was stoned half the time, drunk the other half. One time I got scurvy. I mean, actual *scurvy*, like a sailor on some ship in the nineteenth century. Turns out my body was anemic because I hadn't had anything besides pizza and beer to eat for six weeks."

Lefty thought this over. "Is it contagious, scurvy?"

"No," said Faith. "Not unless you only eat pizza and beer, too."

Lefty looked at his Dixie cup and put it down on the floor of the loft.

"Don't worry, Lefty," Faith said. "That was the old me. The Faith before Benny. When I fell in love with Ben, I put all that behind me."

"How'd you do that, Faith? You just decided to stop being a derelict and everything fell into place?"

"No, silly," Faith said. "It took a while. Part of it was when I found out I was pregnant with Dylan. And Benny wanted to get married. He was different then, too. When we first started dating, he came out of himself. It was like setting off in this new world together, getting married. We both thought we'd turn into different people."

Lefty picked up his Dixie cup, downed his wine.

"Did you?"

Faith reached for the jug, poured herself another cup of Almaden California Mountain White Chablis.

"I don't know," she said. "I mean, I'm not who I was when I was twenty. That's not possible. But I'm not who I thought I'd be when Ben and I left college, moved down to Connecticut to begin our lives together. I still have this wild streak. I feel like I'm in exile, sometimes, like I'm the only person who still remembers who I am."

She carved off a piece of cheese.

"That's why being with Thayer this last week was so great. It was like there was somebody who knew who I used to be. Who doesn't just think I'm some housewife, somebody's mom."

Lefty moved over toward her, sitting very close. The two of them were leaning up against the same hay bale.

"I don't think you're just some housewife," he said.

She looked up at him, momentarily shocked. Then her eyes smiled. "Jeez, Lefty," she said. "You're full of surprises."

He took her hand. "You still have this wild streak, you say."

She nodded. "Yeah, I still have a wild streak." Faith looked at him probingly, as if trying to figure out if he was what he appeared to be. "What about you, Lefty? You got a wild streak?"

"Hell yes," Lefty said. "I got a wild streak a mile long." They stared at each other, dumbfounded, for a moment, then their heads drew close together, and they kissed. It was awkward at first. Then Faith put down her Dixie cup and reached up to hold Lefty's face.

For a moment he drew back. "Hey, Faith, I got a feeling Benny wouldn't like it, the two of us sitting here, like this."

Faith thought about it. "You know what I'm thinking?" she said.

"What?"

"I'm thinking, I wouldn't mind going someplace there isn't so much straw."

Lefty nodded gravely. "It is kind of scratchy, isn't it."

Faith agreed. "It's *very* scratchy," she said.

With its decaying furniture and torn curtains, the old Hitch farmhouse reminded Faith of the sunken *Titanic*. They went into what had once been the master bedroom, taking the nearly empty bottle of Almaden with them. There was a perfectly serviceable rocking chair in one corner of the old room, next to a fireplace. There were still andirons and burned logs in it. Whatever had happened to the people who had once lived here, they seemed to have left quickly.

"Why is this place here?" Faith asked Lefty, looking around the dusty room. It smelled like something rotting.

"Hitches. Ran a sulky track. Husband, wife, three

boys. The bunch of them were killed in a car accident, about five years ago. Just drove off the edge of the road into the river. Some folks say the father did it on purpose. He was kind of a weirdo."

"You mean like he killed them all, his family?"

"That's what people say," said Lefty. "I never knew them."

"Christ," said Faith, unbuttoning her shirt and throwing it on the bed. She unhooked her bra, let her breasts swing loose. "Shit like that just gives me the creeps."

They got into the bed, which squeaked. A large window with a broken pane stood next to the four-poster, and its torn lace curtains drifted toward them in the summer draft. Lefty took off his clothes, put them on the rocking chair. It swayed back and forth, creaking. It's a good thing I'm drunk, Faith thought, looking at Lefty's naked body. Otherwise I'd be perhaps overly thoughtful about these proceedings.

"God damn," said Lefty, and Faith watched him with fascination. There were two Lefties, sitting on top of her. Both Lefties resembled Ben, in many subtle ways, right down to the way they kissed, the feel of their stubble against her breasts. In many ways this wasn't like having an affair at all. It was more like having sex with some other nether version of her own husband.

"God damn," Lefty said again.

"What happened to your wife again?" Faith said.

"Huh?" Lefty said. "What?"

"Your wife. What was her name?"

"Elio," said Lefty. He didn't really want to stop and talk.

"Is she dead?" said Faith, looking over at the fireplace. It wouldn't surprise her a bit.

"No," said Lefty. "Not dead. Just divorced. Lives up north."

The room was spinning. Faith felt herself lifted up on a wave, like she was out in Waikiki. If she closed her eyes she could almost imagine she was back in college. Trying to take a birth control pill every night so she wouldn't get pregnant again. Taking a vitamin C pill every morning to take care of the scurvy. Benny the Worm coming over, telling her he loved her. She felt sorry for him, little Ben Floyd. He probably did.

"Why'd you get divorced again?" said Faith. Maybe this was all a mistake. It was remotely possible.

"Drunk," said Lefty, his eyes all squinchy.

"Who was drunk?"

"Elio," Lefty said. His face was red. "She's. An. Alco. Holic."

At that moment she looked over toward the door. For a single instant, she saw them, the two boys, frozen. Juddy and Dylan looked at her, pale with fear. Lefty couldn't see them. Faith reached out her hand, shook it back and forth, as if to tell them, *No. This isn't me you're seeing. This is only somebody I used to be, a long time ago.* But then they were gone.

"No," said Faith.

"Yes," said Lefty.

"No, no," said Faith. She closed her eyes.

"Yes, yes," said Lefty. His eyes were already closed.

Lefty collapsed on top of her. Faith turned her head and saw the curtains blowing toward her. For a moment she saw the two little boys, her son, her nephew, running past the window, out into the sunshine and away from this place. Again she thought about saying something, but they were already far away.

williams college

A less-popular dorm is Mission Park, constructed entirely of concrete and glass, and located on the outskirts of campus; one resident said that living there is "like being in a permanent episode of *Dr. Who.*"

—*Insider's Guide to the Colleges,* 1996

Williamstown, Massachusetts
Number of applications: 4,674
Percent accepted: 27%
Middle 50% SAT range, 1996:
   600–710V, 650–740M
Most popular major: history
Mascot: the Ephmen

ben Floyd sat in Baxter Dining Hall, drinking coffee, clacking away at the keys on his laptop. Across from him, Dylan pushed his fried eggs around with a fork.

"Did you ever think that eating is disgusting?" Dylan said, with a sudden, unexpected vitriol.

"What?" said Ben, taken by surprise. "Huh?"

"I said eating. It's disgusting. Chewing. Swallowing!" Dylan shook his head. "Man!"

"Eating? Disgusting?" Ben said.

Dylan looked up at his father. "Forget it." A clock on the wall read 8:42. "I better get going."

"What time's your interview?"

"Nine."

"Right." Ben sipped some coffee. "You must be an old hand at this by now."

"An old hand?"

"At interviewing."

Dylan looked miserable. "I'm screwing them all up."

"You shouldn't say that, son."

"It's true. I don't know what to tell them."

"You're not screwing them up."

"You don't know."

"I'm sure you're doing fine. You have to have faith in yourself, Dylan."

Dylan looked angrily at his father. "Faith in myself?" he said, incredulously. "What for?"

"Because," Ben said. "You have a lot going for you."

Dylan pushed his yolk around. "Like what?"

"What do you mean, like what?"

"I mean, like what? Name one thing."

"You have lots going for you," Ben said. He tried to think of something his son had going for him. His glance fell, briefly, to the screen of his computer. "You're a good guy."

"You see, even you can't think of anything."

"That's not nothing, being a good guy," Ben said.

"It is nothing."

"And your grades—they're well above average, and you have the what do you call it, the Ecology Club and all that."

Dylan just shook his head.

"Dylan, you've got to have some confidence. You've got to believe in yourself."

"Why?" Dylan said.

"Because," Ben said. "Because you have a good soul. You had a hard time, growing up. I know you did. But you grew up to be this wonderful kid. You're kind to people. You look out for people. I admire that, son, I really do."

Dylan looked at his father suspiciously.

"I know you think I'm an old fart," Ben said. "Maybe I'm a crummy father, I don't know." He waited for Dylan to contradict him. He didn't. "But don't let the fact that I'm a crummy father cheat you out of college. This is your opportunity, Dylan. To make something of yourself. To get away."

"I know," Dylan said.

"You're going to have the life I never could," Ben said. "You deserve that."

"I'm not having anything," Dylan said. "I'm a fuck-up."

"You're not a— You shouldn't say that."

"I blew my SATs," Dylan said. "I totally blew them."

Ben absorbed this. "What do you mean, blew them?"

"I got mixed up or something. Skipped a line. I got like 300s on them. They aren't going to let me in anywhere. This whole trip is pointless."

Ben opened his mouth and said nothing.

"You can take them again," he said. "Can't you take them again?"

"I can take them again," Dylan said. "But it won't be any different. I know I'll fuck them up again. I'm a loser, Dad. Face it."

"What's wrong with you?" Ben said. "Why do you say things like that?"

"Gee, I don't know," Dylan said. "Maybe I learned it from you." He stood up, pushed his tie close to his starchy blue Oxford collar. "I gotta go."

"Son—" Ben said.

"I said I have to *go*," Dylan said. He left his tray on the table and walked toward a large glass door. Williams students were all around them, although not as many as you'd expect to see at 9:00 A.M. Ben remembered his college days at Middlebury, sleeping late, staying up 'til all hours studying.

He saw now that things were worse than he had thought. It was possible, even likely, that he would soon be in direct competition with his own son for the humiliating position of salesman on Lefty's Pontiac lot next fall. What was wrong with the boy, that he felt so little confidence in the world? It wasn't right for a young man to have such a low opinion of himself. Ben wondered what it was that his son wanted that he had been unable to provide.

At that moment, Allison entered the dining hall with her mother. Chloë had her arm around her daughter's back. The girl looked fragile, like something made of glass that had broken to pieces and been inexpertly glued back together. Together the two women walked like that, toward the place where he was sitting alone.

Polo was driving south again in a Pontiac loaned to him by another one of Lefty's friends, Mack Pullen of Williamstown Pullen Pontiac Mercury Toyota. This one was a 1978 Chevrolet Monza, a rattling four-cylinder hatchback. He didn't mind if they saw him in it at Harvard. If it were possible, in fact, he'd park it in front of Dean Barker's window. Let them see what kind of man he was.

On his head was Juddy's Villanova Wildcats hat. His plan was to wear it in to the interview, let them see how little he cared. He wouldn't try to sell himself. Just be yourself, Juddy had advised. Don't let them think for one second that it makes any difference.

He knew that this new philosophy made no sense, and yet you couldn't argue with results. That girl in Cowboy Bob's had practically thrown herself at him. A day later, Allison down on her knees, begging him for sex. Then Dean Barker calling on the phone. It was all just as Juddy had foretold, like that awful bumper sticker you saw affixed to cars very similar to the one he was now driving. *If you love something, let it go. If it comes back, it's yours. If it doesn't come back, hunt it down and kill it.*

He reached down into the well of the passenger seat and pulled out a six-pack of Budweiser. With a pressurized hiss the can popped open, and Polo took a swig. It wasn't bad beer, if you tasted it.

I wonder who I would have been, Polo wondered, if I'd grown up with Lefty as a father, Juddy as a brother. He'd grown up an only child, his parents both psychologists with a joint practice on Columbus Avenue. His parents were always going on and on about *the life of the mind*, as if the brain had a life independent from your spleen and kidneys. It had been a fine way to grow up, and he loved his parents, but this last week among the Floyd family, Polo had found himself yearning for something he'd never known before. It would have been a great solace in life, to have grown up among brothers. Maybe, if he'd had brothers, he'd be more of a participant in the world by now, less of an observer. Maybe he'd know how to throw a football, to tell a joke, to sail a boat. He pictured himself at a big table, eating spaghetti with his brothers. Everybody laughing. The life of the mind was all right as far as it went, but it didn't tell him how to be a man.

Well, all that is changing, he concluded, increasing speed to keep up with the Boston traffic. If you think about it, it's fortunate he'd had these insights just in time for his Harvard interview. It was a blessing from on high he'd missed the first two. Traffic merged in front of him, and Polo slammed his palm down on the horn. Assholes. Who do these people think they are? Bunch of dickheads and bottom feeders. Who is anybody? He checked his watch. It was a good question.

Lefty sat alone in the Winnebago, looking out the window. It was the second day in a row he hadn't had his waffles. In one hand he held a telephone, the dial tone buzzing faintly in the quiet room. Something was up with Chloë. He thought about the glimpse he'd had of his wife and Ben the other day, walking around Middlebury like a couple. Again he considered the impossible, then ruled it out. Lefty's brother was many things, but at least he was not Lefty.

The sudden absence of waffles from his life, though, was not insignificant. Something about his wife seemed different. Even if she actually went ahead now and made him waffles, there would be a part of him that still wasn't having them. Sometimes the waffles we receive are not the waffles our souls cry out for, especially when the only waffles we receive are actual waffles.

He hung up the phone, considered his own cowardice. As it turned out cowardice was just another word for common sense. Just because you run away from trouble doesn't mean you're stupid. Sometimes it's the bravest thing a man can do, running around screaming.

He went back and sat in the chair again. Well, why not? He didn't have to explain everything. This is how you make yourself nuts, Lefty thought. Analyzing everything until you're frozen.

He picked up the phone and dialed. A moment later a phone was ringing somewhere across town.

Lefty felt his heart pounding in his chest. A woman's voice answered. It sounded like Elio. "Hello?" she said.

Lefty's throat closed. He wanted to say hello to her, say, Listen, I'm in the area. Thought we should get together, just for old times' sakes. It's been a long time. I know that the end of our marriage was not good, but I wanted you to know that when I think about us the end is not all I think about.

"Hello?" Elio said again. It was definitely her. Amazing how people don't change. Her voice was lower than Chloë's, a result of her smoking and drinking. He knew in that instant that Elio still smoked. And if she still smoked, then nothing about her had changed. Twelve years after the divorce and she was the same woman. His heart thundered in his chest.

The line went dead. Jesus, Lefty thought. She didn't wait long. That, too, was just like her. Didn't even give him a chance to speak her name.

Lefty sat there holding the telephone. He thought about his first wife, a drunk. He looked around for his heart medication. Why, he wondered, slipping a glycerin tablet under his tongue, why does everybody hate me?

How very strange, he thought, that it should come to this. He remembered when they were married, right after high school. Ben was still in junior high. It rained that day. Elio walked down the aisle in white, the raindrops hammering against the stained glass. The veil that covered her. Lifting back the veil at the altar, looking into her eyes. How beautiful she had looked then, and how young! The minister, some stranger at his back, saying, *You may kiss the bride.* Elio looked at him with wonder and adoration. Her lips parted, and he kissed her.

"So what do you want to know about Williams?" asked Ms. Guichalarr. She was very pregnant.

"Well," Dylan said, stalling for time. This was the same trick they'd tried on him at Colby. Getting him to ask the questions. As if he wouldn't see through this.

"I guess I'd like to know more about the opportunities for studying away," he said, vaguely.

"Studying away," Ms. Guichalarr said. "You mean overseas?"

"Yes," Dylan said. "Exactly." It was what he meant.

"Well, Williams has two of its own off-campus study programs. We have an agreement with Oxford University which enables our students to study in England during their junior year. And there's the maritime studies program in Mystic."

Dylan thought about this. "What do you mean, Mystic?"

Ms. Guichalarr smiled. "Mystic, Connecticut."

Dylan thought about this some more. "What's involved in the maritime studies program?" he asked. It sounded interesting. It was the first thing he'd heard on this entire tour, in fact, that he could picture himself doing. Dylan saw himself on the deck of a ship, somewhere at sea. Seagulls circling overhead.

"Well, you spend the semester in Mystic, studying sailing, maritime culture, oceanography."

"It sounds great," Dylan said.

"It's very popular. The Semester at Sea."

"I'd like that, a semester at sea." He thought about it. Yes, a semester at sea sounded just like what he was aiming for.

"Well, good," Ms. Guichalarr said. "Actually, study off campus is a very important part of the Williams experience. We have a Dean of Study Abroad who helps coordinate the programs. In addition to the Oxford and Mystic programs, we have an understanding with many other colleges and universities around the world, enabling our students to study virtually anywhere they like."

"Wow," said Dylan. This sounded great. "Like, what are some of the other places people go?"

"You name it," Ms. Guichalarr said. "Cannes. Heidelberg. Florence. Cuernavaca. Sydney."

"Sydney, Australia?" Dylan said, and immediately regretted it. No, Sydney, North Dakota.

"Yes." She smiled. "That's a very popular program for surfers. Do you surf, Dylan?"

He shifted in his seat. "I hope to learn," he said.

Ms. Guichalarr put her hand on her belly and winced. "Nepal," she said, abstractedly.

"There's a program in Nepal?" Dylan said.

"Yes." She looked thoughtful. A moment later she opened the file on her desk and scanned over some of Dylan's materials. "You're going to take the SATs over again, I hope?"

Dylan blinked. "You think I should?"

"Of course you should. It's obvious you had a bad day

or something. Your other grades are very good, according to this. What happened? You get lost or something?"

"I didn't get lost," he said, defensively, then relented. "Well, yeah, I did."

"Of course you did. You're smarter than this."

Dylan looked at her suspiciously. How did she know how smart he was?

"I skipped a line," he said. "All my answers were wrong."

Ms. Guichalarr looked at him. "You're not the first person that's happened to," she said. It was eerie, how sympathethic she was being. There was something unnatural about this kind of maternal generosity. "You should have had the test canceled. After you took it. They'll do that, you know."

"What do you mean, canceled?"

"If you get lost, or whatever, you're supposed to go up to them after the test and tell them. They won't process it." She looked through his transcript. "Anyway, you ought to take them again this winter if you get the chance. We'll need another set of scores out of you before we can give you serious consideration. Your grades are pretty good, overall. You're a good candidate."

Dylan didn't know what to make out of this. "I am?" he said.

"Well, sure," said Ms. Guichalarr. "Your teachers say great things about you. You've obviously done well in school. What, you look surprised."

"I guess I am," Dylan said.

"Why?" she looked at him with what looked like sincerity. Damn these people, Dylan thought. They really were tricky.

"Why am I surprised," he said. "I don't know, I guess I just don't— I don't see myself as a good candidate."

"Well, you should. Your teachers say you're a real mensch."

Dylan's face froze. He didn't know what a mensch was.

"I don't know, Ms. Guichalarr," he said. "I just don't feel like I have a clear sense of—"

"Whoa!" Ms. Guichalarr said suddenly. Her face colored. "Excuse me," she said. "Baby kicked."

"You're pregnant," Dylan said.

"Yes," said Ms. Guichalarr. "I got a little dancer in here."

"That's so cool," Dylan said. He looked at the bulge in Ms. Guichalarr's belly. It was funny to see women wearing maternity clothes, he thought, especially women like this Ms. Guichalarr whose clothes were both clownlike and professional at the same time.

A small but distinct lump moved suddenly and dramatically across Ms. Guichalarr's front.

"Whoa," she said again.

"You can feel that?" Dylan said.

"Oh yeah," Ms. Guichalarr said, looking down at herself. "That was a knee, I think."

"That must be so weird," Dylan said. "Somebody living inside you."

"It's definitely strange." She looked up at him. "You like babies, Dylan?"

"Yeah," he said. "They're cute."

"It says here you don't have any brothers or sisters, is that right?"

"That's right."

There was a long pause while she read something in the folder.

"Your mother is deceased, it says here."

"Yes." He swallowed. "She went to Middlebury."

Ms. Guichalarr was still reading. "Whoa," she said again, more deeply.

"Are you all right?" Dylan said.

Ms. Guichalarr had a funny look on her face. "I think so," she said.

"You let me know if there's anything I can do for you," he said. Dylan was feeling very nervous. With his luck this Ms. Guichalarr was going to go into labor, have to deliver the baby right on top of the desk. He had a sudden vision of himself having to reach in and grab her baby. He hoped the unexpected intimacy wouldn't count against him.

"You know you are a mensch," Ms. Guichalarr said. "That's very kind of you." She took a deep breath. "I'm all right."

"Okay, good."

"So what are you interested in, Dylan?" she said. "Have you thought about a field of study, or a major, or anything like that?"

"I don't know," Dylan said. "I like English. I like music, too."

"Do you play?"

"No," Dylan said. "Just listen." He blushed. "Well, I do play autoharp."

"Autoharp?" Ms. Guichalarr said. "You mean one of those zither things?"

"Yeah," Dylan said. "It's just a hobby. But it's something I'd like to study more. If I came here. Maybe I could take lessons."

"Maybe," Ms. Guichalarr said.

"It's an instrument a lot of people don't take seriously. But it's hard, when you play it for a while. There are a lot of sounds you can get out of one of those things."

"I'd like to hear you play," Ms. Guichalarr said politely.

"Well, if I come here maybe I could stop by some time."

"That would be nice."

There was a long pause.

"You said you liked English, too."

"Yes," said Dylan.

"What authors do you like to read?"

"I don't know. We've read a lot of different ones."

"Which ones do you like, though?"

"Well, I'm not sure. The Romantic poets I liked a lot. Keats and Shelley."

"What do you like about them?"

"I don't know, they were just so alive and everything."

She paused for a moment, then continued. "I know what you mean. And they all died young, too. Keats at twenty-six, Shelley at thirty-two, Byron at forty."

Dylan looked at her. "Where did you go to school Ms. Guichalarr?"

"Wesleyan." She raised an eyebrow. "Are you visiting there?"

"Last stop on the tour," Dylan said. "Day after tomorrow."

"Where else have you been?"

"Yale, Bowdoin, Colby, Middlebury, Dartmouth." He cracked his knuckles. "Supposed to go to Harvard, too, but we got stuck in traffic."

"Those are good schools."

"I know," Dylan said miserably.

"Do you have a favorite poem?" Ms. Guichalarr said. "By one of the poets you mentioned?"

Dylan felt his heart pounding. Here we go again, he thought.

"It's okay if you don't," Ms. Guichalarr said.

He wanted to reach over and push a bead up her nose.

It wasn't okay if he didn't, and they both knew it. "I don't know," he said, his mind desperately searching for one of the poems he'd read. The thing was, he did like the Romantic poets. It had been his favorite semester of school. But now, with the bright lights of Williams College shining in his face, it was impossible to remember anything. The very process of interviewing for college seemed to turn him into the kind of person who could not get in.

" 'Ode to a Nightingale,' " he said quietly.

"Aah," Ms. Guichalarr said. "I love that one. 'My heart aches'—do you remember the opening?"

" 'My heart aches,' " Dylan said. His voice died out. Ms. Guichalarr looked out the window, her hands resting on her enormous belly. Dylan saw a framed photograph of her husband on the corner of her desk. He didn't really look all that old. Christ, Dylan thought. He could be my age.

" 'My heart aches,' " Dylan began again. " 'And—' "

Ms. Guichalarr screamed softly.

Oh my God, Dylan thought, what am I doing? She must think I'm out of my mind.

"My water broke," Ms. Guichalarr said.

"My heart aches and my water broke—"

"No," said Ms. Guichalarr. "I mean, my water. It broke. My actual water."

"Your water?" said Dylan. "Oh, your water."

"My water broke," Ms. Guichalarr said. "My water broke! Jesus Christ. Okay, what do I do? What do I do?"

"Call your husband," Dylan said.

"I'm soaked," Ms. Guichalarr said.

"It's okay," Dylan said, standing up. "You have to go. Call your husband."

"Right," she said, standing. The bottom third of her maternity dress was covered with water. She picked up the phone and dialed. "I guess we're going to have to cut things a little short,'' she said. A tinny voice on the other end of the line spoke. ''Hello?'' Ms. Guichalarr said. ''Honey? It's me. My water broke. I'm going to the hospital. No. *My water broke.* Yes. Okay, I'll meet you there. No, I'm all right.''

''All right,'' she said, hanging up the phone. ''I'm going. Let's stay in touch. It would be nice if you came over and played the autoharp next year.'' She was putting on her coat, strapping a purse over one shoulder. ''I'm sorry I have to—''

''It's fine,'' Dylan said. He knew he wasn't playing her any autoharp. ''Good luck.''

''You're nice,'' Ms. Guichalarr said. She looked at him with a funny expression, then turned toward him suddenly. Her arms were spread. She was getting closer. Ms. Guichalarr looked like she was going to hug him. She was nearly upon him now. Dylan did not know what to do.

She reached him. A moment later her arms were wrapped around him. It was strange, being embraced by a woman in labor. He figured that this Ms. Guichalarr ought to get moving. He felt the warmth of the wet liquid on her dress.

''Okay,'' she said, breaking the embrace. ''You take the SATs again, you hear?''

''All right,'' Dylan said.

''Good. See you.'' And with that she rushed out the door toward the hospital.

He stayed for a moment in the woman's office, looking at the places where they had been sitting. Now that it was too late, the words came to him, as easily as if he were pulling the sword from the stone.

'' 'My heart aches and a drowsy numbness pains my sense, as though of hemlock I had drunk.' ''

There was a puddle on the floor, near her chair. Ms. Guichalarr's husband smiled at him from his photograph, as if to say, Snap out of it, Dylan. It's a world of wondrous things: heart-wrenching, indescribable misery; unplayable music. Astonishing acts of generosity. Drunks and fatsos. The miracle of birth.

Allison walked across campus with her student guide, whose name was Penny. Penny was a blonde woman with shoulder-length hair and bangs, a pink headband, and pink knee socks. There was something a little off about her, but Allison couldn't exactly figure out what. There were dark circles under Penny's eyes.

They had already passed the Hopkins Observatory, which Penny had a lot to say about. She was an astro major. Maybe that was why the woman looked so tired; she had been up all night, squinting into a telescope.

"What are you interested in, Allison?" Penny said, as they walked across the green quadrangle.

"Music, mostly," she said. "Maybe English."

"Good departments," Allison said. "But they're all good, really. You can't go wrong here."

"I heard Romance languages wasn't so hot," Allison said. "Is that true?"

"No, Romance languages are great," Penny said. "You mean like French, Spanish, Latin?"

"Yes. Italian. Portuguese. I think Portuguese is a Romance language, too, isn't it?"

A large group of guys walked by, laughing, shouting, pushing each other. Penny stopped and watched them go.

Allison watched them, too. The two women stood for a moment, as if lost, watching the men.

"I guess so," Penny said.

"Why are they called Romance languages?" Allison said.

Penny shrugged. "I wouldn't know," she said.

She pointed toward the spire of the chapel. "You see that? They drop a watch off the chapel every year at commencement. If the watch breaks, the class is lucky."

"What do you mean, lucky?" Allison said.

"That's the tradition. They're lucky if the watch breaks."

Penny didn't say anything else for a while. Three minutes later they passed the Student Union. "In there's the Dog House," she said sadly.

"Dog House?"

"Yeah. Hot dogs for lunch." Penny shook her head.

"What if the watch doesn't break?"

Penny looked back at Allison. Maybe this was what had been worrying her. "I don't know," she said.

Another group of guys loped toward them, carrying towels. Penny looked at them with her dark eyes.

"The guys here," she said, almost to herself.

"What?" said Allison. "What about the guys here?"

Penny looked ashamed. "I don't know. They're weird sometimes."

"Weird?" Allison said. "Weird how?"

Penny blinked, embarrassed to have spoken out loud. "I don't know what I'm talking about. Forget it."

"No, tell me. This is something I'm interested in."

"Guys?"

"Guys being weird."

"Well, I don't know what to tell you. I'm stumped."

"What do you mean, stumped?"

Penny lowered her voice, embarrassed. "Like, you'll hook up with somebody, okay?, hang out, and then the next day it's like, hello?, they don't even know you."

Allison thought about this.

"Do you think you know anything more about guys now than when you first came here?"

Penny laughed. She sounded bitter.

"They ought to teach a course," Allison said. "Explaining them."

"Yeah," Penny said. "It would have to be a science course, though. Maybe chemistry." She thought better of this. "No, geology." She turned to Allison. "You have a boyfriend, Allison?"

"Yes. Do you, Penny?"

"I don't know. I don't know if you'd call him a boyfriend exactly. It's more like, I don't know, like having a horse or something. Like some animal that lives someplace you have to keep changing its hay."

They were approaching Mather House, the admissions office.

"There are women's groups you can get involved with here," Penny said. "There's WOW and EAT Me."

"Eat me?" Allison said.

"Bulimia and anorexia awareness."

Allison was still thinking about Penny's boyfriend, nattering in his hay bale.

"And WOW—that's Women of Williams."

"Hey, Penny, are you glad you came here? Can I ask you that?"

"Of course," Penny said. "Williams is the best college in the country. Probably the world. Everybody here is incredibly tight."

"Okay," Allison said. "You didn't sound sure, I thought."

"Of course I'm sure. It's awesome here." She looked around. "I'm a little out of it today, I guess. I had a fight with my boyfriend. Or whatever he is."

"I had a fight with mine, too," said Allison. "When we were at Middlebury." She thought. "Well, it started at Dartmouth, but it really got worse at Middlebury."

"I don't know what it is with them," Penny said. "It's like all they want is—oh, never mind."

"What?" Allison said, desperately. "What do they want?"

"Well, what do you think?"

"Yeah, well, I guess. But that doesn't satisfy them either. They're like these big things lurching around without any purposes."

Penny thought to herself. "I meet a lot of nice women through EAT Me."

"Yeah, well, I wouldn't mind understanding them better either," Allison said.

"Who?"

"Women."

Penny mulled this over, then nodded. "Yeah, they're strange, too." She thought some more. "Pretty much everybody is kind of whacked out, if you think about it."

"They are," Allison said.

"It's a miracle we don't all just murder each other, go nuts, strangle people we don't even know, stab them or punch them in the nose. Put glass in their food." Penny blinked, smiled. "Well here we are at admissions!"

"Thanks for showing me around."

"It was fun! I hope you come here," Penny said. "I don't know, Allison. Look me up next fall if you get in. Maybe you and me, we could be friends."

Ben Floyd was still sitting in Baxter. Chloë sat across from him. There weren't many people here now. It was 10:30, the late morning.

A few students still sat at tables, though, reading textbooks, writing in yellow legal pads, tapping away at laptops. A man and his daughter sat at the next table over, having some sort of disagreement. They looked familiar.

"You okay?" Chloë said. "You look a little down."

"I don't know," Ben said. "I'm beginning to think this is all pointless."

"Pointless?" Chloë said, but she didn't contradict him. It sounded as if she knew exactly what he meant.

"You know what Dylan told me just now? He said he thinks he's a loser."

"Oh, that's so sad. He's a good kid. He shouldn't think that."

"That's what I told him. You know what he said? He said he learned it from me. Being a loser."

"Oh, Ben," said Chloë. "The poor kid." She shook her head. "It's amazing anybody ever lives past eighteen. Allison's just as bad, in her own way. On the way in here she was telling me she wants to be a nun."

"A nun?" Ben said. "I didn't know she was religious."

"She's not. But she thinks if she's a nun she won't have to deal with boys."

Ben thought about it. "Seems like a heavy price to pay, being a nun. If she's not religious, I mean."

"I remember that age," Chloë said. "You don't know who you are. I mean, it changes every day. Meanwhile, what does she have to do but ride around on a Winnebago telling these admissions people exactly who she is, explain her precise plans for the future. I feel sorry for all these kids, to tell you the truth. My heart goes out to them."

"You know what Dylan told me? He said he got 300s on his SATs. Says he got lost, or something."

"You're kidding."

"Which means there's probably no way he's getting into any of these schools anyway. Not now that I'm broke. Our only hope was his getting a scholarship." Ben shook his head. "I can't believe this is happening to me."

"You?" Chloë said. "You think you're the one it's happening to?"

Ben's face reddened. "Well, to Dylan and me, I mean."

Chloë looked curious. "Why do you find it so hard to believe this could happen to you? You think you're exempt from catastrophe, or something?"

"What I mean is, I spent my whole life working, making money for my family. I gave up everything else so that my business would succeed. If I'd have known I was going to wind up broke, I'd have lived differently, I can tell you that."

"What would you have done differently?"

"Are you kidding?"

"No. I'm not kidding. What would you have done?"

Ben thought. The answer didn't come to him right away.

"Well, I would have spent more time with him, that's for sure. Gone fishing, played baseball, all that stuff."

"Ah, I see. You'd have been a regular Danny Thomas."

"Forget it," Ben said. "You don't know what it's like, suddenly not having any money."

Chloë's mouth dropped open. "What did you say?"

Ben didn't look at her. "You heard me."

"Oh, Ben," she said, reaching out and taking his hand. "Of course I know what it's like. Are you kidding?"

Ben still didn't look at her.

"No," he said.

"Why do you think I got myself into this mess? Married to Lefty? Living like this? Do you think I'd be like this if I had any money of my own? Seriously?"

Ben looked at her, unsure. "What are you saying? You don't love him?"

Chloë shrugged. "What do you think?" she said.

At the table next to them, a man suddenly shouted. "Well, go on, wreck your life, as if I honestly *give* a good goddamn!" The girl opened her mouth, her lower lip trembling, then stood up and ran from the table. A moment later she stormed out the door. The man looked over at Chloë and Ben, embarrassed. "Sorry, folks," he said. His glance hesitated on them for a moment, then he said, "Say, don't I know you?"

"Yes," said Ben, making the connection. "We've been on some of the same tours together." He cleared his throat. "I'm Ben Floyd. This is my sister-in-law, Chloë."

The man stood up, came over to them. "I'm Captain Bedford." He smiled. "United States Marines, retired."

"Captain Bedford," Ben said. "Would you like to sit down?"

"I appreciate your kindness," the man said. His accent was beautiful. It suggested the deep South, Mississippi perhaps, or Alabama. He looked at Chloë, oozing respect for her womanhood. "If you don't mind."

"No, no," Chloë said. "Sit."

Captain Bedford lowered himself elegantly onto a plastic chair. "I apologize for causing a scene," he said. "Most ungracious."

"Oh, we've seen worse," Chloë said, with a smile. "You think that's bad? That's nothing. You should stick around."

"I should say it is not nothing," Bedford said. "Welly runnin' off like a hare." He looked toward the door, then back at Chloë and Ben. "That's my girl, Welly."

"Lovely name," Chloë said.

"Short for Wellington," Captain Bedford said with a smile. "A family tic. Our firstborn's always named Wellington."

"You're not named Wellington," Ben said.

Captain Bedford glowered for a minute. "That's my brother," he said. Captain Bedford thought about his brother, seemed troubled. "Got himself a dog track, East Texas." He shook his head.

"It's a nice name, Welly," Chloë said.

Captain Bedford grimaced politely. "Where are you all from again?"

"I'm from Connecticut originally," Ben said. "But I live in New Jersey."

"Floyd, you said your name was Ben Floyd?" Captain Bedford said.

"Yes."

"Not the Floyd CyberTech Ben Floyd."

Ben nodded. "The same."

The Captain's face darkened. "I owned some of your stock," he said. "Took quite a bath. Quite a bath."

"Yes," Ben said, humiliated. "I'm sorry."

"Well," the man said. "I'll survive, of course I'll survive. I'm diversified, naturally."

"I wish I'd been."

"You weren't diversified?" the Captain said. He looked at Ben as one would look at a leper. "A bad decision, sir. Putting all the eggs in one basket. A bad decision!"

"I'm from Virginia, originally," Chloë said suddenly. "Now we live in Connecticut."

"Virginia, hm," Captain Bedford said, nodding, shifting focus. "UVA is a good school. Up there in Charlottesville."

"We saw you at Yale, I think," Ben said. "Somewhere else, too. Bowdoin, maybe?"

"Bowdoin," Captain Bedford said, shaking his head.

"What's wrong with Bowdoin?" Chloë said. "It's a fine school, isn't it?"

Captain Bedford leaned his head to one side. "I don't have anything against it," he said. "I just wish my girl would be closer to home." He looked at them as if seeking understanding. "We live down in Athens." Ben and Chloë stared at him blankly. "Athens, Georgia."

"That's where the University of Georgia is," Ben said.

"It is a *fine* school," said the Captain. "What she wants to go stomping around up Nawth for I don't know."

"Well, maybe she wants to get away, see the world," Ben said. "They have to leave sometime."

The Captain looked at Ben crossly. "That's what she says," he said.

"Well, it's true. It's their lives."

"Sir," Captain Bedford said crisply. "I know whose life it is. I am very well aware of whose life it is."

Ben looked at the man, surprised by his sudden bitterness.

"Well, she's not going to learn anything kept on a leash, Captain," Ben said.

The Captain's face turned dark red. "How dare you, sir!" he said, and stood up. "How dare you!"

He bowed toward Chloë with exasperated exaggeration. "Good day, ma'am," he said, and walked away.

Chloë and Ben sat there and watched him storm off.

"Jeez," Chloë said, shaking her head. "Poor kid."

"I guess I put my foot in it," Ben said.

"No, no," Chloë said. She reached forward and stroked the back of his hand. "You did a good thing. That guy hasn't had someone contradict him in his whole life, probably. You know, the marines? You told him what he needed to hear. It's his problem if he won't listen."

Ben put his other hand on top of Chloë's. He didn't look at their clasped hands.

"No," he said. "It's his daughter's problem."

"Welly," Chloë said. "What a name." She put her hand on top of Ben's. Now they had their four hands all in a pile.

"Poor kid."

The two of them sat there in the dining hall, their hands joined. Sounds from the kitchen echoed in the great space.

"Did you ever notice," Ben said, "how easy it is to be a good parent of other people's children?"

"Yes," Chloë said, something in her voice. Their eyes met. "I noticed that. It's easier advice to give than to take, though. What you said about children. Learning to let go of them. Taking off the leash."

They looked at each other for a while. She has such eyes, Ben thought, staring into them. It was amazing how much more beautiful women got as they grew older.

Lefty actually drove the Winnebago right by the place the first time without even knowing that he'd reached his destination. He stopped at the end of the block, letting the thing idle for a moment, as he looked down at the address in his notepad. He squinted at the numbers on the houses. At one time it must have been a nice middle-class neighborhood. It wasn't, now. Some of the lots were vacant, the houses themselves having been pulled down. Other homes were bricked up, plywood over the doors, boards nailed in Xs across the windows, to prevent break-ins. What people would want to break in for, Lefty didn't know. Go in, shoot themselves full of junk, he guessed. Flop dead drunk on an old mattress and eat lead paint, sniff glue.

Judging from the numbers, the house had to be on this block, behind him now. It made more sense to pull over than back up. The Winnebago attracted too much attention, assuming, that is, if it were possible to attract attention on a block devoid of human life.

He pulled through the intersection, then parked the Winnebago by the curb. Even with its engine off, it was not exactly inconspicuous.

Lefty walked back along the street. The upper story of these row homes cut off the sunlight. It was dark.

A dog was barking somewhere, behind these houses. It sounded like the kind of dog that never left its kennel.

He reached Twenty-nine Locust. The house was nearly identical to the others on the block. It didn't look like anyone was home.

For a while he stood there, staring at the run-down building. Torn curtains hung behind a window with bars on it. A mailbox was nailed next to the door.

He walked up the steps. There was her name, taped onto the mailbox: Elio Floyd. How odd, he thought, that I should have given my name to this place.

With an unsure hand he knocked on the door. There was no sound from within.

Lefty waited for a moment, then knocked again. She wasn't home.

Well, what did you expect, he thought. She probably works. Has to support herself somehow.

The court hadn't even required him to pay alimony. It was rare that a divorce was so open and shut. But no court in the world would have asked him to support her. A doctor stipulated that she was an alcoholic, that she was unfit to be a parent. Elio hadn't even asked for shared custody of Juddy. All she wanted, really, was to be left alone to go off and drink. The judge had suggested that she go to AA, get herself some help, but he couldn't force her. Neither Juddy nor Lefty had seen her since.

Once a year he sent her a Christmas card, a picture of himself and Juddy. He kept figuring that the day would come when Elio would want to make contact with her son again, and unconsciously braced himself for her reappearance in his life, but this day had not yet come. Whoever she was now, Elio seemed content to leave him behind.

Lefty remembered their marriage, not for the first time that day. Himself just back from Germany, walking around in his army uniform. The dirty looks he'd gotten then, the hatred he'd received as a vet. Jeez, he thought. Forgive me, man. All I did was get drafted.

The early days of his marriage. Working on the lot. Elio taking night classes. Baking ziti. Playing the guitar. She had a beautiful old Martin she'd picked up somewhere. He remembered Elio drinking her vodka tonics, back in the days when he still drank with her, singing songs that made him laugh.

Lefty was about to head back to the Winnebago when his hand fell on the doorknob, gave it a twist, in a final gesture of fruitlessness. The doorknob, however, turned, and the door opened with a creak.

He looked at the open door. "Hello?" he said, peeking into the house. "Hello?"

It would really be ugly, he thought, to come upon her, dead. He sniffed the air. It didn't smell like anybody was dead in here. Lefty walked into the house. It didn't smell like anybody was exactly alive, either.

Elio lived in what looked like a two-bedroom apartment, the first floor of what had once been a single family's house. The living room didn't have much in it. A television. A beat-up couch. The coiled springs collapsed through the foam. There were some boxes piled up in the middle of the room. On top of them were some bags from a take-out chicken place.

"Hello?" Lefty said again. From outside he could hear that dog, barking.

Jeez, he thought. So this is where she lives. Regular Waldorf-Astoria in here. What were you thinking, sweetheart? Being drunk all the time is really that important to you?

He walked into her kitchen. Cockroaches scuttled away as he drew near. There was the hollow clunk of water dripping from a faucet. The sink contained a bowl of cereal, some milk still in it. Lucky Charms.

A dead plant hung from a hook. It looked as if it had been dead for a long time.

A door off the kitchen led into the bedroom. Elio slept on a mattress on the floor. At one end of the room was a Japanese bureau. He remembered this piece of furniture; she had inherited it from her mother. Supposed to be a valuable antique. Some of the drawers were open, her clothes sticking out. On top of the dresser was a single framed photograph. Next to the dresser was that old guitar, leaning against the wall.

Lefty, he thought to himself. Get out of here, now.

But the photograph captured his attention. What was this, the one object of sentimentality in the place? As he drew near, he saw that it was a picture of his son, taken maybe five years ago. He had stuck it in a Christmas card.

There was Juddy, smiling at the camera. He was wearing his fencing outfit, holding a sword. He couldn't have been more than fourteen years old. His face still had some of its boyish roundness. Recently Juddy had lost this.

He remembered that tournament. It was the first time Juddy had competed. No one had anticipated that he would do much of anything; he was not the kind of boy people expected things of.

And yet he had trounced every opponent. It was amazing to watch. Lefty remembered sitting there in the stands, dumbfounded. It was embarrassing, in a way, to discover this athletic poetry in his son, and to discover it in public. He felt that he ought to have known that his son was capable of such virtuosity, long before anyone, before Juddy himself, perhaps, and yet there he was, one more spectator in a large crowd, astonished by the sudden gracefulness of his child. It was one of the joys and horrors of parenthood, this sudden discovery that your child has a passion for something completely unknown to you.

The place went nuts when Juddy made his final touch. The coach ran over to him and practically knocked him over. Juddy just smiled like it wasn't all that big a deal. He raised his sword Three Musketeers–style and grinned. A flashbulb went off. Lefty felt tears in his eyes. He'd turned to the woman next to him in the stands and said, "You see that kid? That's my boy!" And the woman looked at him like he was nuts. "Then why are you sitting here?" she said, surveying the adoring mob. His teammates were raising Juddy onto their shoulders. "Why don't you go to him?"

Lefty was going to explain it, but as he opened his mouth he realized that no explanation was forthcoming. All he knew is that it felt better to sit here, watching these boys carry Juddy away from him. I don't know, he thought. I don't feel like I have the right. I didn't even know what he was capable of.

There was a sudden click from the other room. Lefty froze. Jesus Christ, he thought. Elio's home.

But then he realized that there was nothing to be afraid of. He wasn't the one living here, in this low place. He'd stopped by to say hello. Since he was in Williamstown. Wanted to wish her well. If she got all bent out of shape, he'd just leave. She'd forget he was even here soon enough.

Lefty walked out of the bedroom, ready to confront her, the woman whom he had once loved.

The room was empty. Whatever it was he'd heard was just some random sound, the settling of the foundation, something collapsing. He had a strange sense of disappointment, of anger, as he realized he'd wanted to say a thing or two to Elio. You don't know what you're missing, he wanted to say. You'd be amazed by our boy now, Elio. He's quite a soul.

On the counter next to the refrigerator was a bottle of vodka, empty. It was the same brand, Fleischman's, that she used to drink. Well, maybe that's not a surprise, he thought. You find something that works, you stick with it. With a sudden irritation he knew now where she was. She must be out at the package store, picking up another bottle. Elio Floyd was getting ready for another big day.

He felt tears in his eyes. He wasn't sure for what. For the young girl he'd married and lost? For his son, who'd grown up without her? For the whole miserable series of decisions he'd made that had brought him here, to this empty place?

God dammit to hell, he thought. It's for me. It's because somehow or other, I brought her to this. It's what I do to everyone I love, if they wait long enough. Leave them in a pool of their own pee. You have to admit, I have the magic touch.

He turned to go, then paused. Lefty went back into the bedroom, picked up the guitar. He ran his fingers across the strings. It was in tune, more or less.

Carrying the guitar by the neck, he left the apartment, closed the door behind him. He walked down the stairs, expecting somebody to yell at him, but again the world was deserted. Lefty Floyd was the only person left in the universe. He wasn't coming back here. Blackbirds sat on a telephone wire. Lefty walked through the empty street, carrying the guitar.

He got into the Winnebago and closed the door, then walked toward the back. There was Allison's bunk, the covers on her bed dissheveled. He placed the guitar gently on the young woman's bed. It looked like it belonged there.

Then he walked toward the galley. An empty box of

Aunt Jemima pancake mix was in the trash. He bent down and picked it up. Some of the powdery mix still clung to the top of the box. He blew on it. The flour drifted through the air like confetti and fell onto his canister of heart medication. He grabbed the canister of capsules and looked at it. The childproof top was slightly powdery now with instant waffle mix.

He remembered dangling from a rope off the side of a mountain, as Chloë looked him in the eyes and thought about letting him fall. He put his hand on his heart and shook his head. It was sad, he thought. The only reason any woman has ever slept with me is because she hates me.

amherst college

Theme houses include "the Health and Wellness Quarter for those who wish to live free from pollutants, and the Zoo, where students cook their own food."

—*Insider's Guide to the Colleges, 1998*

Amherst, Massachusetts
Number of applications: 4,683
Percent accepted: 20%
Mean SAT: 698V, 700M
Most popular majors: English, psychology, economics
Mascot: the Lord Jeffs

the portraits of the past presidents of Amherst College stared down at Polo MacNeil as he sat alone on a pew in Johnson Chapel. They were arranged in loose chronological order, with Zephaniah Swift Moore, Amherst's first president, hanging at one end of the gallery, and proceeding onward to Alexander Meiklejohn on the lower level. The gallery was high above Polo's head, well out of reach. Sunlight slanted through the windows of the church onto the hard wooden pews.

Well at least we know this much, Polo thought. My portrait will never hang here, or anywhere else for that matter, unless there's a special gallery for morons and cretins. He remembered the face of Dean Barker at Harvard, looking at him with curiosity at first, then disappointment, and finally contempt. Well, he'd concluded, based on our conversation here, I wouldn't recommend your proceeding.

The verdict had taken him by surprise. He was so convinced of the economy of his new philosophy that it had never occurred to him that it might have an effect the reverse of the one intended. He'd walked in there with his Villanova Wildcats hat on backward, no tie, his shirt missing a couple of buttons. He told the dean he wasn't sure if Harvard was still on his list. He said he wasn't sure what he wanted to study, "Sociology maybe." He said he was sure there were other schools that would be able to provide him with much the same education as Harvard. Then he belched.

That was the moment that Dean Barker had pushed

back his chair and said, visibly irritated, "Then why, may I ask, are you here?"

Polo felt his face freeze, the mask of feigned slouchfulness falling from him.

"Well," he said, realizing only at this moment the degree of his miscalculation, "I figured I ought to give Harvard the benefit of the doubt."

"The benefit of the doubt," Dean Barker said. "How very kind of you."

"Well," Polo said, his voice fading, "it's a good school."

"Yes," Dean Barker said. "We think so."

"More than good," Polo said. Blood rushed to his face. "The best, in some areas."

"What areas do you suppose those are?" Dean Barker said.

Polo's voice fell to a whisper. "Narratology," he said. "Poetics. Linguistics."

"Ah, yes," Dean Barker said. "I suppose those departments are at least on a par with Villanova, for instance."

Polo took off the Wildcats hat. "Oh, this," he said. "This isn't even mine."

"But you're wearing it," said the dean.

"Not anymore," Polo pointed out.

"Polo, let's be honest. There's something quite strange here. Your academic credentials seem extraordinary— your grades superb, your test scores in the top percentile. And yet, as we sit here, I'm having trouble believing that this is the same young man. It's almost as if this dossier belongs to a different individual altogether."

He leaned forward, accusingly, in his chair.

"Well," Polo said. "I really ought to have showered, I guess."

"That's not what I'm referring to."

Polo thought about it. "Shaved."

"Mister MacNeil—if that really is your name—"

"It is my name," Polo said.

"Well, I find that hard to believe," the dean said. "Come now. Let's be forthcoming. Is this someone else's dossier, Mr. MacNeil?"

"Someone else?"

"Yes." The dean looked angry, then shrugged. "Well," he continued. "Let's just say that you and Harvard have come to a point of divergence. I do appreciate your coming in. I wish you all the best with your future plans."

"But wait—" Polo said. "I'm not who you think I am."

"I think I understand," the dean concluded. "Please. This conversation can serve no further purpose."

The dean stood and showed him to the door. The next thing Polo knew, he was walking, in his beat-up clothes, the Wildcats hat in hand, out through the lobby. Young men and women, wearing their best interview clothes, eager to impress the dean, looked up at him with curiosity and contempt. Man, they thought. That guy is a goner.

So here he sat in Johnson Chapel, while Dylan and Allison were being interviewed at Amherst. Amherst, the number one rated small college in the country, at least according to *US News and World Report*. He hadn't even considered it before. In his desperation he'd asked the admissions office if he could interview today, while he was in town with his family. The secretary just shook her head sadly. Sorry, sir, all the slots are filled.

The portrait of one of Amherst's presidents caught his eye. It was an odd picture, compared to the others, done in a strange El Greco style. He squinted to make out the nameplate. President Ward, it said. The face bore the traces of melancholy.

Polo imagined his own portrait hanging from the gallery, staring down at the future hapless youth of Amherst, then remembered that he would never even achieve this much. It's because I forgot who I am, Polo thought. It's because I let stupid Juddy twist my head around.

He thought for a moment about Juddy Floyd. The idiot. The imbecile. The beer can with hair. How had it come to pass that he, Polo MacNeil, one of the most promising young men he himself was aware of, could have somehow switched places, willingly, with this wheedling orangutan? Polo looked down at his own hands. I did it myself, step by step. At the moment of my greatness I looked at a fool and decided, *Hey, let's swap.*

Now, having made the switch, it was impossible to simply reverse things again. He was stuck for the rest of his days, living Juddy Floyd's life, going to Villanova, perhaps, while Juddy went to Harvard and studied narratology.

Polo made his hand into a fist and punched his own thigh in rage. Still, he was not without recourse. There were other schools, other lives to live, other than Juddy's. What he needed to do was simply return to himself.

Which is who, exactly? Polo thought, miserably. From the high gallery in the empty chapel the eyes of President Ward looked down at him. You don't even know who you are, he said to Polo. You are a man without form.

He heard soft footsteps coming down the aisle behind him. A young woman with black hair sat down in a pew across from him. She bowed her head, hands folded on her lap, and began to pray.

She was wearing a black skirt, a blue knit top. Was it wrong, Polo wondered, to be attracted to someone while they were praying? He looked up at President Ward again. What exactly are the rules now? he wondered.

Polo stared at the strange, fuzzy portrait for a long time.

"Yuh go to school here?" the woman said, suddenly.

Polo wasn't used to hearing human voices. "Excuse me?" he said. He'd heard her.

"Yuh go to school here, I said." The girl had a beautiful Southern accent. It was hard to understand her at first.

"No. Do you?"

"Naw," the girl said. "I'm a prospective. I'm going around, looking at colleges with my daddy."

"Is that right?" Polo said. "I'm touring, too. Looking at all the New England schools."

"That's what we're doin'," the girl said with a kind of exasperated sigh. "One after the other."

"What's the matter?" Polo said. "You don't like what you've seen?"

"I don't know," the girl said. "I don't know where I want to go. It's impossible to figure out." She sounded almost angry.

Polo looked at her. She had a sweet face, a big run in her hose.

"I'm Polo MacNeil," he said.

"Yeah?" the girl said. "I'm Welly Bedford."

"You're not from New England," Polo said.

"Naw," Welly said. "Come from down south, Georgia."

"Georgia," Polo said. It surprised him, what a pleasant word it was to say. They had peaches there. "Emory's in Georgia."

"Yeah," Welly said. She pulled her hair back behind her ears with her middle fingers. The hair stayed put for about three seconds before falling in her face again. "That's where I want to go to school."

"Emory?" Polo said. It was a good school, the best school in the South, probably, unless you counted Duke, maybe Chapel Hill. It suddenly occurred to him: he could go to school in the South. No one would know him there.

"That's my first choice, too," Polo said.

"Yeah?" Welly said. She looked over at him. Her cheeks were very pink. "Well, I wanna go there, but ı'm not sure."

"Not sure about what?" Polo said.

"Not sure I can stand to be so close to my daddy." She shook her head. "He's just the worst."

"I don't understand," Polo said. "You might go to some school other than the one you want, just to get away from him?"

She shrugged. "It's a big thing," she said. "Gettin' away."

"I know," Polo said. "I've been thinking that."

"It's like, everybody I know is going to Emory. Everybody that can get in, anyway." She pushed her hair back again. "Sometimes I think it would be nice to go someplace nobody's ever heard of you. So you can start over."

"I was thinking that, too," Polo said. Actually, he was thinking something else.

"You were?" Welly said.

He got up, sat down on the pew next to her. "Of course all my acquaintances are attending Harvard," he said. "I myself fully expected to matriculate there."

"Harvard," Welly said, shaking her head.

"But I was just reconsidering, just as you found me sitting here, in contemplation."

"You were?" Welly said. "Spooky."

"Yes. I was thinking how limiting it all is. Harvard. New England. It's all so small somehow!"

"I been thinking that since we got here," Welly said. "All these little places seem the same."

"For years and years it's been assumed that I would go to Harvard, just as my father and grandfather did. But why shouldn't I go where I want? Why shouldn't I go to Emory? It's my choice, isn't it?"

"It is," Welly said. "We ought to be allowed to live our own lives."

"Where do you really want to go, in your heart?" Polo said.

"Emory," Welly said, without hesitation. "It's got everything. Coca-Cola came along a couple years ago, dumped a big truck full a money on the place."

"Then why not go there?"

"Aw, hell, I don't know," she said, annoyed. "'Cause my daddy wants me to go there, that's why. 'Cause he's so stupid!"

"Your father is too insistent on Emory, then? That's the problem?"

"Yeah, it's like I want to go someplace else, just to bug him. I'm so tired of his horseshit, you know? Man oughta have a pitchfork or something, toss it around with."

"And that's why you've been looking at schools in New England? Not because you wish to go to school here, but—"

"To piss him off," Welly said, and nodded. "I don't know, some of these schools are all right."

"Which ones?"

Welly smiled. Her grin was lopsided. "Well, Bowdoin would tick him off the worst I guess."

"Bowdoin?"

"Yeah, on account of that Civil War guy. The one that won Gettysburg, he went there."

Polo thought. "Joshua Lawrence Chamberlain," he said. "The Hero of Little Round Top. Served as Bowdoin's president."

"Yeah, the Captain would just about blow his stack if I went there. But any of these school would do it. Harvard and Yale would get his goat pretty good too, I think!" She laughed. The laughter echoed in the empty chapel.

"Well, I don't know, Welly," Polo said. "It's not for me

to say. But I don't think this is how you should live your life."

"What?" Welly said. "What do you mean?"

"You can't make all your decisions based on what's going to annoy your father the most. Sooner or later you have to leave him behind. College is a pretty good place to start."

Welly nodded. "He'd just be so smug about it, me going to Emory," she said.

"Well, let him be smug if he wants. You can't spend your whole life running from it, his being proud of you."

She looked at Polo's face, seeming to see something there.

Polo reached over and took one of her little hands.

"It's really all right if you want to live your own life, and not someone else's," he said.

Welly looked at him. Her lower lip fell about a quarter of an inch.

Polo moved toward her quickly and placed his lips against hers. She didn't move for the first few seconds. Then she made a soft mewing sound. Her hand raised to touch his cheek.

Polo pulled his face back from hers. Her black hair was soft.

"Well, God damn," Welly said. "That sure came out of noplace."

"It did," said Polo. "I hope you don't mind."

"Naw," Welly said. "It was swell. You're okay." She looked at him with that lopsided grin. "Say, you like blow jobs and junk?"

Polo thought for a second. "I have known them done," he said.

"Well, hell," Welly said. She looked up at the portraits above them. "You think we can get up in that gallery place?"

Polo thought. "There must be stairs."

"Yeah, probably." Welly stood up, took his hand.

Polo stood up too. A strange sense of peace had settled upon him. Of course, he thought, happily imagining this Welly with her legs in the air. His heart leapt with joy as he returned to a place long familiar.

"That would be cool," Welly said, as they began to climb toward the gallery. "If we both went to Emory."

Juddy watched as his Uncle Benny walked across the Amherst campus. If I'm going to do it, Juddy thought, I've got to do it now. He got up and ran toward his uncle. "Hey," he called. "Uncle Benny."

"Hello, Judson," said Ben. He seemed thoughtful.

"Whatcha doin'? Just walkin' around?"

"Yeah," said Ben. "Taking in the campus."

"Man, this is some hill, eh?" Juddy said.

"Yeah," said Ben, despondent. "It's some hill all right."

"You wander around here in the dark some night, it's all over."

"It's all over," Ben said.

Juddy looked at his uncle. "Hey, Uncle Benny, you okay?"

"I don't know," Ben said. They had reached the steps of Johnson Chapel. It looked like a good place to sit down. "Yeah, I'll be okay."

Juddy looked up at his uncle. It was funny to have a close relative that he almost never saw.

"I heard about your trouble," Juddy said.

"Yeah? Which trouble is this?"

"Your business," Juddy said. "I'm real sorry, man. That sucks."

"Yeah, it sucks all right. I don't know. I'll land on my feet."

"Sure you will," Juddy said. "There's lots of jobs."

"I know," Ben said. "It's tough, starting over when you're forty. But I'll find something. I have to, if I'm going to send Dylan to college."

"Aw, don't worry about him," Juddy said. "He's pretty crafty. He doesn't know it, of course, but he's got something."

Ben nodded. It was strange how well Juddy seemed to understand his cousin.

"I'm glad you see that in him," Ben said.

"Sure I see that in him," Juddy said.

"I wish he saw it in himself."

Juddy appeared to think about this. "Yeah, well, you never see yourself," he said. "Way I see it, we never know shit."

Ben nodded grimly.

"You know I always liked Dickweed," Juddy said. He sounded embarrassed. "Dylan, I mean."

Ben looked over at his nephew. They shared some of the same genetic makeup, himself and Juddy. You had to look hard, but it was there. It was strange to be speaking this way to a seventeen-year-old. He wished he were able to speak to his own son this way.

A group of Amherst students walked past. Below them and to the right was the village green. It looked like a good place to go to school, this Amherst. You could learn things here.

"I'm sorry, man," Juddy said. "I didn't mean to call him Dickweed. That's just the name he had when we were kids, used to play together."

Chimes began to play from the stone steeple of Stearns' Chapel, far behind them. A professor carrying a heavy briefcase puffed up the hill toward them.

"Hey, Uncle Benny, how much do you know about these Ventura Monmouth people?"

"What? How much do I know about them? What do you mean?"

"You've got their prospectus, right, Uncle Benny? Their annual reports, all that junk?"

"I got them. My briefcase is full of them."

"So, did you ever read who's actually on the board of directors? All their names, I mean?"

Ben was about to say something, then paused. His nephew had something in his voice he hadn't detected before. He scrutinized the young man for a moment and considered, momentarily, the vague possibility that Juddy was not who he seemed.

"You should check it out," Juddy said.

"What?" Ben said. "Who's on the board?"

"I'm just saying you should check it out, you know? It might be, like, educational." He smiled. "Hey, Unk, ya wanna brewdog?" He lifted a ring of Buds toward his uncle.

At that moment, a young woman walked briskly down the stairs from the chapel. She wore a black skirt and a blue top. In one hand, trailing in the wind like broken spiderwebs, were the torn legs of her pantyhose.

A moment later Polo MacNeil came down the steps, whistling. He didn't see Ben or Juddy. He seemed happy. Ben followed the young man with his eyes, wondering what Polo had to be happy about.

A moment later, he turned back to his nephew, only to find that Juddy wasn't there anymore. Even now, Juddy was vanishing in the distance, walking away across the campus with a half-dozen beers dangling from one hand.

"*Whssht-whssht*," Juddy said, quietly.

*   *   *

"Okay, Dylan, good luck now," said the interviewer, whose name was Mrs. Bavender. "*Huck.*"

"Okay," he said. Mrs. Bavender stood up.

"*Huck,*" she said again.

"You know what works," Dylan said, "is drinking some water while someone puts their fingers in your ears."

"Oh, I'll be all right," said Mrs. Bavender. "I'll hold my breath."

"Well, you should do whatever works for you," said Dylan. "Each person has to find their own solution."

"There's tru-*huck*— Excuse me. There's truth in that."

Dylan stood in the door. "All right then," he said.

"Good luck. We appreciate your interest in Amherst."

"Thanks," Dylan said.

"*Huck.*"

"You know, if you want I can do that," Dylan said.

"Do what?"

Dylan swallowed.

"Put my fingers in your ears."

Mrs. Bavender, who wore a lot of tweed as well as a pearl necklace, looked thoughtfully at him.

"I'll hold my breath," she said.

Dylan wasn't sure if his interview was over. He stood there in the door, watching the woman hold her breath. Her cheeks puffed out a little; her complexion slowly reddened.

A long period passed with Dylan standing in the door, watching Mrs. Bavender hold her breath. Even if she wanted him to leave, she wouldn't be able to say anything about it at this particular moment.

She exhaled suddenly, gasping. Mrs. Bavender looked at the files on her desk, then up at Dylan.

"*Huck,*" she said.

"Guess you still have them," Dylan said.

"Yes," said Mrs. Bavender. She seemed to withdraw into herself. "That thing you mentioned, the ears, that works?"

"Every time," Dylan said.

"Okay, fine," she said. "What do I ha—*huck*. Have to lose."

She poured some water from a Poland Spring bottle into a coffee cup.

"All right then," she said. "How do we do this again?"

Dylan came back into her office and stood behind her. "You drink the water," he said. "Really slowly."

Mrs. Bavender began to sip the water from her cup.

"Now I put my fingers in your ears while you sip," he said. He reached forward into the woman's hair and found her ears. He inserted the tips of his pinkie fingers into her ears.

The office was nearly silent, and in that silence all sorts of hitherto unnoticed sounds came to Dylan. He heard Mrs. Bavender swallowing, the water squirting down her esophagus. He heard her exhaling into the coffee cup, her breath blowing against the water. He heard people in offices nearby, talking. People like himself, being interviewed for college.

He became aware, suddenly, that he could feel Mrs. Bavender's pulse beating through her eardrums onto his fingertips. It was a strangely intimate moment. Her hair felt soft against his hands.

"Ahhh," Mrs. Bavender said, putting down the coffee cup. Dylan removed his fingers from her ears. There was a soft pop, as if from tiny suction cups.

"There," he said. "It worked, didn't it?"

They both froze for a moment, pausing to see if there would be the sound of another hiccup. They waited for it, but nothing came.

"Success!" Mrs. Bavender said. "That's great."

"I told you it would work," Dylan said.

"I've never heard of that," Mrs. Bavender said. "So you put your fingers in your ears while you swallow water."

"Yup," said Dylan.

"Only problem is, I guess you need somebody's help when you do it. You can't do it if you're alone."

Actually, Dylan knew of two ways of drinking water alone while you had your fingers in your ears. One of them was to hold the rim of the glass with the bottom of your palms. The other was to use a straw.

"Well that's a good thing about the hiccups, I guess," Dylan said. "They bring people together."

They both thought about this.

"All right then," Mrs. Bavender said. "I'll make a note of this on your file. *Good with hiccups.*"

He laughed as if this were a big joke, but as he walked down the corridor he didn't see why this had to be impossible. The fact that he was willing to stand there looking at the back of her neck, the place where her pearls were linked together with a silver clasp, the pulsing earwaxy sense of her eardrums against his fingertips, all of these ought to count for something. Did it not demonstrate that he possessed a certain human kindness, a willingness to engage in socially awkward behavior in order to bring a stranger solace? Well, maybe it did, but these were not the things that there were places for on the forms. There wasn't a hiccups portion of the SAT. Not that there shouldn't be, everyone would agree to that, but there wasn't. Right now it was just math and verbal.

He walked down the hall, feeling a sudden rush of anger at the world. Enough already, he thought. Enough.

In the distance, from a place far behind him, he heard a soft sound. *"Huck."*

*   *   *

"Hey, kid," said Uncle Lefty, sitting in the waiting room. "How'd it go?"

"It sucked," said Dylan. "What did you expect? She got the hiccups."

Lefty was thoughtful for a moment. "Did she try holding her breath?"

Dylan didn't answer.

Lefty seemed surprised by his nephew's sudden vitriol. "I'm sorry, Dylan. That's a shame, when the person you're trying to talk to starts up with the hiccups."

"Oh, shut up," Dylan said.

"Boy," said Lefty. "You sure got a bear by the tail, kid. I'm telling you."

Dylan looked around. "Where's Dad?"

"Aw, he wanted to go back to the 'Bago. I had to move it. Ben asked me to escort ya."

"So he's not here." Dylan shook his head. "Figures."

"Dylan," Lefty said. "You gotta relax, boy."

"Listen, Uncle Lefty. We both know I'm not getting into college, okay? If it's all right with you, why don't I just work on the lot next year? I know how to change the oil on a Pontiac. Rotate tires."

Lefty looked at his nephew, surprised his sights weren't any higher than living the kind of life that he himself was living right now.

"Come on, kid," Uncle Lefty said. "You don't want to wind up like me."

"Yeah, well, I don't think I've got a choice."

They were outside now.

"So," said Lefty. "You're a desperado, then. A desperate character?"

"Leave me alone."

They were passing the old observatory, a yellow octagon. A fence stood near one of the walls.

"Hey, whyn't we sit down, me and you?" Lefty said.

"Sure," Dylan said, sitting down on the fence. "Whatever you want."

Lefty sat down next to him.

"So you're pretty pissed off at everything, is that right?" said Lefty.

"Leave me alone."

"You've pretty much decided everything sucks, is that about the size of it?"

"Everything does suck," said Dylan.

Lefty sighed. "Yeah, I guess that's true. If you think about it. Everything sucks. Can't argue with you there."

Dylan looked at his uncle, wondering what the catch was. Adults wouldn't agree with you so willingly unless they had something up their sleeve.

"So what's the answer, then?" Lefty said. "If everything sucks. Just give up, I guess."

Dylan rolled his eyes.

"What?" said Lefty. "Isn't that pretty much your philosophy? Everything sucks, so you might as well give up."

Dylan looked away. "I don't have a philosophy."

"Yeah," said Lefty. "Well, you should."

"Like what?"

"I don't know. You got to find out something for yourself, kid. You want to know what I believe in, I'd say you have to believe in yourself. Especially if the world sucks. If there really isn't anything out there besides, you know, drunks and morons, you might as well try to be a force for good. Do what you can."

"Gee, Uncle Lefty," Dylan said. "That's deep."

Lefty looked a little deflated. "I'm telling you. You have to love people."

Lefty looked at the young man. He had the sudden desire to tell the boy about Chloë, about his sudden suspicion that his own wife did not love him. Actually, it wasn't so much that she didn't love him that hurt as the possibility that she'd been intentionally trying to give him a heart attack, that she actually thought her life would be better if Lefty turned bright purple while his tongue stuck out. Lefty stared at his pudgy fingers, wishing he had the ability to explain himself. It would have been nice, to have been able to talk to someone. He had the sudden urge to explain his view of the world.

"That's the only thing there is in life," Lefty said sadly. "To love people, to forgive them."

"Hey, Uncle Lefty?" Dylan said. "Is it okay if I throw up now?"

Lefty wasn't surprised. This was typical, when you tried to share the concerns of your heart, to receive contempt, scorn, and ridicule.

"I'm not kidding, Dylan," he said, unbowed. "You have to love people, always."

"Yeah. Well, I guess you were teaching Mom that lesson last time I saw you."

Lefty opened his mouth but didn't say anything for a moment.

"You think I don't know about that?" Dylan said. "You're wrong. Juddy and I saw you, in that old house. We were there!" He reached forward and shoved his uncle in the guts. Lefty tipped backward, his arms flailing, and fell off the fence, onto his back.

"Ow," said Lefty. "That hurt."

"You want to know what that was like, to see you there, doing it with her? You think maybe that's why I wound up like this, a loser? You think maybe?"

Lefty was trying to untangle his legs from the fence. "Help me get up," he said.

"We saw you, you *idiot*," Dylan said, and began to storm off. After a moment he turned back to his uncle again, and said, "We *saw* you!"

Uncle Lefty lay on his back, looking up at the blue sky. He didn't feel good.

Ben sat on the front steps of the Winnebago holding the annual report of Ventura Monmouth, printed on rich, creamy paper. The company name was printed in dignified green script, along with their corporate motto: *A Catalyst for Cash.* Jesus, Ben thought. How stupid can I be? There was his brother's name, in black and white. *Lawrence Floyd. Board of Directors.*

He put the report back in his briefcase and snapped the clasps closed. He stood and walked back across the Amherst campus, wondering what he should do now. Should I just walk up to Lefty and punch him in the nose? Get a gun from somewhere and blow his brains out? Put glass in his food? It was incredible. For the last week he'd been riding around with the man who had ruined him. What had he ever done to Lefty that Lefty should be so dedicated to destroying his life? Was there any kind of revenge on him that even now would provide him with satisfaction? He felt his heart beating quickly. Before this moment, revenge had never been part of his vocabulary.

He walked back to the steps of the chapel and sat down. It was getting late in the day. Pretty soon, Ben thought, they would all have to pile back in the Winnebago, drive to some campsite for the night. Tomorrow it was down to Middletown, Connecticut, for Wesleyan, and then home, to his nebulous, contaminated future.

"Hey," said Chloë, walking up the chapel steps toward him.

"Hey," said Ben. "What are you doing here?"

She shrugged. "I don't know. Looking for you, I guess."

Chloë sat down next to him. The skies were turning pink.

"It sure is beautiful here," Chloë said.

"Yeah. I guess."

Chloë looked at him. "Hey. Are you okay?"

Ben sighed. "No," he said. "I'm not."

"What's the matter?"

He wasn't sure he wanted to talk to Chloë about it. After all, she was married to Lefty, even if she didn't like him.

"Everything," Ben said.

Chloë reached over and took his hand. She raised it to her lips and kissed it. "Poor Benny," she said, then let go, as if convinced she'd acted, for a moment, like an insane person. She laughed, almost to herself. "Poor Chloë, I mean."

Ben took her hand again. "Chloë's all right," he said.

She smiled. "Look who's talking," she said. Their eyes locked for a moment.

"What are we going to do?" Ben said.

Chloë smiled a wicked smile, and shrugged.

"I don't know. What do you think?"

Ben looked over at her and suddenly wondered, What the hell is this about? Am I attracted to her? Am I thinking about having an affair, with my brother's wife? Isn't that how we got into this mess in the first place, years and years ago? Is it possible that people can live their entire lives and learn exactly nothing?

"I don't know what I think," he said.

"You know what I'm thinking," Chloë said. "I'll tell you what I'm thinking. I'm thinking—we should do it."

"Do it?" Ben swallowed. "You're thinking we should— do it?"

Chloë nodded. "Yeah," she said. "What the hell."

Chloë's hand was warm. Ben's mind was reeling. It was wrong, this much he knew. And yet, what difference did right and wrong make, at this hour? He was really going to refrain from getting involved with this smart, sexy woman, out of respect for his brother, the brother whom he'd just learned had dedicated his life to ruining him?

Chloë squeezed his hand. "You're thinking too much," she said.

"I know," said Ben.

"Let me ask you something. Did you go out with a lot of women, at Middlebury?"

Ben grimaced. It was supposed to be a smile. "No. Faith was about the only woman I really saw."

Chloë looked at him. "And you haven't really dated since she died, right?"

Ben shrugged. "I keep meaning to."

"Uh-huh. So Faith was really the only woman in your life."

Ben nodded. "Yeah," he said. "I guess that's true." He looked embarrassed. "I guess that's pathetic, huh."

"That's wonderful," Chloë said. "To have had that one great love."

"It could have been wonderful," Ben said. "If I didn't mess it up."

"Oh, Ben," Chloë said. "Stop it. Faith made her own choices."

"I don't know," Ben said. "I think I helped her along."

"Oh, stop," Chloë said. "She was an adult, Ben. She made her own decisions."

"I guess."

Chloë followed Ben's gaze, over the hills of Amherst toward the town. The sun was disappearing over the Berkshires.

"What's your best memory from college?"

"What?"

"You know, the thing you remember the best from that whole time in your life."

"I don't know."

"Well, what's the first thing that comes to mind?"

"The first thing. I'm trying to think of something besides studying, drinking. Well there was this one night, just before I graduated. I was the opinion page editor of the Middlebury *Campus*, you know, the paper. And on that last night, this must have been the middle of May I guess, we put the last edition of the paper to bed before we graduated, turned off the typositor, turned out the lights of the *Campus* office, and went outside. It was five A.M., and the sun was coming up and we all went over to the editor's house and had pancakes. I left there, I guess it was like six-thirty in the morning by then, birds were singing, there was light all around and it occurred to me then that I should ask Faith to marry me. So I went over to Weybridge and woke her up and proposed."

"And she accepted."

"No, she thought I was nuts and told me to go to bed."

"So you went home."

"No, so I climbed into bed with her and we made love."

Chloë smiled. "That's nice."

"We were lying there afterward when she turned to me and said yes."

Chloë put her arm on Ben's shoulder.

"You loved her a lot, didn't you?"

Ben nodded.

"You haven't been in love with anyone since she died."

Ben nodded again.

Chloë stroked his shoulder, ran her fingers up to his ear and touched the side of Ben's neck.

"Do you think it would be hard, to fall in love with someone else?"

Ben took her hand.

"No, I don't think so," he said, quietly. "I'm just a little worried about our motivations, that's all."

"Our motivations?"

"I just want to make sure that if anything happens, it's not because we're trying to hurt Lefty. I don't want to do this if this is about Lefty."

Chloë turned toward Ben, moved closer to him. Her hair fell against his neck. "Ben," she whispered. "This isn't about him."

They sat there for a very long time, not quite kissing. He felt her breath on his face.

"What should we do?" Ben whispered.

"I don't know," Chloë said. She pulled back from him, looked around nervously. "Maybe we wait for an opportunity."

"An opportunity," said Ben. It was hard to believe this was happening. He had forgotten what it was like, having someone who liked him.

"Tomorrow, when they're all off on their tours. I'll meet you in the Winnebago. Okay?"

Ben nodded. "Okay," he said.

Chloë leaned forward suddenly and kissed him. She put her hand on the back of his neck. Ben felt her breasts pressing against his chest.

The sun was nearly gone now. Students on their way to dining halls passed them by.

Chloë stood up, breaking the embrace. She looked around her at the beautiful campus. "I hope Allison comes here," she said. "I could get to like this place."

"Well," Ben said, his voice hoarse. He looked at the spire of the chapel above him. It was square, wooden, strangely austere. "It's supposed to be a good school," he said, but in the same moment it occurred to him that he did not remember, exactly, where they were.

Allison sat on the quad, playing her guitar. *Down in the valley, valley so low. Lean your head over, hear the wind blow.*

This Martin twelve-string was a beautiful instrument. She still wasn't sure why Lefty had gotten it for her. He said he'd driven around Williamstown while everyone was doing the Williams tour, saw it in the window of a pawn shop. It was a little sad, to have a guitar from a pawn shop. It had belonged to someone else.

Lean your head over, lean your head low. Lean your head low, dear, lean your head low.

She liked Amherst. It was like going to college up in the middle of the sky. Maybe this would be a better place to go than Middlebury after all. Her memories of Middlebury were all dented now, tied up with her aggravation with Polo. She remembered going in to her interview without having slept with anyone. The whole time she was trying to answer the interviewer's questions, she was thinking, Can he tell? Does he know that I'm a child?

What was the story with boys? she wondered. She felt sorry for them sometimes, the way they were constantly at the mercy of their penises. Like some slobbering husky dog always yanking on its leash. It was no wonder they were disgusting. That was why she liked boys, out of sympathy, mostly. You had to admire the way they pretended to act like humans.

She thought about Dylan, who seemed so decent, considering what he had to work with. She was glad to have gotten to know him on this trip. It would be sad to part tomorrow.

"Allison," said a voice.

Oh, thank you, God, she thought.

Chloë sat down on the bench next to her daughter.

"Oh, it's you, Mom," Allison said.

"You sound disappointed."

"I'm not."

"Everyone's waiting for you, honey."

"Okay," said Allison. "I guess you want me to get going."

Chloë shrugged. "Soon," she said.

Allison looked at her mother.

"Are you okay, Mom?"

"Okay?"

"Yeah. You look kind of out of it."

"Do I? I don't know. I've been thinking."

"About what?"

"All sorts of things. You, me. College. The future."

"Yeah, well, me too," said Allison. She strummed her guitar.

"That sounds pretty."

"It's a beautiful guitar. I can't believe somebody would pawn it."

"Well, you never know. Somebody needed the money, I guess."

"Yeah. It makes it a little sad, maybe, that someone had to pawn their guitar, especially a Martin." She looked at the guitar, which had fingernail scratches around the soundhole. "You can tell it's been played a lot."

The twilight was falling on the campus. It was time to leave. From the remains of Stearns' Chapel, a bellringer rang chimes. Allison looked toward the chapel. Dylan was walking over the ridge toward the camper.

Allison held the neck of her guitar.

"Hey, Mom," she said. "Can I ask you something?"

"Sure, honey."

"What would you do if you were in love with two people at once?"

Chloë's face flushed. "I don't know," she said quickly. "That's hard, when that happens. Has that happened to you, honey?"

"I don't know," Allison said. "Maybe it's not that I'm in love with two people at once. Maybe I'm in love with someone other than the person I'm going out with. Can you imagine what that's like?"

Chloë nodded. "I can imagine it," she said.

Allison looked at her mother. "Mom, do you like Polo?"

"Like him? Sure, I like him."

"Would you want me to marry him?"

"Marry him?" Chloë looked like she had swallowed her tongue. "You want to marry him?"

"I used to want to," Allison said. "Now I'm not sure."

"Why not?"

"I don't know. The longer we're together, the less I feel like I know him."

"I understand." The shadows were lengthening. Above them in the purple sky stars were beginning to appear. "No, Ally, I don't want you to marry Polo."

"Why not?"

"I can't say, sweetheart. He's just not who I see you with."

Allison strummed a chord. "I'm not sure," she said. "I'm not sure I see me with him either. Isn't that weird? To be with somebody and not want to be with them?"

Chloë nodded. "It's weird all right," she said. Allison put the Martin back in the case.

"I guess we have to go, huh."

"We should, honey. It's getting dark."

Allison closed the latches. They started walking north across the quad. There was the sound of stereos playing from dorms.

As they walked, Chloë had a sudden recollection of her

daughter's first week of life. The sad vigil she and Gary endured in the hospital. The baby's heartbeat sky-high, all those tubes and wires connected to her tiny arms and legs. Where is that child now? Chloë thought. Where is that mother? She looked at the stars above them and thought of Planet X.

"Hey, Mom," Allison said. "Why do you think Lefty bought me this guitar?" She stumbled for a moment, and the Martin rang inside its case.

"I don't know, honey," Chloë said. She put her arms around her daughter, to steady her. "It's a mystery."

They were driving south toward Connecticut. Lefty was behind the wheel. Dylan sat in the rear of the Winnebago, looking out the window. Everyone else was in their bunks, the folding doors pulled shut.

"Hey, son," said Ben, sitting down next to the boy.

"Hey, Dad," said Dylan, glancing up at him.

"How you doing? You okay?"

"I'm all right," said Dylan.

"I just wanted to say—" Ben said, stuttering. Oh my god, Dylan thought. Here comes trouble. "I just wanted to say I'm sorry."

Dylan nodded. "Thanks, Dad. But you don't have to apologize."

"I didn't know how much you loved her."

Dylan paused. He suddenly realized he wasn't sure exactly what they were talking about.

"How much I loved her," Dylan said.

"I mean, I never even met her. I wish you'd brought her over. Introduced me to her. I mean, it's my fault for not being more open. It's just I've been working so hard." Ben let his head collapse onto his hands. "Working all the time, for nothing."

"It's all right, Dad," Dylan said.

"It's a terrible thing, to lose someone you love, so young."

Dylan nodded. "It's terrible all right," he said.

"You never get over it. Not really."

"I guess not."

"This Brenda. She was in your class?"

Dylan paused. Like headlights shining through fog, some vague idea of the subject of their conversation began to appear. They were talking about his girlfriend, Brenda. Who had died so suddenly. When she had been bitten by a diseased chimpanzee.

"No, Dad," he said. "She wasn't in my class, not exactly."

Ben took his son's hand and held it. "I want you to know I'm going to be there for you. Okay?"

"Okay, Dad," said Dylan. "Thanks." It was touching, actually, the way his father was reaching out to him, even though he was all broken up about the death of someone imaginary.

"I'm serious," Ben said. "I'm going to change. You'll see."

"It's all right," Dylan said.

"You think it's too late?" Ben said. "For me to be a good father?"

Dylan didn't know what to say. "No," he said.

"Good," said Ben. "Good." His face jerked suddenly with his nervous tic. "You know, we should talk more. Share our feelings. It's no good, keeping everything inside. From now on, no more secrets between us, all right?"

"All right," said Dylan.

"Whoo," said Ben, rubbing his hand across his face. "This is hard."

"Hey, Dad," said Dylan. "You really don't want there to be secrets between us?"

Ben looked at his son. "Is there something you want to tell me, son?"

Dylan heard the sound of the tires humming against the road beneath them. It seemed like they had been living on this Winnebago for a long time.

"Yes," he said. "There's something."

"What is it?"

Dylan tried to find the words. He thought about his mother and Uncle Lefty, lying there in that old farmhouse. Running from the scene with Juddy, wrestling by the stream. *You listen to me*, Juddy said. *We never tell anybody about this, ever. You understand?*

"What is it, son?"

Dylan felt his heart beating in his throat. He suddenly had the feeling that his entire life was leading up to this point, to the words he was about to say.

"I really loved her."

Ben opened his mouth and shut it. Tears came to his eyes. He reached out and hugged his boy. Dylan felt his father holding him. No one was more surprised than Dylan about the sudden turn of events.

"Oh, Dylan," he said. "Oh, my poor boy. I'm so sorry."

"It's okay," Dylan said, but even as he said it, he choked. Tears were coming to his eyes. He was getting all broken up about an imaginary world.

"It's a terrible thing," Ben said. "To lose someone you love."

wesleyan university

Students tend to stay on campus as, according to one student, the surrounding community of Middletown is "the deadest town I've ever been in all my life."
—*Insider's Guide to the Colleges*, 1998

Middletown, Connecticut
Number of applications: 5,482
Percent accepted: 36%
Mean SAT, 1996: 620V, 660M
Most popular major: English
Mascot: the Cardinals

t hey spent the morning in Hartford visiting the Mark Twain House, and bought some T-shirts. Then they got back on the Winnebago and passed lakes and streams and shopping malls, a Bess Eaton doughnuts, then drove up a hill and under a bridge. There was a slightly sad sign: WELCOME TO MIDDLETOWN: A MAJOR SEAPORT OF THE 18TH CENTURY. On their left was a submarine museum, then a Dunkin' Donuts, then a traffic light. On the right was a group of buildings that looked like a science-fiction penitentiary. WESLEYAN UNIVERSITY, a sign read. ARTS CENTER.

They turned right on High Street, passed the Honors College with its long white columns, the Malcolm X House and DKE and the Romance languages building. There were columns and widow's walks. Chloë held a map in one hand. They turned right on Wyllys Avenue and came up behind the hideous Arts Center complex again and parked the Winnebago in a parking lot near the admissions office.

It was just before 3:00. Polo put on his last clean black turtleneck. Allison wore a peasant skirt and a sweater. Juddy put on a sweatshirt that read BUM, then slung his fencing equipment in a bag over his shoulder. Dylan donned a blue oxford shirt and a tie. Ben wore a tie and a V-neck sweater. Lefty wore a vinyl windbreaker. Only Chloë stayed in her old things. She was going to stay here, she said, on the Winnebago, feeling as she did a little unusual.

Allison was ready to go before the others and walked out into a field in the Arts Center with her guitar and sat down to play. It was a strange scene, this long green field, surrounded on three sides by the cubical buildings of the arts complex, made of badly poured concrete and limestone. It must have looked very modern twenty years ago, she thought. On the fourth side of the field was the street with the Winnebago, the old buildings of the college towering behind it.

Allison sang, *"The river is wide. I cannot cross 'oer. And neither have I wings to fly. Build me a boat that can carry two. And both shall row, my love and I."*

"Whoa," said a voice. "That's like, so retro!"

Allison looked up. A young man carried an oddly shaped drum. He had beads, several earrings, blue eyes.

"Thanks," Allison said.

"It's so retro, it's outré!" the young man said.

Allison nodded. She started to play again. *"I leaned my back up against an oak, thinking it was a trusty tree. But first it swayed, and then it broke, and so did my true love to me."*

The young man began to play the African drum with a strange drumstick that had a right angle in it. A moment later several other students walking nearby came and sat down in the field next to them. Two of these were other African drummers, a man and a woman. The third was a man with a blonde crewcut who played the trombone.

"Yikes," said the man with the trombone. "It's so utterly—something!"

Allison sang. *"Oh, love is handsome, and love is kind, just like a jewel when first it's new. But love grows old, and love grows cold, and fades away like the morning dew."*

They all sang the chorus together, except for the trombonist. They smiled at the words, as if they had a meaning other than the one intended.

A moment later two other students came along. One carried a strangely shaped gong. The other had a bamboo flute. They listened to the music, then began to play.

It was getting harder and harder for Allison to hear the Martin. This wasn't necessarily all bad. It was a strange and wonderful collection of instruments around her. Well, damn, Allison thought. Maybe this is what college is like, everybody playing gongs.

A woman with a set of bagpipes approached them. She stood several feet behind the group, placed the reed in her mouth, and began to blow. A tremendous blast issued from the pipes.

Everyone else stopped playing, and looked at her.

"Hey, man," said the first African drummer. "Cool your jets."

The bagpiper stopped, looked dejected. "Sorry," she said, and walked away. The others looked at each other with sarcasm and disbelief.

"Some people," the drummer said.

"Hey, man, you're good," said the guy with the gong.

"Thanks," said Allison.

"I love that guitar," said the female drummer. "You don't see many old Martins like that."

"My stepdad got it for me," said Allison.

"Whoa," said the trombonist. "He must be pretty cool."

There was a thundering honk from the Winnebago. Lefty rolled down the window. "Hey, c'mon, kid! Slap some bacon on a biscuit! We're burnin' daylight!"

"Who's that," the drummer said, wrinkling her nose.

"That's him," Allison said.

"Whoa," said the boy with the earrings. "He's so totally—postmodern!"

"He's postmodern all right," Allison said, standing up.

"Are you going to the jam on Indian Hill?" said the Indian flautist. "You heard about it?"

"No," Allison said. "I didn't hear about it."

"Tonight's the full moon," the flautist continued. "Harvest moonrise, same time as the sunset. A bunch a us are going up to the cemetery, to make a bunch a noise, you should come."

Allison looked ashamed. "I'm not sure if we're still going to be here then. We probably have to leave right after my interview."

"Interview," the trombonist said. "You're like, a prospective!"

Allison nodded miserably.

"No way!" said the female drummer. "You look just like a Wesleyan woman!"

"Well, maybe," Allison said.

"You come here, you can major in ethnomusicology," said the flautist. "That's our thing."

"Ethnomusicology?" Allison said.

Lefty honked the horn of the Winnebago again.

"Yeah." She pointed around the circle. "Navatzio here does African drumming, Rob's in the jazz band. Spiro and Helene are African drummers. Tim there is in the Javanese gamelan."

"Gamelan?" Allison said, vacantly.

"Gong orchestra," Tim said. "From Bali."

"Ah," Allison said.

"I'm working on a piece," Tim said, "called, *I Tim Am Now a Channel for the Music That Comes Through the Light*."

"Are you?" said Allison.

"And me," said the flautist, "I'm doing Indian flute."

Allison looked around at them. A Wesleyan woman, she thought. They said I looked like a Wesleyan woman.

"Who was the bagpiper?" she said.

They all shrugged. "Some weirdo," the flautist said.

"I have to go now," Allison said, putting her guitar back in its case. "But you're all really nice. I hope I get to see you next year or something."

"You should go here," the flautist said. "You'd like it."

"Don't forget the jam tonight in the graveyard. If you

head toward the athletic center, you'll see the driveway. Or you can take the shortcut through the tennis courts."

"Okay," Allison said. "I'd like that."

The group of students looked at Allison for a moment, as she walked away from them toward the Winnebago. Then they turned back to their instruments and began to play.

"**H**ey, everyone," said the guide. They stood by a kiosk on College Row. "My name is Phoebe, I'm your tour guide."

Phoebe had shoulder-length hair that had been dyed bright blonde at one point. It had grown out now, though, so that her hair was blonde only from her ears down. The whole top third was brown.

Juddy, Allison, Polo, Dylan, Ben, and Lefty stood in a wide semicircle. Phoebe wore a loose orange T-shirt and black jeans. Phoebe had giant black boots on, too, the kind you'd expect to see on someone jumping out of an airplane.

Phoebe dropped a pencil and leaned over to pick it up. As she did so, among the six people in the tour only Juddy failed to notice that Phoebe was (a) not wearing a bra and (b) had some kind of tattoo on her breast.

Phoebe stood up. "So this is College Row," she said. "The oldest part of the college. All of these buildings are made of Portland brownstone. You're standing in front of North College, which is where admissions is, and next to it, South College, which is the president's office. The top of South College holds the Butterfield Carillon, which has the world's only rosewood clavier."

"What's a carillon?" said Lefty.

"Bells," said Phoebe. "They're pretty. I'm one of the

bellringers, so if anybody's interested you can come with me after the tour and I'll play."

"That sounds great," said Allison.

"I've got an interview at four," said Polo.

"Mine's at five," said Dylan.

"Whatever." Phoebe turned and walked toward the chapel. It struck Dylan that she was the first tour guide he'd seen who walked forward.

They walked past South College. Juddy's fencing equipment rattled in its bag. "On your right," Phoebe said, "the Douglas Cannon."

On a brownstone pedestal were two bronze fixtures that at one time had held a very small cannon. A plaque affixed to the base of the pedestal read THE DOUGLAS CANNON: BORN IN OBSCURITY • REARED IN STRIFE • TEMPERED BY TRAVEL • NEVER DISCOURAGED • HOME AT LAST.

"I don't get it," said Lefty. "Where's the cannon?"

"It's been stolen," Phoebe said.

"That's too bad," said Ben.

"It's supposed to be stolen," Phoebe explained.

"Who stole it?" asked Polo. "Vandals?"

"No one knows who steals it. Various people. Every now and again it shows up. Then someone steals it again. Last time anyone saw it, it had been given as a gift to Andrei Gromyko. The Soviet foreign minister. Wesleyan's president had to get Senator Spoont to ask for it back. It was kind of a scandal."

They stood around looking at the empty pedestal.

"So did you get it back?" Lefty said. He looked concerned.

"Oh, sure," said Phoebe, leading them onward. "But then someone stole it again. I think it showed up for a couple minutes when President Bennet was inaugurated. That's Wesleyan's president. Then it got stolen again."

"That's some cannon," Lefty said, nodding.

"It's kind of every student's ambition," Phoebe said. "Someday, to steal the Douglas Cannon."

"You hear that, Welly?" said a voice. "You come heah, someday yuh can swipe a lil' ol' cannon."

Ben recognized the voice. Oh, no, he thought. Please let it not be.

"Hey, folks," said Phoebe. "You want to join the tour?"

Captain Bedford shrugged. "I guess."

"Hi, Polo," said Welly, smiling at him.

"Greetings," Polo said.

"You know her?" Allison said.

"Yes, we met at Amherst."

"We spent an afternoon together," said Welly, with a big sigh. "I'll never forget."

"On your right is Memorial Chapel," Phoebe said. "Built to honor Wesleyan's casualties in the Civil War."

"Well we oughta set a while in there," Captain Bedford said bitterly. "Think about that bastard Sherman."

"What do you mean you'll never forget?" Allison said.

"Hello, Captain," Ben said.

"Ah, Ben Floyd," said Captain Bedford. "I want a word with you."

"You do?"

"Indeed." Captain Bedford looked around. "Where's your wife?"

Lefty put his hands in his pockets.

"My wife?"

"That woman, I thought she was your wife."

"You mean Chloë? My sister-in-law, Chloë?"

"Your sister-in-law you say," Captain Bedford said.

"We had a good talk," Polo said to Allison. "Welly and I did. In the chapel at Amherst."

Welly giggled. "We did! We had a talk!"

"On your right is the '92 Theater." Phoebe pointed to

a building covered in thick ivy. "This was originally the college library, transformed into a small theater by the class of 1892. It's one of two theaters on campus, the other being the larger and more sophisticated CFA theater in the Arts Center."

They looked at the old building.

"I love talking," said Welly.

"Next building is Orange Judd Hall, home of the psychology department."

"Doesn't look orange," said Captain Bedford, suspiciously.

"Orange was his name," Phoebe said. She looked at her watch.

Allison looked at Polo and crossed her arms. "I'm glad you got to talk to Polo," she said to Welly. "He's quite a conversationalist, isn't he?"

"He's very sympathetic," Welly said, grinning.

"What did you say?" said Ben. "You wanted a word with me?"

"Yes," said Captain Bedford. "If you don't mind."

Ben looked like the Captain was about to strike him. "I said I was sorry."

"Yes, indeed," Captain Bedford said. "Well, if you don't mind I'd like a word. In private. Sir."

Dylan looked at the man with aggravation. Just once, he thought. Just once I'd like to see my father punch somebody in the nose.

"Come on, folks," Phoebe said. "We have to keep moving."

Ben looked at Dylan helplessly. He didn't want to leave his boy.

"Dad, it's okay," said Dylan. "I don't mind."

"Go on, Ben," Lefty said. "Sock 'em."

Allison walked quickly toward the front of the group.

Somehow it figured that things would end this way, the adults punching each other in the face.

"All right already," Ben said. He stepped off the path. "I'll meet up with you later, Dylan."

Welly didn't notice as her father left the tour. She walked next to Polo, looking at him with undisguised desire.

Dylan walked on, without his father.

From a building on their left, at the end of the large green, a bunch of naked guys jumped up and down on a roof.

"Hey," Juddy said. "What's that?"

Phoebe glowered. "Chi Psi," she said, and shook her head. "A frat."

From the windows of Chi Psi came the sound of Lynyrd Skynyrd.

"Hey," Juddy said. "This Chi Psi. They let anybody in?"

"I don't know," Phoebe said, turning right at the end of Judd Hall and moving the tour up a small hill. "I think you have to get chosen."

Juddy shook his head. "Figures," he said.

"Oh, Juddy," Polo said. "I'm sure they'd let you in. Once they hear about your fencing and everything."

There was the sound of glass breaking from inside the Chi Psi building. As they walked up the hill toward Olin Library and the Science Center, Juddy looked over his shoulder toward the fraternity. His foils were heavy in the athletic bag. He felt a strange sensation in his gut, as he watched the naked, yelling guys throw a couch out a window. It was homesickness.

Chloë took off her shirt and bra and brushed out her hair. Then she stepped out of her jeans and underwear and looked at herself, briefly, in the full-length mirror on the Winnebago's wall. Well, here I am, she thought. It wasn't a bad body. We've had some good adventures together, you and I, over the last fifty years. You think this is bad? We've been through this and worse. Sometimes she felt as if her body were some old pal she'd served with during the War. *You and me, we were in the big one together.*

From outside came the sound of Javanese gamelan, bagpipes, and bongos. She peered out the window and saw a bunch of kids playing instruments in a field. Someone was flying a kite. A dog was chasing a Frisbee. There wasn't any sign of Ben yet.

Chloë walked over to her daughter's bed and picked up the guitar. It was a beautiful old instrument. She sat down on the side of Allison's mattress, let her red fingernails strum the strings. Chloë had played the guitar years ago, back when she and Gary were married. It was something she'd let go of, though, especially since Allison was the musician now. It was sad, if you thought about it, that she'd lost the gift of music.

She played a chord. "O.K.," she sang. "*O.K. Corral, corral.*" It was the song she'd heard in that old movie the other day. "*Wyatt's lady fair, he left her crying there, he broke his vow, and rode away to Tombstone.*"

She stopped playing, sat there for a moment with one breast falling down over the top of the guitar. I feel like a painting, she thought. The realization did not cheer her. From outside came the music of young people.

Phoebe, the tour guide, walked with Allison, Dylan, Polo, Juddy, Welly, and Lefty through a dark tunnel. There was surreal and chaotic graffiti on the walls, in layer upon layer, like the hieroglyphics of a doomed civilization.

"These are the famous West College tunnels. They

connect the ten Foss Hill dormitories and run all the way from Foss One, across the street from the Science Center, to the other side of the campus at Foss Ten, across from Mocon.''

''Mocon?'' said Allison.

''The dining hall,'' said Phoebe. ''Looks like a flying saucer.''

''Excuse me,'' Polo said. ''My interview is at four.''

''Okay,'' said Phoebe. ''We ought to send you guys on your way. Next exit we pass I'll tell you where to go.''

''Okay,'' said Dylan.

They walked onward through the dark tunnels. On the wall were various messages, including *The beds are too narrow here*, and *Do not imagine that you can survive in the vampire economy*, and *To see the sky again*. There were the prophesies and drawings and jokes and hogwash, one phrase written atop the other. The net effect was somewhat frightening, especially since many of the lightbulbs down here appeared to be broken or missing.

Ahead of them came a churning, looming sound. They walked past a dimly lit room, suds on the floor.

''Laundry,'' said Phoebe.

Just past that it was even darker. There was a faroff sound of bells and bumpers.

''Pinball,'' said Phoebe.

They passed a room lit only by the red glow of the Fireball machine. A man with dirty clothes and a beard stood there, juking.

''Some of these guys are real addicts,'' Phoebe warned. ''They hoard quarters. Forget about doing laundry.''

A sign ahead read EXIT. ''Okay,'' Phoebe said, turning to Polo. ''You go up these stairs, you'll come out at the end of Foss Five. Go up toward the observatory, then go down the hill. You'll see it.''

Polo started up the stairs.

"I'm going with you, Polo," Welly said.

Allison watched the girl scurry after him.

"If you wish," said Polo, pretending to be casual.

"You think they have a chapel here?" said Welly. "I'd love taking a look at the chapel. Compare it with the one at Amherst."

"I already showed you the chapel," said Phoebe, annoyed.

"Not the inside," said Welly.

"I think I'll head back, too," said Lefty. See how Chloë's doin'. You okay on your own, Allison?"

"I'm okay," said Allison, in a small voice.

"She's not on her own," said Dylan.

"That's right," said Juddy. "You still got me!" He grinned.

"And me," said Dylan.

Lefty, Welly, and Polo vanished up the stairs. The others entered a passage completely devoid of light.

For a long time they walked through the darkness. Sound echoed and reverberated in the pitch-black space. At one point, as Allison stumbled, Dylan heard her cry out.

"Hey," he said. "You okay?"

"I'm all right. I just can't see anything. Is that you?"

He felt her take his hand.

"It's me," he said.

"Is anyone else there? Hello?"

There was silence. Phoebe had ditched them.

"Oh my god," Allison said. "We're lost."

Dylan held her hand. "We're not lost," he said.

They walked forward through the dark. At the end of a long passage they suddenly saw the red glow of an exit sign.

Dylan and Allison, fingers joined, walked through the tunnel toward the light.

"I wanted to tell you I'm sorry," she said, softly.

"About what?" Dylan said. They were getting near to the exit now.

"About Brenda. Juddy told me the news. I don't know how you're managing to keep going."

They opened the door. Light from outside shone down the staircase.

"Allison, listen," Dylan said, as they walked up the stairs. "There isn't any Brenda."

"What?" said Allison. "You mean she's okay?"

"No. I mean she doesn't exist. I made her up, just so you wouldn't think I was stupid."

They reached the top of the stairs. Juddy was sitting there, waiting for them.

"There isn't any Brenda?"

"No. I just made her up."

Allison looked at Dylan. "So you're saying there isn't any Brenda?"

Dylan nodded. For the first time in a week he felt happy. "No Brenda," he said, and smiled.

"You," Allison said, thinking it over. "You son of a bitch." She reached back, grimaced, and slugged him.

Dylan fell back down the stairs.

"Jesus," Allison said, storming away. "I give up!"

Dylan got to his feet and limped up the stairs. Juddy was waiting for him at the top.

"What did I tell you, Dickweed," said Juddy. "I told you I was going to do you a favor."

"A favor," Dylan said. "Thanks a million, Juddy."

"Oh, don't worry about her," said Juddy, looking after Allison, who was still storming away from them. "She's crazy about you."

"What makes you think that? She hates me now. You understand?"

"Now, now, Dickweed. She wouldn't have punched you if she didn't love you."

Dylan looked at his cousin. "You're insane, aren't you?" he said.

Juddy smiled. "Yup," he said.

"**N**ow then," Captain Bedford said. "Let's finish this business."

Ben took off his sweater, folded it over the arm of a bench at the edge of the long green.

"Fine," Ben said. "Give it your best shot, Bedford."

The Captain looked at him, and laughed.

"You're serious, aren't you, sir. Prepared for fisticuffs, are you?"

"I don't know if I'm prepared," Ben said. "I just want to have done with you, all right?"

"Oh, for heaven's sakes, stop," said Bedford. "Cease and desist." He looked at Ben with derision.

"Come on," Ben said. "Take your best shot."

"Mr. Floyd," Bedford said. "I'm a former captain in the United States Marines. You're supposin' I'm unaccustomed to the arts of combat?"

"Shut up," Ben said. "You know somebody ought to take a pin and pop you like a balloon."

Captain Bedford laughed heartily. "Exactly!" he shouted. "That is what you have done, precisely!"

Ben lowered his fists somewhat. "I have?"

"Stop," Bedford said. "Let us be seated." He nodded toward the bench. "Like civilized gentlemen."

Ben sighed. "Whatever." He looked at his watch. "I have to go soon, actually."

"Indeed, well you should go as you please. It wasn't my intention to get you all riled up."

"Well, what was your intention?"

The Captain sighed. "Well, I suppose I wanted to thank you for your words the other day. They weren't totally ignorant."

"They weren't?" said Ben. He looked at this strange man with the red face and the string tie. "They weren't."

"I apologize for responding in a manner that was gruff. It's not in my nature to take criticism, I reckon."

"Well, I just told you what I was thinking. Maybe it wasn't any of my business, I don't know."

"But you spoke the truth. The only way to get Welly to live her life is to give her some responsibility."

"Well, I'm glad you see it that way. She'll be happier, going to a school of her own choice."

"But that's just it. I told her about my change of heart, that I wanted her to make her own decisions. The change in her character has been enormous. The last day or so she's been walkin' around like some kitten, snagged the catnip!"

"Well, that's great, Captain. You'll be glad she's made her choice. Whether it's Bowdoin, Colby, Dartmouth, or whatever."

"But that's just the thing, Floyd. Now she says she's going to Emory."

"Emory? In Atlanta?"

"Exactly."

Ben looked at him blankly. "Well," he said. "I'm glad it's all working out."

From the Chi Psi house behind them came the sound of a couch being pushed out a window and falling onto the sidewalk.

"Now then," said the Captain. "I've been thinking. I've got a little business, Bedford Smithfield, perhaps you're familiar with it."

Ben nodded. It was not a little business.

"Well, the fellow I've got running it, he doesn't know a damn thing. I've got a mind to put you in charge, have you run the show. Does that sound interesting?"

Ben nodded. It sounded interesting. "Captain Bedford."

"Jack," the Captain said. "You call me Jack."

"Jack—" Ben said.

"No, no, don't thank me. You're a good man. I can see that. Those varmints up at Ventura cut you off, no reason. They'll regret that. You'll do well with our little company, there's plenty to do." Captain Bedford stood up. "Don't thank me," he said.

"Thank you," Ben said. "Thank you."

"I said don't thank me," Bedford said, shaking his head. "Now let's get out of here. Sooner I'm out of this Wesleyan the better."

A beer keg came sailing out a window and rolled down the green grass.

"Thugs," Captain Bedford muttered. "Look at them."

"Yeah," Ben said, turning with him to look at the fraternity house. "Bunch of vandals." There was loud music, the sound of glass breaking, something exploding. A woman screamed. The two men stood there looking at the house, wishing that they were young.

"Okay, Mr. Floyd," said Polo. "Thanks for walking us down."

"Hey, no problem," said Lefty. "Nice campus they got here, reminds me of that Epcot Center. You think that, this place looks like Epcot?"

"Mr. Floyd," said Welly. "It doesn't look anything like Epcot."

"Well, I've never been there, so I wouldn't know." He scratched his head.

"It was nice to meet you," said Welly.

"We'll see you," said Polo.

"Okay," Lefty said. "Good luck, kids!"

Welly and Polo walked toward the admissions office. Lefty watched them recede, then headed in the direction of South College. It was a beautiful day. The sun was going down behind him now, behind the big graveyard beyond the observatory. He walked toward the pedestal next to the flagpole. There were the green fittings for the missing cannon.

He stared at the place where the Douglas Cannon wasn't. Strange tradition, he thought, some cannon that kept getting stolen. But colleges seemed full of such things. Throwing watches off of steeples. The Babson Anti-Gravity Stone. Gamaliel Painter's cane.

He turned around and looked at the sun going down behind the observatory. It was a lovely thing, the round-roofed observatory atop the hill. It would have been nice, he thought, to have gone to school at a place like this. It would have been nice to have spent a few years talking about narratology and metaphysics, instead of demonstrating the intricacies of antilock brakes and air bags.

At that moment a bell in South College pealed, loudly. He stopped to listen to it ring.

That girl, Lefty thought. Phoebe, her name was. He would walk back to the Winnebago in a moment, find Chloë. But first he would climb these stairs, go all the way up to the top. He didn't think he'd have this opportunity again in life, to watch a young woman, ringing bells.

Ben walked across the campus, whistling. He passed Judd Hall, the '92 Theater, Memorial Chapel, South College, North College, some old athletic building that looked defunct. There across Wyllys Avenue was the Winnebago. A woman on Rollerblades, ski poles in hand, rushed past him. Ben started to cross the street and watched the woman glide toward a line of dormitories on the hill. She must be training for the ski team, he thought.

He thought about Chloë, lying naked in her bed, waiting for him.

Ben reached the other side of the street and paused. There was something back there. He waited, stared toward the place where she had gone. He remembered the lines of her skis, trailing across that frozen pond in Vermont, coming to the place where the ice had broken.

He looked at the Winnebago. Chloë was inside. Do you think it would be hard, she'd asked, to fall in love with someone again? No, I don't think it would be hard at all. He thought about Chloë, her wonderful curves, those sweet eyes with the lines around them. He remembered the feeling of her fingers against his neck.

They could live in the country, in the suburbs around Atlanta. With any luck he'd be able to do a lot of the work for Bedford Smithfield from home, send it all in via modem. On the days that he did have to leave her, he could bring things home after work. Flowers. A chicken. This time he wouldn't put work ahead of his love. They'd take trips—Venice, Nepal, Alaska. They'd sit on deck chairs on cruise ships drinking rum. Every couple of months Dylan would come home, Dylan and Allison. It would be amazing to watch them grow, become adults.

It would be the easiest thing in the world, to live this life. All he'd have to do would be to walk into the Winnebago and make love to her. To do to his own brother what his brother had once done to him.

The skier on her Rollerblades returned down the street. She rushed past Ben, stabbing the pavement with her poles. Ben felt the whoosh of air as she passed him by.

He thought of Lake Dunmore, the surface crashing open.

Ben felt himself slowly turning. Son of a bitch, he thought. He took a step forward, back in the direction he had come. A moment later he had crossed the street. Son of a goddamned bitch.

The Winnebago faded behind him. Ben scuffed his feet angrily against the sidewalk. You see? There's nothing in the world worth having, he thought, that you can actually put your fingers on.

He walked back down College Row, unsure now of his destination. He thought about Faith, how he'd lost her twice. Once when she'd fallen through the ice. And the summer before that, when she'd slept with his brother. Ben shook his head. Even now it made his cheeks burn. That had been the worst time in his life, much worse than this. The only good thing about the whole affair, if you could call it good, was that Dylan never found out about it. No matter what else happens, Ben thought, at least Dylan still had the image of his mother the way she was— young, uncorrupted, still true. He was proud of this much, anyway. He had protected his son from shame.

A moment later he saw the tour guide, Phoebe, walking toward him. In one hand she held the keys to the bell tower.

"Hey," she said. "What happened to all your friends? Your family?"

"All my friends?" Ben said, forlornly. "I thought they were with you."

"Not anymore," Phoebe said. "We went into the tunnels together, that was the last I saw of them."

"Why? What happened?" He looked alarmed. "Where's my family?"

Phoebe shrugged. "I don't know, man," she said. "They went into a long tunnel. They didn't come out."

*   *   *

"You're going to like Emory," Welly said, sticking her thumbs inside the waistband of her panty hose, sliding the black hose down her thighs. "Atlanta's a great town."

"That's what I've heard," said Polo. He looked out the window of the Middletown Motor Inn, toward the highway, then closed the curtains. "I heard it's a great town." He took off his pants.

"You know what they call it? The Harvard of the South," Welly said. She pulled her sweater off over her head, reached around to unhook her bra.

"The Harvard of the South," said Polo. He unbuttoned his shirt, pulled off his underwear and socks.

"I hope it's okay with you that we blew off your Wesleyan interview. I mean, now that you know you aren't going here."

"Aw," Polo said. "What's an interview, anyway?"

"Emory's got distribution requirements, though," said Welly. Polo sat down naked on the edge of the bed. Welly got down on her hands and knees.

"I don't mind distribution requirements," said Polo. He held her face with his hands. "Gives you a chance to get more well rounded."

"They have seven areas," Welly said, pausing for a moment. She reached forward with one little hand. "Tools of Learning, Historical—excuse me—Historical Perspectives of the Western World, Natural Sciences and Math—" She didn't speak for several moments.

Polo felt his eyelids close. He fell backward, supporting himself against the bed with his elbows. "Historical Perspectives," he said.

"Boy, look at you," Welly said. "You've sure got one, all right!"

"Thank you," said Polo, his eyes still closed. He tried to imagine what he looked like. He envied Welly her ability to see him.

"Then there's Aesthetics and Values."

"Aesthetics—" Polo said quietly.

"Aesthetics and Values," Welly said. What a wonderful, miraculous world, she thought joyfully, this world with men and women in it.

"Values," Polo said. "Oh God yes! Values!"

Polo fell backward on the bedspread.

"Okay, hang on for a second. Ready?"

There was a sound.

"Yow," said Polo.

"Hokey smokes," said Welly, laughing. "Boy, you're really something. You okay?"

"Uh-huh," said Polo.

"I'm just going to bounce up and down here, if that's okay."

"Fine, fine."

"What else am I forgetting? Oh, yeah. Individuals and Society."

"Individuals," Polo said, whispering.

"Oh, man," Welly said, breathlessly. "Man. Are you okay? Okay. Where was I?"

"Individuals," Polo said, his eyes turning red, squinting, "and Society."

"That's like economics, I think. Economics and, whoo. Sociology. Whoo."

"Wait," Polo said. "Wait."

"What's the matter, am I going to lose you? Okay, wait, Polo. Hold on. Can you hold on?" There was a sound not exactly like a cork popping off a champagne bottle. "Please wait, Polo. Okay? Are you waiting?"

"I'm waiting," Polo said.

"Do you want to blow me for a little while?"

"Sure," said Polo. "If you want."

"You just lie there, I'll sit on your face. Is that all right?"

"That's fine," said Polo. "I'll just wait."

Welly walked up the length of his body on her knees. "Okay, I'm lowering the boom!" she said.

Polo said something that was not discernible.

"You're awfully nice," Welly said. She thought. "What am I forgetting? Of course, Health and Physical Education." She clutched on to her own breasts. "Oh, yeah, and you got to take a writing course."

"Nhg," Polo said. "A wrtn crz."

"Those, those, those," Welly whispered. "Those are the—those are the core core core courses."

There was the sound of a key in a lock. Welly turned to look over her shoulder.

"Holy shit," she hissed. "It's my *father*."

"What?" said Polo. He looked up, not sure where he was.

"My father. Hurry. Get out of here. He'll kill you."

The door, unlocked, swung forward, but it was restrained by the draw-chain. "Welly?" Captain Bedford said. "You in there?"

"I'm here!" Welly said. She picked up all of Polo's clothes in her arms, stuffed them into his chest. "Just a second!"

"Open this door," the Captain said.

"Go out the bathroom window," Welly said. "Hurry. I'm not kidding, he really will murder you."

"Who are you talking to?" the Captain shouted. "Open the door this instant!"

Polo stumbled into the bathroom, turned on the light, and shut the door. He pulled on his pants and underwear.

"Just a second, Captain, I'm coming," said Welly. "I'm not even decent!"

Polo opened up the bathroom window. He heard the sound of the chain on the motel door being drawn.

A moment later he was standing outside the Middletown Motor Inn, his shoes in one hand. He ran toward Washington Avenue until he had put some distance between himself and the motel. He paused near a Dunkin' Donuts to put his shoes on.

Well, now what? he thought. Talk about leaving the job half done. He was hornier than ever.

He looked to his right, where a large iron gate stood over the Indian Hill Cemetery. The sun was going down.

Allison, he thought. Of course. The big jam. He crossed the busy street and entered the graveyard.

Well, she'll be glad to see me. Now that I'm my old self again. It would be nice for her, sleeping with me. He smiled and began to run through the headstones toward her.

Captain Bedford stepped into the motel room. His daughter was wrapped up in a sheet. There was a tube of KY jelly on the floor.

"Welly," he said. "What's going on here?"

"I was just going over some things," Welly said, out of breath.

"What things? What things you were going over?"

Welly's cheeks were red. Her hair was tangled. Sweat trickled down her temple.

"Distribution requirements," she said. "At Emory."

"Welly Bedford," the Captain said. He looked around the room, his hands gathering into fists. "Not again." He rushed toward the bathroom, found it empty, with the window open. "Not again!"

He stood there by the bathroom and turned to face his daughter, his hands on his hips. "What am I going to do with you?" he said. "What?"

"But, Daddy," Welly said, sitting down on the bed. Tears gathered in her eyes. "I thought you *wanted* me to go to Emory!"

*   *   *

Dylan sat in the waiting room of the admissions office with a black eye. He couldn't believe some of the courses they offered here. EN 310, Construction of Teenagers. PSYC 363, Dramaturgical Approach Psychology. PHYS 384, Particles, Space-Time, and Symmetry. He couldn't imagine taking a course where you couldn't even understand the title. Maybe that's what you learned by the end of the semester, what the hell it was you were studying.

There was no one else in the waiting room. It looked more or less like all the waiting rooms he'd seen so far, at Yale, Bowdoin, Colby, Middlebury, Williams, Amherst. He was forgetting one. Brown? Had they gone to Brown? He couldn't even remember now.

He wasn't sure what he was going to say about the black eye, if they asked. Maybe he could work it into his interview. Well, you see, this girl I have a crush on punched me because she found out that my dead girlfriend was imaginary. Maybe that's why I should get into college. Because this girl I like slugged me.

No, that's not it. For the hundredth time that week, he wondered, Why should these people care about me? What about me is worth paying attention to? I'm just an American kid. I'm a mess.

It was sad, sitting here, the end of the day. It was strange he hadn't seen Polo or Welly yet. Their interviews were supposed to be over just as his got under way. It was possible they'd crossed paths, something like that.

He remembered coming home from Juddy's house, that hot summer day, driving back home after the terrible thing they'd seen. He and Juddy had spent an hour skimming stones under the covered bridge. His dad had shown up at the end of the day, late as usual, tired. They drove back home, Dylan's cheek leaning against the window. He wanted to warn his father about what he had seen, wanted to unburden himself of the whole awful business, but he had held his tongue. It was the one thing he could do, to do anybody any good. So he said nothing, not then, not even in the terrible months that followed. Even at the funeral, his father putting the rose on the casket, he'd kept his secret.

It struck him now, as he sat here, waiting for another opportunity to explain himself to a stranger, that it was a kind thing he had done, that it was not the way most people would have behaved in the situation. It had been his own choice to bear this burden. This single action, his refusal to open his mouth and hurt his father, maybe this is what made him unique. I ought to tell these bastards, if they ask me, Dylan thought. They want to know why I ought to go to college, I can tell them. I spared my father sorrow.

He saw them, the blurry figures sprawled upon that beat-up bed. Uncle Lefty's face. *You have to love people and forgive them.*

He'd left Uncle Lefty yesterday, walked away from his idiot prophecy and crossed the Amherst campus. Then he'd heard something. Allison singing. He remembered sitting next to her during that class at Colby. That crazy guy standing at the front of the room. *Ridiculous the waste sad time stretching before and after.*

Without deciding to, Dylan suddenly stood up. God damn, he thought. Maybe I'm in the wrong place.

Moments later, a young woman opened the door of the waiting room, reading a file folder. "Dylan Floyd?" she said. There was no response. "Dylan Floyd." She looked up from her folder, to take this young man by the hand, snap him out of whatever reverie he was in.

But the waiting room was empty. The interviewer at Wesleyan looked around the room suspiciously, then turned around, letting the door close softly behind her. Whoever this Dylan Floyd was, she guessed he wasn't coming.

*   *   *

Ben stood in the bell tower. It didn't have any bells in it.

"It's not what I was expecting," he said to Phoebe. "It looks kind of like a classroom, only, I don't know, more run-down." In the middle of the room was something that looked like an organ, except that instead of keys it had long wooden poles, arranged in tiers like the black and white notes of a piano. At the ends of the wooden keys of the clavier were heavy wires that ran up to, and through, the ceiling. An ivy-covered window stood in one wall. There was a small door in the wall opposite this. Next to the door was a smaller version of the clavier that stood in the center of the room, a set of tubular practice chimes. A ladder ran up another wall and disappeared into a trapdoor in the ceiling.

"The bells are up there," Phoebe said, nodding toward the ceiling. "In case you were wondering."

"Are they?" Ben said. "Do you mind if I look at them? I've never seen bells, not like this anyway."

"Be my guest," said Phoebe. "I have to practice something anyway." She sat down at the practice clavier and started punching out a melody. The music rang very softly on the small tubular bells. Ben, meanwhile, walked over to the ladder and climbed toward the ceiling. When he reached the top, he shoved the trapdoor open with one hand, then stepped through the hole and into the tower.

All around him were giant bells, covered with verdigris, hanging from an iron frame, painted orange. Wires ran down from the clappers, through the floor, toward the clavier below. The cupola had diagonal slats cut through it, so that light could shine in. The western side of the bell tower was bright with slanting light. Wind blew through the slats.

On the sides of the bells were inscriptions. FOR THE MAN OF PHILOSOPHY WHO WOULD SEEK TO LEARN ABOUT THE SOURCE OF

REASON, I RING, read one. FOR THE MAN OF RELIGION WHO WOULD SEEK TO KNOW HIS GOD, I RING, read another. There were perhaps twenty-five bells in all. The smaller ones didn't have inscriptions. But the big ones did, each one cast around the rim. The largest bell, nearly five feet wide at the base, read, FOR THE MAN OF POWER, WHO WOULD SEEK NOT TO BE MASTERED BUT TO MASTER, I RING. As he stared at this behemoth, it suddenly swung in its cradle and the clapper struck the girdle of the bell with an enormous, brain-shattering OOONNNNNNGGGGG.

Ben could not hear for a moment, as the bell resonated both inside and outside his skull. His heart was beating quickly from the sudden surprise. He climbed down the ladder, back toward Phoebe. "Hey," he said. "What's the big idea?"

"Sorry," she said, smiling wickedly. "I couldn't resist."

"You bonged me," Ben said, hurt.

Phoebe shrugged. "It happens," she said.

"What's in here?" Ben said, pointing to the small door by the practice chimes.

"Attic of South College," said Phoebe. "There's a mattress in there. I sleep up here once in a while. If I've been studying late."

"You study here?" Ben said.

Phoebe nodded. Looking at her at that moment, Ben saw something in the girl. She spent most of her time up here in the bell tower. He felt sorry for her.

At that moment there was a knock on the door. "Hello?" said Lefty. "Can I come in?"

"Hello, brother," said Ben. Lefty walked into the room. He looked at Phoebe. "Where is everybody?"

Ben thought about Chloë, lying in her bed, alone, back in the Winnebago. He thought about Ventura Monmouth, cutting him off. He thought about his wife, Faith, lying in his brother's arms.

"They're all up in the tower, Lefty," Ben said. "You should take a look around, it's amazing."

"They are?" Lefty said, eyeing the hole in the ceiling.

Phoebe looked at Ben with an odd expression.

"Sure," said Ben. "All the children are waiting for you. Go on up!"

"Okay," said Lefty, grabbing the ladder. "I want to see them."

As Lefty climbed the ladder, Ben reached into his pocket. Lefty reached the trapdoor and stepped through. "Wow," they heard him say. "Look at all the bells."

Ben handed Phoebe a fifty-dollar bill. "Go on," he said. "You're sure?" Phoebe said.

Ben nodded. "Give him the works."

"Hey," Lefty said, from overhead. "Where is everybody?"

Phoebe began to punch the clavier. One after the other the bells swung in their harnesses, gonging against the clappers. It was a tremendous noise, a joyful, ringing cacophony. Mingled among the ringing aftertones was the sound of Lefty screaming.

Phoebe kept playing and playing. I guess she wants to give me my fifty bucks' worth, Ben thought. The young girl had a strange expression on her face. It was as if she'd been waiting her whole life for an opportunity like this.

A moment later a pair of legs appeared in the trapdoor. Lefty was squirming and rushing blindly, like he'd kicked over a bees' nest. His feet kicked around wildly, trying to find the ladder. Phoebe kept on playing.

As Lefty fell off the ladder and plummeted the ten feet onto the floor, Ben realized what song it was the young woman was playing. *Tis a Gift to Be Simple.* You know, Ben thought, as his brother writhed on the floor. I always hated that song.

"Ohhh," Lefty moaned, from the floor. "My ears. My ears."

"Here," Ben said, walking over to his brother. He put out his hand. Lefty clasped it, slowly got to his feet. When Lefty was standing upright again, Ben reached back and made a fist. A moment later he punched Lefty in the jaw. Lefty went down again.

"All right, that's it," Phoebe said. "I don't mind bonging this guy, but if you're just going to punch each other, I'm out of here." She looked angrily at Ben. "Is that what's going to happen now, you're just going to punch each other some more?"

Ben nodded. "I guess," he said sadly.

"Fine," Phoebe said. "Have a ball." She walked toward the door. "Pull this shut when you're done," she said, and left.

Ben turned his back and walked to the window. "Son of a bitch," Ben said. "Goddamn stupid-ass son of a bitch."

"What," Lefty said, moaning from the floor. "What was that for?"

"For everything," Ben said, looking out the vine-entangled window. In the distance he saw the Connecticut River, snaking south.

"What?" Lefty said. "I can't hear anything."

"You what? You can't hear anything?" Ben turned to look at his brother again.

"What?"

Ben leaned over and yelled into his brother's ear. "FOR EVERYTHING."

Lefty sat up, holding his ears. His hair was going in all directions. "I can't hear anything," he said. "I'm deaf."

"Why, Lefty?" Ben said. He kneeled down next to him, shook his head. "Why'd you do it?"

"What?" said Lefty.

"Wreck me? Why? Why do you hate me?"

"What?"

"Why'd you sleep with her, Lefty? What difference was it to you?"

Lefty whispered. "You didn't want her."

"Why'd you shut down my company? Call in the loan?"

Lefty's voice grew even softer. "To take you down a peg."

"Why'd you ruin me? Destroy everything I care about?"

"Because," Lefty said, his voice nearly silent. "You went to college."

"What? Because I what?"

Lefty looked at the floor, his head ringing. Ben didn't think his brother was going to say anything more.

"Because," he said finally. "Because the old man sent you to college. Instead of me."

"What?" said Ben. Now he was the deaf one.

"Because the old man sent you to college!" Lefty shouted. "Why you, instead of me? Why you?"

Ben didn't say anything.

"You think I liked it, getting drafted, being in the army? Why'd I have to go into the army, spend two years in goddamn Germany, while you got to sit around on your ass, drinking beers in a frat house? Why?"

Ben looked at his brother. "Ah, Lefty," he said. "For Pete's sake."

Lefty held his hands to his ears. "I'm deaf."

"Jesus," Ben said. "We could have been friends, me and you, if it hadn't been for this. We could have been good brothers."

There were tears in Lefty's eyes. He looked at Ben, his rival for so long, wondered if they could ever untangle their lives enough to forgive each other.

"What?" he said.

*   *   *

A dark figure moved through the cemetery. Allison sat by herself at the top of a hill. I'm probably early, she thought. Those other kids will be here soon. Then we'll make some music.

It was a little creepy sitting here by herself. Indian Hill was the largest, oldest graveyard she had ever seen. Most of the gravestones were over six feet high, made of the same brownstone as Wesleyan. In every direction the cemetery stretched, a vast city of the dead.

Polo could see her sitting alone at the summit. He imagined what was going to happen when he reached her. He would kiss her, take her shirt off. It would be good if he could get her to do that thing that Welly had done, he thought. The little hello.

As he got closer to her he felt a strange ripple of anger. He thought about the months and months she'd made him wait, turning him down, saying that she wanted to wait for marriage. As if she were serious. Then, the moment he'd decided to swear off sex, that's when she says she's ready. It was obvious now that she had only been toying with him, trying to keep him down. It wasn't fair that someone should resist him, especially not his girlfriend. She was going to have sex with him now, whether she wanted to or not. And of course she'd want to, what was he even thinking. He was really a lot of fun.

"Hold it right there," said a dark figure, standing behind a gravestone.

"What?" said Polo. He kept moving toward Allison. She was less than a hundred feet away now.

"I'm serious. You keep away from her."

"Who is that? Dylan? Come on, man, get lost."

"It's not Dylan, dude," said the voice. "You're all messed up."

Juddy stepped out from behind the tombstone. He was holding his fencing sword in one hand, the tip pointed toward Polo's chest.

"Juddy," Polo said, with relief. "What are you doing?"

With a sudden spring, Juddy jumped forward. It was like something Polo had once seen in the Joffrey. Juddy had an unexpected grace. He held one hand aloft. The other pointed the sword at Polo. The tip of the sword jabbed against Polo's shirt.

"You think this is funny, Polo? I think you're wrong."

"Juddy," Polo said. "Come on. Quit it. I got a date to keep."

"Exactly," said Juddy. "That's exactly what I'm telling you. I think you oughta leave the girl alone."

"What are you talking about?" said Polo. "Come on, brother. You're in my way."

Juddy pushed Polo backward with the point of his sword. "I'm not your brother," he said.

"I'm warning you, Juddy, back off!" said Polo.

"No, Polo," said Juddy. "I'm the one warning you."

And he pushed Polo back again with the sword. Polo took a step backward.

"What, you're going to slay me with your fencing sword? That's your idea?" Polo reached down and removed the button tip of the sword from his chest. "This thing can't hurt anybody."

In response, Juddy suddenly swept through the air with the sword. He leapt forward. Polo stepped aside, narrowly avoiding Juddy's blow. Juddy had anticipated this, though, and was now in front of Polo again. Polo reached out to grab the sword, but in that instant the sword rushed through the air again. Polo jumped high in the air to avoid being slapped in the shins with it.

"God dammit, Juddy," Polo said. "Quit it. Come on, get lost."

"I don't think so," said Juddy. "I think you're the one getting lost. You let Allison go, dude. She's meeting people."

"Meeting people?" Polo shook his head. "Aw, this is nuts."

"Yes," said Juddy. "It's nuts." And with that he jabbed his sword forward again. Polo stepped aside.

"What happened to that thing you said in the car," Polo said. "About you and me, having so much in common?"

"What was it I said we had in common?" Juddy said. "Can you remember?"

"Yeah," Polo said, slightly crestfallen. "You said we were both assholes."

"Well, guess what," Juddy said. "Turns out I was only half right."

He jabbed forward again. The thrusting sword stabbed deftly into Polo's fly, which was still open in the wake of the debacle at the Middletown Motor Inn. Juddy smiled suddenly, and pushed the sword harder against Polo's groin. Polo fell backward against a large brown gravestone. ELIJAH WINSLOW, read the stone. LOST AT SEA.

Juddy pulled back the sword. "Pretty good," he said. "For a sword that doesn't even have a tip."

"What's your problem, Juddy? What do you care about Allison and me?"

"I'll tell you the truth, Polo," Juddy said. "I don't think you're right for her."

"You don't—what?"

"Naw. I don't think you're right for her at all. She needs somebody else. Somebody she can trust."

"I like her. What are you saying? I'm nuts about her!"

Juddy shook his head. "You're nuts about yourself, dude."

"You're insane."

"You know, everybody keeps saying that," Juddy said. "You think I should get counseling or something? It's possible."

"Counseling would be a good start, Juddy."

"Hey, remember when Allison was all upset the other day? When she tanked her interview at Middlebury? What were you thinking then, when you let her run off cryin'? Your idea was, what? She'd be happier if she was crying her eyes out?" Juddy shook his head. "I tell you, Polo. You're a real disappointment."

"Juddy," Polo said. "What do you want, man? Do you want money?"

Juddy laughed. "Hey, man! You're cracking me up!" He shook his head. "Actually, what I was kind of hoping was, you'd let me chase you all over this friggin' graveyard. You think I could do that, chase you around?"

"Leave me alone," said Polo. "You leave me alone."

"Naw," Juddy said. "I don't think so." He jabbed his sword forward suddenly. Polo scurried out of the way. The sword stabbed against the old headstone. Juddy jumped onto the top of a stone and leaped through the air. Polo rolled over and scrambled to his feet, but Juddy was already there. He jabbed the sword at Polo's calves. Polo jumped. Juddy spun around and sliced his sword downward. Polo ran to the left. A moment later, Juddy was behind him. It was infuriating. Wherever Polo turned, Juddy seemed to be there, a moment ahead of him.

Juddy laughed suddenly. "Whoo, man!" he said. "You're funny, dude!"

"All right," Polo said. "I'll do whatever you want. I swear to God."

"Too late," said Juddy, who again thrust forward with his sword and snagged the inside of Polo's fly.

"What are you going to do?" Polo said. He fell backward against a long marble stone. Juddy's sword dug into his groin.

"Sorry I had to do this, man," Juddy said. "What can I tell you? You're just not a nice guy."

With a flick of the wrist, Juddy moved the point upward. It snicked to the top of Polo's crotch, resisted for a moment against the metal button that fastened Polo's pants closed. A moment later there was a soft ripping sound, followed by the sound of something metal rolling around on a tombstone.

Juddy had cut off the button that held up Polo's pants.

"Now get out of here," Juddy said. "Leave here, and never talk to Allison again. Got it?"

"Okay," Polo said. He bent over to pick up his button.

"Sorry, dude," Juddy said, knocking the button with his sword tip. "That belongs to me." He slapped the tip of his sword against the button and tiddlywinked it into the air. His free hand snapped forward and caught the button.

Polo's eyes opened wide in horror. His pants started to fall down.

"Adios, amigo," Juddy said.

Polo, grabbing the top of his pants, ran from the graveyard, down the hill toward the college.

Juddy looked toward the top of the hill, where his stepsister was silhouetted against the scarlet sky. He made the sign of the *J* in the air with his sword, and said "*Whssht-whssht.*" Then he looked down at his thumb. He remembered the feeling of the knife cutting his skin, pressing his thumbtip against Dylan's.

"Okay, Dickweed," he said softly. "You take it from here."

Allison sat alone, watching the sunset, unaware of the duels of men.

* * *

Ben descended the steps of South College, opened the front door, and walked outside. The sky above the university was crimson in sunset. A man from Buildings and Grounds was lowering the flag down the pole. The pedestal for the missing Douglas Cannon was bathed in purple shadows.

A man walked toward him. It took Ben a moment to recognize his son. He seemed different.

"Hey, kid," Ben called. Dylan looked down the sidewalk of College Row, went to his father.

"Hey, old man," Dylan said.

"How'd your interview go?"

Dylan shrugged. "I don't know," he said. He looked toward the observatory at the crest of Foss Hill. "I gotta go somewhere. Meet up with some folks."

"Okay," Ben said. "Hey, what happened to you, son? You have a black eye."

"Yeah," he said. "Allison punched me." He looked at his father's hand, which was bruised. "What happened to you?"

"Nothing. I had to punch your Uncle Lefty."

"Yeah," Dylan said, nodding. "I know what that's like. I had to punch him yesterday." Dylan's father looked strangely proud of his son. "And what happened with Captain Bedford? Did you have to punch him, too?"

"No," Ben said. "He didn't want to fight. He wanted to thank me. Offered me a job."

"You're kidding," Dylan said. "You?"

"Yeah," Ben said. "Me. Wants me to run a company he's got. Bedford Smithfield."

"Whoa," said Dylan. "I've heard of them. He's *that* Bedford?"

"It's a good job," Ben said.

"That's great," said Dylan. The ramifications of this

began to become clear to him. Things were going to be all right. For a moment he had the desire to rush forward, hug his father. "That's really good, Dad," he said. "Maybe if I retake my SATs, I can actually get into college."

Ben nodded. "And maybe I can actually pay for it."

Dylan had the desire to say or do something. He wanted Ben to know that he understood some things now that had eluded him. It had been hard. Dylan didn't figure he had made things a lot easier. The only thing he had ever done for his father was to be silent.

Dylan thought about it. It would be nice, the two of them embracing, father and son, here by the old chapel, the sun going down behind them, a moment of forgiveness and reconciliation. It would be something they would remember for the rest of their lives.

Instead, Dylan said, "Well, listen, I gotta go."

Ben thought he understood his son's destination. "Yeah, well, I gotta go somewhere, too," he said.

"Okay, well, anyway. See you later."

"Okay," said Ben. "See you later."

Dylan nodded, then turned his back. Ben stood there and watched his son walk, then run, across the great green lawn, toward the graveyard.

She was nearly asleep when he finally came to her. Chloë had put the guitar away, had crawled into bed in the Winnebago and covered her naked body with the sheets and a blanket. She was still on fire, waiting for him, but the coals had died down a little. It seemed sad, that she had to wait so long.

It was a mistake, and she knew it. The long period of waiting had given her the chance to realize this now. It was a repetition of the exact same sin that had ruined this family in the first place. And yet, it wasn't her fault, the things that had happened years and years ago, between people that weren't even alive now. She was just one woman, waiting for the chance to be with a man that she liked. That didn't mean she craved destruction.

It was funny, she thought, lying there in the dark camper, how the realization that this was all a vast mistake didn't in any way lessen her desire to commit this act. *If I had to do things all over again, I would repeat every action.* Every one of these long talks in college cafeterias and student unions across New England, each of these lovely walks along college hills. This final, doomed moment, waiting to make love to him in the Winnebago while the rest of the family was away, was worth it all. She knew that each of these gestures led to the same place, which was pain and longing and separation, and yet there was nothing she regretted.

She thought for a moment about Gary, about her former life, now nearly forgotten, but felt no guilt. *Go on,* he'd say, if he were alive. *Isn't that what we're here for, feasts and loud music and stolen moments? Live your life, sweetheart,* he'd say to her, *what the hell. Search for Planet X. Tear the joint to pieces. There's plenty of time later to be dead.*

Chloë heard the door open, his steps coming down the center of the camper.

"Chloë," he said. "You in there?"

"I'm here, darling," she said. "Come to me."

She heard him unbuckle his pants, the soft collapsing sound of his clothes falling to the floor. The partition to her bunk opened, and he moved toward her in the darkness, wrapping his arms around her.

"My love," she said. "At last."

Their skin brushed softly together. He kissed her neck, then her breasts. Chloë moaned. "Oh, Ben," she said. "My love."

"What?" Lefty said. "What?"

Chloë opened one eye.

"My love," she said.

"I'm a little deaf right now," Lefty said.

"I said my love," Chloë said. She could barely see his face in the darkness.

"What?"

"What are you doing, Lefty?" Chloë said.

"I'm lying next to you, sweetheart," he said. "I'm lying next to the woman I love."

"Uh-huh," Chloë said, moving away from him slightly. Damn, she thought. It all figures. It all makes perfect sense.

His face lowered to her breast again, and he kissed her.

"What happened to your face?" Chloë said. "You're bruised."

"Ah, nothing," Lefty said. "Got into a fight."

"You're kidding. Somebody punched you?"

"I don't blame him, the guy who punched me," Lefty said. "I was out of line."

"Poor thing." She felt sorry for him, suddenly, sorry for everything.

"It's nice to find you here, waiting for me."

"I wasn't waiting for you exactly," Chloë said. "I was just resting."

"What?"

"I said I was just resting."

"Oh." Lefty moved closer to her. "What do you think, you want to make love, honey? I think we got time, before everybody gets back."

"I don't know," Chloë said. "I'm not sure I'm in the mood."

"I can help you get in the mood," said Lefty. "I can help."

Chloë thought about things. "I'm hungry," she said. "Can I eat something first?"

"You want to eat something, then make love?"

"Let me make myself something," Chloë said. "Then we're going to have a talk." She swung her feet onto the floor, pulled on her pants, then a T-shirt. She opened the partition.

"You think we need to talk?" said Lefty. He didn't like the sound of this.

Chloë nodded. "Yeah," she said. "We need to have a long talk."

"Okay, fine," said Lefty. "I'll just lie here. You make yourself something, then we'll talk."

"Good," said Chloë. She went into the galley.

Lefty lay naked in Chloë's bed. It was a good place to be. He wondered how many more times he'd get to be in it. Maybe not as many as he'd thought.

"Dang it, Lefty," he heard her say. "We're all out of waffles."

Lefty wasn't all that surprised, now that it was upon him. If you thought about it, maybe they'd *never* had waffles, never, not even once. Lefty sighed, thinking about Chloë, thinking about Faith, thinking about Elio. It was possible, it occurred to him, that a man could live his entire life without ever eating real waffles, and not even know it.

Dylan walked through the old graveyard. He didn't see Allison. The sun was setting over Middletown.

He followed a road that seemed to be twisting toward the top of the hill. It was spooky, this place, a little like being lost. Now and again he thought he heard music coming from somewhere higher up. He reached into the pocket of his pants and pulled out the compass. North, it said.

Dylan came to a section of the cemetery where three large mausoleums were dug into the side of the hill. They were huge brownstone arches, twenty feet high. He had never seen such elaborate tombs before. In giant letters above the tombs were the names of the dead: CHAUNCEY, MÜTTER, ALSOP. There were a lot of people buried here, maybe six in each mausoleum. Dylan read the dates for Richard Alsop: 1761 to 1815.

Each of the three mausoleums had an iron door, secured with a heavy chain. The doors had small circular windows in them, so you could peer in if you wanted. Dylan thought about it, stepping forward and squinting through the windows. It was something he wanted to do, but it seemed a little too scary.

In the distance he heard the sound of that strange music again, floating in the air. There were people singing. One of the voices belonged to Allison.

Dylan walked in a straight line toward the central mausoleum, MÜTTER. He stood before the iron door. He looked in the window. On the walls on either side of the tomb were marble slabs. Well, Dylan thought. They're in there.

He said, softly, "Hey." His voice echoed hollowly in the tomb. *Hey*, a voice did not say back.

Dylan turned his back on the dead and walked to his left, climbing farther up the hill. The sky ahead of him, in the east, was bluish black with oncoming night.

At the summit of the hill was a great round place with no tombs. A dozen young people were gathered there, playing drums, flutes, guitars. They were singing: *Bottle of wine, fruit of the vine. When you gonna let me get sober? Leave me alone, let me go home. Let me go home and start over.*

He walked up toward them. Allison was sitting to one side, alone.

"Hey," Dylan said.

"Hey," Allison said. She looked at his black eye. "Aw, Dylan, look what I did."

"I deserved it," he said.

"Yeah," said Allison. "I guess." She touched it with her fingers. "Does it hurt?"

"No," said Dylan. "It's fine. You'd be surprised."

Allison looked around her at the others. "You know what, Dylan? I think I want to go to school here. I want to go to Wesleyan."

Dylan felt a pang for a moment, for he knew that they would not be together next year, not after he'd walked out on his interview. Still, perhaps this did not matter. He took her hand.

"Hey, man," said a guy with long hair and little John Lennon glasses. He handed them a large bottle. "Have some."

Dylan took the wine bottle, raised it to his lips. He didn't really know what wine was supposed to taste like. He figured it was good.

Preacher will preach, the musicians sang. *Teacher will teach. Miner will dig in the mine.*

Allison leaned her head on Dylan's shoulder. He raised his hand to touch her hair. It was soft.

"Hey, look at that," somebody said. One by one musicians stopped playing. The song died out.

The moon was rising over the campus. It was dark, blood red, and huge. Dylan had never seen a moonrise before.

"Boy," Dylan said. "That's really something."

From a great distance they heard the sound of bagpipes. It sounded like "Amazing Grace." Pipes were really quite beautiful, Dylan thought, if they were far enough away.

The rising red moon bathed the college and the graveyard in soft light. The young people sat at the crest of the hill, silent in wonder.

Epilogue

Number of colleges and universities in the United States: **2,167**

Number of these that are in New England: **357**

Average percent increase in SAT scores for those who take the test a second time: **25%**

Average number of colleges applied to by typical senior: **6**

Average '97 cost, including room and board, per year, of private college: **$29,300**

Percent by which college tuition is expected to rise in the next 20 years: **8%**

Projected inflation rate, same period: **4%**

Percent of students needing some financial aid in 1997: **72%**

Average coat size, 18-year-old American male: **38**

Average trouser size: **34 waist, 32 inseam**

Average bra size, 18-year-old American female: **34B**

Percent of 18-year-old females who say they are "on a diet": **74%**

Percentage of New England College alumni jobless one year after graduation: **19%**

Most popular book among college students, 1970: *The Catcher in the Rye*

Most popular book, 1990: *The Far Side*

Percentage of students admitted to their first-choice school: **18%**

Percentage of college students who say they are "haunted by a nameless, lurking dread": **97%**

AMHERST • HARVARD • YALE • MIDDLEBURY • BOWDOIN
DARTMOUTH • COLBY • WILLIAMS • WESLEYAN

COMMON APPLICATION

Application for Undergraduate Admission

Personal Data

Legal name: _____ Floyd _____ Dylan _____ Benjamin _____ Male
            (Last)   (First)   (Middle)   (Sex)

Are you applying as a ☒ freshman or ☐ transfer student? For the term beginning: Fall 1999

Permanent Home Address: 199 Camden Hills Drive
                        (Number and street)

Camden   Camden County   NJ   08101
(City or town)   (County)   (State)   (Zip code)

If different from the above, please give your mailing address for all admission correspondence.

Mailing address: _____
                            (Number and street)

_____
       (City or town)   (County)   (State)   (Zip code)

Telephone at mailing address:_____ Permanent home telephone: 609-555-8338

Birthdate: 06/22/81
           (Month/day/year)

Citizenship: ☒ U.S. citizen

                ☐ U.S. Permanent Resident visa. Citizen of: _____

                ☐ Other citizenship. Please specify country: _____

If you are not a U.S. citizen and live in the United States, how long have you been in the

country? _____   Visa type: _____

Possible area(s) of academic concentration/major: English, American Studies

Special college of division if applicable: _____

Possible career or professional plans: Unknown

Will you be a candidate for financial aid? ☐ Yes ☒ No If yes, the appropriate form will be

filed on: _____

Name of applicant: Dylan Floyd   Social Security #: 166-81-6867

The following items are optional:

Place of birth: Meridan (City) CT (State) USA (Country)   Marital status: Single

First language, if other than English: _____   Languages spoken at home: _____

If you wish to be identified with a particular ethnic group, please check the following:
- ☐ African American/Black
- ☐ American Indian, Alaskan Native
- ☐ Asian American
- ☐ Asia (Indian subcontinent)
- ☐ Hispanic, Latino
- ☐ Mexican American/Latino
- ☐ Native Hawaiian, Pacific Islander
- ☐ Puerto Rican
- ☒ White or Caucasian
- ☐ Other (specify: _____)

Educational Data

School you attend now: Camden Hills High School   Date of entry: 09/94

Address: Camden (City)   NJ (State)   08101 (Zip code)

Date of secondary graduation: 06/99

Is your school: ☒ public
  ☐ private
  ☐ parochial

College counselor

Name: Mrs. Midgely   Position: Director, College Counseling

School telephone: 609-555-2477   School fax: 609-555-2478

List all secondary schools, including summer schools and programs you have attended beginning with the ninth grade:

Name of school	Location (city/state/zip)	Dates attended
Camden Hills Middle School	Camden, NJ 19977	09/92–06/94
Camden Hills High School	Camden, NJ 19977	04/94–06/99

List all colleges at which you have taken courses for credit. Please have an official transcript sent from each institution as soon as possible.

Name of school	Location (city/state/zip)	Degree candidate?	Dates attended?

Name of applicant: Dylan Floyd   Social Security #: 166-81-6867

Test Information

Be sure to note the test required for each institute to which you are applying. The official scores from the appropriate testing agency must be submitted to each institution as soon as possible.

SAT I (or SAT):

Date(s) taken: __10/97, 10/98__

Score: Verbal: __277__   Verbal: __650__

     Math: __350__   Math: __520__

SAT II (Subject Achievement Tests)

Dates: __10/98__   Dates: _____   Dates: _____

Subject: __English Lit__   Subject: _____   Subject: _____

Score: __590__   Score: _____   Score: _____

ACT:

Score: Verbal: _____

     Math: _____   Science: _____

     Reading: _____   Composite: _____

TOEFL

Date taken: _____   Score: _____

Family

Mother's full name: __Faith Catherine Conklin__

Is she living: __no__

Home address if different from yours:

Street: _____

City: _____   State: _____   Zip: _____

Occupation: _____

Name of business or organization: _____

College (if any): __Middlebury__   Degree: __B.A.__   Year: __1980__

Professional or graduate school (if any): _____

Degree: _____   Year: _____

Name of applicant: __Dylan Floyd__   Social Security #: __166-81-6867__

Father's full name: __Benjamin Steward Floyd__

Is he living: __yes__

Home address if different from yours:

Street: _____

City: _____ State: _____ Zip: _____

Occupation: __Director, Software Development__

Name of business or organization: __Bedford Smithfield, Inc.__

College (if any): __Middlebury__ Degree: __B.A.__ Year: __1980__

Professional or graduate school (if any): _____

Degree: _____ Year: _____

If not with both parents, with whom do you make your permanent home: __father__

Academic Honors

Briefly describe any scholastic distinctions or honors you have won beginning with the ninth grade:

Honor Roll, third marking period (Nov/Dec), senior year, 1998.

Voted "most improved GPA," Camden Hills HS faculty, fall 1998.

Extracurricular, Personal, and Volunteer Activities:

Please list your principal extracurricular, community and family activities and hobbies in the order of their interest to you. Include specific events and/or major accomplishments.

Activity	Grade level or post-secondary (PS) 9 10 11 12 PS					Approximate time spent Hours per week	Weeks per year	Positions held, honors won, or letters earned	Do you plan to participate in college?
Ecology Club	X	X	X	X		2	36	Treasurer (tenth grade)	Yes
Drama Club				X		12	10	"Grampa," You Cn't Take It W/U	Yes

Name of applicant: __Dylan Floyd__ Social Security #: __166-81-6867__

Work Experience

List any job (including summer employment) you have held during the past three years

Nature of work	Employer	Dates of employment	Hours per week
Lawn Maintenance/Landscaping	self	06/92-09/98	12

In the space provided below, briefly discuss which of these activities (extracurricular and/or work experience) has had the most meaning for you and why:

I enjoyed the experience of mowing lawns for my family and for my neighbors' families as well. It was a pleasure to help lawns look their best. Also important to me was the process of learning to invest the funds I gained from my lawn maintenance business in a manner that showed awareness of what money can do. I gained greatly from the experience of mowing lawns and am glad I had this opportunity, because over time I was able to invest some of the money I earned into a better mower, which in turn made my business a better one. Most of all I liked the fact that I was able to work independently and on my own. It is a good thing to be one's own boss and to have the ability to make those decisions that most effect one's own situation, and the situation of mowing lawns for other people as well.

Name of applicant: <u>Dylan Floyd</u>   Social Security #: <u>166-81-6867</u>

Personal Statement

Please write an essay (250–500 words) on a topic of your choice or on one of the options listed below.

1) Evaluate a significant experience or achievement that has special meaning to you.
2) Discuss some issue of personal, local, national or international concern and its importance to you.
3) Indicate a person who has had a significant influence on you and describe that influence.

The person who has had the most significant influence on me is my father, Benjamin Steward Floyd. He has been my father since my birth in 1981, and during the time that he has been my father we have both changed a great deal, both as a father and a son.

My mother, Faith Catherine Floyd, died in 1988, as a result of her taking her own life. This was the worst thing that ever happened to us as a family. For a long time I wondered, what will happen to us, will we ever be able to go on? I also wondered for a long time who was to blame. My father kept on going. He is not an emotional man really and does not express his feelings with ease. Even when he needs to. Sometimes I have been very upset that he was not able to talk about things with me, esp when I needed to the most. And yet every day he went into work and kept on working hard to enable me to have the life he wanted me to have.

He met with a serious setback last year when the business that he started went bankrupt on account of my uncle Lefty, and yet even this did not have him stop his hoping for me. Over time, his optimism and belief in things working out have paid off and he has now got a job as the director of a software development company, Bedford Smithfield.

Name of applicant: <u>Dylan Floyd</u>   Social Security #: <u>166-81-6867</u>

If you would have looked at my father over the last few years there are times when you would have thought his goose was cooked, and yet if you look at him now you'd see someone doing all right.

What has been the same, however, throughout all this time is the fact that he loves me. Even though he doesn't say it exactly. Once in a while he has said it, which is good, but most of the other times he just looks at me and I look at him and I know what he means.

He would never say this about himself but as far as I am concerned he is a hero and the person who has had a significant influence on me.

My signature below indicates that all information in my application is complete, factually correct, and honestly presented.

Signature _Dylan Floyd_   Date _1/1/98_

Name of applicant: Dylan Floyd   **Social Security #:** 166-81-6867

Chloë stood next to the trailhead with her daughter. Chloë wore a huge backpack. A rolled-up sleeping bag and tent were affixed to it with bungee cords. Allison wore a small daypack.

"Okay," Chloë said. "Here we go."

Allison didn't say anything. A sign read, SPRINGER MOUNTAIN TRAIL. MOUNT KATAHDIN, MAINE, 2160.4 MILES. A moment later, the two women were on the Appalachian Trail, headed north.

"A journey of a thousand miles," Chloë said, "begins with a single step."

They passed rushing streams, oak trees, and cedar. The young woman walked in front, ahead of her mother, who carried the heavier burden.

They walked for about an hour before Chloë stopped. "Sorry, Allison," she said. "I need a break."

"It's okay," Allison said. "I can use some water."

They broke out the water bottles and split a candy bar. Chloë looked down the trail that lay before her.

"What do you think, Mom?" Allison said. "You gonna make it?"

"I'll make it," Chloë said. "What I've heard is that the first week or so is the hardest. After that it's just a matter of walking."

"Well, I guess this is where I leave you, then," Allison said.

"It's okay," Chloë said. "I appreciate you getting me started."

"How long do you think it'll take?"

"Depends," said Chloë. "If I hike alone I'll make better time. If I meet up with people, that will slow me down."

"Still, it's a couple of months, right?"

"Yeah. It's the second week of May, it'll be September or October before I reach Maine."

Allison sipped some water. "I wish I could do the whole thing with you."

"Me too," said Chloë. "But you have to get ready for school. I don't want you showing up at Wesleyan exhausted."

"Well, I'd still like to do it."

"Someday," Chloë said. "Maybe."

Allison put the cap back on her water bottle. "How close does the AT come to Wesleyan?"

"I don't know," Chloë said. "I don't think it's close."

"Oh, well," said Allison. "Too bad for you I didn't go to Dartmouth, huh?"

"Oh, I'm glad you're going to Wesleyan. You fell in love with the place the second you set foot there, didn't you?"

"I don't know," said Allison. "But it did feel like home, I guess."

"Well," said Chloë, picking up her backpack, "I guess this is home for me for a while."

"Yeah," said Allison. "You want me to phone Lefty or anything for you, let him know you got off okay?"

Chloë thought. "I don't know," she said. "Now that we're separated I think he's going to have to fend for himself. Might as well make an even break."

"Well, I could call him for you, if you want."

Chloë shrugged. "Yeah, I guess you could do that. Just see how he's doing."

"Okay."

The women looked at each other. "I guess this is it, then, huh," Allison said.

Chloë nodded.

They drew close together, embraced. Allison thought it was funny to hug her mother in her giant backpack. She suddenly seemed like a very large person.

"I love you, kid," said Chloë.

"I love you, too, Mom."

"You knock them dead at Wesleyan. I'll call you from Maine."

"Good luck on the trail," said Allison.

They looked at each other, awkwardly, unwilling to turn away.

"It's okay if you meet somebody on the trail," Allison said. "I mean, it's all right even if it slows you down a little."

Chloë nodded. "Thanks," she said.

"Okay," said Allison, and began to walk away. Chloë watched her daughter going back down the trail for a while, then she turned her back and began her long journey north.

Mr. Floyd Dylan
199 Camden Hills Drive
Camden, NJ 08101

Dear Floyd:

Thank you for your application for admission to Yale University. I regret to inform you at this time that we are unable to offer you a position in the class of 2003.

We received over 13,000 applications for the 1300 spaces available in our freshman class. While we are grateful for the high degree of interest in Yale University, we also regret that many promising students must be turned away. This is no reflection on your accomplishments as a young scholar, or as an individual, but more a result of our record high number of applications.

We wish you the best of luck with your post-secondary education, Floyd, and thank you for your interest in Yale University.

Sincerely,

Vincent Kugelmaus
Assistant Dean, Admissions

Welly Bedford went up to her professor after class. "Excuse me, Dr. Peacock? Can I ask you a question?"

"Darryl," Dr. Peacock said. "You call me Darryl."

Welly giggled. "Darryl," she said. "I wanted to know if I could discuss the assignment with you?"

"Oh, this first assignment is nothing to fret about, uh—Wellington, is it?"

"Welly," Welly said.

"Welly," said Darryl. "It's not even graded. It's just to get your creative juices flowing. That's important for your Emory education, to be in touch with that side of your brain."

"Okay," said Welly. "But I'd still like to talk to you about it. We're supposed to write about our earliest memories of—what?"

"Of being male or female." He cleared his throat. "Female, in your case."

"Okay," Welly said. "But I'm still not sure I understand."

"Well, we are examining gender roles in this class," said Darryl. "Trying to understand them. So a natural place to begin is with our earliest memories of ourselves as gendered individuals."

Welly licked her lips. "Okay," she said. "I think I can write about this. Still, would you mind it if we met and talked about the assignment? I have a couple of different ideas."

"Sure," said Darryl. He reached into his tweed jacket

and pulled out a small datebook. "I'm free this afternoon, if you like. Say, three o'clock?"

"Three o'clock," Welly said. "That sounds good."

"All right," said the professor. "I'll see you then. You bring your ideas to my office and we'll talk about them."

"Okay," said Welly. "I'll see you later, Dr. Peacock."

Dr. Peacock smiled. "You call me Darryl," he said.

Mr. Dylan Floyd
199 Camden Hills Drive
Camden, NJ 08101

Dear Dylan:

I'm writing to inform you that we cannot offer you admission to Bowdoin College.

While we are aware that this may come as a setback to you, let us assure you that we have great respect for your accomplishments, as expressed in your application and dossier. We had over 3,600 applications this fall for the 420 spaces available. As a result, many deserving students have had to be denied admission.

We thank you for all the interest you showed in Bowdoin College, and wish you the best of luck with your future educational plans.

Sincerely,

Chip Gladstone
Associate Director, Admissions

Elio Floyd woke up from a strange dream. She had been sitting in a large room. A man at the front of the room called upon her, asked her for her name.

She sat up on her mattress. Outside it was still dark. She walked out to the kitchen, went over to the sink, poured herself a small glass of Fleishman's vodka. In a single swallow, she kicked back the shot.

Elio saw herself reflected in the toaster. Her face seemed strangely distorted, ovoid. She left the kitchen and walked to her bedroom. She thought about turning on the television but did not.

On the dresser was the picture of her son she had received at Christmas several years ago. She picked up the picture of Judson, holding his sword aloft.

Elio lay down on her mattress again, stared at the ceiling. It all seemed like a long time ago. For a moment she thought about getting out of bed, playing something on her guitar, but then it came back to her. She had left the Martin someplace she could not quite remember, and now it was lost.

Mr. Dylan Floyd
199 Camden Hills Drive
Camden, NJ 08101

Dear Mr. Floyd:

It is my unfortunate duty to inform you that we are unable to offer you admission to Colby's class of 2003.

Your transcript was impressive, your essays well written, and your recommendations superb. Nevertheless, due to the extremely competitive nature of this year's record-high number of applications, we are unable to admit you.

We appreciate your interest in Colby and wish you luck.

> *Sincerely,*
>
> *Marcus Drink*
> *Dean of Admissions and*
> *Financial Aid*

Monsieur François de Salignac de la Mothe Fenelon looked angrily at Juddy. "Non, non, non!" he shouted. "Ze attack is all wrong!"

"I don't know, Monsieur," Juddy said, looking at the point of his épée sword. "Somehow I can't get into this."

"Into zees?" the coach said. He took off his cap, emblazoned with the large crimson *H* and threw it on the floor. "Monsieur Zhuddy cannot get *into* zees?"

"Is good with sabers," said the new assistant coach, Ruki, coming over to talk. "Why not switch to saber? Is good!"

"Monsieur Zhuddy, he is not zee saber type, is he not?" François de Salignac de la Mothe Fenelon said, hopefully. "It is not hees speciality. Monsieur Zhuddy, he has the grace. The poetry of ze épée."

"Well, gosh, Coach Ruki. I'd be willing to try!" said Juddy.

"Non, non, non!"

" 'Course I'd need me a saber sword."

"Is good," said Ruki, handing Juddy his own saber. "He tries! Makes big slice!"

"You will not play ze saber," said François de Salignac de la Mothe Fenelon. "You must not!"

"Well, hell," Juddy said. "Coach Ruki here seems to think I can do it!"

"Can do it!" said Coach Ruki. "Can do if he tries!"

"Please," said François de Salignac de la Mothe Fenelon. "Judson. I ask you this as I ask my own son. Do not do this thing to Harvard."

Juddy held Coach Ruki's saber in one hand. It was a whole different feeling. He raised the sword into the air.

"*En garde*," Juddy said.

Coach Ruki smiled. "Is good," he said.

Mr. Dylan Floyd
199 Camden Hills Drive
Camden, NJ 08101

Dear Dylan:

I regret to inform you that you have not been selected for admission to Dartmouth College.

We had an extraordinary number of applications this year—over

8500 for the roughly 1000 spaces available. While we have made every effort to be fair, it is still not possible to offer admission to every qualified student who applied. Clearly you are a promising young scholar and will find other education opportunities available to you.

We thank you for your interest in Dartmouth College, and wish you the best of luck with your future plans.

Sincerely,

James Rothchild
Assistant Director, Admissions

Polo drove his car into the lot and parked in the back, behind the service bay. A large banner blew in the wind: BOY DO WE HAVE A DEAL FOR YOU. Lefty came out of the showroom a few minutes later, looking at his watch.

"You're late!" Lefty said. "Again!"

"Sorry, Lefty," Polo said. "Had a little problem with my alarm clock."

"I'll give you problems," Lefty said. "I've got a showroom full of people waiting to take test drives, and nobody to help them!"

"What about Whizzer?" said Polo. "He's on today."

"Don't you worry about Whizzer," said Lefty, angrily. "You worry about Polo MacNeil. You worry about one sad son of a bitch who will be out of work if he doesn't shape up. Is that clear?"

"Yes, Lefty," said Polo.

"I said is that clear?" Lefty said. He leaned into Polo's face like a drill sergeant.

"Yes," Polo said. "It's clear."

"Now get going." He stood in the lot and watched Polo scurry off to the showroom. Immediately upon entering, Polo was beset by a couple who had a lot of questions about minivans.

Whizzer came out of the service bay, wiping his hands

with a rag. "Hey, boss," he said to Lefty, who was still standing there in the lot.

"Hey," Lefty said.

"You want me to work in the showroom today? We're just standing around back here."

"Nah," said Lefty. "You take it easy."

Whizzer looked toward the showroom. "How's the new kid working out?"

Lefty shrugged. "I don't know. Not good, I guess."

Whizzer put the rag in his back pocket. "Not gonna make it, huh?"

"I don't think so," Lefty said, and put his hand on his heart. "College boy."

Mr. Dylan Floyd
199 Camden Hills Drive
Camden, NJ 08101

Dear Mr. Floyd:

On behalf of the staff of Admissions at Williams, I regret to inform you that we are unable to offer you a position in our class of 2003.

We at Williams are dedicated to preserving the small and intimate nature of our campus. As a result, we were able to admit fewer than 500 of the nearly 5000 students who applied this year. We respect your accomplishments, however, and wish you the best of success with other opportunities.

Sincerely,

Lorraine Guichalarr
Dean of Admissions

Ben and Dylan walked away from the car, piled high with suitcases, steamer trunks, a stereo, CDs in boxes, a computer. In their hands they carried their rods and reels and the tackle boxes.

•

They walked down the path to the edge of Lake Dunmore. The August sunshine played off the clear waters.

Ben adjusted the tension on his Browning reel, then snapped a Rapala lure into the swivel. He cast out into the lake, waited for a moment, then reeled it back in with a jerking motion.

Dylan decided to try his luck with a Heddon Zarapuppy, and tied on the lure. A moment later there was a soft plunk in the lake, ripples heading outward.

They reeled their lines back in, cast again. Ben took off the Rapala after a while and replaced it with a Rat-L-Trap floater. Dylan untied the Heddon lure and tried a Tiny Torpedo. After a while he untied that one and put on a spoon. They weren't biting.

Ben took a break after a half hour and sat on the bank, his back against a tree, watching his son cast and reel in. It was a beautiful thing to watch, the young man casting.

A pair of loons out on the lake laughed and cackled. They looked over at Ben and Dylan. One of the birds bobbed its head.

"You ready for tomorrow?" Ben said.

"Yeah," Dylan said. "It's not far from here, right?"

"About a half-hour drive north."

"Yeah," Ben said. "I'm ready."

"I can't believe you're living in Painter," Ben said. "They'll probably give you my old room."

"Is that where Mom lived?" Dylan said.

"No, I don't think so," said Ben. "She was in Weybridge, at least when I met her."

Dylan's rod bent suddenly. "I got a strike," he said, reeling in. "No, wait." He looked at his father, slightly ashamed. "I'm just snagged."

"Pull on it, you can probably get it loose."

"I know, Dad."

Dylan pulled on his line. The reel made an unpleasant clicking noise.

"Shit."

"Be patient," Ben said.

Dylan's face flushed, as he felt the shame of being snagged in front of his father. He could see the place where the lure was caught, on a submerged log about twenty feet offshore. The lure glittered silver against the rotting old trunk.

"Give it time," Ben said.

"I am giving it time," Dylan said.

"We're in no rush," said Ben. "We don't have to go anywhere, do anything."

Dylan yanked on his line again and the lure came loose suddenly and hurtled toward him, its hooks spinning around in the air. The lure sailed high and imbedded itself into the bark of the tree above Ben's head.

"Fish," Ben said. "You're supposed to be catching fish."

Dylan didn't laugh. He reeled in the loose line and walked over to the tree and dug the spoon out of the bark. It took him a while to get it free.

"I can't believe I didn't come up into the mountains more when I went to Middlebury," said Ben.

Dylan was trying to get his line untangled.

"Promise me when you're at Middlebury you'll save time to do stuff like this, come up here, go fishing."

Dylan wasn't listening.

Ben sat there and watched the lake. On the opposite shore a small cabin sat on top of a hill. The bricks in the chimney were painted blue.

"Try a Hawg Frawg," said Ben.

"Dad," said Dylan.

"Whatever."

Dylan sank a large metal weight into a speckled plastic

worm. He tied the worm to his line, then cast out. He waited for a moment after the lure hit the water, letting it sink. Then with a series of jerking movements, he hopped the lure over the bottom of the lake.

They would not have many more days like this together, Ben thought.

A large fish crashed out of the water, splashed back in on its side.

"I got a strike," Dylan said excitedly. "I got a strike."

"Smallmouth," Ben said.

"Okay, what do I do?" Dylan said.

"Don't reel him in all at once. Wait. Let him run with it."

"Okay," said Dylan. They could see the tremendous bass thrashing in the water, just below the surface.

"You're doing fine," Ben said. "Stay with him."

The fish swam away from the bank. Dylan felt the fishing rod coming out of his hands.

"Steady," said Ben.

"You take it, Dad," Dylan said, afraid.

"You're doing fine," said Ben.

"Dad," said Dylan.

The reel clicked under the stress. Dylan held on to the rod with both hands.

The fish swam to the left and right. Dylan began to reel it in. It was a huge fish, easily nine pounds.

"I think I got him," Dylan said. "I think I got him." Slowly the creature gave up the fight.

Dylan reeled it out of the water, clasped it below the gills. "Hey look, Dad. Look at me."

Dylan looked at the young man, holding his enormous fish. He felt all right.

"Boy," Ben said. "That's a nice one."

author's note

This is a work of fiction. No resemblance between persons living or dead is intended. The colleges in this novel differ, as necessary, from their counterparts in reality, and the situations located at each institution herein are intended to be neither representative nor emblematic of the institution in question. I am exceedingly grateful to the staffs of the bureaus of public information at the colleges mentioned in this novel for all their help, without which this work could not have been completed. I also want to thank the following individuals: Doug Archibald, Sandy Maisel, Patrice Franko, Charles Conover, Susan Kenney, Peter Harris, Barbara Sweney, and Karen Oh, as well as Kris Dahl and Jamie Raab, for whose vision and support I am especially thankful.

The statistics that form the epigraphs to each chapter (except where noted) are from the 1998 *Insider's Guide to the Colleges*, compiled and edited by the staff of the *Yale Daily News*. The statistics on the epigraph of the Epilogue are a series of inventions, half-truths, and just plain lies.

A portion of the proceeds of this book will go to the J. Richard Boylan Scholarship in the Humanities at Johns Hopkins University in Baltimore.

The author would be pleased to correspond with readers through the publisher.

CPSIA information can be obtained at www.ICGtesting.com
Printed in the USA
LVOW072251290313

326563LV00004B/6/P

9 780446 674171